more . . .

"A special brand of zaniness. . . . IN MILDRAGO-VITCH AND SUGHRUE, CRUMLEY HAS TWO OF MY ALL-TIME FAVORITE LITERARY CREATIONS."
—Tulsa World

"THIS IS THE REAL DEAL, FOLKS . . . CRUMLEY HITS THE MARK IN HIGH-ACTION STORYTELLING."
—Clarion-Ledger (Jackson, MS)

"THE REUNION OF SUGHRUE AND MILODRAGO-VITCH IS THE LITERARY EQUIVALENT TO FIVE CHERRY BOMBS IN ONE TIN CAN. . . . Once again Crumley's talent and originality shine . . . reminiscent of Jim Harrison or James Lee Burke. . . . This powerful novel will stick with you long after the motor shuts down."
—BookPage (NJ)

"Crumley can punctuate the detective's quest with short bursts of the staples of P.I. fiction, sex and gore, and make each one fresh and vivid and unforgettable . . . . AS CHANDLER SAID OF DASHIELL HAMMETT, HE CAN WRITE SCENES THAT SEEM NEVER TO HAVE BEEN WRITTEN BEFORE."
—Twentieth Century Crime & Mystery Writers

BORDERSNAKES

Novels by James Crumley:

Bordersnakes
The Mexican Tree Duck
Dancing Bear
The Last Good Kiss
The Wrong Case
One to Count Cadence

JAMES CRUMLEY

BORDERSNAKES

WARNER BOOKS

A Time Warner Company

WARNER BOOKS EDITION

Cover illustration by Christopher Zakarow
Cover design by Rachel McClain

Warner Books, Inc.
1271 Avenue of the Americas
New York, NY 10020

Visit our Web site at
http://warnerbooks.com

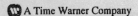 A Time Warner Company

Printed in the United States of America

Originally published in hardcover by The Mysterious Press.
First Printed in Paperback: September, 1997

10 9 8 7 6 5 4 3 2 1

for
Martha Elizabeth

Author's note:

For reasons of my own, I've played fast and loose with the geography of two of my favorite places, West Texas and Northern California, and I beg the reader's indulgence. Thank you.

As we climbed out of the plane the automatic runway landing lights snapped off, leaving us in the soft desert darkness surrounding the small field.

"Castillo, Texas," the pilot muttered, nervous, removing the dark glasses he always wore for night flying. "Who the fuck lives out here?"

"*Mojados*—that's wetbacks to you gringos—three kinds of drug smugglers, six different breeds of law dogs, and every kind of criminal ever dreamed up," the guide answered grimly.

"And over there?" the pilot said, waving his glasses at the smoky, smudged lights across the Rio Grande.

"Enojada?" the guide said, amazed. "Bordersnakes, man."

"Who's that?"

"Shit, man," he finally said, "*nobody* knows who they are. And nobody with any fucking sense gives a shit."

From a conversation with C. W. Sughrue

Part One
Milo

MAYBE IT WAS THE GODDAMNED SUIT. TAILOR-MADE Italian silk, as light and flimsy as shed snakeskin. Or maybe my whole new clean and shiny wardrobe looked strange under my battered old face. A thin knit shirt under the suit coat, woven leather loafers—without socks, of course—and a soft Borsalino felt fedora that made me look like a Russian Black Sea summer pimp. Not bad, though, I thought. For a pimp.

But obviously I had violated more than the dress code in this run-down shithole called Duster's Lounge, a code that surely included a rap sheet at least two pages long, five years' hard time, and all the runny, jailhouse tattoos a man's skin could carry.

Or perhaps the 'roid monkey leaning beside me on the battered bar fancied himself a fashion critic. He sported winged dragons and skulls on the bulging arms hanging out of his muscle shirt, an oversized switchblade in his right hand, and the slobbery leer of a true critic. Whatever, he played with my left cuff until the switchblade pressed into the soft fabric. For the third time in the last two minutes.

"What the fuck you doing here, old man?" he muttered in a downer-freak's growl. "What the fuck?"

I hadn't even had a sip of my beer yet, my first beer in almost ten years. I tried to turn away peacefully again, smiling tensely without speaking, but the big jerk recaptured my cuff with the point of his knife. Goddamned Sughrue. He'd love this shit. But he wasn't here. As far as I knew, he could be dead. *But what the hell,* I heard him think, *nobody lives forever.* Gently, I slipped my cuff free.

"Kid, you touch my suit with that blade again," I said calmly, "I'm going to shove it up your ass and break it off." Maybe he'd think it was a joke.

At least he laughed. His voice broke like an adolescent's when he brayed. He honked so loud and long that the steroid acne across his shoulders threatened to erupt. Somewhere in the dim bar, this kid had an audience.

I checked a group of glassy-eyed young men of several races, sporting bloody new tattoos on their arms and military haircuts, who had surrounded two pitchers of thin, bitter beer and one professional woman old enough to be their grandmother. Fort Bliss, I guessed, and the first payday pass of basic training. A half-dozen Sneaky Pete day-drinkers occupied a couple of other tables in the decrepit joint at the desert end of Dyer Street. No problem there. Then I saw the big kid's audience at the shadowed edge of the dance floor: two beefy guys showing lots of ink who could have been tired electricians, unemployed roughnecks, or ex-cons. I addressed them politely.

"Excuse me, gentlemen," I said loudly, "perhaps this *vermin* belongs to you?"

The beefy guys made a mock glance over their broad shoulders, then turned wide gap-toothed grins at me. Several day-drinkers chugged their beers and slithered out like greasy shadows. The bartender sidled into the cooler. Then the biggest hunk of beef stood up, laughed, and hitched up his greasy jeans.

"Truth is, sir, Tommy Ray, there," he said, still grinning, "he don't much belong to nobody. Seems like the best part of the kid ran down his momma's leg." Then he paused and glanced at his pal. "Unfortunately, that'd be my momma, too."

"Sorry to hear that," I said, then turned back to the bar to reconsider my new life and wardrobe. And other pressing matters. Such as: why had I brought my ancient bones and new wardrobe into this particular bar on this particular October day in El Paso, Texas? Ten years without so much as a beer, and there I was about to die before I even had a sip of the Coors longneck sweating in front of me.

So I took off my new hat and reached for the beer. Tommy Ray giggled like a fool and missed my cuff this time when he tried to pin it to the scarred bar with the blade, saying, "What was it you were going to do, old man?" Then he raised a double tequila with the other hand, chugged it, and tossed down a small draft beer to douse the flames.

While he had his head tilted back far enough to stretch his thick neck, I slapped him across the face with the hat and hit him in the windpipe as hard as I could with my right fist. Which should have been hard enough. I'd come into my middle fifties sober and solid. I ran, I pumped iron, and worked the bags, heavy and speed, three times a week. I was still six-foot and two-twenty, with a rock-hard Milodragovitch head. But this kid, like many kids these days, was a monster. Maybe only six-three but a solid two-eighty, with a chin like a middle-buster plow. Even bigger than his big brother. And he stood between me and the sunlight. Grinning.

I cut an eyebrow with a jab, hoping to blind him, then wrapped my right fist in the soft hat and hit him in the face with three straight rights that didn't faze him, didn't even make him stop smiling.

Then I hooked him in the gut. Big mistake. My wrist bent and nearly dislocated. So I grabbed the beer bottle and smashed it against the slimy brass footrail. My first beer in years spattered across the dry wood floor and deeply stained my beautiful new loafers. Maybe the beer would cover the blood. Sure as hell, I'd have to cut this kid just to get out the door; and as much as he deserved to be taken out of the gene pool, I didn't want to be the one to do it. About the time I stopped drinking, I also decided that I'd seen too much death in my life, much too close.

Tommy Ray stepped back into a crouch, his close-set eyes bunched so tightly I might have poked them out with one finger. But his eyelids were probably iron-hard, too. He waved the blade in front of his belt, then rushed me, clubbing at my head with his left and trying for an underhanded sweep with the right. But I caught his left on my shoulder and blocked his sweeping arm with my forearm, a pair of shocks I felt all the way to the bone, then I rolled out, raking the broken bottle across his chest.

Tommy Ray stopped long enough to look down and find his right pectoral, complete with the strap of his muscle shirt and his nipple, flapping off his chest. Then a sheet of blood flowed across his ribs.

In his dazed pause, I meant to drive the beer bottle into his face, then run, but his big brother stepped between us, and the pal pinned me from behind, wrapped me almost gently in his arms. "Easy, old man," was all he said.

"Goddammit, T.R.," the brother said, taking the knife from him, "you fucking asshole." Then he turned to me, grabbed my wrist with one hand, and jerked the beer bottle out of it with the other. "Ah, shit, man, I'm sorry. The fuckin' kid's got the IQ of a spit-warm beer. But he's my little brother. He's just funnin' you . . ."

"Gut strokes are not funny, buddy," I said.

"I can see how you might feel that way," he said sincerely, "and I really am sorry. I should've stopped this shit before somebody got hurt . . ."

"Hurt?" the kid growled as he tried to press the flap of flesh back to his chest. "The son of a bitch cut my fucking tit off, Rock!"

"You ain't hurt," his brother said, laughing calmly. "We'll just sew the fucker back on. Good as new . . ."

Which was the last thing I heard. Tommy Ray slipped to the side and launched a long, slow, looping right hand over his brother's broad shoulder. The fist looked as large as my head and it crunched into the side of my face with a sound like a melon thrown off a speeding truck. I sure as hell wished I had found C. W. Sughrue before I decided to fall off the wagon in this particular wreck.

When I came back to some semblance of consciousness, I found myself still facing afternoon. Late afternoon. The same day, I dearly hoped. The shadows of the rough, prickly mountains that split El Paso like a primitive, sacrificial dagger had only reached the hard-packed parking spaces in front of Duster's.

At least I was in my car, my new Caddy beast, and I had the steering wheel to help me sit upright. As I did, my loafers and hat fell off my chest.

"Jesus," I muttered, "fucking kid musta knocked me outa my shoes."

"True enough, man," came a voice from beside me. "And he got Dancer, too, with the back of your head. Dropped him like a cold dog turd. Then I had to hit T.R. about nine times before he went to one knee." Big brother held up his right hand. The two middle knuckles were jammed halfway to his wrist, a long deep tooth-cut split the knuckle of his index finger, and his other fingers splayed brokenly from the crooked hand. "Fuckin' kid always could take a punch."

"Where's he now?" I asked. When I turned to look around, the wobblies resumed residence in my head, so I had to close my eye. The right one. Tommy Ray had sealed the left one for me. Perhaps forever.

"Police took him to the hospital," he said. "Maybe they'll hold him for a while. And with any luck his probation officer will violate him for being drunk. So we're safe for now." Then he laughed wildly.

"Police?" I said. "How long have I been out?"

"A good bit," he said. "One of my brothers took the call, wrote it up as a wash, but he left me to keep an eye on you. In case you died. Or something."

"Your brother?"

"Big family, the Soameses, seven brothers," he said. "Half cops, half crooks, half crazy."

"How do you get half of seven?"

"I guess your head's all right, man, you ask a question like that," he said. "Sammy Ray drowned in Grenada."

"How's my eye look?"

"Hamburger," he said, "rotten hamburger. Or maybe bloody dog shit. Nothin' a couple of stitches can't fix."

"Thanks," I said, "but I meant the eyeball."

"Me, too," he said, then giggled drunkenly. "It's ugly, but it's okay. And the socket's intact. That's the important part. You've probably got a concussion like a barrel cactus. But the eye will be okay. My old man used to box a little. A ranked heavy for a few minutes, before the booze got him. I worked his corner some when I was a kid."

"Thanks," I said, and extended my hand. "Milodragovitch."

He waved his bag of bones at me and said, "Rocky Soames. Rocky Ray. It's a family tradition."

"Lost fistfights and suicides," I said, "that's my family's tradition."

"Nothin' you could do about it, man. When T.R. gets behind a handful of downers, somebody has to get hurt," he said, then grinned. "Usually several somebodies."

"Well, fuck it. Next time I decide to have a beer I'll bring a hand grenade," I said. I would have grinned back at him but it hurt too much.

Rocky drove me back to the Paso del Norte Hotel and kindly helped me to my suite. We drew some odd looks as we crossed the lobby, but I crossed some palms, and the looks disappeared. We had plenty of help the rest of the way. After that it was all gravy. A house doctor brought codeine and a half-circle of stitches for the corner of my eye. The bellman took my bloody suit off to the cleaners, then fetched coffee for me, a large glass of tequila for my new buddy, and an extra television set to roll beside my king-sized bed so I could see it with my single working eye.

"Thanks again," I said to Rocky as he took his leave. "And tell your little brother that I ain't ever been hit that hard in my whole fucking awful life."

"Shit, man," he said, "everybody tells him that."

I had to laugh. Maybe it was the drugs. A little later, codeine smooth and toweled warm from a hot tub, I slipped naked between cold expensive sheets. I thought about ordering a scotch the size of West Texas, then knew I shouldn't drink it without Sughrue, and wondered where the fuck he had hidden from me. And why.

When I finally found him three weeks later outside a rock-house convenience store in the tiny West Texas town of Fairbairn, we had both changed so much we didn't even recognize each other. But at least I'd found his hiding place.

Earlier that afternoon, five hours on the interstate east of El Paso, I decided to take the scenic route and turned south on a narrow pāved strip that wound through the dry, scrub-brush foothills of the Davis Mountains. In spite of the barbed-wire fences flanking the pavement, I couldn't imagine soft-footed steers grazing across the thin grass scattered among sharp rocks. Maybe sheep or goats. But the rusty, four-string barbed-wire fence couldn't hold a goat. Or even the world's dumbest walking mutton.

After thirty minutes on the little highway without seeing a soul—not even a buzzard—I spotted a small herd of long-horns among a patch of thorned brush hopelessly trying to crawl up the genetic ladder toward treedom. When I stopped to stare at the cattle, they stared back, their wild eyes perfectly at home in that reckless landscape, their gaze as rank and rangy as the African breed that began their bloodline. I wondered how the hell those drovers managed to herd these beasts from West Texas to Montana in the 1880s without Cobra gunships.

Then I began to see people: a welder hanging the blade back on a grader that had been scratching a firebreak out of the stony scrub; two Mexican hands greasing a windmill under a sky swept pale, polished blue by the constant wind; an old woman in a tiny Ford Escort running her RFD route, bringing the mail to the scattered, shotgunned mailboxes along the road.

At a Y intersection with an even smaller highway, I had to stop to let a funeral cortege pass, though I couldn't imagine a graveyard in the middle of this nowhere. The next vehicle I met was a pickup that contained three teenage boys with faces painted like clowns under their broad cowboy hats. I don't know what I'd expected in West Texas, but I began to suspect that I had wandered into a fucking Fellini film.

Then came the tourists as I climbed past slopes of juniper and scrub oak, and higher still into the improbable gray rock peaks: a busload of ancients turning into a picnic ground already occupied by several families in vans; a couple of drug-store cowboys drinking beer at a turnout; and a group of hikers who looked like retired college professors. Then I saw the MacDonald Observatory rising from the mountain ridge like an escaping moon.

Too weird, I thought, too fucking weird. So I stopped at the next wide spot in the road to collect myself, wondering what I'd done, wondering what the hell I was doing in West Texas.

I had been born and raised in the small western Montana city of Meriwether and, except for my time in the Army, had always lived there. It had taken only a month, but now I owned nothing, just a rented mailbox and a telephone number that rang at an answering service. I had destroyed my past, abandoned my parents' graves, said goodbye to the few friends still alive, then flew to Seattle to buy a new car. I had visions of exotic convertibles, crouched low to the road, faster than death, more surefooted than a Revenue Agent. But now that I could actually afford one, I didn't fit in the little bastards anymore. A Porsche salesman pointed me toward a Cadillac Eldorado Touring Coupe, nearly two tons of Detroit iron driven by three hundred horses out of a thirty-two-valve V-8, a car big enough for my butt and my head, a trunk the size of a small country, and a Northstar engine that nailed my ass into the driver's seat when I stuffed the accelerator into the fire wall. And the Beast held the road in a screaming corner. At least as fast as I cared to push her. But I had to wait a week to get the color I wanted with a sunroof. The salesman tried to sell me a Dark Montana Blue, but I assumed I'd given up sentiment in my middle age, so I waited for Dark Cherry.

That's where the trouble started. In Seattle. Still not drinking, just waiting for the sunroof, I decided that the new ride deserved a new wardrobe. A couple of tweedy blazers, maybe, a pair of cords, maybe new boots. So I dropped into a store a couple of blocks from the Four Seasons, found a tall, elegant lady with a British accent, who sold me five thousand dollars worth of Italian foofaraw, including a two-hundred-fifty-dollar felt hat that she claimed could be pulled through a napkin ring, then nearly fucked me to death. I was so sore driving from Seattle to El Paso not even the eight-way power seat took the strain out of my groin. But it was fun. In my drinking days, I might have married her, lived with her, or tried to love her. But I already had enough ex-wives, ex-roommates, and ex-lovers to last me a lifetime. Oddly enough, I'd taken a vacation from love about the same time I began my long rest from drinking.

But down in this moonscape I decided I'd rested long enough. So I pulled into the next unpaved turnout and dug into my elegant road provisions: I fired up a fancy English cigarette, a Dunhill Red, and cracked a bottle of Mexican ale,

Negra Modelo, then stood in that relentless fall wind smoking and drinking like a civilized man, suspecting that soon enough I'd be back to Camel straights and cheap shots of schnapps anchored by cans of Pabst, living like the drunk I'd always been. Or maybe not. Ten years dry and sober without the crutches of cigarettes and meetings—it hadn't been a waste of time, but it hadn't been constant entertainment, either.

All the high-class fixings burned my tongue like fried shit and made me dizzy and reckless. I loved it. But I didn't have another beer. I guess it was a test. I guess I sort of passed.

All I had was an address on the single main street of Fairbairn, a dying town about halfway between Marfa and the Mexican border at Castillo, a town killed by cattle prices and the closure of a military firing range. I drove past the address twice, not believing my own eyes or notes. Once the Dew Drop Inn must have been the best motor court in town. Eight native rock cabins with Spanish tile roofs and tiny garages stood in a shabby half circle around a patio filled with Russian thistle tumbleweeds and ancient dust, and the cabins looked as if they hadn't been occupied since WWII. A small cafe and beer joint perhaps once had adjoined the office. But now a shabby convenience store filled that space. It advertised ICE COLD BEER and HOMEMADE TAMALES, two major West Texas staples, it seemed.

As I parked in front of the store, a darkly brown man stepped out. He looked rope-wiry and rank in a flat-brimmed hat, jeans, and only a vest in spite of the sharp wind. A knife the size of a small sword dangled from his belt. I couldn't see his shadowed eyes, but his mouth pursed as if to spit when he passed my Caddy with the temporary tags. Fucking tourist. Then he climbed into an ancient GMC pickup and rattled away.

Inside the store, blinking against the sudden shade, I paused as the tall blonde behind the counter rang up a candy sale and made change for a couple of young Mexican-American kids. She looked up, her mouth moved as if to ask if she could help, then tears filled her eyes and she rushed around the counter to hug me long and hard, as if I were her long-lost father. She even whispered "Milo" against my shoulder.

Shit, I had driven two thousand miles to be attacked by a woman I had never seen before. But I didn't say anything. My life had always been like that.

After a long moment, the woman realized that I wasn't responding in kind, so she stepped back, wiping her eyes. "Milo," she said, "it's me. Whitney. C.W.'s wife."

"Wife?"

"Whitney. From Meriwether. I used to work for . . . for C.W.'s lawyer friend," she said, then paused. "You know. Solly . . . I guess they aren't exactly friends anymore."

Then I realized who she was. One of Lawyer Rainbolt's endless stream of tall, blonde, perfectly lovely, and damn smart legal secretaries. After Wynona died in a bout of gunfire, for which Sughrue blamed himself, he had split for Texas with her baby boy, Lester. This woman had started dropping into my bar, the Slumgullion, shyly asking about Sughrue, but not often enough to make me remember her name. That woman was just barely visible beneath the face of this one. Her darkly burned face with a fan of hard-sun wrinkles winking white at the corners of her blue eyes looked nothing like the one I remembered. What time couldn't do, Sughrue and the West Texas climate had. Still lovely and surely still smart, even though she *had* married the crazy bastard, her face no longer even vaguely resembled the distant, professional mask I remembered. This was the face of a woman who would kick your ass and give you an hour to draw a crowd.

"Whitney . . ." I said. "I'm sorry, but is that your first or last name?"

In answer, she laughed, bright silver peals that chased the shadows from among the half-empty shelves. "I could tell that you never remembered my name," she said, smiling, then added proudly, "Whitney Peterson . . . well, Sughrue, now," and shook my hand. "I'm so glad you're here. C.W. will be so happy to see you. You just missed him, you know."

I should have recognized the knife, I thought. "I didn't know . . ." I said.

"Oh, we didn't tell anybody," she continued. "We didn't want anybody to know. We did it in the hospital . . ." Then she paused; a shade fell across her face. "I better let him tell you about that," she said quietly. Then she grabbed a tablet off the counter and began to draw. "Let me show you how to find the place. I'd call, but he won't have a telephone in the house." She tore a sheet off the tablet, handed it to me as if it were the winning ticket for a lottery I hadn't entered, then dropped her eyes and added, "When you get out to the trailer, tell him I'm right behind you. Just as soon as I can get Dulcy to relieve me. I'll bring dinner. And tequila. And some more beer. And we'll have an evening of it . . ."

Her wrinkles deepened with sadness, as if she meant to weep again.

"Is there any place to stay in this town?" I asked, to bring her back to this moment.

"Oh, you have to stay with us. You must. The trailer is a double-wide. With an extender. We've got tons of room . . ."

Eventually, I convinced her that unannounced guests deserved to pay for their own space. So I left, loaded down with tamales, ice, and beer, and took a room at the only open motel, the Cuero, named I assumed for the dry creek that skirted the tiny town, and followed her map south and east of town.

The rough mountains had ended north and west of Fairbairn, but they had left a score of rocky echoes trailing into the desert. Scuts of wispy clouds troubled the afternoon sky, flirting with a half-moon rising. On the parched flats between the outcroppings, the desert wind picked up strength, moaned and rattled, shifting even the weight of my new Detroit Iron as I rode south and east, following Whitney's directions, trying not to think about what she had said, the H-word.

Hospitals had already taken enough of my friends. My people had a history of living until somebody killed them. Usually themselves. But Sughrue's mother had died of lung cancer years ago. And his crazy father of a benign brain tumor. So without thinking it, the worst came to mind. If the bastard was dying, I told myself, I wouldn't tell him why I'd come hunting him. No matter what. And I wouldn't cry, either. At least not sober.

I turned onto a dirt track a couple of miles past a pretty little roadside park, stopped to open a wire gap, then eased the Beast down a one-lane track, rutted and rocky, that led between two rusty barbed-wire fences across a flat pasture where a dozen antelope grazed on invisible grass, then through another gap, across another pasture. This one rolling toward the blue mountains beyond. And filled with tiny horses grazing. Those little horses were my last straw. All over again. I grabbed another beer. My second of the day, of the decade. It worked just fine, just wonderful. And I ignored the fucking little horses flittering like gnats at the corner of my eye.

Once through the last gap, I glanced back at the trail of dust I'd left, in spite of driving slowly, as it fled before the ever-rising wind. Then at the road ahead. More of the same. Winding over a couple of small ridges and around another heap of rocks, I found Sughrue's double-wide permanently installed and sided with rough boards nestled in a small depression, as if seeking lee shelter from all the winds that might blow. Some sort of unfinished frame structure stood in front of the trailer and a metal shed behind, with a windmill and horse trough beyond that.

I parked in front, honked the horn into the wind without response, then walked up to the trailer's steps. The frame structure turned out to be a grape arbor of some kind, standing over a patio in progress, Mexican tile set directly on the hard-packed ground. The marker strings hummed in the wind, and the dead vines rattled, almost blotting out the pumping grind of the windmill. I turned back, surveyed the thorny brush—greasewood I guessed from reading western novels—scattered with dwarf mesquite.

A child's voice shouted "Yo!" from the corner of the house, and I turned quickly enough to catch a glimpse of a small figure darting around the corner. Before I could take a step in that direction, though, a brown blur swept from under the steps, a forearm as hard and unforgiving as sun-dried leather locked around my throat, and I could feel the point of a knife blade under my ear. Actually, the point was too sharp to feel. What I felt was the slow trickle of blood down my neck. Another goddamned suit for the cleaners.

A voice hissed, the breath beside my face smelling of dried beef and chilies, tequila and lime and fear, a whisper as roughly soft as a wood rasp in white pine.

"Who the fuck are you, buddy?" it said, then the forearm eased slightly off my throat.

"It's me, you fucking idiot," I gasped. "I gave you that knife."

Everything stopped for a moment. Then released.

"Milo?" Sughrue said as I turned. He slid the twelve-inch blade of the full-sized Ruana Bowie back into its sheath. "What the hell are you doing in those clothes?"

I might have asked the same thing.

It was the guy from the parking lot in front of the Dew Drop Inn. Except he had exchanged his jeans for a loincloth and his hat for a leather string around his forehead holding back the long sun-bleached hair. Up close I could see a puckered scar that divided his ridged abdomen. And Sughrue's blue eyes in this rawhide stranger's face.

The beef had been whittled away, the stocky body now fence-rail thin instead of cornerpost solid, the eyes as wild and shifty as those of the longhorns, the old laugh lines of his face washed out, blown away. When he finally smiled, I thought his face would crack.

"Goddammit," he said, "you got your fucking money." My insane mother had convinced my father to keep my inheritance in trust until I was fifty-three so I wouldn't squander it on wild women, whiskey, and trout streams. As my father had. "You finally got the money." Sughrue hugged me so hard he nearly knocked the breath out of me. "So how is it? Being rich?"

I didn't bother to answer but nodded at the scar. "Your wife said you'd been in the hospital," I said when he turned me loose. I pointed at his scar. I swear he flinched.

"It's nothing," he said quickly.

"Nothing?"

"Had a little trouble up in New Mexico," he said, trying to smile. "Nothing serious. I'm fine. Never been better," he went on as Baby Lester crept quietly around the near corner of the trailer to wrap his brown arms around the corded leg of his adopted father. Baby Lester wasn't a baby anymore. Just a smaller version of Sughrue, silent and wary, and dressed like his foster dad. He would have looked at home on one of the dwarf horses. "This is your Uncle Milo," Sughrue said to Lester, and the small boy shook my hand solemnly. "Why don't you grab us a couple of beers, son?" Sughrue said. "Unless your Uncle Milo is still on the wagon . . ."

"I just fell off today," I admitted as Lester went up the steps to the front door.

As soon as it closed behind the boy, Sughrue turned to me, asking with a wolfish grin that only hardened his icy blue eyes, "How the hell did you find me, old man?"

"I hired a private eye," I said, laughing. The bark that escaped his thin smile didn't exactly resemble laughter. "Just a joke," I explained.

My eye had taken several days to open, but it had healed long before the sick headaches expired. Just using the telephone brought the dizziness back. Driving and talking became drug experiences. Just as I was about to give up on Sughrue, quit and drift with my tail between my legs, I found a mailman to buy and he came up with an address for Baby Lester from a rocking horse his grandmother mailed to him.

Earlier, the grandmother wouldn't give me the time of day. She claimed not to have the slightest idea where Sughrue had taken her grandbaby. In fact, she offered to hire me to find him. Both her children were dead, she said, and it was that son of a bitch Sughrue's fault. And now her only grandbaby was gone. She had blood in her eye and vengeance wearing down her teeth, she said. But I didn't believe a word of it.

"You taught me," I said. "I found the post office bar." Something about working for the Postal Service drove me to drink. And other acts of madness.

"Shit," Sughrue said dryly. "I kept telling Grammy not to mail that fucking rocking horse. But I guess it was too late by then, wasn't it? Pretty slick, Milo."

"I learned it from you," I said, but he didn't seem amused.

Baby Lester arrived with two bottles of Dos X's, which Sughrue promptly opened with his teeth.

"Some shit don't change," I said as he handed me the icy bottle. But he didn't even smile. "Whitney said she'd bring out dinner and some more beer just as soon as somebody named Dulcy came to work."

"Fucking Dulcy is hanging at a jackpot rodeo up by Alpine," Sughrue said, which probably explained the little cowboy clowns. Then he spit on the ground, adding, "She'll be pig-drunk and crotch-sore for the next couple of days. Whitney'll have to close early. But she won't. Stubborn woman. Dammit."

"Well, you married her," I said. "Congratulations."

"Fuck you," he said, then almost smiled. "Let's get out of the wind. Love this country, man, but hate the fucking wind."

"Ambiguity," I ventured. "Always your strong suit. Love a stubborn woman, but hate being married to her . . ." But the joke died before we took a step.

Sughrue and I had been buddies from the moment we met in the early seventies. He showed up in Meriwether chasing a pharmacist from Redwood City, just weeks after I had opened a PI office because the sheriff's department had terminated my deputy's job for lack of morals. I didn't believe punchboard and poker games were mortal sins or that a couple of sad half-breed whores threatened the moral fiber of Meriwether County. When Sughrue checked in with the police department, an old pal of mine sent him to me, since Sughrue's California license didn't buy doodley-squat in Montana.

So I completed his search for the pharmacist, and Sughrue confronted him. The guy had a fugitive warrant on him, so we could have taken him anytime and any way we wanted. But Sughrue wanted to be kind, let the old boy have one last drink and one last piss. Rather than go home, the pharmacist hanged himself on his knees in front of the urinal, and the resultant lawsuits drove Sughrue out of California. So instead of returning to Moody County in South Texas, where he'd been raised, he came to Montana. Other people had come for worse reasons.

We'd partnered for a time, long enough for him to qualify for his Montana ticket, then we got into a moral argument about one of our clients—something about fucking runaway wives—and that turned into a drunken fistfight, which I lost. Only Tommy Ray ever hit me harder.

We parted ways. Badly. The next time we crossed paths, in a bar in Paradise, Montana, I broke his right collarbone with a pool cue and, with him one-armed and hurting, managed to fight him to a draw. When we got out of the Saunders County jail the next morning, we decided that not being friends was too much trouble. So we were buddies again.

Out of the wind, for Sughrue, meant another flat tile patio under another grape arbor behind the trailer, where we sat, mostly silent, drinking beer and smoking my cigarettes—he decided to quit quitting, too—until the sun hit the horizon and the wind fell. Then in the sweet dusky light he built a tiny smokeless fire and squatted, sipping slow beers until deep-dark-thirty, when Whitney's lights came bouncing up the trail.

After dinner, Sughrue put the boy to bed, leaving Whitney and me on the patio. I stirred the Indian fire as we listened to Sughrue's voice reading to the boy. It sounded like Dickens.

"Doesn't sound like Dr. Seuss," I said, quietly, as I cracked two more beers. "More like *Hard Times*."

"C.W. thinks that children's books don't prepare children for the real world," she said, not a hint of judgment in her voice, no more than when she added, "He's crazy, you know."

"He's always been crazy," I joked.

Whitney's pale eyes darkened as tendrils of flame ate the small dry wood, then she stood abruptly. "I'm going to bed, Milo," she said. "Maybe he'll talk to you."

"Don't mean to interfere, ma'am, but you ought not to marry a man who won't talk to you," I said, stupid now I suppose with drink. "Sorry. None of my business . . ."

"I married him so he wouldn't die," she answered like a woman who knew, "but I can't make him live." Then she said good night and trudged into the trailer as if climbing the steps of a gallows.

I wanted to put my hand under her slim elbow and help, but knew better. I'd done enough marital work in the old days, to smell the rift between them even before I heard it, and during my marrying years, when I had been known as the Dick Butkus of domestic relations, even I could recognize sadness in a good woman.

Looking back over my five marriages and four divorces—one of my wives died in a car wreck with three sailors before we could get divorced—sometimes I wanted to track those women down to ask what we had done wrong. But I knew better than that. What we'd done wrong was to marry. The marriages are just flings and larks and hangover refuges. At least my only son was lucky. His mother, Ellen, had married a decent man who raised him well, and when I stopped in San Francisco on the way to El Paso from Seattle to see the boy and his wife, they treated me like an aging uncle, some distant and dimly remembered relation, whose company they enjoyed but didn't quite understand, but for whom they honestly cared. It was a lovely gift, and I thanked them for it, an act I perhaps had too often neglected during my earlier years.

Sughrue broke the thought when he stepped outside, unscrewing the cap on a bottle of tequila. He took a pull, then handed it to me. I took a sip, prepared for liquid fire, but touched a soft smoky taste almost like a good single-malt whisky. Not bad. I had another, then stared at the blue horseshoe on the label. Sughrue slipped a skinny joint and a kitchen match from his vest pocket, then fired them both.

"Not bad," I said, passing him the tequila. "And I wouldn't mind a hit off that doobie, either, but I want you to know that if you're going to continue to jerk me around and avoid talking about this shit . . ."

"What shit?" he asked blandly enough to piss me off.

"This," I hissed, suddenly angry, slamming my hands against the rocks of his shoulders, "this hiding out shit . . ."

"You too drunk to drive that hog, Milo?" he said. I shook

my head, still angry. "Let me put my pants on," he said mildly, "then let's take a ride, old man."

His story about getting shot drifted like the trip he'd made that day through the Rio Grande Valley north of El Paso, back in town after a long, ugly chase to catch a bail jumper, a child molester who had once been a citizen. There was that. And the fear that the bastard would slither through the system, more trouble than he was worth.

But mostly the wandering, afternoon road trip was about Wynona, Baby Lester's mom. Sughrue still blamed himself, though nobody else did. And on his way to see the sunset over the desert, Sughrue stopped for a six-pack in a New Mexican beer joint and somehow got involved in a hassle between the bartender and a group of El Paso Chicanos, led by a tall, loud kid.

Words were exchanged. Then the big kid whipped a cheap, snub-nosed .38 out of his back pocket and snapped a round at the bartender, a loud, stinky pop that smashed an old Coors sign. The second round clipped right between Sughrue's fingers, between the little finger and the ring finger on his right hand, right through the beer can, and into his gut.

In that moment the motes dancing on the shafts of sun shivered with the cloud of gun cotton, wadding, and unexploded powder grains, not to mention the fucking lead, plus the vaporized beer from the murdered can. But by the time Sughrue let this random madness roar through his mind, before he could step forward, the flattened .38 lead had tumbled through the edge of his liver, several loops of gut, and his left kidney, where the spent round died like a lost marble.

Between midnight and sunrise Sughrue stopped talking; we sat on a picnic table at the little rest area just up the road. Stone Corrals, it was called, I learned from the sign as I pissed on it. A short ride from the trailer. Sughrue loved the Beast but couldn't stand to be inside too long. When I walked back to the table, he took up the tale again.

"So they took the kidney and a couple of feet of intestine," he said jauntily, then gunned a beer. "The only telephone number in my wallet was Whitney's." He sounded embarrassed. "The hospital called her. I didn't want to call anybody. I don't know. Maybe I was ashamed. They say it happens that way sometimes. Maybe I wasn't too lucid. I don't fucking know. Anyway, she came down, hung around, and finally said it might cheer both of us up to get married. So we did."

"So what the hell are you doing out here in the middle of nowhere? Playing cowboys and Apaches?"

"I came down this way once," he said softly, "on a job, and I liked the country. It suits my personality." Then he stopped and pointed his finger at me. "You ever realize that you and me, we've always lived close enough to the border to run if we have to?"

"Sounds right," I agreed, and he just let it hang there. "So what's the problem?"

"What the hell are we running from, man? What are we afraid of?" Sughrue paused, then walked away for a moment, hitting on the tequila bottle, then back to the cooler for a beer. He offered me a drink, which I declined. Another test maybe, but maybe I just needed to be a little sober, now. Then Sughrue turned away from me. At first I couldn't hear him, so I moved closer.

". . . all the customers ran, everybody ran, but the *cholos,* the kids, those fuckers dragged me out back to the edge of the irrigation ditch, then the big one stuck the pistol in my ear and pulled the fucking trigger, pulled the fucking trigger with the barrel in my ear . . ."

"I don't understand," I said, quietly.

An easy breeze rattled the stunted trees among the rocks. Stars and a half-moon filled the night sky with enough light to see a small herd of desert white-tailed deer grazing in the shadows across the highway. They raised their soft noses and flickering ears at a rattle of gunfire from the south.

"What the hell is that?" I asked.

"Hollywood blanks," he answered. "Some asshole is rehearsing a western movie around here. On the old pieces of the gunnery range. Down by Castillo. Fuck 'em."

"Fuck 'em?"

"They don't know a thing about gunfire," he said softly.

"Or having a thirty-eight stuck in your ear?"

"You're dead right there, bro'."

"What happened?"

"The goddamned firing pin shattered," Sughrue said. "I heard it. Broke like an ice crystal. I still hear it. Then the big guy threw the pistol away."

He was talking but wasn't getting to it. I knew that much. Pushing wouldn't help. It had taken two years and ten thousand drinks to get the story of his Vietnam troubles, particularly the one that nearly got him sent to Leavenworth. I didn't have either the time or the liver for this one.

"Yeah," I said into the silence.

"So I rolled into the irrigation ditch," he said. "The guy who shot me wanted to come after me, but the other guys, they were dressed out and didn't want to fuck up their good clothes. What the hell, they said, I was one dead fucking gringo already.

"I didn't disagree with them, either," he continued. "I floated along, drifting and dreaming. I might still be there, but I bumped into a head gate. Climbed out, walked back to the van, and drove myself to the hospital down in El Paso."

"Nobody picked you up?"

"Drunk, wet, bloody in the middle of the afternoon," he said, "who would pick me up?" Then he looked at me and laughed. "You would, you dumb son of a bitch. Even if you didn't know it was me. Asshole."

"Thanks."

"You're welcome."

It passed for a joke between us.

Until he told me what he had been working toward.

"I heard them talking, Milo. I've got just enough border Spanish to understand a little. Somebody hired these fucking guys to kill me," he said flatly. "Some son of a bitch."

"Who?"

"They didn't say and I couldn't think of a soul who'd want to. Still can't."

"What'd the cops say?" I asked.

"Fucking cops," he answered. "Not much. Couldn't find the piece. Told me I was crazy. According to the bartender, the *cholo* was just some drug dealer passing through town.

Nobody would dare testify, even if they could find him. And according to the Luna County Sheriff's Department, if I wasn't crazy or drunk or stoned, or all three at once, it was just some hangover from my troubles down here a few years ago."

Sughrue stopped. I knew that sorry story. It had ended where this one began. With the death of Wynona Jones.

"The fucking DEA ran Dottie and Barnstone all the way to Coasta Rica, so I didn't have any friends. And all kinds of law, they're still mad at me. If the licensing rules weren't so fucked down here, man, I'd never have gotten a ticket to work.

"So the official stance is that since I'm not dead," Sughrue growled, "it's not their problem. So fuck it."

"And if you're dead? Fuck that, too?"

"Right on, brother," he muttered. "But I ain't dead. And I know the bastards are still looking for me."

"So let's find the bastards," I said. "They'll tell us who hired them." In the old days, Sughrue could make a rock talk. "Then we'll know who."

"You're big on finding people, Milo," he said softly. "Hell, you couldn't even find me."

"Not quite true, Sonny."

Sughrue bowed his head, then turned away from me, whispering, "I think Whitney'd leave me, man. She for damn sure would. I owe her big-time. And Lester loves her like fire."

Not just Lester. I had to think about that. This was Sughrue's first marriage, maybe his first longtime live-in love. The child seemed deeply attached to Whitney. If Sughrue was going with me, I needed him whole. Not looking back all the time. And I owed him, too, so it was an easy decision to make.

"Okay," I said, "I'll do it without you. I'll find them. Then you can stop hiding."

"No," he pleaded, then grabbed a sob before it escaped into the dark air. "Fuck that. I can't afford any more debts."

I wouldn't even guess what had happened in the hospital to make Whitney think she had to marry Sughrue, but that was the debt Sughrue had trouble carrying. Maybe a little anger would help.

"Your sorry ass ain't the boss of me," I said.

Sughrue turned, tears glistening in his eyes, his fists knotted. He remembered the line. He'd said it to me just before our first fight. "Goddamn you, Milo."

"Goddamn you," I said. "Fucking coward. Tell the woman the truth. Maybe she won't leave."

"What fucking truth?" he shouted. The whitetails scrambled toward safety, bounding rocks with flags waving, as the echoes of his scream rattled the stillness.

"That somebody shot you in the guts, and you got scared. For the first time in your life," I said, calmly. "So welcome to the human race."

"I'm not scared of you, asshole."

"I didn't put a round in you," I said. "Plus I'm your friend. And except for the war, your oldest friend."

The breath Sughrue took seemed to suck all the fresh air out of the night. He took a step toward me, nearly cocked a fist.

"I've got a pool cue in my pocket," I said.

"No, you don't. It'd make that silly-ass suit hang wrong," he said. Then Sughrue smiled.

"It's an Italian cue," I said, "light, troublesome, fashionable, and ineffective."

Sughrue finally laughed.

"I'll talk to her," he said. "I can't promise anything, except that I'll talk to her."

"She loves you, Sughrue," I said, "and she's a damn smart woman. She'll do the right thing. Trust her. And if she won't let you go," I added, "I'll still go alone."

"Why are you doing this, old man?" he asked.

"I want something from you."

"What?"

"I want you to help me find a banker."

"What for?"

"Well, you know. A long time ago I tried to throw all my guns away . . ."

"At least you got rid of the ammo," he said.

"And out of the business. Something I had to do, I guess, a promise I needed to keep," I said. "Too many people got hurt . . ."

"Tell me about it," he said.

"But when I find this son of a bitch," I said, "I want you to hold him while I take a double-bitted axe to him. Chop off his hands at the wrist and feet at the ankles. Maybe some other parts, too."

"Jesus, man. What'd he do?"

"He stole my father's money," I admitted, "stole it with a computer."

"But the car, the clothes . . ."

"I sold everything he didn't steal. The office building, the bar, the rent property. Everything. I've got enough money to chase him for a couple of years," I said, "living good. Maybe even three. Then after that . . . who knows? Maybe I can sell the Caddy . . ."

"Sell your wardrobe first," he suggested.

"But I'm going to catch the son of a bitch, even if I have to do it on Social Security."

"You never paid much Social Security," he said. "Shit, man, you're crazier than I am."

"Just older," I said, "and slower. It took me almost two years to get mad."

My father, trapped in a bad marriage, in love with another bad woman, had shotgunned himself before I was a teenager. My mother hanged herself with her queen-sized panty hose at a fat farm in Arizona while I was a teenager in the Korean War. As they say, shit happens. I learned to live with it. But she had hated my father so much, she took it out on me for being his only son. She and her lawyer managed to convince him to tie the family money, principal and interest, in trust until I was fifty-three.

During my years as a deputy sheriff, a private investigator, and a bartender, I could forget about the money. Mostly. The drink helped, I think, a little bit. Then the chore of sobriety helped, too. It was just a thing in my future, assuming I had one in those days, something like a lottery ticket. Hell, when I got to the bank on my fifty-third birthday only to find the trust department in a furor over the disappearance of Andy Jacobson with the money wire transferred into the Bermuda Triangle of Caribbean banks, three million plus dollars of my father's money, I just accepted it, like some Zen warrior,

took the punch, and walked back to the bar, went behind the
stick still wearing my three-piece courtroom suit, and
worked my shift. Without a word.

The FBI did their job, sort of, found out that Jacobson—a
paunchy, balding little banker guy with bad skin and worse
breath who got his job because he was married to one of his
bosses' ugly daughters and who used to lean on my bar and sip
cheap draft beers and treat me to his coltish giggle as he reported the ups and downs of my unavailable trust fund—had
slipped out on his fish-eyed Christian wife and was hosing
some beefy lady poet out at Mountain States College. But that
was a dead end. The lady poet turned out to be operating on a
pretty good set of fake identification, which they found in her
apartment, and a pretty good life story. According to her, she
had been a stripper, bartender, lady wrestler, and bouncer in
the Bay Area. She had even managed to publish a chapbook of
poetry and work a couple of temporary replacement teaching
jobs on the fake paper. But academics are easy to fool. As far
as anybody could tell, she'd never been photographed or fin-
gerprinted, and her alias, Rita Van Tasselvitch, didn't show up
on anybody's computer AKA lists. Whoever she was, she and
Jacobson had simply disappeared. As soon as the feds started
babbling about a vague mob connection, I knew my money
was long gone. In their minds. But not in mine, not yet.

After poking around her colleagues in the English Department at Mountain States, most of whom were on her side and
blamed Jacobson for corrupting her talent and intelligence
with money, I gave up that trail and sued the bank, but it
looked like a long haul to nowhere. A year drifted past, another six months, then one afternoon it hit me so hard I nearly
took a drink. I poured a dozen shots, then dumped them down
the drain. Then decided to hunt up Sughrue. He used to say,
"Anybody who speaks badly of revenge ain't never lost nothing important." If anybody could find Jacobson, the large
lady poet, and the money, he could. But faced with his story, I
didn't mind standing in line behind Sughrue for my shot at revenge. Hell, I had nothing but lots of time and a little money.

Back at the trailer Sughrue offered the extra bedroom
again, but I knew what was coming when he went to bed—

angry words, tears, the slap of bare flesh—so after we promised to meet for breakfast in Fairbairn, I left Sonny to the rest of his night. But in the rearview mirror as I drove away I saw him heading for the desert horizon, a rough blanket over his shoulder. Followed moments later by Baby Lester's tiny figure. Then Whitney's larger one. It was a family, I suppose, three people wrapped in raw wool, huddled on the desert floor, praying for sleep without dreams.

At ten the next morning, when we gathered around a table at the local cafe, El Corazón del Leon—The Lionheart, I think—everybody looked tired. Even in fresh clothes. Whitney, beautifully haggard in jeans and a worn cotton work shirt. And Baby Lester, now dressed like a normal child on his way to preschool. Even Sughrue had changed out of his Apache drag. I had tried to tidy up but not too hard. I managed a white suit and an Italian silk shirt in a pattern that resembled dog viscera, but shaving had been beyond me.

"I don't know if I can eat with that thing hanging on your chest," Sughrue offered as the waitress walked toward our table. "Who're you supposed to be this morning? Don Johnson?"

"My hangovers don't have names," I said, woolly worms under my skin. At least that hadn't changed. The waitress was very polite to me. As if I might be a television star.

After a breakfast of eggs and chorizo, fresh tortillas and peppers, aided by streams of strong coffee, at least the Sughrue family looked like human beings. Or some West Texas version of them. And I felt less like an animal.

Nobody had much to say. Sughrue's duffel was waiting in the back of the truck. Whitney didn't say a word through breakfast, not even as Sughrue tossed his gear in the trunk of my Beast, then played goodbye grab-ass with Lester. But after the boy climbed into the truck and Sughrue into my ride, she hugged me dry-eyed, then held my shoulders.

"I know you don't know anything about me, Milo, but I grew up too pretty for my own good," she said, surprising me with a story instead of a plea to bring him back alive. "My mother always envied me," she continued, "and my father was afraid to touch me after I started my periods. And the men I've tried to love have always been afraid of me. Or even worse, prettier than me. It hasn't been fun. Except for Sonny. And that's probably because he's always been too crazy to be afraid."

I didn't know what to say, so I kept my mouth shut.

"But now he's afraid, too," she added. "Last night, after you left, he went out into the desert to sleep with the snakes and the thorns, instead of spending his last few hours with me. Then Lester went. Then me. Too fucking crazy." Then her voice hardened. "If you bring the son of a bitch back, Milo, bring him back whole."

Hey, lady, I wanted to say, I'm not some fucking spirit doctor. Sometimes love made me angry. Even when I wasn't involved in it. "I can't promise anything," I said sharply, then quickly apologized. "I'm sorry. I'll do my best."

"Just be his friend," she said. "He needs a friend. I'm tired of being his only friend." Then she put a hand on my shoulder. "And one more thing."

"What's that?"

"When you find the son of a bitch who shot him. Cut his fucking nuts off, okay. Then kill him." She kissed me sweetly on the cheek and climbed into the pickup.

As Sughrue and I drove north toward the interstate, he asked me what Whitney had said.

"She said we were assholes, buddy," I answered. "But you were the worst."

"Boy," he said mildly, "she's sure got you pegged." Then he actually smiled. "Let's see what this fucking Beast can do."

And he smiled as I showed him.

We had lunch at a place called Chope's in the Upper Valley, across the New Mexican border north of El Paso, then eased up to La Esperansa del Mundo. On the way, I made him loan me the S&W .38 Airweight out of his duffel. He wanted to know why. "I've heard what you think you remember," I said. "Now let's see what you really remember." Two pickups were parked outside the small adobe building.

"Let me handle this," Sughrue said as he held the bar door open for me. "These people have different ways . . ."

The two beers I'd had with lunch hadn't killed the worms yet. "Fuck you," I said. "You've handled it enough."

Inside the pleasant cozy place, two old Mexican-American farmers sat at a table covered with Schlitz cans and tobacco flakes. The bartender gave us a narrow look, then turned back to his Spanish soap opera on the television. He didn't need or want our business. I ordered four cans of Schlitz, which he reluctantly brought.

"What are you doing, man?" Sughrue asked as I carried the cans to the farmers' table.

I sat the beers and myself down. "Excuse me," I said. "You gentlemen look like regulars. Maybe you were here the day some asshole put a round in Señor Sughrue over there?" The old boys looked at me as if I were crazy, then hustled out the door without speaking as I carried their beers back to the bar.

"See what I said," Sughrue whispered.

"Just exactly what I wanted," I said in a loud voice. Then I stepped around the bar and switched off the television. "Hey, bartender," I said, "maybe you remember that day?"

Sughrue started to say, "He's not the guy who was . . ."

"*No habla English, señor,*" the bartender said.

"Good," I said, flashing an old badge at him. "You *habla* F-B-fucking-I?"

"Hey, man, I wasn't even here," the bartender said with a Texas accent. "Didn't you hear what . . ."

"I don't care what he says," I said. "He was fucked up that afternoon. It's you I care about. We're going out back to look around for a minute. When we get back, you best have your shit stacked in an orderly pile, señor, or you're looking at a bus trip south of the border."

"Jesus," he squealed, "I'm a fucking citizen. I was born in Dallas."

"That's never stopped us before, amigo," I said, "so get your story ready. We'll be right back."

Then I led Sughrue out the back door of the bar to the junky verge of the irrigation ditch that branched through the cotton and chili fields. He didn't much want to go, but he went anyway, caught up in the act.

"You got another one of those needle-dick joints,

Sughrue?" I asked as we stopped beside an abandoned culti-
vator.

"What?" he said. "Sure. Why?"

"I'm asking the questions," I said. "Smoke the son of a
bitch before that guy calls the cops. Then sit down."

Sughrue smoked like a stove for a few minutes. I watched
the pale blue sky rent with contrails, watched small groups of
cotton pickers glean the machine-swept fields, watched the
slight breeze unburden the cottonwoods along the ditch of
their last leaves.

"Hey," he said shortly. "It's hard to get stoned while
you're watching, Milo."

"I don't have time for this sensitive shit," I said. "Sit the
fuck down. Close your eyes. And breathe deep."

Sughrue did, as docile as an old dog.

As soon as he calmed down, but before he calmed down
too much, I shoved him on his side with my foot. He
protested, but neither too loudly nor too long. When I stuck
the Airweight into his ear, he nearly jumped out of his skin,
but he kept his eyes tightly closed.

"Oh, fuck, man," he muttered. "It's loaded."

"Damn right," I said, though I'd unloaded it. "It's supposed to be. Keep your fucking eyes shut, gringo. The next
sound you hear is the next to last one you'll ever hear . . ." I
cocked the .38. Sughrue curled into a ball, holding his gut.
"What's next?"

"What?"

"The sound. What is it? Ice breaking on Flathead Lake?
The Meriwether during spring thaw? A martini glass . . ."

"That's it. That's the one."

"Goddamn son of a motherfucking bitch. Piece of shit," I
growled. "What's next? What? Goddammit, what?"

"I don't know," he said, then opened his eyes.

"Look around," I suggested, "then come inside. Let's have
another beer."

Before Sughrue came in, I had time to apologize profusely
to the bartender, whose name was Teo, buy him two beers,
and discover that he had a brother-in-law who had worked
sugar beets in Wyoming and apples in eastern Washington,

which nearly made us neighbors. In the western scheme of things.

"Pretty sneaky," Sughrue said, smiling, "but it didn't work, asshole. The only thing I remember is that I shit my pants when the firing pin shattered. Isn't that lovely."

"That's something," I said, laughing so the suddenly terrified bartender could laugh. "Let's look at some highway," I said. I overtipped the bartender, then we left.

"What's next?" Sughrue asked as we pulled back on the road.

"Your New Mexico license is still good, I hope?"

"For another six months," he said.

"Good," I said. "I'll hire a lawyer in Las Cruces, who then will hire you, then maybe the fucking sheriff's department won't shoot us on sight."

Sughrue thought about that. I slid a tape of Gregorian chants into the tape deck and let it carry us softly away toward the seat of Luna County.

We were winding under Interstate 10, looking for the markers to downtown, when Sughrue sat up abruptly.

"The tree," he said. "When he threw the piece away, it hit a fucking tree." Then he turned to me. "You son of a bitch."

"Don't flatter me," I said, turning the car around. We could always hire a lawyer.

"I wasn't," he said. "I nearly shit my pants again."

With Teo's rickety ladder and his approval, Sughrue found the cheap revolver in surprisingly good shape lodged in the rotten crotch of the second cottonwood in the line along a shallow subsidiary ditch.

"All right," Sughrue shouted to me where I sat in a webbed folding chair. He tipped the piece off a pencil and into a baggie. "Now you can get off your ass, Milo, and do something."

"Like what?" I said, happily buzzed. But then I knew. I didn't like it, but I knew.

By noon the next day, and thanks to the house dick at the Paso del Norte, we had our Las Cruces lawyer, Teddy Tamayo, a retired district court judge, a short, stout old man who had worked his way through college at New Mexico

State and law school in Albuquerque as a professional wrestler known as the Masked Avenger across the border in Juárez. Teddy thought we were a couple of pretty funny gringos, and he offered to take my retainer just as soon as he managed to stop his mad chortling. And checked my Montana references. For once, my old buddy, Jamison—the decent man who had mostly raised my son and who was now chief of the Meriwether Police—came through with the right words.

As he handed me a receipt for the cash, Teddy looked up at my partner and said, "Mr. Sughrue. I have heard it said that you were the man responsible for the death of one Joe Don Pines."

That would be Wynona's former stepfather, and Baby Lester's father, and a capital slimeball, by all accounts.

"I heard he killed himself," Sughrue answered.

"Unfortunately, men like that never do," Teddy said, laughing, then added, "Many people owe you thanks."

"Nobody owes me anything," Sughrue said, then stepped out of the office.

"Did I hurt his feelings?" Teddy asked.

"He ain't got none," I said, then left, too.

The next part seemed harder.

When Sughrue and I walked into the dingy air of Duster's at four-thirty, I made sure we covered the dress code: windbreakers, jeans, and T-shirts; steel-toed work boots for balance; and a criminal air about our eyes. Sughrue didn't have any tattoos, but I had a blurry patch of gunpowder burn on my right forearm that might have been a tattoo once. Or at least a grease spot. I was glad because, in spite of Rocky's prediction that the law might keep his brother this time, Tommy Ray leaned on the bar. At least he only had one usable arm. They had bound the other to his chest with a scraggly body cast. From the looks of it, T.R. had already seen action.

"Hey, Tommy Ray," I said as we pulled up beside him. "Buy you a tequila?"

His head turned like a giant boulder toward my voice, then he stared at me for a long time. Behind me Sughrue whis-

pered, "You didn't tell me how fucking big he was, Milo."
But I had.

Then suddenly T.R. grinned, his giant teeth exposed like
a bad dog's, a broken one gleaming in front. "Hey, dude,
how's it hanging?" he said. "You're the old fart who hit me
with his hat." T.R. reached up to scratch the scab on his eyebrow where I had cut it with the jab. Nobody had taken out
the stitches yet. One came away with T.R.'s dirty fingernail.
"Let me buy the drinks," he offered.

"You're too big to argue with," I said. T.R. laughed
wildly, but Sughrue didn't crack a smile. Not even when I introduced him, as usual: *Sugh,* as in sugar; and *rue,* as in rue
the fucking day.

The greasy bartender came over to tell us that if we were
going to fight he wouldn't serve us, but when T.R. grinned at
him as if he were a bar snack, the bartender bought the first
two rounds. So we drank a bit, chatted about bar fights we'd
won and lost. Except Tommy Ray couldn't remember losing
any.

"How's the tit?" I finally asked. T.R. explained that the
stitches kept tearing out, which is why the doctor put him in
the body cast. Then he added with a grin that it was one *bad*
scar but he was having trouble deciding what kind of tattoo
to have around it.

"Dripping blood," Sughrue said under his breath. But T.R.
heard him and said he'd already rejected that one. "Teeth, I
think," he said, then wondered where my hat was, how it had
weathered the tussle. Soon it became clear that he admired
my Borsalino. I went to the car and made him a gift of it.
Even though it perched on his huge close-cropped head like
a beanie, he kept it. I could always get another hat, like a
lawyer or a gun.

"Hey, you seen Rocky around?" I asked.

T.R. gunned his tequila, then sloshed a large measure of
beer into his mouth. "Shit, dude," he said slowly, "Rocky's
really mad at me. For hittin' you. You bein' a retired officer
of the law and all. He said if you wanted to push it, I'd be
doin' hard time right now. So these days, when Rocky comes
around, I got to take off, go someplace else." Then Tommy

Ray shook his head sadly. "But he don't come around much anymore."

"Why's that?"

"He's inna hospital," Tommy Ray said seriously, poking his finger into his mouth to touch the broken tooth. "Might lose his hand . . ."

"Jesus Christ," was all I could say.

"Worse than a snakebite," Rocky said, nodding toward his right hand propped up on thin hospital pillows. "And my own little brother, too. Ain't that the shits. God knows where he had that mouth." Then he paused. "Doc says he might have to take the finger. Maybe the hand."

"I'm sorry," I said. "You didn't have to step in."

"Yeah, I did," he said. "Family. And what the hell. I knew better."

The little television on the wall murmured as *Jeopardy* came back after the commercial break. Rocky turned the sound up with his left hand. His right was wrapped in a gauze ball the size of a melon with a drain hanging out and an antibiotic drip plugged into the inside of his elbow. As we watched, he muttered the questions under his breath. He knew most of them, too. Like Sughrue usually did. It made me wish Sonny had come inside, but he said he'd had enough of that particular hospital, even if it had been the scene of his marriage.

During the commercial break before Final Jeopardy, I told Rocky that I'd paid his hospital bill.

"What the fuck did you do that for?" he asked.

"I don't know," I admitted. "An old friend of mine says I have a too finely developed sense of responsibility. Whatever, it's done."

Rocky thought about it, then shook his head. "Shit, it's not even T.R.'s fault. I knew the fucker was infected. But I was down in Culiacán setting up a run." Then he stopped. "Into California, man. I don't shit where I live. Besides, it'd be embarrassing for one of my brothers to have to pop me . . .

"After it was set, I got to drinking tequila and sampling the product, ignoring my fucking hand. Doc says that might've done it. So it's nobody's fault but my own. No reason for you to pick it up."

"Like I said, Rocky, it's done," I said. "And I never heard of a dope dealer or a hospital giving the money back." Rocky laughed shortly. "Besides, I've got a favor to ask."

"What kind?" he wanted to know. Really wanted to know. So I laid it out for him.

"Shit, man," he said, "it ain't like the old days. All these fucking computers, you know. Cops gotta log on and log off and leave an electronic trail all the way. I just don't know. But I'll call Jack—he's pretty tight with the DEA—maybe he can figure a way to do it.

"You still at the same place?" he asked. When I nodded, he said, "Must be nice."

"It ain't home."

As I opened the door, he said quietly, "Hey, man. Paying that bill, that'll draw some water with Jack. And thanks."

Jack was a skinny wire-cable of a guy wearing a bushy moustache and a ponytail, red-eyed and unshaven. But he looked like his brothers around the eyes, and I assumed he had been working undercover, so I was going to open the door. Then Sughrue demanded some ID, and we nearly lost our help right there. I cooled them off, and we handed over the cheap .38 and told him what we needed. He didn't like it, but he said he'd try. Then he took five hundred for expenses.

Jack didn't get back to us for four days. But we didn't mind. Sughrue and I spent them quietly, driving up to the Upper Valley in the mornings to jog for an hour along the levee roads along the Rio Grande. Sughrue was in great shape. He could nearly double my distance in the hour, and come back to the Caddy barely sweating. He'd been running in the desert, he said.

"Getting ready to vamoose?" I said, joking.

"Milo, I've got food, water, weapons, and ammo cached all the way to the border," he admitted. "They come for me, man, I can make it across the desert to Castillo then across the border to Enojada in twelve hours. Eighteen carrying Baby Lester on my back."

"What about Whitney?" I asked, but he just climbed in the Caddy without answering.

In the afternoons, we read or watched television, waiting soberly for Jack to call.

But he came to the hotel in person.

I poured him a large drink, which he poured down his throat, then another, without effect. "All right," he said, his thirst quenched, "you were right. The money helped. It's all gone, but this is what I've got." And he had plenty.

Teddy Tamayo had pulled some strings in Las Cruces and gotten him a copy of the ballistics report from the sheriff's department. This was the piece. And it still had a serial number. According to the ATF computer the revolver had been bought at a pawnshop in Austin by one Raymundo Lara. He even had the address. Then the bad news. It had been reported stolen ten months before Sughrue was shot. The fingerprint guy also had some good news and some bad. He was able to draw some latents off the weathered surface; but as far as he could tell, whoever had handled the revolver last had burned his fingerprints off.

"It could be any of ten thousand assholes along the border," he said.

"No, just one," Sughrue said, then walked into the other room.

"Thanks," I said. "How's Rocky? When I called yesterday, the hospital said he'd checked out." Jack just looked at me. "Well, how is he?"

"Three-fingered," he said sharply. "And as far as I can tell, Mr. Milodragovitch, you ain't exactly worth it." He didn't say it, but I could hear "bad cop" in the bottom of his voice.

"Hey," I said. "I didn't start the beef with your little brother. He could've cost me my eye, he could've gutted me, he could've killed me. So back the fuck off."

"Just stay away from my family," he said softly.

"And one more thing, Jack," I said. "You want to muck around in my past, ask somebody who knows. Leave the asshole county mounties out of it. Call the fucking chief of police in Meriwether. Jamison."

"Maybe I'll do just that," he said. "But if I were you, asshole, I'd get the fuck out of town. And take your partner along. He's even less popular than you are." Then he left.

"What the hell was that all about?" Sughrue asked from the door.

"A clash of personalities," I said. "How far's it to Austin?"

Damn near six hundred miles, as it turned out. And most of it in the cold, windy rain. But by noon-thirty the next day we tooled up South Congress toward the capitol, our trip a blur, slowed only by a quick detour to the graveyard where Sughrue's grandparents were buried down by a little town called Kyle. The norther had passed on southeast, leaving blue skies and sunshine, Austin all rain-washed limestone and shining glass.

"Anybody ever tell you that the Texas state capitol building is taller than the one in Washington?" Sughrue asked, oddly excited. I knew he had mixed feelings about Texas, but as we drifted through the Hill Country, where I hadn't seen many actual hills, Sughrue recounted some good memories of Austin. Mostly involving music, drugs, and women. But most places are like that. If you were there during the sixties.

"Washington State?" I said to torque him a bit for bragging about Texas all night.

"D.C., you jerk," he said. "Bet you didn't know that."

"Interesting," I said, staring at the capitol building across the river. "Anybody ever tell you it was pink?"

You would have thought I had called his poor dead Avon Lady mother a whore. From his stories, I knew she was the best gossip in Moody County down along the Muddy Fork of the Nueces River, where Sughrue had been raised. And that she didn't exactly live celibate after Sonny's father drifted west when he came back from WWII.

"Just look at it," I said among his spits and sputters and useless denials. "The fucker's dog-dick pink."

"It's the light," he said, then sulled up on me. All the way to the Hyatt Hotel by Town Lake.

After we unpacked in the suite, I poured my first drink in

days, then let it set on the desk as I took out the telephone book.

"Sughrue," I said. "Raymundo Lara is listed."

"No shit?" he said, then came in from his room. He picked up my Scotch, but I took it away from him. I'd failed that test. The first sip of the Macallan single-malt was worth the wait. This time.

"You know," I said, "sometimes I forget why I quit drinking."

"You were a fucking drunk," Sughrue pointed out.

"Must have been the cocaine made me drink like that," I said.

"Or maybe the crank," he said. "You were a Hoover. You're lucky to be alive, old man."

"What's with this 'old man' shit?"

Sughrue paused, swirled his Scotch, then sipped it, before he answered quietly. "You're a serious man, Milo," he said, "and it always made you seem older. And you always took care of people. Like you cared more about that sort of shit than I did."

Then he sipped the malt whisky slowly again. "I've always felt like a kid around you," he said, "so that makes you older."

I reached into my bag and found my favorite sap, the one with the circle of lead in the head and a piece of spring steel in the leather handle. "Next time you call me 'old man,' kid, I'm going to break both your elbows."

"Guess we have to get divorced right now, old man," he said, then grinned.

"Maybe you haven't noticed," I said, "but I'm not married."

"Good point," he said. "Maybe I can catch Whitney at the store . . ."

"Go ahead," I said, "this is a good hotel. We've got two telephone lines." Sughrue started for his room. "Hey. How come you don't have a telephone in the trailer? The lines run all the way out there."

"I tried, man. But every time the son of a bitch rang," he said, standing in the doorway, "my fucking heart stopped. I don't even know why." Then he closed the door.

Moments later I heard the murmurs of his heart as he talked to his lady-love and his boy-child. I tried Lara's number, but nobody answered. At least it hadn't been disconnected.

So I kept trying the number through the afternoon as we cruised Austin, following Sughrue's directions, sightseeing through his past on the soft afternoon, more like spring than fall. Turned out Sughrue hadn't really spent much time in Austin for twenty years. Things had changed.

We went for a bar-burger lunch out by the Low Water Crossing at a beer joint called the Lakeway. Not only had it obviously been attacked by yuppies—we could tell by the awnings and the chi-chi menu posted outside—but it was closed, too. So we ate across the street, in a place that seemed to think it had invented funk, sitting under a tin roof on a deck that jutted out over the blue sparkling water. The drinks seemed overpriced but they were large, and the food just average, but the waitress was lovely and cheerful, and it was pleasant until some pissant on a tremendously noisy jet-ski decided he had to show his stuff to the small crowd of late lunchers. Halfway through our sandwiches we gave up, Sughrue muttering under his breath about some people's children.

"Tonight we'll find a chicken-fried steak," Sughrue promised as I listened to Lara's number ring unanswered.

"Great," I said, "but I'll bet we'll find yuppies there, too."

"Chicken-fried steaks are bad for your heart," he said, Texas proud.

"Let's have two," I said, "apiece."

We took the Low Water Crossing across the lake and then got lost among expensive houses. A shortcut, Sughrue called it. At least we found a place to wash the road dust off the Beast. As we were sitting outside on a bench like a couple of turtles soaking up the soft fall sunshine, I remembered something.

"Did you leave your Browning under the front seat?" I asked Sughrue.

"Yeah," he answered sleepily. "Why?"

"Won't they be worried?"

"Hey, man, this is Texas. Everybody's got a pistol under the front seat."

"What do you think people carry in Montana?" I asked. "Horse turds?" But he was already asleep. I could see that I was going to have trouble with Texans. They seemed a bit self-centered to suit me. Particularly Mr. Chauncey Wayne Sughrue. For a guy who supposedly hated it, he seemed awfully much at home.

When we got to the corner in south Austin where his grandfather had built a little house stick by stick, Sughrue couldn't believe it. Some asshole had built a strip mall right on top of it, complete with a convenience store staffed by Paki's.

"Jesus," he said, "there wasn't anything here. Nothing at all. Now look at this. Goddammit. When the old man lost his place down between Kyle and Buda, he took a job with the state, him and my granny. They went out to the state farm on Webberville Road . . ."

"In most places, Sonny, the state farm is where they keep minor-league criminals."

"Retards, down here," he said.

"You mean the mentally challenged?"

"Them, too," he said, but he was someplace else. "He raised hogs for the state, bacon and ham and sausage for all the institutions around Austin back then. Had all these big retarded guys helping him. My mother was always nervous around them, but they just seemed like big kids to me."

"And you were a big kid, too?"

"Started paying adult prices at the movies when I was eight," he said, smiling, "and buying beer at twelve." Then he cracked two beers out of the backseat cooler. "Hey, Milo. If we wrap this shit up quickly, maybe . . ."

"Maybe what?"

"Maybe, we can take a turn down to South Texas, Moody County, maybe . . ."

"This ain't a vacation," I said, but I had a large swallow of cold beer and gave in to his disappointment. "But we'll try," I said, and Sughrue smiled so broadly, we didn't drive by Raymundo Lara's address. We took the rest of the day off. And the evening, too.

But I didn't stop trying Lara's number. The last time I tried, as we had a midnight drink in the bar on the top floor of the Hyatt, he still didn't answer. I thought about driving past the house, but I had made it this long without a DUI, and somehow I didn't think Austin, Texas, the place to begin. It might have been worth it, though. At least to Lara.

Before sunrise the next morning Sughrue ran me halfway around Town Lake. When we finished, he wanted to brace Lara at six o'clock in the morning, before work, but I insisted on a little background first. And a lot of coffee.

We worked the usual routines—the city directory, the library, the county courthouse, the credit bureau—only to discover a lot of boring details, none of which made him sound like the sort of guy who would need a cheap .38: Lara was current on his credit cards and mortgage; a registered voter; honorably discharged from the U.S. Army; thirty-six years old; once divorced, twice married, most recently to a woman named Analise Navarro from Del Rio, whose only court record was an action to revoke her license to cut hair.

"Why would they do that?" I asked myself.

"Nine times out of ten," Sughrue said, "it'd be for dealing coke out of her chair."

We checked for convictions but found none.

Because Raymundo was bonded, we assumed he had no police record, either. He had been a computer programmer before he took the job as a loan officer at a small state-chartered bank on the Bastrop Highway south of the airport, Pilot Knob Farmers Home Savings and Loan. It was interesting that he had been born in El Paso, and he'd paid cash for his house.

So we had some cards printed up that said we represented a local insurance agency—even used the right name—then bought a couple of cheap suits and plastic briefcases, rented an anonymous Dodge van, and walked up the stone path of the nice little native rock three-bedroom bath-and-a-half ranch-style in a corner lot in a neat northwest Austin neighborhood off Shoal Creek Boulevard.

"Did I used to do this for a living?" I asked Sughrue as I rang the doorbell. "Or did I just do it for fun?"

"Fun," Sughrue answered nervously as I pushed the button again. "Oh, shit," he said, peering around the corner of the house. "Phone line's cut," he whispered. Then we both smelled it at the same time—cold copper blood, sharp gunpowder residue, death—and strolled casually back to the van.

"What now?" Sughrue asked as we drove slowly away. "Call the cops?"

"You've got family," I said, "so I'll go in tonight. Whatever's in there will keep. And this is our only chance to see it."

It had been so long since either of us had broken into a place, neither of us had a set of lock picks. Jeweler's tools are almost as good. I had to find different places to buy a black jumpsuit, black sneakers, a watch cap, camo paint, plastic gloves, and two handheld radios. It took the rest of the day, a dozen conversations with survivalist Nazis all over central Texas, and most of our portable cash, so we didn't get to case the neighborhood as well as I would have liked before dark. At least Lara's house was rock-solid and silent, and his neighbors didn't keep outside dogs.

None of that seemed to matter, though, when I rolled out of the van as Sughrue slowed to take the corner. I was so scared—not nervous, scared—I couldn't catch a breath as I rolled sideways for a sudden but absolutely necessary piss among the weeds beneath the front shrubbery, thinking *invisible* as hard as I could. But I was out of practice. I felt like a giant steaming dog turd. So much for in and out in fifteen minutes. It took that long to make myself belly around the house to the back door, which was thankfully unlocked. My hands were shaking so badly I couldn't have unlocked the expensive dead bolt with the key.

Once inside the closed porch, the odor of violent death was nearly overpowering, even stronger than the Vicks I had rubbed under my nose. I slipped into the kitchen, which was full of expensive appliances, and closed the blinds against the slanting shafts of the streetlight, then crept into the dining room, where the blinds were already tightly closed. Before I could turn on the flashlight, though, I heard a hushed belch, then the slow click of dog paws coming from the hardwood hallway.

I played dead, or maybe I fainted, then heard quiet padding across the dining room carpet. Suddenly, a soft, warm "whoof" came from the darkness above my face, a large tongue lapped at my face, and Sughrue's harsh whisper boomed in my ear. "Ready?" he asked through the earplug.

"Fuck no!" I hissed back, then switched on the flashlight.

An old Black Lab bitch stood over me, breathing hard and wet, her grizzled muzzle in my face and her front legs braced widely. Even in the hooded red light, I could see the dark crusted blood on her shoulder. I scratched the old girl's ears, then eased her out of the way so I could stand up. She circled once, painfully, then curled in my spot and stared at me mournfully. But when I moved away to search the house, she hobbled after me.

An hour later, when Sughrue, lights off, whipped around the corner to pick me up, Sheba—as her name tag said—was still with me, wrapped in a clean beach towel. I had taken one that Lara had stolen from a South Padre hotel.

"What the fuck?" Sughrue wanted to know. "And where's your watch cap?"

"In my pocket," I said. "I puked in it. Turn at the next corner. Then let's have some headlights. And find me a fucking telephone booth."

It took so long to locate the Emergency Veterinarian Clinic in north Austin that Sheba fell asleep in my lap. She didn't complain, though, when I took off her tags and carried her to the front door and tied her to the knob with a leash I'd found hanging on the closed porch. Then back to the telephone booth to call the vet.

A young woman answered, "Dr. Porterfield. How can I help you?"

"Hey, hey, doc," I stammered, only half-faking. Then I told her that she had a dog named Sheba with two gunshot wounds tied to the front door. The vet must have had a walk-around telephone, because I heard her sigh in exasperation when she opened the front door. When she began to curse me and shout about calling the cops, I started to explain that

I hadn't shot the dog, but she wouldn't have believed me, so I hung up as the vet shouted something about AKC numbers and how she'd have my ass in a sling. But as I climbed back in the van, sighing, I knew that it was already deep in a bloody sling. "Hotel room, Sonny, and whiskey."

And he did it just right, didn't say another word until after I showered the dog blood and slimy fear-sweat off my suddenly old and ungainly body. Even then, all he said was, "That bad, huh?"

"You don't know the half of it."

The slick bastards who had tortured and killed the Laras hadn't made many mistakes: the cut telephone line; a single blood track from the woman's nipple; and the floppy disk they left in the laptop computer.

They must not have found what they wanted, though, because the whole house had been professionally, painstakingly tossed, everything put back in place, neatly, but not too neatly. The homicide detectives wouldn't buy the murder-suicide setup for too long.

But it would look good for a minute. Cocaine and whiskey glasses were scattered across the bedside tables. And it looked like an enraged killing. The barrel of the single-action western-style revolver, a Ruger Blackhawk .44 Magnum, had broken off half a dozen of the woman's teeth at the gum line when somebody jammed it into her mouth. And Lara had taken his round in the temple, sitting on the toilet naked, as if in terrible remorse.

"They made one other mistake," I said to Sughrue in the sitting room between our bedrooms. "They shot the dog. With a twenty-two. And I couldn't find one in the house." My hands were still shaking so hard the ice rattled as I held up my empty glass for Sughrue to fill.

"Are you going to be okay, man?"

"I feel like a fucking ghoul, but don't worry about me," I said. "Worry about the bastards who did this." I gulped air, but my lungs still smelled of corruption. "When I started this shit, Sonny, I thought I needed you to help me find that pissant banker. He doesn't seem so important now."

"We don't have a single police connection here," he said,

"and this is going to be a large homicide investigation. They'll put your ass inside the walls at Huntsville. Haven't you had your felony fix tonight?" he asked.

"Not hardly," I said. "It's my first in ten or fifteen years." Sughrue poured me another splash of whiskey. "You can go home anytime you want."

"Maybe they'll let us be cellmates," he said. "I wouldn't miss that for the world. Maybe we can even learn to like mascara and tattooed Nazis." Then he leaned forward. "So I'm in for the duration, Milo."

"Thanks," I said, "but I still feel like shit. A fucking ghoul . . . wandering around the house with a hat full of puke in my pocket."

Sughrue took care of it for me, stuffed it in a plastic bag with my jumpsuit, gloves, underwear, and shoes and socks. He promised to get rid of it on his predawn run.

I knew better than to try to sleep until all the drink was drunk. And me, too, I hoped. I also knew that sometime after the trembling in my hands stopped, the pictures behind my eyes would start. Sughrue meant to stay up with me, but at sunrise I sent him out to run, then took another shower. It didn't help. So I opened the drapes to watch dawn break over downtown Austin and the pink capitol.

The force of the .44-Magnum round had blown the woman—I couldn't say her name, even in my head—half off the bed, leaving her ruined head clotted to the bedroom carpet and her hips propped on the bed, her naked vulva exposed to the stinking air. The shock of death had been so sudden that her body hadn't had time to void itself. The large drop of blood on her right nipple could have come from the blow-back, but with the barrel of the large revolver in her mouth, maybe not. Careful not to step in the dried puddle of brain matter, bone splinters, and blood, I had taken the red lens off the flashlight and examined her breast as closely as I could stand. The blood had come from a single crusted hole in her nipple no larger than a pinprick.

I couldn't imagine her pain. Once as a teenager, a kitten had hooked my nipple with a sharp claw. I had gone to my knees as if struck by lightning. Just thinking about her as the sun flashed brightly off the narrow lake brought the acid remains of my stomach back into my throat. I barely made it to the toilet before I gushed good whiskey into the porcelain throne.

From the look of Lara's white face and blue penis, a drop of blood congealed at the crusted slit, resting flaccidly on the fuzzy toilet seat, I guessed that he had died before the .44 round. Maybe of a heart attack, facing the sort of torture his wife had suffered. Then, I suspected, they had wrapped his hand around the Magnum and pulled the trigger with his dead finger. Whoever these guys were, they didn't mind getting their hands dirty.

But I thought I'd worry about that tomorrow, so I took to my bed with the rest of the whiskey. When it was empty, I thought about hitting myself in the head with the bottle. But I didn't have to bother.

When I emerged from my cocoon at ten I forced myself into swim trunks, my old running shoes, and a U of Montana Grizzlies sweatshirt. I waved silently at Sughrue in the sitting room, then stumbled outside to jog at a slow amble down the gravel footpath alongside the lake. I used any excuse to walk, or sit down to watch the children in their light winter clothes feeding the ducks. The perfect weather had held, blue cloudless skies, cool dry air. But still the hangover and nightmare sweats poured off me in torrents.

So many runners and families clotted the path, I supposed I had slept into the weekend. A fact I confirmed in the Jacuzzi back at the Hyatt as the Austin *American-Statesman* Sunday comics floated past me. Some people's children, I thought, as Sughrue always said. Several young mothers basked in the warming sun as their kids paddled about the pool. I wadded up the comics so I could drop them into the trash on my way into the hotel.

"Sir," came a nasal voice beside me. I turned.

"You talking to me, lady?"

"My boys weren't through with those," she said.

"Then why the hell did they throw them in the Jacuzzi?"

The woman was slim and tall, mid-thirties, pretty in a brit-

tle, bleached-blond, expensively buffed way, but for reasons
I didn't really examine I decided her jutting breasts had experienced the miracle of silicone. Either that, or a true miracle.

"They didn't," she claimed in her abrasive Texas accent.
"Maybe the wind blew them in."

I started to say something ugly—I didn't need this shit—
but paused when she batted her eyelashes at me and smiled.
She didn't want to fight; it was just the accent. A couple of
small boys, maybe six or seven, true cottonheads, stepped up
behind her, dripping water. As if on cue, the boys shook their
heads like white dogs, and cold drops of water flew. I
flinched and the woman squealed, fussed her boys back into
the pool, then grabbed a hotel towel off her chaise longue
and started drying my chest and shoulders.

"Thanks," I said, taking the towel away from her. I noticed
that she hadn't bothered to dry herself, but let the drops stand
on her remarkably tight, tanned skin. I felt as if I had wandered into a commercial. "Let me buy you another paper," I
said as I daubed at her wet hide like a fool.

"Let me buy you a drink," she said, then extended her
hand, the one without the giant rock and the wedding band of
diamonds. "Maribeth Williamson," she added.

"Milodragovitch," I answered, shaking her firm little
hand.

Without turning loose, she told her boys to wait at the pool
for her, and led me toward the patio tables above the pool,
saying, "Is that Russian?"

"My great-grandfather claimed to be a Cossack," I answered lamely as we had a couple of Bloody Marys, which
she charged to her suite, then we discussed our personal his-
tories.

Or, more accurately, mine. During the next half hour, I decided that her habit of squealing whenever I said "Montana"
or "private investigator" and her chainsaw Texas accent
might be considered attractive, maybe even terminally cute,
in some circles. Such as the ones her forefinger made on my
palm. And the circles I was thinking about: my tongue
around the nipples of those amazing breasts, around the
furred freckles above her pubis.

I don't remember exactly how it happened, her call or mine, but before we split we agreed to have a couple of "sundowners," as she called them, in the bar at the top of the hotel. So I raced to my room and stepped into the glass-sided shower, maybe having one of those acid flashbacks Sughrue talked about, or neatly hooked through the foreskin. An evening with a woman like Maribeth could wipe some of the dreams clean. Who was I to look a gift woman in the mouth. Or anyplace else. I tried to push the Laras to the dead rock bottom of my mind.

After the shower, I was all for room service and a nap till sundown. "I've got a date," I told Sughrue, but he wasn't impressed and insisted we had to get out of the suite so the maids could clean. I dressed in real clothes, jeans, a Deerskin flannel, and cowboy boots, then let him lead me to a place called Cisco's, where after two plates of *migas,* even Sughrue was ready for a nap.

But the maids were chattering in our suite, so we took the Saturday and Sunday Austin *American-Statesman* and an alternative weekly called the *Dark Coast* down to the patio.

After the waitress—another one of the good-looking long-legged coeds of which the hotel seemed to have an inordinate supply—took our orders, I glanced through the meaningless newspaper lies of the Lara killings. They were still withholding the names until the next of kin were notified. Then I broached the subject of my date.

"Don't complain," he said when I finished my story. "Maybe you got lucky."

"You don't understand," I told him. "I felt like I was dealing with a woman from another country. Maybe even another planet."

"Texas women only come in two types," he said, then went back to the paper.

"What types?" I finally had to ask.

"What?" Sughrue said, bored already with my love life. "Oh, that, man. Some of them are terrific, the kind of women who can match you drink for drink, smoke for smoke, fuck you stupid, and piss standing up."

"How the hell they do that?"

"I didn't say they'd let you watch," he said.

"Wonderful. What about the other ones?"

"They'll chew you up like an old hunk of side pork and not even bother to spit out the rind," he said. Then held up the *Dark Coast*. "I think I was in the Army with the guy that runs this paper."

"In Vietnam?"

"Nope," he said, "just before that. My third hitch. I was playing ball and covering sports for the base paper at Fort Lewis . . ."

"Your third hitch?" This was new information to me.

"Yeah," he mumbled, blushing. "I did two before Vietnam. Between football vacations at various junior colleges under various names."

He didn't seem to want to talk about it, so I asked about the guy he thought he knew.

"Carver de Longchampe. Can't be two guys with that name," he said. "And I think he went to school at UT. Econ, maybe. He wanted to be a draft dodger, but he couldn't find a dodge before Vietnam. Shit, the Army wouldn't even let him out when he confessed to being both a Communist and a homosexual. Even though it was true. One hell of a good guy, though. The only other admitted dope smoker on base." Then Sughrue smiled. "When I told him that my single chance at the straight life had been torpedoed by nigger music and Meskin smoke, he knew what I meant." Then he laughed. "One hell of a guy. I kept the rednecks off his ass."

"Sonny Sughrue," I said, "cracker by day, protector of the deviant by night."

"Something like that," he said with a fond smile. "I heard that when the Army decided they needed another faggot pinko in Vietnam," he continued, "he finally split for Canada. Took some balls. Guess he came back when Carter let them off the hook."

"Doesn't sound like the sort of guy who would have any police contacts."

"I don't know," Sughrue said. "His editorial this week is about the Austin Police Department. Seems they actually investigate hate crimes against gay people."

"Maybe he's got a computer, too," I said, tapping the floppy disk copy in my shirt pocket.

"What the hell made you look in the computer?" he asked.

"Slumgullion's may be an ancient shot and beer-back shithole dive—fried mush and fresh side pork, too, if you please—but it was a gold mine for years," I said. "Hell, even back when Gene Currier was keeping both sets of books, he worked on the first IBM PC."

"Fucking perfect," Sughrue said, raising his Bloody Mary. "Sometimes I really miss Montana. You know, I was working the salmon fly hatch once up by Fish Creek. Couldn't catch a cold, even though I could see the damned trout rising right at my knees. But then I looked over on a gravel bar, and there was that giant cop—you remember him?"

"Smolinski," I said, "the one they once called 'Animal'?"

"Yeah, but he looked peaceful that day. He had some chick sitting on a driftwood log while she gave him a blow job standing there in his waders. It was that lovely cross-eyed girl who used to cocktail at the Riverside . . . what was her name?"

"Arlene," I said.

Thus the afternoon passed, trailing shining memories of our misspent youths and middle years through the drinks, as we talked of old pals and home, good times and bad, and blessed survival of witless, benighted fools. Maybe the worst part about being sober was not having any new drunk stories to tell.

Maribeth beat me to the top-floor bar, which for some reason was called the Foothills, but I wasn't late. Sundown waited and the end of the fine afternoon. It was early November somewhere else, but in Austin that day it might have been spring. Maribeth wore a red sundress, busy with exotic blossoms and vines, that made her skin glow, so I kissed her on her glossy lips, then refused to apologize.

"You're properly tuned, cowboy," she said.

"Thanks," I said, meaning it. "Forgive me, but I've been standing in a dark wind too long, sitting on my own lap too fucking hard . . ."

"And?"

"Tomorrow morning I go back to the job, love."

"Which means?"

"Sometimes my work is like war, so this might be the last fun I ever have," I said.

"Which means?" she said again.

"My turn for questions," I said. "Were you trying to pick me up at the pool?"

"I hear old guys are sometimes grateful."

"I wouldn't know," I said. "You know Austin?"

"I grew up here."

"If you're not doing anything else, Maribeth Williamson," I said, then tossed my car keys on the table, "I'd love it if you'd take the keys to my brand-new Cadillac and drive me deep into the sunset."

She considered it for a moment, then smiled. "My boys are already at their grandmother's. Tomorrow morning at ten I'm due in divorce court to fight over custody and a lot of money. I'm supposed to have dinner with my lawyer, but I think he's trying to fuck me . . . So I'm sort of going to war, too." Then she grinned and picked up the keys.

"You're a gift, darling."

"And don't I love it," she said, laughing and laughing as she took me away.

Like most middle-aged white American males I grew up during the years when nobody except fundamental Christians and other bigots knew exactly what to think about "the love that dare not speak its name." Working my side of the street, though, I didn't exactly see the best side of any segment of the population. Mostly, they were just there. Faggots, butt-fuckers, cocksuckers, nances, flits—they're just names. Beyond the insults, you find people. Real people. Maybe a little sadder than everybody else. But on the whole, as we've come to find out recently, not nearly as dangerous to small boys as some Catholic priests.

So I was prepared to meet Carver D, as he called himself in his gay persuasion, but I'd never met a Texas Communist before. Nothing prepared me for that.

In spite of their past history and friendship, Carver D was a little wary of Sughrue. Maybe the world had taught him to be wary of everybody. Instead of meeting at the newspaper office, Carver D insisted on meeting at a small beer joint east of the interstate in what looked like the deep dark heart of a bad neighborhood. Gang turf, I suspected, although I had only seen "gang turf" on television. Whatever its denizens called their neighborhood, it was surely enemy territory for a couple of white boys in a Cadillac.

"Maybe they'll think we're pimps," Sughrue said as we parked next to a lime-green '62 Lincoln limo with suicide doors and a personalized plate—CARVER D—on the caliche lot in front of the board-and-batten shack called Flo's Blue Heaven.

"You talking about my new clothes or my new car?"

"Right," he said, then climbed out. "Sorry you gave up weapons, old man?"

"I didn't give up weapons, asshole," I said, following the mad fucker into the blackness of the beer joint. "Just bullets." Then I checked the sap in my sock. It felt just fine.

A single white face glowed at the rear of the tiny bar. We walked toward it. Closer, we could see that a large black gentleman with close-cropped gray hair and a military bearing shared his table. Even in the dim light, Carver de Longchampe looked dead. Or dying. His bloated face floated over a body that seemed to be a large pile of mashed potatoes covered by a once-expensive and once-elegant white suit that could have covered a small truck and might have been retrieved from a vegetable dump. His deep, rumbling voice had been hoarsened by the cheap bourbon from the brown paper sack at his knee and by years of the same Gitane smoke that turned his fat fingers into small yellow tubers harvested from a graveyard. His large brown eyes, as melancholy as prunes in Cream of Wheat, shone with secret knowledge and sparkling wit, and when he smiled, you wanted to laugh.

"Sergeant Sughrue. What a pleasant surprise," he said, waving his thick fingers at him, then turned to me. "This man," he said to me, "may have saved my life. But that's a trifle in the larger economic scheme. He saved my pride, which is a much more precious gift, as I'm sure you understand." Then he paused, adding, "Great suit, Mr. . . . ."

I introduced myself and held out my hand. It disappeared into his soft soiled paw.

"I want one just like it," he said. "Sit down and tell me what you want, Mr. Milodragovitch."

"What makes you think we want something, Carver D?" Sughrue said.

"And what makes you think you've got it?" I added.

Carver D just laughed, sloshed whiskey in his glass, lit one Gitane from another, then said quietly, "Everybody wants something, gentlemen, and I've got it all."

The black gentleman chuckled, his first sound of the afternoon. It wasn't pretty.

Carver D certainly had some contacts. In that single morning, somehow he had learned that Sughrue had worked for the Department of Defense Intelligence Agency after the Vietnam War. In lieu of a stretch in Leavenworth. "Faggot underground," he said. "That should scare the shit out of the straight world," he said, with laughter. So I had no way of knowing if he was telling the truth.

It didn't matter, though. After Carver D decided that we were what we seemed and wanted what we wanted, he said he'd get right on it. He stood, leaning heavily on a black-thorn stick, and promised to meet us later that night. His driver helped him out the front door of Flo's and behind the suicide door of the Lincoln.

We gathered at a beer garden near the capitol. A hangout for country-lawyers-cum-politicos, shirttail lobbyists, and what was left of Austin's left, Carver D said. But it seemed to me to be filled with collegiate riffraff, spiced with skate-board punk trash.

"Times change," Carver D mused. "Do you realize that teenagers control a full one-quarter of the GNP? If they just had politics again . . ."

Carver D and Sughrue talked for a full hour, nonstop, as they guzzled whiskey chased with pitchers of beer and chomped on enough nachos to feed a Mexican village for a week. Quite an unlikely pair to be running a military post weekly newspaper. Sughrue had been there because he actually had a degree in English, some newspaper experience, and it was a more interesting job than checking out basketballs and towels at the gym like the rest of the football team. Carver D had been there because nobody else would have him around.

Their pasts successfully recounted, Carver D got down to business before Sughrue got too drunk to read. From a pocket not readily visible in his refrito-splattered suit, Carver D withdrew a sheaf of folded papers.

"Don't ask where I got this," he said, then handed us copies of the Lara homicide report. "This is all they've got right now."

"Jesus, they're not buying this murder-suicide shit, are they?" I said once I had scanned the report.

Sughrue stuffed his copy into his back pocket without folding it. "Fucking fairy tale," he said.

"Please," Carver D said. "I lost my wings years ago."

"I thought you said the department here was straight," I ventured.

"Within reason," Carver D said, then waved his empty platter at yet another leggy Austin coed. "So what does that tell us, gentlemen?"

"Some captain is on the take?" Sughrue suggested.

"Or the feds stepped in," I added.

"All that water out in the Gulf," Carver D said, "and all those desert miles along the Mexican border. And you know what the ladies down here say . . ."

"What?"

"They love champagne, Cadillacs, cocaine, cowboys, and cash," he said as the waitress slid another platter of nachos under his raft of chins.

"Carver D," she added, "you are a fool. Lying to tourists like that." Then she smiled with the face of a young woman who had never even taken an aspirin.

"I was born and raised in Moody County," Sughrue said.

"Where's that?" she asked, then flounced away.

"When we were at Fort Lewis," Carver D said, "I seem to remember that you claimed to be from New Mexico, Sughrue."

"Well, I am. Sort of," Sughrue answered.

Carver D laughed like crazy, then said, "Son, no matter

how much you deny it, you are a Texican to your bare-bone butt."

"And damn proud of it, too," I added.

Sughrue grabbed the pitcher, then stormed off for a refill.

"He hasn't changed much," Carver D said, sucking down another cubic foot of smoke. "What happened?"

"Vietnam," I said. "He fucked up. Fragged a family on Canadian TV. That's how the DIA got their hands on him."

"He didn't seem the type," Carver D mused.

"Then some other shit came down over the years," I continued, "and a few years ago his lady got killed, and he took her boy to raise. Most recently, though, he got gut-shot in New Mexico, married in the hospital, then went to ground for a couple of years. Now we're on this crazy chase across Texas."

"On your way to Hades, I suspect," he said, "like everybody else who ever stopped in."

"I guess he's never had much of a chance to change," I said. "He is what he is."

"There's that," Carver D said. "Those silly boys at Fort Lewis were going to either beat me or butt-fuck me to death. I've seen my share of violence, my friend, but Sughrue was something else. He kicked over a double bunk, grabbed a pole, and laid waste. If it hadn't been for me, he would have killed those boys. As it was, he scared them so bad they begged us to lie to the MPs. And never tried to get even. Even with me."

"Sonny can be a handful."

"Those guys all went to Vietnam," he said softly. "Only Sughrue came back in one piece—if you can call it that. Sometimes I have to admit to myself that maybe Canada was a mistake . . . but that's heavy water under the bridge of sorrows and lost highways . . . all the young boys gone for soldiers . . ."

Then he pushed the nachos away, made the whiskey bottle bubble, and looked at me seriously. "I see you're not a drinking man, Mr. Milodragovitch."

"I have been," I said, "and probably will be again. But that night at the Laras' house burned most of the fun out of it."

"Fun?" Sughrue said as he set the pitcher on the table. "What the fuck is that?"

"What about the floppy?" I said.

"What about my suit?" Carver D said, sounding drunk for the first time.

I handed him a thick envelope, saying, "First-class round-trip ticket to Seattle, enough cash for a week in a four-star hotel, and two made-to-order Italian suits."

"By gad, sir, you have style!" he exclaimed. "*Panache!*"

"For a Montana hayseed," Sughrue said, actually sounding pleased that I'd impressed his old buddy.

"I grew up with whorehouse money," I admitted.

"So did I," Carver D said, "but I never learned how to properly squander it."

Sughrue started to say something about my lost fortune, but he stopped when he saw my face. Perhaps I hadn't completely gotten mired in his search for vengeance, hadn't lost my purpose.

"As much as I'd love to, Mr. Milodragovitch, I can't take your gift so generously offered," Carver D said sadly. "Like many of my generation I never leave the Austin city limits." He chuckled and set the envelope on the table in front of me. "As for the floppy disk you copied," he added, "it took my cyberpunk boyfriend twenty-seven minutes by the clock to break into the file, but the information is encoded and locked behind a password, and since Lara once served his country as a cryptographer for the Army Security Agency, I'm sorry to say that Pinky suggests that it could take a National Security Agency program to break the code. And nobody has hacked into *their* computers for some time.

"According to another friend, though, the disk probably contains records of money transfers. And some bad news: God and the DEA will figure it out before you do. Or perhaps I should say 'we.'

"Because in exchange for your story, should there ever be one, we'll keep after it," Carver D said, then waved at a young skateboarder with orange hair sprouting from one side of his head, who came immediately to help heave Carver D to his feet. "And remember: Follow the money."

"Who said that?" Sughrue said. "Marx?"

"Chandler, I think," he said, then leaned heavily on his cane and the young man as he fondly helped Carver D up the steps and out of the beer garden.

"I think he liked you, old man."

"But he loves you, kid. Let's go back to the hotel and sip good Scotch until we figure out what to do next."

"I thought you had another date, Milo."

"It was a maybe," he said, "a perhaps."

But when we got back to the room, Maribeth had slid a note under the door. Her husband never made it to divorce court. He dropped dead on the steps of the courthouse. Which made the divorce superfluous. And she thought perhaps spending the night together so soon might be unseemly. But she had left some telephone numbers: Austin, Crested Butte, La Jolla, and someplace called Port Aransas.

"Should I send flowers?" I asked Sughrue after reading the note aloud.

"Damn straight," he said. "You've got style."

"Guess that's a no," I said, and we laughed our way up to the bar, only to find it closed.

Over the telephone the next afternoon, the president of the Pilot Knob Farmers Home Savings and Loan, Travis County's newest state-chartered bank, sounded so country I expected him to have a cowlick, tractor grease under his nails, and cowshit on his boots.

Leon Firth didn't disappoint me too badly later that afternoon. He ran his bank business out of a double-wide trailer not even as nice as Sughrue's. And although his nails were freshly manicured, his hand was roughly callused and work-hard when I shook it. But I hadn't counted on the Texas affection for hair spray: a cow's tongue couldn't have mussed that hair-helmet; maybe not even a gun butt. I thought I detected a stirrup scuff on the inside of his expensive ostrich boots, but he could have spilled aftershave on the pebbled vamp. The stuff certainly smelled as if it might have scoured leather.

I also had my shit together: two days' growth of beard; a stretch limo with a cellular telephone rented for cash and driven by Carver D's large black friend; my eyes bloodshot from one of Sughrue's powerful needle-thin joints; and the night before I'd slept in my most expensive suit.

"So how can I help you, Mr. Soames?" Firth asked, after a white-haired woman who looked like his grandmother had served the coffee in china cups. If she wasn't his grandmother, surely they went to the same hairdresser.

"I want to open an account," I mumbled.

"What sort of account?" he asked, smiling at me with capped teeth.

"Ever' kind you got, buddy."

"Every kind?"

"Checking, savings, CDs, annuities," I said. "The whole fucking ball of wax. But I have to have instant access to the money. Can you dig it, man?"

Firth looked a little worried, but strove bravely forward. "How much did you plan to deposit?"

"Three and a half million," I said, "give or take a couple of hundred K."

"Give or take?" he said, suddenly interested.

"In cash," I said.

"Excuse me, sir," he said carefully. "Can I see some identification, please?"

"It's in the limo," I said, "with the cash."

Firth stood up, touched his hair as if it might have escaped somehow during our brief conversation. "I'm sorry, sir," he crooned, "but I suspect you'd be happier at some other financial institution. We don't handle deposits like yours."

"Hey, man," I said, standing also. Checking my back and glancing nervously out the window. Reaching under my suit coat, then cursing under my breath when I didn't find a piece. "I'm in a bind here, asshole. I'll pay ten cents on the dollar. Add it up, sucker. Three hundred fifty K. For nothing."

"I'm truly sorry, sir," he said, moving around the desk toward me. He must have hit the panic button. "But we just don't do business that way."

"The fuck you don't," I said. The door opened behind me, and the burly guard I'd seen in the bank put his hand on my shoulder. "What do you think I am, you fucking hayseed? The fucking FBI? And tell your boy that if he touches me again, I'll jerk his arm out of the socket and shove it up his ass."

"Please, sir, don't make us call the law."

"Here," I said, picking up the telephone on his desk. "I'll call for you. You boys got 911 out here in the sticks?" The bank guard tried to grab me in a wrist-lock come-along, but I was already spinning, so instead he caught my elbow in the nose. He sat down abruptly. "Big mistake, kid," I said. Then kicked him smartly in the ear.

"And you, too," I said to Firth, whose hands scrabbled at a desk drawer, then stopped. "Don't be an idiot," I said, stepping around the desk and pinning his hand in the drawer with my thigh. "Take it easy. It's just a fuckup. Obviously, my people didn't talk to your people yet. I'll be back tomorrow." Then I stepped back to release his bleeding hand. "And by the way, Leon, the next time you try to pull a piece on me, man, I'll kill you, your family, and everybody you ever said hello to."

Then I mussed his hair and left.

"What do you think?" Sughrue asked me over the cellular telephone from his rental unit parked down the highway as the limo pulled out on the road.

"Oh, man, they stink like fried shit," I said back.

"I think you're right, Milo," Sughrue said. "I watched in the spotting scope as some guy with a bloody nose and a grandmotherly type just ran to their cars. And some other guy is standing on the back steps trying to comb his hair and use his cellular telephone at the same time."

"Perfect," I said into the telephone. And meant it. Then I ran down the glass barrier between the driver, Hangas Miller, and me. "Mr. Miller," I said. "You look like a man who has perhaps seen some military service."

"Three tours in the Southeast Asian war games as a senior master sergeant, Third Marines, sir," he said in a voice that sounded as if he carried a small grenade in his throat. "But call me Hangas, please sir."

"I'll call you Hangas if you call me Milo," I said. He nodded with a smile, and I slipped forward to the jump seat. "Things didn't go exactly as planned in there, so the rest of

this could be fucked, too. How deeply you want to be involved in this shit?"

"Any friend of Carver D's is a friend of mine," Hangas
said softly, holding his hand over his shoulder. I shook it. It
felt like a brick. I slipped five hundred in twenty-dollar bills
into it.

"We better do this after dark. So let's drive around till
then, act like we're trying to lose a tail, but not too seriously.
Then drop me at the Omni Hotel," I said, "and park as close
to the lobby door as you can, like I'm on my way right back
out. Be generous with my money. A couple of minutes later,
some people are going to come around . . ."

"What kind of people would that be?"

"You know the kind. Too much money, not raised right," I
said. "And not nearly as tough as they think they are."
Hangas, who could probably drive his hand through a cinder-
block wall, smiled like a man who was just exactly as tough
as he thought he was.

"Trash," he said.

"Uncle Tom 'em a little bit," I suggested, "then sell me
out. Don't take the first price, though. And if they want to
muscle you, sell me out immediately."

"Are you sure?" he asked, astounded and disappointed.

"I don't want you to get hurt," I said. His laughter sounded
like an avalanche. "But if you want to shuffle up to the room
behind them . . . far be it from me to step on your fun,
Hangas."

Hangas drove the limo aimlessly around Austin as the
grandmother and the bank guard did a pretty good job
switching a front-and-back tail. Sughrue and I thought we
had it set up pretty good. I'd rented two connecting rooms
and the one across the hall at the Omni, and we planned to
take whoever showed up when they tried to go into the room
I'd rented in Rocky Soames's name, thinking that not even
these guys would want to chance gunfire in a fairly crowded
hotel, and that a scuffle, if we controlled it quickly, might go
unnoticed.

But as usual the bad guys didn't behave. Which I guess is
their job.

Hangas had just done a U-turn on South I-35 at the Onion

Creek Parkway exit when the cellular telephone rang. It was Sughrue.

"Milo," he said, "we've picked up company: two cowboys in a blue Ford four-wheel-drive pickup; two Hispanic suits in a white Lincoln; and two yuppie types in a Taurus. So stop fucking around, man. Act like you're going someplace, before they make me . . . Fuck it, man. They're looking too hard, seen too much of me, man. I'm outa here. I'll stay on the Parkway, take the next exit, if the assholes don't follow me."

"Plan B, huh?" I said.

"What's Plan B?"

"I thought you had one," I said.

"Asshole," Sughrue said, cursing as he thought. "Let's go to the parking lot at Mt. Bonnell. There's always a crowd up there this time of the afternoon, drinking beer and getting ready to watch the sunset. Tell Mr. Miller to take Riverside to the Mo-Pac, then Bull Creek to Mt. Bonnell Road. Fuck it, he'll know the way. And that should give me time to get there."

After I gave Hangas the change in plans, I told him to stop at the next convenience store. Preferably one with a lot of lights and maybe a cop car, so I could get the aluminum suitcase out of the trunk.

"If you don't mind, sir, I'll get the suitcase," Hangas said. "There's something back there I need, too."

Hangas found a place at the corner of Lamar and got a golf bag and my suitcase out of the trunk, while I bought a carton of Camel straights and a case of Coors as blithely as a wino on a lark. In the backseat, I dumped the suitcase, then changed clothes as quickly as I could. Up front, I could hear Hangas rattling through the golf clubs.

"You don't look like a golfer," I told him, glancing into the front seat. Hangas had pulled a heavy cane out of the bag. He twisted the handle, which opened into a shotgun breech, into which he dropped a 12-gauge buckshot round. "And that doesn't look exactly like a nine iron."

"Carver D calls it his asshole driver," he answered, slipping the cane under the seat. "He's not crazy about people playing through."

"Well," I said, "I'm not up on the etiquette of the game, but I can see why they might not."

Then Hangas and I got in an argument.

Which I finally won. But not easily.

When we got to the Mt. Bonnell overlook, the afternoon had faded to dusky gray, that time of day when the black road eats the headlights and the ashen air turns impenetrable. Sughrue's ghostly figure leaned against the hood of his Japanese rental, his hands wrapped in hard leather work gloves. I slipped the spring-handled sap into my right back pocket.

Hangas pulled into the lot and, much against his wishes, let me climb out with the case of beer and my aluminum suitcase, which I cached in the trunk, and then he drove slowly away. He had to wait while the grandmother and the bank guard rolled past as if they hadn't a care in the world.

By the time the rest of the convoy arrived, Sughrue and I were mounting the steps to the overlook itself, where a half dozen college students watched the final act of a fairly mediocre sunset. They looked at Sughrue and me oddly when we stopped next to them. When I opened the case of beer and told them to make themselves at home, they remained suspicious, but they did grab a couple of beers.

On the parking lot below, the bad guys had a short conference. One of the Hispanics, a tall thin guy who looked as quick as a snake, seemed to be in charge. After a moment they came up the hill, the yuppies and the bank guard in the lead, the cowboys circling through the cedar scrub, scrabbling in their slick-soled boots. And the two suits split up, hanging outside and behind the other groups.

"So this is Plan B?" I asked Sughrue as he cracked a beer.

"Goddammit," he hissed, "that skinny fucker could be the brother of the asshole who shot me."

"We couldn't be that lucky," I said, but Sughrue didn't hear me. He was long gone into his private madness.

The yuppies, who dressed like male models but who had the eyes of fundamentalist linebackers, flanked us on the overlook while the cowboys struggled with the knee-high brush. I didn't see Sughrue move. Nobody saw him move. But the nearest yuppie's head flew back as Sughrue broke his jaw with a short uppercut. The big kid was unconscious when he flopped over the low rail to hit the downhill slope.

"What did you say!" Sughrue screamed after the fact. Even crazy, the fucker was still smart. If we needed it, the college kids would remember the scream, then the punch.

The other yuppie had seen too many Bruce Lee movies. Sughrue blocked his sweeping sidekick with his left elbow, then kicked him on the offside knee. Behind me one of the girls puked as the bone and cartilage exploded with a wet crack. Except for that, their whole group stood, stunned, motionless as Sughrue popped the bank guard in his swollen nose and hooked in the gut.

Thanks to their vanity, the cowboys still hadn't made it to the overlook. I slapped the first one in the middle of his forehead with the sap, then dropkicked him in the chest. He rolled downhill in a cloud of dust. But the other grabbed for a piece under his denim jacket. I had to leap downhill to whap him on the elbow with the sap. Then we got tangled in each other's limbs and rolled down the hill, too, the poor cowboy's broken arm flapping and grinding all the way to the parking lot.

Where, goddammit, Hangas had come back, crouched in his immaculate chauffeur's uniform, the shotgun-cane across the hood of the limo, covering me as I lifted the Glock from under the cowboy's Levi's jacket, unloaded it, and threw the rounds one way, and the pistol another. The pistol bounced off the asphalt in the wake of the first cowboy, who was busy cutting thuds into the waning light down the road. I had lost sight of the two Hispanic guys. I thought I saw one of them following the cowboy along the brushy edge of the roadway.

"Sughrue!" I shouted. "Look out for the skinny guy!"

"*Cuidado!*" Hangas shouted, aiming the cane into the darkness behind me.

I dove behind a low stone wall just as two silenced rounds skipped off the pavement behind me, then I rolled and caught a glimpse of the skinny guy bounding through the shadows like a deer. Brake lights flared down the road, and a car roared away. Just about then Sughrue came down the steps, the sick yuppie over his shoulder.

"Looks like this is our guy," Sughrue said, then dumped

him into the backseat of his rental. "At least this is the one in the best shape. And I got all the plate numbers. So let's hit it before those college kids call the cops."

"Hangas," I said, "thanks. Now disappear."

"Not with my grandbaby, you don't," came a nasal woman's voice. Grandma stepped into the light, a hit man's special—a silenced Colt Woodsman .22—locked in a combat grip. Nobody suggested that she didn't know how to use it. Or that she wasn't ready to pull the trigger. "He's just hired help," she whined, "he don't know shit from wild honey."

But Sughrue had already spun, the Browning appearing in his hand. I knew he wouldn't wait for conversation but would depend on a head shot to prevent her from pulling the trigger. So I stepped between them.

"Nothing here worth dying for, Granny," I said, holding out my hands.

"Get out of the fucking way, Milo," Sughrue said flatly.

"What the hell are you doing out here, Granny?" I asked her. "Playing cops and robbers? You oughta be home in the rocking chair with your knitting."

I knew Sughrue wanted to put a round into her. Through me, if necessary. And the old woman nearly pulled the trigger when I called her Granny.

"Knitting, my ass," she said. "I oughta put one right in your eye, dipshit." Then she lost heart, let her hand drop. "You boys just fucked my retirement, you know. They don't have much social security in my line of work."

"Give her the kid, Sonny," I said, and heard him huff as he propped the yuppie over his shoulder again, carried him to the old woman, who let the boy lean on her shoulder as they walked away.

Just at the edge of the light, though, she stopped and gave us something. "Everybody in this shit is hired help," she said. "Even me and Leon. Everybody but Rogelio. He's a bordersnake. He belongs to the Baron."

"What fucking Baron?" Sughrue shouted.

But the old woman just shrugged.

So after a couple of chores, we fled Austin with its pink capitol building and hard-skinned old women. Carver D fed our information back in to the police department the next morning, but the Firth family had cleaned out the bank and, unlike Sughrue and me, fled to quieter climes where extradition could be a problem. I thought about trying to convince Carver D to pick up Sheba from the vet clinic, but he shuddered so deeply I decided on an anonymous cash contribution to the Humane Society in Sheba's and Dr. Porterfield's names and another, smaller one to the emergency vet clinic.

As we drove away, I watched them in the rearview mirror, Carver D rolling his great soft body into the backseat of the Lincoln limo as Hangas closed the suicide rear doors.

But Sughrue never looked back, not once, all the way to Rocksprings, where we paused to establish a base camp from which to investigate Ana Navarro's past before pressing on to El Paso to dig in the remains of Ray Lara's.

While Sughrue tried his border Spanish on Ana Navarro Lara's widowed father in Del Rio, I examined the silver-framed photographs propped on the crude shelves. Like the rest of the tiny tin-roofed adobe house, the pictures were immaculately clean and polished. A wedding photo that looked as if it had been taken in the previous century sat next to a snapshot of what I assumed was Señor Navarro as a young *vaquero,* straddling an uncovered saddle tree cinched to a piebald hip-shot pony. His sockless feet were encased in *huaraches* with spurs strapped to them and stuck into bare wooden stirrups. This old boy had been the real thing. Several double sets followed the progress of two girls: confirmation; *quinceras* and proms; high school graduation; then nothing, nothing more.

I looked over at the old man. He squatted on the rough tile floor, a hand-rolled cigarette dangling from his lips, his knotted fingers braiding a rawhide lariat, and his milky eyes trying to follow Sughrue. When Sughrue finally got the formalities over and mentioned Analise's name, the old man popped the finished end of the leather rope against the tile. It rang in the small room like a gunshot. Then his eyes filled with tears. A fine mesh of deeply cut wrinkles etched his Indian face, a maze of arroyos that scattered the tears to salty mist before they floated to the red tile.

There was plenty. This might be life or death for us, but Señor Navarro's sorrow seemed more important. We apologized our way out the door, then we stood like fools in the dirt street just outside the rickety gate, without a clue again.

As far as I could tell, Del Rio was a third-world country, peopled by the very rich and the very, very poor. And none of our usual sources of information existed in this world. We'd found the old man almost by accident, because he did not exist on gringo paper: no telephone, no city directory listing, no voter registration.

But we had found an Ana Navarro in the high school yearbook collection in the tiny local library. Luckily, the part-time librarian remembered that she had grown up down by the tracks. Of course, not many trains troubled the tracks these days, but they still divided things. So we found a taxi driver, Tony Vargas, who couldn't believe we didn't want to cross the border to Ciudad Acuña. But he found the right neighborhood eventually. Perhaps it took longer because he seemed to enjoy the notion of being driven slowly around town by two gringos in an El Dorado. While he sucked down free cans of Tecate beer.

"Tony," Sughrue finally said, "get your fucking nose out of that beer can and help." Tony heaved his red-eyed face and sweaty, stubby body out of the backseat, blinked in the cold wind, then gave us a gap-toothed golden smile. "*Me amigo,*" Sughrue continued, "I know these people. Somebody in this neighborhood, probably on this block, takes care of this old man."

"*Sí,* but who?"

"I'll give you another fifty-dollar bill to find her," Sughrue said, "and give her two fifty-dollar bills to talk to us."

Tony shuffled in the dirt, oddly reluctant suddenly. "My friend, why should this person who perhaps does not even exist," he mumbled, "receive more money than myself, who you know is your friend?"

"Okay," Sughrue said softly. "Two fifties if you find her. Nothing for looking."

Tony grumbled like a man who had been outbargained. "Nothing for looking?"

"*Nada,*" Sughrue said, "not one fucking penny."

"But I have no coat, señor," he said in a great imitation of a waif.

"Then you should hurry."

Tony grinned, then trotted away on his short legs like a man who knew exactly where he was going. After a moment, he came back with a middle-aged woman who was trying to untie her apron. "Perhaps if we could sit in the lovely car," he said, "so Señora Alvarez . . ."

Sughrue laughed as I hadn't heard him in days. "Tony, my friend," he said, "Why don't you drive us around the barrio while we talk to Señora Alvarez."

Tony's smile came like a sunburst into the cold, blustery afternoon, so we mounted my Dark Cherry steed.

Afterward, Tony would have it no other way than that Sughrue and I meet his wife and children and his mama. Then Sughrue had to drive the family around the block. Five or six times. Then we waited while he let Tony drive his family, including his ancient mother, around the block.

"Mr. Sughrue," I pointed out, "you've just given my brand-new and damned expensive Cadillac to a Mexican cab driver who reeks of marijuana, tequila, and chicanery . . ."

"Chicanery?"

"Like you," I said. "What if he doesn't come back?"

"Where the hell's he going to go, Milo?" he asked, half-pissed. "He lives here. Like that old *vaquero* this afternoon. He fucking lives here. What? Are you becoming a bigot in your old age? I've seen you take puking, dying winos home to live with you for months at a time."

"Okay," I said, "but sometimes they were you." Down the block, Tony turned the corner and drove toward us gently. "I give up."

But it wasn't quite time yet. There was some drinking with Tony's friends, who looked as much like criminals as he did. And some singing with some other friends. Then an encounter with the local police, who wanted to know about the strange gringos in the Caddy. But Tony handled that for us. Since we had left most of the cash, all of Sughrue's firearms, and the smoking dope back at the motel in a little town called Rocksprings, I wasn't too worried, so I let the two Mexican-American cops search the car, after they asked politely. They were just doing what they thought of as their job.

· Lately the goddamned government had decided to suspend due process for the duration of the war against drugs. Given the right set of circumstances and the proper narco shitheel, if they found a roach in the ashtray of my ride, left there by a hitchhiking hippie deep into bad karma, they could confiscate all my goods without a hearing, a charge, a conviction, or recourse.

I couldn't see walking one hundred twenty-three miles back to the motel. Driving was quite enough. I was very happy to see the little motel when we finally got there just before daylight. I woke Sughrue and told him that I liked him a lot better when he was morose. He laughed, agreed with me, and staggered out of the car toward his room.

"Goddammit, Milo," he said at the door. "Remember the old days?"

"What?"

"When you were serious and I had all the fun?"

"What's changed?" I said.

"Nothing," he said happily, then he stumbled to bed.

I poured a drink and stepped outside to watch the sun try to burn through the clouds to expose the place these Texans called the Hill Country. I'd seen bigger snowdrifts, I thought, and just about that time a blast of freezing rain slapped me in the face. I could have sworn it was seventy degrees when we'd checked in.

Señora Alvarez had told us that Ana's little sister, Connie, sent a check every month from Kerrville, where she had married a rich old gringo who owned a motel and a ranch and some other things, she didn't know what. Señor Navarro hadn't spoken Connie's name since she married the old gringo. Señora Alvarez didn't know anything about the troubles between the old man and his daughters. She just cashed the checks and took care of Señor Alvarez. As she had promised.

So with that knowledge firmly in hand and four hours' sleep behind us, Sughrue and I checked out of the motel in

Rocksprings and drifted east again, easing down back roads as the cold rain, which threatened to become sleet again, hammered the Beast. Sughrue, suffering the deserved pangs of a tequila hangover, slumbered in the backseat, leaving me to myself.

Truth be told, I really liked being on the road. Even if it was Texas. I had folding money in my pocket, a great ride under my ass, and a fucking purpose.

Even though I grew up with money and a generous father, once he was dead my mother, who beneath her East Coast affectations was a mean-spirited and miserly drunk, kept me on a short financial leash. Which had something to do, I suspect, with me quitting high school at sixteen to enlist in the Army. Although she constantly threatened to report me for the forged birth certificate I'd used to join, she never did. Not even when I went to Korea. Not even after I wished she had. So I spent most of the rest of my life scrabbling for money, or waiting for it. I took the GED before the Army turned me loose, then worked my way through college at Mountain States, doing the night shift pulling the green chains at the local lumber mill and spending summers gandy dancing for the railroad, then joined the sheriff's department the day I graduated. After they allowed me to resign ten years later I took up my private license, scuffling for money in various legal and illegal ways, until I couldn't carry my own weight anymore. Then another eight years working for Gene Currier, tending bar, until Sughrue loaned me the money to buy into the Slumgullion.

So I got by, but I hadn't owned a great ride since I bought a chopped and channeled, bored and stroked '49 Merc, Midnight Black with a white leather tuck-and-roll interior, when I got out of the VA hospital in San Francisco. A beautiful ride. Which I wrecked outside Susanville, California, showing off for a blackjack dealer from Reno. And purpose? Shit, I thought, driving through the small town of Hunt, I'd never had a purpose. Just a drifter, a saddle tramp without a horse, a bindlestiff without a blanket roll. A drunk with no good reason to drink. For a moment I was almost thankful that Andy Jacobson had lifted my daddy's money. Then I shook my head. Maybe I wasn't actually thankful. But he was going to be one sorry son of a bitch.

"Where the fuck are we?" Sughrue grumbled from the backseat.

"Hunt-fucking-Texas," I said.

"Sorry," he said. "Kerrville is just down the road. You're going to love Kerrville, man."

Señora Alvarez said Connie Navarro had married money, and in a town the size of Kerrville, money shouldn't be too hard to find. But as strangers, it seemed best to sneak up on it. So we figured that the place to begin was the bar at the most expensive motel in town. Once we spotted it, a giant limestone chain outfit that looked more like an old Spanish garrison than a motel, we parked under the ramada. Sughrue wandered around the cluttered lobby as I walked over to the registration desk. Before I could finish filling out the card, Sughrue slipped up behind me, grabbed my elbow, and jerked me away from the desk.

"What the hell is going on?" I asked.

"Take a look," he said, pointing to a corner where cowboy memorabilia had been supplanted by an African landscape, the centerpiece of which was a mother giraffe, her neck lovingly stretched down to a baby. "What kind of people would stuff a baby giraffe?"

"Same kind of assholes that would kill one," I said.

"Let's find another place."

"Right," I said. "And some new transportation, too. I don't want to end up in somebody's trophy case." Suddenly Austin didn't seem far enough away, and prudence a necessity.

We rented a storage space for the Beast, a Lincoln Town Car for me, and a Ford Escort for Sughrue. The moment with the giraffes still bothered him. So much he didn't even complain about having to drive the smaller car. After looking at several places we finally found the Guadalupe River Lodge, another maze of stone buildings nestled deep in the cypress and sycamore shadows along the river.

Sughrue and I checked into the lodge separately about four in the afternoon, agreed to meet in the Cypress Tree Piano Bar shortly so we could pump the bartender from different directions. But the bar didn't open until five, and the rat's ass of a bartender, a bald-headed guy who wore a string tie and a black sliver of a moustache, was one of those little guys who had either seen or done everything. A perfect waste. But he made a great martini. So fine that I sensed destruction at the end of this olive trail. I had two, then went back to the room and called down for a steak and salad, leaving Sughrue to try his redneck charm on the little shit.

"The little fucker's name is Albert," Sughrue said when he stopped at my room about ten. "His pimp moustache is dyed. Just like his remaining hair. Supposedly, he once was the welterweight champ of the Pacific fleet. He hates niggers, pepper-bellies, Yankees, the Dallas Cowboys, lesbians, faggots, Marines, and me."

"How the hell does he keep his job?"

"He's a great bartender," Sughrue answered. "He handled three cocktail waitresses, the bar customers, and me. Without breaking a sweat." Then Sughrue sighed drunkenly. "And he cut me off. Thank god."

"You make a scene?"

"No, I got drunk. You know that second-day hangover drunk?" he said. I nodded. "Well, when I tried to sing along with the kid playing the piano, Albert suggested that a dozen beers and a dozen shots of tequila were probably just right for a fellow my size. Management policy, he said."

"So how should I work him?" I said as Sughrue opened the door.

"A fucking ball-peen hammer," he said, then wandered down the hall toward his room.

At the nearly empty bar, decked out in my best Montana rancher duds, I ordered a single-malt Scotch from Albert, sipped it, and complimented him on the martini he had made for me earlier that afternoon.

"It ain't hard," he said in his squeaky voice. "Sir."

"You'd be surprised," I said, but he had already scooped up my C-note and gone to make change.

Several expensively casual couples leaned against the baby grand piano on the other side of the room. The kid, as

Sughrue had called her, turned out to be a tall willow switch of a girl with a husky contralto far too knowing for her years, as was the elegant black sheath that draped a little loosely over her slim hips, as if she had borrowed it from her mother. Her black hair was in a twenties bob, as if she came from a simpler, happier time. Or hoped to go there.

The couples sitting around her piano bar were tipsy in a rich and controlled manner; the goldfish tip bowl was filled with five and tens instead of ones. The women's laughter was high and thin but not in the range of giggles yet. The men could still raise an eyebrow at the kid, but only one at a time, and not always the right one. They all seemed to be having trouble trying to suggest a song title that the young girl hadn't already played for them. The girl's smile seemed real, as did her occasional husky laughter, but she looked tired, perhaps bored, her bright eyes shining among black circles.

I took the fifty out of the change Albert stacked on the bar, then wandered over to the piano, where I stuffed it into the tip bowl, which caused a momentary silence.

"Play something you really like, ma'am," I said, then drifted back to the bar.

"Righto, old chap," came a voice from the couples. "A delightfully wonderful notion."

What the hell was a British accent doing in Kerrville, Texas? I asked myself, thinking I'd probably find out as soon as the camel-hair sport coat made it to the bar.

Western art, it turned out, as the Englishman told me. The piano player noodled happily, covering some Elvis, a few Beach Boys tunes, a bit of the early Beatles, and some Eagles cuts.

By this time, I knew about the Englishman's galleries in Paris, London, Beverly Hills, and Scotsdale, where he lived. I knew his wife; three of his friends, who ran a local gold exchange and jewelry factory; and a big guy who dealt in Mexican art, named Ed Forsyth, who looked a little like Howdy Doody and who told me he was friends with the motel's owner, which was what I wanted to know, but I didn't realize it.

When the piano player wrapped up her evening with a

painfully slow and touching version of "Poor, Poor, Pitiful Me," a Zevon tune that Linda Ronstadt had covered, or so she said, the art people drifted away.

The piano player pulled up a stool just down the bar from me and began to count her money just as Albert offered me, the last customer, the last call. "Thanks," I said to her, "that was a great set. Can I buy you a cocktail?"

"Let me have a setup, Al," she said without looking up from the bills she was counting. Then she raised her shockingly blue eyes, a tilted smile matching her raised eyebrow. "I'm Kate," she said, "and you're old enough to be my father."

Albert set four fingers of Irish and a pint of Guinness in front of her. Then four fingers of the Macallan in front of me.

"Grandfather," I said as I paid.

Kate laughed that wonderful laugh again. And we finished our drinks in silence. But I knew we'd talk, eventually.

The next night, after a day of exhausting the usual sources, we still weren't any closer to Connie Navarro. So I sent Sughrue on a tour of the local night spots, such as they were, then met him in the Cypress Tree just before midnight.

Kate, who was wearing a long straight blond wig tonight and a high-necked black sheath, which made her look like a surfer chick escaping from a Catholic girl's school, smiled and nodded when I came into the bar. But she was talking and laughing with Sughrue, who was sipping a tequila and washing it down with Shiner beer. It seemed time to lose our cover. I took my drink over to the piano to sit on a stool next to Sughrue.

"Hello, Grandpa," Kate said quietly as I sat down, chuckling deep in the beautiful pale column of her neck. "Good to see you again."

"You told her," I said to Sughrue.

"I told her nothing," he said without looking at me. "But if she asked, man, I would tell her everything."

"Great," I said. "And give her my Cadillac, my cash, credit cards, and . . ."

"All your cocaine," Kate whispered breathlessly, then segued from the show tune she was playing into something the

Cowboy Junkies might have done to Billie Holiday's "Cocaine Blues."

"And you look like such an *innocente*, Catrina," Sughrue said.

"Substitute teacher by day," she said, "femme fatale by night." Then she laughed bitterly. "Honey," she snapped, "there are neither innocent nor guilty in my life. Just lots of victims and damn few survivors."

Sughrue and I looked at each other, considering the bitterness of that remark, while Kate excused herself to slink toward her break.

Then somebody touched my arm. When I turned, Ed Forsyth stood there grinning at me like a feral pup, sharp teeth shining among that plague of silly freckles. We reintroduced ourselves. As I shook Eddie's large hand, I realized that I had dismissed him too lightly the night before. His expensively tailored cowboy clothes hid his true nature. Eddie was a big boy, one of those pleasant-faced ugly guys; a goon at first look, but his knuckles were knotted with scar tissue and gristle, his arms were as big as small tree trunks, and his wide, sloping shoulders supported a thick, brutal neck. Eddie had a pair of slick scars, one on the back of his right hand and another on his left wrist, where I suspected that prison tattoos had been removed.

I introduced him to my partner, nodded to Sughrue so he would take a read on Eddie, who invited us to join his table for a taste or two. He indicated a round table in the corner where the people from the night before had gathered around an old man and his young wife. I promised we'd be there in a New York minute.

"Waxahachie minute," Sughrue said as Eddie walked away.

"What's that?"

"Same thing with a Texas twist," he said. "What's that jailhouse trash want with you?"

"Maybe they teach art appreciation at the Big House now," I said. "Maybe last night I told him about my last hole card, the Charlie Russell pencil sketches sitting in my safety deposit box."

"He's sure to want to fuck you out of them somehow,"

Sughrue said. "That boy never did an honest day's work in his life."

"You can bet on that," I said. "But let's see where it takes us."

"At least he's got some cocaine," Sughrue said. "And a postnasal drip the size of Yellowstone Falls." Then he raised his eyebrow at me. "Worried?"

"Not yet," I said, "and it's been ten years."

The older gentleman in the cashmere blazer, whose name, according to his card, was Lyman Gifford Gish, had a thicker and more attractive veneer, which meant, as far as I could tell, that he'd never done time. But I bet that he'd come close during the savings and loan rip-off. The largest and most successful crime ever committed in America. America, hell; the world. Because L.G. claimed to be a retired banker. Retired, hell. Old whores retire; crooked old bankers just get a change of venue. But since L.G. was married to Consula Navarro late of Del Rio, I forced myself to be nice to the old man.

Consula herself was a piece of work. She had a short-legged, chunky body crammed into a little number right out of the Frederick's of Hollywood catalog and a chubby, mean version of Analise's face. But she reeked of sexual fire. Hell, even her ostentatious fur stank of animal musk. So much I couldn't tell if she had heard about her sister's murder. But as I listened to her telling Sughrue the lie of her life, I decided she hadn't heard. Nobody's that tough. Connie came close, though.

So when the bar closed at midnight, Sughrue and I joined the rich, desperate parade across the river to L.G.'s four-thousand-square-foot stone and glass house on the bluff. It also counted, I suppose, that Kate asked to ride along with us to show us the long winding way across the Guadalupe to perdition.

Kate admired the Lincoln, claiming she had never been in a nice American car before, as she hunkered on the front seat with her feet beneath her, then lit a joint. "You guys aren't cops, are you?" she asked through a veil of dope smoke, then extended the number toward me.

I started to wave it off, then assumed we were looking a long reckless evening dead in the pale, shrunken face, so I took it from her like an old professional hippie, and hit the sucker till I nearly choked. Before I could stop, though, Kate grabbed a little camera out of her purse and snapped a photograph of me. The camera might have been small, but the flashbulb blinded me so badly I thought she had burned my lashes off.

"Jesus," I said, stopping in the middle of the road. "You do that a lot?"

"Only when I do drugs with strangers," she said, then giggled and handed the joint to Sughrue.

"That's fucking dangerous," I said.

"Why? You guys gonna shoot me?"

"If we don't die in a car wreck first," I said.

Then Kate laughed again, and I realized that her charm and grace came from shyness overlaid with drugs. I don't know how I missed it. I'd been that way often enough myself. Then she fixed our noses with two blasts of coke so pure my face froze. And I didn't care anymore.

L.G. had a sleepy white-coated Mexican standing at the apex of the circular driveway. When he opened the door for Kate, she rattled at him in Spanish, then headed for the wide carved front door.

"What'd she say?" I asked Sughrue as we followed her.

"She told him to be careful with the car, man," he answered, "because we're cops."

"You look like cops," Kate said, leaning against the door. I'd never been much for tall, skinny women, but in the muted light of the entrance, her long, limber body striking exactly the perfect graceful edge of the arc, Kate was truly beautiful. And she leaned into my shoulder, her breath soft on my neck.

"I've seen that look before, Grandpa," she whispered, "and I'd advise you to keep it to yourself." Then she laughed and whipped off the long blond wig. Beneath it, her dark hair had been clipped to the skin. She grabbed my hand and rubbed my palm against the stubbled scalp. It was as soft as the bones of her head were hard.

"Jesus," Sughrue said. "Give it up, Milo. You look like a man who's just been gut shot."

I didn't ask him how he knew. I just followed her inside when he held the door for us.

One of the things with which I tried to replace drinking during the dry years was books. I read so many that I couldn't always keep them straight. And I could never remember endings, either. But images, they stayed with me sometimes. In a novel called *Waltz Across Texas,* I remembered what I thought the telling image of rich Texans at play. When these old boys in the novel ran out of ice, they cut cubes of frozen steak to cool their bourbon and branch. Not on my worst day. Never.

But if L. G. Gish had run short of ice, he would have bought an ice house. Sughrue and I had never seen anything like this. And between the two of us, we'd seen some shit. A hog calling, a pig wallow, a Polish wedding, and Saint Paddy's Day in Butte. But nothing like this.

Eddie took a framed Russell Chatham landscape print off the den wall—one of the Headwaters of the Missouri series, I thought—set it on a table, then dumped an ounce of sparkling pure coke in the middle. He didn't cut a line, he cut an endless spiral. Then handed out silver straws. The joints were machine rolled, loaded with slivers of hash, and served on silver slavers. They were also deadly. We tried to limit ourselves to two hits an hour. And had to fight off the two Mexican bartenders who must have been ordered not to let any of the guests see the bottoms of their glasses.

Oh, and the guests. Turned out we had stumbled into a regular Wednesday night hump-day party. Between one A.M. and four, twenty people must have drifted through. Almost all of them out-of-towners, it seemed. Lawyers, doctors, politicians, and various members of the idle, vacationing rich. Not all of them criminals. But not a single one that I'd let sleep in the chicken house. Sughrue and I took turns mixing and standing on the deck over the river, even though the norther hadn't completely blown itself out.

Neither of us had a chance to talk to Connie Navarro. She had jammed herself into another nifty little number, all slits and lace-up strings, fishnet hose, and tiny four-inch heels. In one way or another, she spent the evening attending to L.G. When she wasn't engaged in dancing displays of her blunt sexuality with various men in front of her smiling husband, she sat on the arm of L.G.'s leather chair, touching him fondly, laughing warmly into his hairy ear.

Well, hell, even criminals can fall in love. And as far as I could tell, neither of them touched a drug. They barely drank. Kate did some drugs, though, drank champagne from the bottle, and broke some old boys' hearts. She had changed into cutoffs and a long-sleeved denim shirt tied below her small breasts. She didn't mix much, though, just hung out in front of the stereo, earphones clamped to her lovely head, dancing with her eyes closed.

Eddie played host, his goofy grin tightly pasted to his face. He did some cocaine, but never really fired the end of a doobie when he had a hit. He spent some time trying to pump me, but you can't bullshit a bullshitter. I led him to believe that my family money had been supplemented by the sort of real estate scams and sharp deals only allowed the idle rich. And former deputy sheriffs.

But when I didn't have his attention, Sughrue did. They circled each other like a pair of bad roosters. I knew it wouldn't take much to set them off, so I made Sughrue promise good behavior on Baby Lester's head.

Then about four-thirty the party dimmed, and the whole point of it became clear. Connie wandered over to the stereo, slapped in a blues CD, then slipped off Kate's earphones. They began to slow dance together. L.G.'s eyes brightened and he licked his lips like a lizard. Now I knew which motel he owned. Sughrue and I glanced at each other across the suddenly still room, nodded, then went over to cut in. He took Kate; I gathered the ruthless sex machine of Connie into my arms. I couldn't tell from the look on her face if she wanted to arm wrestle, leg wrestle, fistfight, or fuck.

"Down home," I heard Sughrue explain to Kate, "when women dance together, it means they want a man to ask them."

Kate barked once, then giggled, saying, "Where I was raised, when hogs dance, snakes fuck."

"You're not as stupid as you look, Montana," Connie said. "Are you?" Then she hooked her wrist around my neck and pulled me tightly against her body, which was as hot as a banked fire. She was as strong as a monkey.

"Connie, I was down in Del Rio a couple of days ago," I said when I got my breath back, "talking to your daddy."

She didn't miss a beat. "My father doesn't usually talk to gringos." Even her breath was hot.

"Well, actually we didn't talk all that much," I admitted. "But you and I should have a conversation about . . ."

"About what?"

"Your little sister," I said.

"Goddammit," she said, "fuck." Just for a beat did she search for a plan. As we whirled, I saw Eddie step toward Sughrue. But Sughrue swung Kate into his arms before he could say anything. Kate shivered as if she'd stepped on a banana slug.

"Checkout time at the lodge is three," Connie said. "Complain about your bill. Ask for the manager," she said. "Now get the fuck out of here before L.G. sics Eddie on you."

"Lady," I said, "Eddie'll never know what hit him."

"Probably your crazy friend," she murmured, smiling for the first time. "He's wanted to all night." Then in a normal voice she added, "Thanks, Montana." Then chuckled as she walked over to Kate, who was still standing in the circle of Eddie's arms, a sick look carefully hidden on her still face.

L.G. heaved a terrific sigh as Sughrue and I thanked him for his hospitality. "Anytime," he said, but he didn't mean it.

"So what happened?" Sughrue said as we waited for the attendant to bring back the car.

"I'm not sure," I admitted as the Chicano pulled up and held the door open for me. "But either way, we're out of here tomorrow."

"Too bad," Sughrue said, staring at Eddie standing in the open door and giving us the look. Then Sughrue cocked his finger, pointed it at Eddie, and fired. "Too fucking bad."

I slipped behind the wheel, but the Chicano held the door for a moment, talking through his smile as if giving directions. "Watch that one, señor," he said. "He is a master of the sucker punch."

"Thanks," I said, and handed him a twenty. But he waved it away. "For your children," I said, and he took it.

Sughrue wasn't in his room when I got ready to check out of the lodge the next afternoon, but he'd left a note saying he'd meet me at the car rental place at four. I glanced at my bill, then squawked for the manager. Connie came out of her office, all spiffy in a gray linen suit with matching heels.

"Come into my office, Mr. Milodragovitch," she said. "I'm sure we can work this out."

Connie's office looked as if it belonged in a southwestern art gallery. So did she. In her expensive working clothes, manicure, and perfect hair she looked like a woman in charge of a Fortune 500 company, her inner beast sheathed in Irish linen.

"So who the fuck are you, and what do you want from me?" she asked once she was seated behind the redwood slab of her desk, fingering an obsidian knife with a clay handle. It looked as if it were meant to cut out men's hearts. For fun, not in religious sacrifice. She didn't offer me a chair, but I took one anyway.

"Look," I said, "I'm not the enemy. I'm no threat to your life . . ."

"You goddamned well better not be," she said passionately. "I'll cut your fucking head off."

"I hope it won't be necessary," I said, "because I have some sad news. Your sister and her husband are dead. Murdered." At least she caught her breath for a second, rose and stepped over to the glass wall to stare at the shaded river. "I'm sorry," I added.

"Don't be, Montana," she said without turning. "Ana's been dead for a long time. Maybe since the day she changed her name. Certainly since she hooked up with the *co-caíneros,* the day she met Ray." Then she turned to face me. "Does my father already know?" I nodded. "At least there's that." Then she sat down, leaned on the desk, and looked at me sadly. I thought she was going to talk about her sister, but like many people dealing with grief, Connie decided to talk about herself.

"I did everything right, you know," she said, running her

thumb across the glass blade. "Finished high school. Worked my way through college making tacos in San Marcos. For six years. Got my degree in accounting. Straight A's all the way through. Didn't get married to some *cholo,* didn't get pregnant.

"The first job I got—a good job with a national accounting firm—some needle-dick white-bread fraternity boy told me to work on my accent and to buy some new clothes. Something a little less flashy. Then he showed me his little white chipmunk of a dick, and told me to get on my knees. I was still a fucking Meskin chick from Del Rio whose father couldn't even speak English.

"I grabbed his pecker, all right," she said calmly, "nearly jerked it out by the root. But goddammit, I almost got on my knees."

"But you didn't," I said. "It doesn't do much good for me to apologize for either my gender or my race," I added, "or the world. But I'm sorry."

Connie looked at me for a long second, then almost smiled. "Then I went to San Antonio and had some fun," she said. "Caught the clap, had my uterus yanked out my vagina. Some other shit. Tried to go home, but *papá* threw me out of the house.

"The next real job I had that didn't take place after dark or in a bar was here, in the laundry, shaking farts out of sheets. Now I'm vice president of the company, and when L.G. dies in bed some night," she said softly, "I'll have it all. So don't fuck with me. I'll have Eddie turn you into fertilizer."

"I suspect Eddie's got his own problems right now," I said. She looked puzzled, then smiled.

"I'm sorry to miss that one," she said.

"Right," I agreed, "but this has nothing to do with you." She raised an eyebrow. "Aside from the fact that Ray was a sleazeball and ran a money laundry, what do you know about him?"

"Not much," she said. "Ray was a bordersnake. He belonged to one of the *familias,* big families that control the drug trade on the border. He was too nice a kid, I bet, so they changed his name and sent him to college."

"What was his name?" I asked.

"I've only heard it once," she said. "But it was German, not Spanish. Bachmann, Hoffmann—something like that. A lot of those old northern Mexican ranch families have English or German names."

"He have any brothers named Roger?" I asked, but she shrugged. "What about your sister?" I asked. "What sort of woman was she?"

"A girl," she answered sharply. "A girl who liked to have fun. A little girl always afraid of the dark. And she hated to be afraid. So of course everyone loved her, loved to take care of her, help her make decisions. Shit, she couldn't finish her degree because she couldn't decide on a major. When she met Ray, she was working as a hostess in a place in north Austin, one of those theme places. She was too dumb and lazy to cocktail. She got the job because she was fucking the bar manager, sharing him with Kate . . ."

"Kate knew her?"

"I think she and Kate were in love," she said flatly, daring me to make something of the dancing scene. "Or maybe Kate was in love and Ana was having fun. Who knows? Who cares?" Perhaps I had the wrong expression on my face because she quickly added, "Whatever L.G. wants, L.G. gets. Till the day he dies."

I stood up, asked one last question. "So where's this *familia* that Ray belongs to?"

"A little town across the border from Castillo," she said. "Enojada. But I wouldn't cross the border there and go around asking a bunch of questions. By the time those border-snakes get through with you, you'll be begging them to cut off your head. Try El Paso. Hell, at least it's sort of Texas."

"Thanks for the advice," I said.

"I'd ask you to drop in after L.G.'s dead, Montana," she said, "but somehow I suspect you're going to beat him to hell."

"And thanks for the offer," I said, ignoring her prediction. "But when I go to bed, I like to make love, not war."

"Trust me, amigo," she said, almost smiling, as she grabbed my bill and signed it. "It's all the same."

"I hope not," I said, not exactly sure, though.

The desk clerk gave me an odd look when I handed her the bill that Connie had signed. I reached for my billfold.

"It's on the house, sir," she said. "Come back an' see us, you heah."

"At these prices," I said, "I can't afford not to."

Her look got even odder. Texas seemed to be full of pretty women. And tough women. But cheap irony seemed to be wasted on some of them. Maybe life down here was too hard on women for them to appreciate irony of any sort.

When I got to the Lincoln, Kate sat in the front seat, painting her toenails. A variety of backpacks and duffels were piled in the backseat. She wore a white nameless ball cap, baggy pants, and a shapeless purple cotton sweater that had slipped off her shoulder. I leaned in the open window and kissed the cool, clear skin in the hollow of her collarbone.

"What the hell are you doing here, girl?" I said.

"I've worn out this town," she said, concentrating on her tiny little toenail, "and I've never been to Montana."

"I'm not going to Montana," I said.

"You will eventually," she said calmly. "Where are we going first?"

"Good question," I said, then threw my bag on top of hers and climbed into the driver's seat. "I thought I locked the car."

"Not very well," she said, reaching into the large purse at her feet to pull out a professional-quality slim jim. She smiled shyly, then said, "I had a misspent youth."

"As far as I can tell," I said, "you're still having it."

When I drove out of the parking lot, Kate put her feet out the window for her toes to dry and her head in my lap.

"I'm a lesbian, you know," she said.

"I'm not sure you know what you are," I said, "and even if you are, honey, I sort of like the idea of being in love with a woman I can't fuck. Seems pure and simple, somehow."

"Believe me, it's not," she said, then she tilted her cap over her eyes and fell promptly to sleep like a tired kitten.

Sughrue looked a little tired himself. But not sleepy. He leaned against a wall outside the rental office, his bag at his feet. A scrape high on his right forehead had already stopped bleeding. But his T-shirt, jeans, and windbreaker were unsoiled. And his big smile unbroken.

We transferred a dazed Kate and her bags to the backseat of the Beast, settled our bill, then drove out to Interstate 10 and headed west.

"How'd it go?" I asked.

"A draw."

"A draw?"

"Yeah," Sughrue said. "I promised I wouldn't kill the son of a bitch and L.G. put the over-under quail gun back in the trunk of his Mercedes and promised to tell the hospital that Eddie fell off a cliff." Then Sughrue laughed so loudly that Kate stirred on the backseat. "Where'd you get her?"

"I'm not exactly sure."

"Where's she going?"

"With us," I said. "Guess she's been living too hard."

"Tell me about it," Sughrue said, then groaned softly. "How'd it go with Connie?"

"She suggested we not go down to Enojada . . ."

"From what I hear, that's good advice," Sughrue said, "and it's a little too goddamned close to the house for my comfort."

". . . and that perhaps Raymundo Lara was born under another name," I said. "Maybe Carver D will turn another favor for us."

"Maybe," Sughrue said. "Or maybe the El Paso narco guy can help."

"I don't think so," I said. "He checked up on me in Meriwether and didn't like what he heard."

"Nobody likes a crooked cop, Milo," Sughrue said. "Particularly when they don't even get paid for it."

"I always did get it wrong, didn't I?"

Sughrue smiled again, touched his scrape, and said, "Let's stop first chance. Stretch our legs, maybe have a beer."

"Shit, Sughrue, we've been in the car ten minutes."

"Yeah," he said, "but Eddie got in a couple of body shots before he went down. I could use a beer, maybe see if I'm pissing blood yet."

Damaged kidneys or not, I could tell Sughrue was hurting, and Kate was sleeping like the dead, so we stopped in Junction. One drink turned into four or five, which, when mixed with a couple of Florinal 3's out of Kate's grab bag of drugs, turned into darkness. My road pals were nodding out over their drinks before sundown, so I bought us a bag of tacos and found a motel, where we crashed like a small litter of sick puppies.

Everybody seemed fine the next morning after the miracle of twelve hours of sleep, so we were full of coffee, biscuits, and country gravy and rolling west again with the rising sun at our backs, the Beast purring beautifully, eating that long gray ribbon of highway. The norther had petered out, the blue sky bloomed, and the landscape lapped clean again outside the windshield.

Sughrue resisted it until nearly nine o'clock, but he tilted his seat back. Kate, who hadn't said ten words since the afternoon before, except to complain when the bartender carded her in Junction, disappeared into her portable CD player and earphones, and also disappeared beneath the contents of her bags. They seemed to have exploded. The backseat looked like the bottom of a teenage girl's closet. Her sleepy eyes drooped slowly and soon she joined Sughrue in his major nap.

About noon, I fed my charges in Fort Stockton, when they finally awoke. As we pulled back on the seemingly endless interstate across West Texas, Kate leaned forward between Sughrue and me.

"I hate to be a pest," she said brightly, "since I'm riding free and all that. Hell, you guys haven't even tried to get a blow job, or make me jack you off, or anything. That usually comes in the first thirty minutes. But do you mind if I ask where we're going?"

"No," I said, then looked at Sughrue. "I don't mind, do you?"

"Not at all," he said, "but I'd like to hear some more about these blow jobs we didn't get."

"Ha, ha, ha," Kate said, then ran down her window and spit. "Sometimes bad sex is better than bad jokes."

"When?" Sughrue asked, then turned around in his seat.

"All right," Kate shouted, smiling. "Where the fuck are you guys going?"

"El Paso City," Sughrue said.

"Oh, shit," she moaned. "I fucking hate El Paso. After Mom died, every time the General got stationed in Central America, he sent me and my big sister to boarding school there."

"The General?"

"My father," she explained. "He was really just a bird colonel, but they gave him a star and made him a brigadier before he retired. Just to be nice, maybe. But maybe because he held the line on Iran-Contra. My mother always called him '*El General*.' Even when they were kids. Her family owned the ranch next to his family's. It was a joke. Kind of. Maybe he was kind of bossy even then, but I don't think my father was ever particularly militarily minded. He just wanted to get off the ranch. It can be boring if you're not born for it." Then Kate paused. "Maybe you guys can drop me at the ranch," she said quickly, then slapped me on the shoulder. "But you have to promise, promise, promise you'll pick me up before you head back to Montana. I'll love you forever if you promise, Grandpa."

"You'll love him forever, whatever," Sughrue said. "All the girls do."

"Especially the ones who call me Grandpa."

"I don't know your name, man," she said. "Or yours, either, tough guy."

It seemed a little odd to introduce ourselves at this point, but we did it with a certain amount of grace. Her name was Katherine Marie Kehoe.

"So where's this ranch?" I asked.

"The Castellano Ranch. Just down the road," she said, "between Fairbairn and the border. The General loves having me around. But I make him nervous. And he's too sweet to complain. So we spend all our time drinking our way through his wine cellar. It's a blast. One of these days I'm going to get him stoned, too. You goddamned betcha . . . I'll bet he's really sweet and funny when he's stoned."

Sughrue and I glanced at each other, but we couldn't tell what question we wanted to ask.

"A sweet and funny general?" was what we finally decided upon. In unison.

"Maybe *charming*'s a better term. That's it," she said,

"charming. And maybe a little shy." Then, as if she'd never thought of it before in the clutter of her mind, she said, "I guess shy can be mean, you know, like if you're a kid, or something. You're sweet, Grandpa, and shy, too." Then she chuckled and kissed me wetly on the neck. "It's not much out of the way. Really. Take the next exit and head south." Then she added with that West Texas dismissal of distance, "It's only about seventy miles." Kate began madly repacking as Sughrue and I looked at each other again.

Sughrue's face was suddenly quiet, unmoving. I couldn't read it. Had no idea what he was thinking. I wasn't sure what I was thinking, either. But we'd find out.

Finally he said, "Funny place to grow up."

Kate paused in her scramble to say, "Well, I didn't exactly grow up there. But it is a funny place to call home."

I couldn't tell what Sughrue thought of that, either.

North of Fairbairn, after a long silent ride south from the interstate, I suggested a farewell road beer. Sughrue cracked them for us, and we toasted our brief friendship, and Kate gave me the ranch's telephone numbers. It seemed there were several spreads that ran from south of Fairbairn to the Mexican border. I gave her the answering service number in Meriwether. And promised not to go to Montana without her.

Then I asked her about Analise Navarro.

"What?" she said, her mood suddenly dark, then desperately chatty again. "Sure, I knew her in Austin. She was an okay chick; a little confused about her sexuality. I think her mother's brother used to dandle her on his knee. That happens a lot more than people think, you know. Connie doesn't know what the hell she's doing, either. Something happened there, too. But Ana was okay. I liked her. Till she married Ray."

"Ray?" I said, fishing.

"Ray Lara," she said, glancing around like a trapped animal. "After that she had too much cocaine and too little sense. She never thought Ray gave her enough money. So she started dealing when they got back from the honeymoon. She bought a little hair salon and dealt out of there. Dumb." Then Kate paused, pointed up ahead. "There it is, boys. My hometown."

As I had noticed before, there wasn't much in Fairbairn, fair or otherwise, just five hundred people sprinkled across a dusty plain with hazy mountains in the distance and deeply cut arroyos that only ran in the occasional rain. They weren't running that day. Sughrue didn't even glance at the Dew Drop Inn when we passed.

So we rode in silence south toward Mexico past the ornate locked gate that opened to the Castellano Ranch, until Kate screamed to stop at an unmarked cattle guard secured by a barbed-wire gap. Kate insisted on opening it, and we drove through on the rutted track. Where it dipped into a dry wallow about one hundred yards inside the fenceline, the track suddenly became a nicely graveled road. Two young *vaqueros* in a pickup with one M-16 and one heavy scoped deer rifle racked behind their heads came across the plain to intersect our path, until Kate leaned out the car window and waved at them.

It must have been five miles to the house, a huge rambling adobe that had faded to its natural desert color. A line of foreign poplars bordered the road, their needs fed by an irrigation ditch. And a large greensward watered by an underground sprinkler system surrounded the house in that rocky scrub-brush desert. The main house was large enough to be the clubhouse of a small country club. We parked in the circular drive beside a brand-new Dodge pickup and a Toyota 4Runner with a logo painted on the side: RATTLESNAKE PRODUCTIONS.

"Oh, god. That's probably Suzanne's car. She's making a movie, you know," Kate prattled nervously, "but what an odd name for her production company. My god, she hates rattlesnakes. And the General . . . Oh, shit, I'll be in the middle again . . . sometimes they just hate each other . . ."

A long porch stretched across the front of the house. Two tall, lean men stood up from a small table to examine the approach of our Beast. One of the men was dressed in starched khaki, a leather bomber jacket, and a blue gimmie cap with gold braid on the bill. The General, I assumed. The other, a dark-faced *vaquero,* looked as if he could be the younger brother of Señor Navarro of Del Rio. His faded jeans and blanket-lined jacket hung on his lanky frame with a working cowboy's grace.

As Sughrue and I climbed out of the Beast, the men stared at us with the narrow eyes of land barons who have just caught some peasant interlopers. Then Kate popped out of the backseat and both men smiled broadly. Within moments, the *vaquero* had picked up Kate's baggage and the General had Sughrue and me gathered around the table with mugs of dark, chicory-laced coffee served by a darkly silent, stone-faced woman with bright blue eyes who seemed not to approve of us. Then the General sweetened our coffee with expensive brandy and began to whip us with charm.

Brigadier General Kehoe, U.S. Army, Retired, a tall, lean gentleman of the old schools—West Point, Georgetown Law, and the War College, among others—had the soft-spoken, slow cadences and sweet gentility of a southern poet. The General had spent most of his career at various embassies throughout Central America, so he had the graceful manners of a diplomat rather than those of a military man. Within moments of being introduced to him as Kate's bene-factors, friends, and working private investigators, the General had Sughrue and me babbling like enlisted men in the presence of their commanding officer.

I found out things about Sughrue's nine years in the Army that I'd never known. And discovered, much to my chagrin, that in spite of my Korean War experience and the fact that the General wasn't much older than me, I was still deferen-tial to a fucking officer. Sometimes our basic training betrays us.

We were thick as thieves and in the middle of our third cup, more brandy than coffee now, when Kate came back out on the porch trailed by a preppie kid, an old rumpled drunk, and her older sister, Suzanne: a taller, more rounded version of Kate, elegant in black and silver—high-heeled boots, tight leather pants, and a soft, draped sweater gathered at the waist by a silver concho belt. Her short jet-black hair framed a striking face of light toffee and Irish cream, widely spaced metallic green eyes, and a generous mouth as red as fresh blood. When Suzanne stepped through the screen door,

Sughrue knocked over his chair and I spilled my coffee as we rose for introductions.

The introductions were short and not very sweet. Kate let us know that Suzanne was writing and directing a western movie, and the kid trailing her, who looked like an Ivy League sophomore and whose name we missed, was the first AD and an assistant producer. And the rumpled drunk turned out to be Sam Dunston, a Hollywood icon who had written and directed a dozen wonderful westerns. I shook his hand and told him how much I loved his movies.

"I know," he said, "I know. You thought I was fuckin' dead. Hell, everybody thought I was dead. I even thought I was dead . . ."

Murmuring something about script changes, Suzanne took Dunston's arm to lead him back into the house. Sughrue and I had been examined, found wanting, and dismissed by a superior being. On that note, the General's fabled charm failed him.

"Goddammit, Suzanne," he growled. "These men are Kate's friends and my guests. The least you can do is make a little polite conversation."

After a long uncomfortable silence, Suzanne gave her father a look that would have frozen a rattlesnake in midstrike, then said quietly, "Father, the air out here reeks of brandy and violent militaristic nostalgia. Two of my least favorite topics of polite conversation. So if you don't mind, I think we'll return to our work."

Dunston burst into the next silence like a man looking for a drink. "You know, General Kehoe, making a movie is a little like starting a small war . . ." But Suzanne had him firmly by the elbow, and his last words were lost by the slamming of the screen door. Which left the preppie kid on the porch. He lifted his small hand in an apologetic wave, then hurried after his boss.

The General muttered some vague apologies, grabbed the brandy bottle, then almost ran to the Dodge pickup, and was nearly out of sight before Kate caught her breath.

"I told you they didn't get along," Kate said, close to tears. "And Suzanne's been working toward this movie all her life . . ."

"You want to go to El Paso with us?" I asked.

"No," she answered quickly. "No, now that I'm here I better stay. I'm the only one who can make peace when they're like this." Then she bit her painted thumbnail. "It'll be okay. Really. At dinner tonight he'll go down to the cellar. He's got a really great wine cellar, you know, and try to impress her, you know, like always, so we'll drink nine hundred dollars worth of wine, and drive out to Momma's grave in the moonlight, then everything will be all right . . ."

Kate kept reassuring us all the way out to the Caddy, then made me promise again that I'd take her to Montana. Which I did promise.

As we drove away, she stood in front of that lonely house on the plain, waving goodbye like a little girl. In the distance, her father leaned against his pickup at the top of a slight rise. He seemed to be looking back at the house.

"Jesus," Sughrue said, then sighed. "I'd hate to leave my worst enemy out here."

"What are you talking about?" I said. "You live out here."

"Yeah," he said, "but I'm the only crazy person living at my house. Did you see that housekeeper look at Kate? Like Kate was a housefly and she was the swatter. And her father is obviously as nervous as a chicken in a dog run."

"I sort of liked him," I said.

"Fucking officers. And, Jesus, did you catch the big sister act? Her shit don't stink or melt in her mouth," he said. "But by god I've seen that woman someplace. I just can't think of where . . ."

"Maybe on the silver screen," I suggested. "She's good-looking enough."

"She looked mean as a blacksnake whip to me, man, with a barbed-wire popper," he said, then paused. "Hey, if you don't mind, I'd like to spend a night or two at home. Okay?"

"Okay by me," I said. "But I'm going on to El Paso. I've already got a reservation at the Paso del Norte tonight."

"What the hell are you going to do in El Paso?"

"Just nose around gently," I said. "You got a way to get to town?"

"Sure," he said. "I'll ride in on the Frito Bandito. You sure you don't mind?"

"Nope," I said. "It'll take me a while to cover all my chores. Transfer some cash, put some Texas plates on the Beast . . ."

"No," Sughrue said. "Register it in New Mexico. Use my P.O. box number in Chamberino, or Teddy Tamayo's address in Las Cruces."

"Okay," I said. I wanted to check with Teddy anyway. And Jack Soames, and Carver D's cyberpunk boyfriend.

Sughrue smiled again, almost a whole man, as we passed an ostentatious barred gate marking the fake entrance to the Castellano Ranch.

"You know," I said. "Dunston made a wonderful cavalry movie called *Demon Ride*."

But Sughrue wasn't listening. "I know that goddamned woman from someplace . . ."

When I dropped him in Fairbairn at the store, Whitney was glad to see him. She was so effusive and Sughrue as shy as a mountain Apache, I excused myself to use the pay telephone outside. It was time to check messages back in Meriwether.

"Anything?" Sughrue said as he unloaded his gear from the Beast.

"Nothing," I lied. Whitney looked as if she could use him around the house for a couple of days, so I drove away, leaving them with smiles as tentative as neon in the sunshine.

I stopped in Alpine for a beer and to use the telephone again. I had some messages at home—a bundle of them from my old pal Jamison, Meriwether's police chief, and two from the FBI—which didn't lead me to expect good news.

Jamison told me that some cop named Soames on the El Paso force had called last week to check up on me. "Milo, I told him the truth," he said.

"What's that?"

"I told him that you were all right," he said, "as long as you kept your hand off the bottle and your nose out of the coke. He mentioned you were drinking when he saw you last."

"That's right," I said. "I've had a drink or two. Even a bit of blow . . ."

"Don't tell me."

"It's out of your jurisdiction, asshole," I said. Jamison and I were friends. For a long time. But not always. He had married my favorite ex-wife, and I owed him for raising my son. "And thanks, buddy."

"You're welcome," he said. "But then the calls got serious three or four days ago. Somebody killed his brother, Milo, and now he really wants to talk to you."

"Which brother?"

"He didn't say," Jamison said. "But he did mention that whoever pulled the trigger—two in the back of the head, one in the ear, and one in the mouth—had tied him to a chair and cut the rest of the fingers off his right hand . . ."

"Shit, fucking shit," was all I could say. "Why don't you call him back, Jamison, tell him I'll meet him in Teddy Tamayo's office in Las Cruces at five tomorrow."

"That doesn't sound good."

"It's not," I said. "But if I'm in trouble, it's with the family, not the law. Jesus wept fucking blood. What the hell does the FBI want with me?"

"Oh, that."

"Yeah, that."

"They found your banker buddy's girlfriend."

"Great," I said. "Did she have my money?"

"Don't think so," Jamison said. "They picked up her body floating in the Copia River. Up in Cocachino County in Northern California. A week ago Friday night, I think." He shuffled some papers, then found the date and told me. "Some fishermen saw her come off the bridge. But she was dead when she hit the water."

"How long? And how?"

"About four hours," he said. "Somebody tied her hands over her face, then tried to blow her head off with a twelve-gauge. You got an alibi?"

"Sure," I said. I'd been prowling the Laras' house that night. "Sughrue was with me."

"Who'd believe that criminal son of a bitch?" he asked. "And what the hell are you doing hanging around with him?" Then he paused. "Oh, fuck. You guys aren't looking for Andy Jacobson, are you?"

"No," I said.

"You lying sack of shit," he said. "Where are you?"

"Somewhere in Texas," I said, and hung up.

I went back to the bar, toyed with my beer. And with the notion of going back to get Sughrue. I had made the mistake of using Rocky's name at the Pilot Knob bank, and I'd face that music by myself. But on my turf, not Jack's. I had a second drink, then called Teddy Tamayo to set up the meeting. He didn't like it, but he was my lawyer. Then I got out the map and looked for a road into Las Cruces that didn't take me through El Paso. It didn't look easy, but I found a way. It was easier, though, than looking Jack Soames in the eye was going to be. Walking the borderline.

Teddy Tamayo was, as I came to find out, one of the most honest and upright men it had been my honor to meet. And not just for a lawyer. Teddy was dead solid straight. But even he advised me not to tell Jack the whole story. I did, though. Sat there with Jack hating me as the light faded in Teddy's office and told it all. Even taped it. And gave Jack the tape.

"I can't tell you how sorry I am," I said as he dropped the tape in his shirt pocket. "I never had a brother, Jack, so I don't know what it means to lose one. It was my fault, and whatever you want to do with me . . . well, it's okay with me." Then I handed Jack my father's old Colt Army revolver that had gotten him expelled from Harvard and a new box of .45 rounds I had bought that day. "It's registered to me. And given my family history, the law won't have any trouble believing in my suicide."

Jack had sat silently through the long story, the hate coming off him in waves. Now he stood and slammed his hand into Teddy's solid adobe wall, then turned, pointed his finger at me, and said in a harsh whisper, "Let's take a ride, you son of a bitch."

I quieted Teddy's protests and went with Jack.

When we got to the freeway in Jack's unmarked unit, he turned west instead of east, and we rode without a word. All the way across New Mexico to the Arizona line, where he turned around and drove back to Las Cruces, where he parked in the lot behind Teddy's office next to my car and handed me the pistol and the box of shells.

"You took one hell of a chance, man," he said.

"It was the only one I had," I admitted. "If I'd run or whined, you'd have popped me. Eventually."

"Fuck, I still may," he said. "Rocky was a criminal all his worthless life. Shit, he wouldn't even pay his fucking child support. The family had to stop gathering at Christmas 'cause Rock and I would get in a fight every time. But goddammit, he was my little brother. Shit . . ." Then Jack leaned his head against the steering wheel. "I think I know who we're looking for, now. Xavier Kaufmann Hurtado. You put it all together for me. But he lives in Mexico. If I lure the fucker across the border, will you pop him?"

"I don't think so," I said. "I gave that up."

"Not even to save your own ass?"

"Probably not."

"Shit," he said, then raised his head. "What about your partner?"

"He thinks he would," I said, "but I don't know . . . He might beat him to death, but I don't think he would drop the hammer in cold blood. Hell, he couldn't even pop Joe Don Pines, and he really hated him."

"Yeah, I heard about that," Jack mused. "How did he get the bastard to jump out that window?"

"I never asked," I admitted.

"Well, who the fuck is going to do it?" Jack hissed.

"Let's get him across the border first," I suggested, "then maybe we can draw straws."

"Let's hope Rocky didn't give him your name before they cut off the rest of his fingers," Jack said. " 'Cause you're my bait, amigo."

"Okay," I said. Which is how I went into the drug business.

Sughrue didn't show up at the Paso del Norte for four days. When he did he looked like a new man, looked as if he had even put some flesh back on his hard bones. I don't know what I looked like after four days in bed, sick with a spiritual flu. The only good news was that I couldn't stand the taste of whiskey. Thought perhaps I'd never be able to stand the taste of whiskey again. When I finished telling Sughrue the story, he put his half-finished beer on the coffee table, where it sat until we checked out of the hotel.

It wasn't hard for me to look and act like a drug dealer. I'd known enough of them over the years, even worked for them when money got short. Working for drug dealers was one reason I had a pretty good fake set of identification that claimed I was a retired deputy sheriff from Grand Forks, North Dakota, back when it seemed I might have to run for the border at any moment. Using that paper, I rented a Mercedes convertible and an ostentatious modern house off Scenic Drive above El Paso, splashed a lot of expensive money and cheap talk around the local hangouts and nightspots that Jack suggested. Looking for Xavier Kaufmann. I had to snort a lot of cocaine with people I didn't know, or even like very much, as usual. And lie a lot. And not drink too much.

At first it seemed like a lark, coke without a dozen cocktails, a drug experience I'd missed in the old days, but after a few days it began to seem like a real chore. But I maintained. As did Jack, who took a bunch of comp time, and Sughrue, who stuck to him like a cocklebur, and three retired cops Jack said he could trust—they took on the tedious chore of surveillance for the first three weeks. I wore a directional beeper in my shoe, and they stuck with me. But just about the time they got bored, I got drunk.

Which is how I ended up in the desert west of El Paso digging my own grave, barefoot. While Xavier and Rogelio Kaufmann Hurtado and their walleyed thug watched. With my backup nowhere to be found.

I had started the evening at El Cuerno Oro, a local hangout out on the edge of the desert that seemed to cater to both DEA agents and drug smugglers. Jack had told me that my fake name, Milton Chester, had finally shown up on the DEA computer with more bells and whistles than Sughrue's, and Jack suggested I should stop by the Golden Horn at least once a night. Dutifully, I did.

Just after sundown the place was almost empty. None of my new coke buddies or my future narco pals were around. Just a couple of cattle ranchers at a table and a blonde in a suit at the bar, her purse hanging off the back of her chair, her wallet open in front of her. Between the coke and the anxiety of waiting for somebody to try to kidnap or kill me, I'd lost ten pounds and twenty years. And any interest in sex, I thought. So I said *fuck it* and ordered a Bombay martini. Which my trembling fingers sloshed over the rim of the glass before I got it to my lips.

"Terrible waste of good gin," said the blonde, but I just nodded, gunned the martini, and ordered another. As the bartender fixed it, I went to the john to fix my nose in the hope that the trembles might cease.

They did. So I drank the one I had, then ordered another. To sip on. When I tried to pay, the bartender nodded toward the blonde.

"It's my birthday," she said, then slid her wallet down the bar, open to her California driver's license. "Take a look," she said. "I hate to drink alone on my birthday."

I guess I knew better, but I looked anyway. No bells went off, so I let her slide onto the stool beside me. She had large, friendly eyes and a wide, generous mouth, and she smelled of money. "Come here often, sailor?" she asked, and I made the mistake of laughing.

Four or five martinis later, when she said quietly, "How would you like to get laid on my birthday, honey?" I laughed again. But she didn't. She just smiled.

"Where?" I said, glancing around at the now empty bar.

"We could start in the ladies' room," she whispered, leaning her unfettered breast heavily against my arm. She was naked under the suit coat.

"Shit," I said, stupidly. "What could happen to a guy in the ladies' room?"

"You could come in my mouth," she murmured closer to my ear, then drew my hand under her skirt, up her silky leg to her crotchless panty hose, where she was wet and warm. "There'd be no harm in that, would there?" Then she stood up, and with a final nice touch, left her wallet open on the bar, her purse still hanging on a bar stool, and walked toward the restrooms.

I heard the back door open. Two ordinary-looking guys came in, one about my size, the other bigger. They waved at the bartender and chatted familiarly. While I headed for the ladies' room.

I should have realized that I'd fucked up when the blow job was too good, too professional. But just as soon as the thought came, so did I. And a thin, sharp needle plunged into my thigh, so sharp and thin I didn't really notice it until I realized I was completely paralyzed, conscious but without muscular control.

I had to watch without resistance as the blonde quickly stripped me out of my clothes. All of them. One of the ordinary-looking guys put them on, and the larger, walleyed guy lifted my body like a baby's and dumped me into a rolling hamper. Then somebody else loaded the hamper into the back of a delivery van within ten feet of the cop covering the back door, a van that deposited me at my own back door.

The Kaufmann brothers had swept all the bugs out of my house and dumped them into a glass of vinegar on my rented table, where they released the occasional bubble like insects losing air out of their thorax. Then they taped my lax body, naked, to a rented wooden captain's chair in the dining room, and gave me another shot. Whatever it was, it was wonderful. I went from paralyzed to bright-eyed and bushy-tailed in a few seconds.

Rogelio, the younger brother, smiled at me as he pulled on surgical gloves. The walleyed thug didn't smile. Xavier didn't need gloves. He didn't have any fingerprints. But he hung back in the shadows anyway, a soft-spoken shade. Then Rogelio frowned. "Hey, this is the guy told Leon he was Rocky Soames."

The thug—I never did get his name—said something in Spanish.

"Maybe you killed him too soon," Xavier answered him in almost accentless English. "Like Raymundo." Then he turned to me. "I hear you been looking for me, man," he said.

"And trying to do business in my town," Rogelio added. "So who the fuck are you, man?"

Okay, I was dead whatever I did, and I'd probably earned it. It was almost a relief after the last three weeks. I had spent enough time in police interrogations to know that you don't tell the cops anything. Period. Ever. Not one word. So I decided not to talk to the crooks, either.

That lasted about twenty seconds. Or just as long as it took Rogelio to plug in his toy, an electric stencil cutter with a long needle soldered to the end, and watch the current heat the needle red-hot. Suddenly I realized what had happened to the Laras. And knew why Ray Lorenza had died before he could tell them about the floppy disk in the PC. When Rogelio brushed it across the head of my penis, I nearly fainted.

But when he stuck it up my dick, I convulsed so wildly that the rented chair exploded into pieces around me. I nearly got away in their surprise. At least I got in one good lick on Rogelio's upper arm with a chair leg before the thug wrapped me in his huge arms. So Rogelio could pound on me at will. Or till his arms got tired.

Within minutes, I was back in the same condition. Except that now I had some new scars and sore teeth. And somebody had thought to bring a metal chair from the kitchen.

"Jesus," Rogelio said, wiping sweat off his face and smiling. "That must've hurt, man." Then he looked at Xavier, who nodded, and his little brother didn't have any trouble doing it again. This time I had neither a swoon nor a convulsion to blanket the pain. Not the next time, either. At least I didn't have a heart attack.

Nobody likes to show their ass. But the truth is, I soiled myself. Twice. Then told them a story. Then another story. And another. But I don't think I told them everything. And didn't tell them my name. Somehow it seemed terribly important to hold on to my name. But the fucking bastards didn't believe me. No matter how many stories I told, they would not believe me.

But I guess at some awful moment I gave up Sughrue's story.

"Hey, look man," Xavier said softly from the edge of the room as the thug cleaned me up with a dish towel, his giant fingers so oddly gentle I could have kissed his face, tongued a fly speck off his walleye, anything. "This isn't about some dude I shot, up in New Mexico, this Sughrue guy. It can't be. Nobody would go to all this trouble." Then he turned to his brother, who was sweating nearly as badly as I was as he burned hairs off his arm with the needle. I could smell the burning hair even through the stench of my own voided bladder and bowels. "You wouldn't do that for me, would you, *hermano*?"

Rogelio smiled, then said, "Of course not, brother mine."

"Good," Xavier said, but his eyes narrowed slightly as if this wasn't the right answer. Then to me he said, "If I had wanted to kill this Sughrue person, he would be dead. As you are dead, my friend. As a favor to a friend, you understand, I just shot him a little bit. So he was supposed to live."

Somewhere I registered the lie, not that it would be of any use. Like the distrust and lack of love between the brothers. They were too smart to let me use that.

"Do him again?" Rogelio asked, almost whining, pulling a cocaine inhaler from his pocket and sniffing deeply.

"No. I don't think so, little brother," Xavier said. "You like it too much. It's not good for your mental health. And it gives me bad dreams."

"Fuck it," Rogelio said, grinning, "let's take him to the desert. Let him dig his own grave."

So they did.

"See," Rogelio said as he tossed me a long-handled spade and pointed to the center of a bare, sandy spot. "We aren't uncivilized. We've picked some easy digging for your last chore."

"No such thing as easy digging," I said, "or bad pussy." Nobody laughed. None of them had ever done any serious digging. I didn't know much about their sex lives. Except that something was terribly wrong with Rogelio.

The long ride to the desert had restored me slightly. At least I was getting used to being naked. I'd never got used to the pain that burned to the center of my groin. And I had a weapon in my hands. I would die, sure, but I'd take at least one of these fuckers to hell with me.

Xavier, with arrogantly empty hands, was a black shadow in front of the van's headlights. Rogelio, holding a silenced MAC-10 submachine gun, which probably meant it was a .380, and the thug, with a Glock automatic pistol, stood on opposite sides of the grave site. I plotted out the grave and began digging slowly but steadily, pitching the sand close to the thug's feet. He stepped back, moved slightly to the left.

"Hey, Rogelio," Xavier said, "stand back. Don't let him throw sand in your face." His face was shadowed by the lights, but I could hear the taunt in his voice. So could his brother. Who just grunted, and clicked off the safety of the MAC-10.

"This *maricón,* he's the one gonna have sand in his face," he added, then stuffed his nose again with the inhaler.

I worked steadily, long enough for them to get bored, long enough for my muscles to loosen and the sweat to turn from clammy to clean and hot and angry, and to get down far enough past my knees to have a little leverage, then tossed the shovel handle-forward on the ground in front of Rogelio.

"What the fuck you doing?" Rogelio said suddenly, as if just waking up.

"I got to pee," I groaned, lying—I didn't think I'd ever pee again—leaning my hands on the side of the grave, as if standing up hurt. Which it did. But I'd sweated out most of the gin and the drugs. But not the shame. "I really got to pee."

"Piss in your own grave!" he shouted.

"Suck my dick, *maricón* !" I shouted back.

"Suck on this!" Then Rogelio stepped toward me with the submachine gun. Xavier started to say something, but he was too late.

Using my hands I levered myself straight up as if about to jump Rogelio as he advanced, but I came down with both hands on the shovel blade, and the handle leaped into Rogelio's crotch so hard it lifted him off the ground. As I twisted to land flat on my back in the shallow grave, Rogelio fell to his knees and pulled the trigger of the MAC-10.

A couple of rounds just missed my head, thudding into the side of the grave, but as the clip emptied, the MAC-10 lifted up and to the side, stitching the large, kindly thug from his knee to his walleye. He dropped the Glock at his feet and toppled sideways.

Xavier recovered quickly and dove for the pistol. He and I reached the Glock at about the same time—because I had paused to grab the shovel. He had just locked his fingers around the Glock when I cut his hand off like a snake's head with the shovel blade, clean off at the wrist. Xavier rolled away screaming. For most men that would have been it; I would have taken his head, too. But he scrambled to his feet and fled for the van.

The Glock was slippery with blood when I shot at his fleeing shadow. I missed him, but I got the headlights with the next two rounds. Then jerked two clips off of the thug's shoulder holster. And made it back to the grave as the sound of a heavy assault rifle started chugging from the darkness beside the van.

I stayed down.

"Give it up!" I shouted from the bottom of my grave. "I'm going to put a round into your little brother!"

In the starlight I could see Rogelio still kneeling above me, trying to hold his nuts with one hand, trying to eject the empty clip with the other.

"Give it up now!" I screamed, and reached to pull the skinny fucker into the grave with me.

The kid was dead before I touched him; his brother sprayed the grave site with a full clip. I heard the sound of a fumbled reload. Then the firing of the engine. I scrambled out from under Rogelio's body in time to throw the rest of the clip at the van. I heard the steel *prang* of my rounds against the van's body but must not have hit anything important because it kept going.

Maybe the fucker would bleed to death before he got to El Paso. But I couldn't count on it. I stripped the thug of his bloody clothes, jacket, and his oversized shoes, threw them on, then took the MAC-10, the fresh clip, an ugly switchblade, and the cocaine inhaler from the kid's body, shouldered the shovel, and, at the last moment, gathered some other things I didn't want anybody else to have. Not Xavier, because he'd be back. Not even Sughrue. This was mine.

Then I found the dirt track and jogged away from the

lights of El Paso, the warm glow over the moonless eastern sky. Jog a hundred steps of pure fire, then walk two hundred, sobbing. When I had to lie down I stepped off the sandy road, then backtracked through the brush and buried myself in a thornbush beside the track.

Nobody showed up but a roving Border Patrol Suburban, and I would have died before I talked to them.

Just before daylight, I had to go to the ground hard before hypothermia put me down for good. I slipped as far as I could into the brush, which frankly wasn't too far. When I looked for a place to dig my hole, I spotted the corner of something projecting just above the blow-sand. I dug around it with my hands just long enough to find out that somebody had buried a fucking bale of cotton. And a six-pack of Bud cans. What kind of people steal a bale of cotton? Or abandon beer in the desert? I didn't want to think about it, I just guzzled a warm beer. Dug another shallow grave and lined it with wads of cotton pried from the bale with the switchblade. Drank another beer and lay down to die. Or dream. Or just sleep till dark. In spite of the cocaine. If I dreamed, I didn't want to remember it.

That night outside Columbus, New Mexico, I found a farmhouse circled by a field of stalks, guarded by two mange-ridden dogs they must have kept to fox *mojados,* wetbacks crossing the desert toward the false promise of America. I couldn't kill the fucking dogs, even though I wanted to and tried, but I did manage to trap them in an empty ramshackle garage long enough to gobble a pound of raw hamburger and an onion, to steal clothes without bullet holes or blood, and to find a pair of shoes that moved when my bloody feet did. Almost sixteen dollars in piggy-bank change and three cans of peach halves. I had simply become a smarter, more feral animal than the dogs. I buried the bloody clothes and the MAC-10, which was too bulky to carry under the too-tight clothes, but there were other things I still didn't want to give up.

When, surviving on freestone Melbas, I got into Columbus later that night, the only pay telephone I could find was under a bright streetlight hanging off the post office. That

wouldn't do. I hiked back to dig up the MAC-10 and the si-
lencer, hiked back to town, shot out the streetlight, then went
back to bury it again. Perhaps that was when I lost my mind.
Finally. Perhaps because I hadn't peed in over twenty-four
hours, I was dying of uremia. Or at least I assumed something like that.

When I called collect the only safe person I could think of
south of the Montana line, Teddy Tamayo, I woke him up.
He complained, mightily, but he came, drove me to Deming,
bought me a truck stop breakfast, then another, and checked
me into a motel. He even found me a junkie doctor who
would make a house call that time of night, an elderly blue-
faced white guy who hadn't had a medical license since the
fifties and who had to dig a vein out of his white, wormy old
toes so he could fix in front of me because his old hands
shook so badly he couldn't stick a catheter up my dick. So
the old boy fixed me, too, then rammed the rubber tube
home. As I nodded off behind the Mexican brown heroin, I
dreamed the bloody urine ran out of me into a plastic bag as
if I were bleeding to death.

Part Two
Sughrue

Fucking Milo. The old fart stands over there next to the cliff watching a pod of gray whales about half a mile out through the spotting scope, leaning to stare into the cold, blunt face of the Pacific. The sundown sea is calm today, with a thrilling blush of fire that glistens like molten blood on the flat, sullen slopes of the easy swells, then fades to black with the passing tilt of a wave. One of the whales spouts, a trail of breathy waters like a sigh hanging in the stolid air. Milo grunts. I can tell by the hunch of his shoulders that he feels as if he's been hunted nearly to extinction, too.

He's not been himself since that night. Maybe it was soiling himself in fear before other men. That must have robbed him of something terribly important to his idea of being a man. Or maybe it was the simple insult of the pain. But I think I can guess what he's really mad about: when he spilled his guts, the assholes didn't believe him. Milo always really hated to be called a liar. Once the Kaufmanns did that, they were dead men. Or so we hear. Rogelio's body disappeared, as did the large nameless Mexican. So nobody slept in Milo's shallow grave. Jack heard from his DEA buddies that Xavier Kaufmann died of blood poisoning somewhere deep in the interior of Mexico.

At least the old fucker is alive. That counts. Milo didn't notice it for a couple of days—guess they hurt him so badly he couldn't look himself in the eye; I was like that in the hospital, Whitney said, the day she told me to marry her or die, and he still hasn't said zip-minus-shit about it—but the curly tar-black pelt that used to cover his head like a dead animal is now clipped to the bone and streaked with long shafts of pure angel white. And something small and dangerous lurks behind his eyes, hides in his rare smiles. As far as I can tell, Milo's handling his violation at least as badly as I did mine.

Okay, so we fucked up. But the Kaufmanns ran a pretty slick scam, and Milo chose that night to get hammered on gin martinis, tough drinks in the best of times. Once a shrink friend of mine, who specialized in drunks, told me that he could spot a gin drunk across a crowded room. Of course, the shrink was wasted on Absolut vodka at the time. Maybe if Milo had been drinking anything but Bombay martinis, he wouldn't have fallen for the hooker's birthday-blow-job routine.

Perhaps I shouldn't joke about it, but sometimes shit is too heavy if you don't make light of it.

Jack and I sure didn't have any jokes that night. By the time we figured out that something was wrong, the bar had filled with a batch of early evening hard-drinking big guys with guns. It wasn't the sort of place you wanted to pull a piece, unless you could find perfect cover from the cross fire when the good guys, and the bad, saw a pistol waving in the air. Jack said it had only happened once before, when a demented DEA agent and former Dallas Cowboy fan had tried to plug Tom Landry on the big screen television. The final toll was sixteen wounded, not one of them an innocent bystander. So we did the only thing we could think of: we set fire to the Golden Horn.

In the resultant confusion, we took out the guy wearing Milo's clothes, and the hooker, too, when she objected, stuffed both of them in the trunk of Milo's rented Mercedes, and drove them back to the house off Scenic Drive.

My viscera flinched when I saw the long needle soldered to the sharp point of the stencil cutter lying on the table. Jack and I ignored the blood and the splintered chair as we stared at the needle and knew the old fart was dead. Maybe we even prayed he had died easy.

Within five minutes we knew everything the guy in Milo's suit and the hooker knew, which was jack shit. Fucking hired help from California. I wanted to cut their fucking heads off anyway, but Jack talked me out of it. So we locked them in the garage, then sat around for three days with our thumbs up our asses, working the telephones and planning an assault on Mexico we knew we'd never make. Jack had five kids from two marriages and another in the oven with his girlfriend; I had Baby Lester, and Whitney now. Only men who are done with their family lives can do *The Wild Bunch* number, can walk into a hail of gunfire, grinning like Warren Oates or marching with the peace and dignity of Bill Holden.

Just about the time Jack and I had gotten sick of blaming ourselves, and each other, Teddy Tamayo left a message for Jack at the police station.

On the afternoon I got shot, a Saturday, I spent the heat of the day cruising the Upper Valley of the Rio Grande in Norman's classy VW van, easing back and forth between El Paso and Old Mesilla, New Mexico, foxing the sun in cool Mexican beer joints with slow, sweaty beers, and smoking Detroit needles, skinny doobies, on the comfortable curves of the back roads, the tape deck cranked all the way to the sky as Zevon, Seger, Ely, and Waits wailed rock and roll into the blind maw of the ancient sun.

Perhaps noticing that I was staring a half-century dead in the eye, I wondered if I should regret my taste in music, wondered if it was infantile, as a woman once told me, but I simply could not resist all that wonderful madness, that reckless joy and pain. Truth to tell, I wondered about a lot of things these vacation afternoons. My hair had gotten skimpy, gray streaks among the blond, but god help me I still loved the blessed *mota* smoke, still loved the fuzzy stoned light in the middle of the afternoon. I had been living as straight as I'd ever managed, given my life, working hard and taking good care of Baby Lester. Hell, I was even putting money away for the kid's college. But I simply couldn't live too straight all the time. I had to bend, crooked, occasionally.

My other choices seemed limited: twelve-stepping like a ghost into a boring future; or becoming one of those old mutt-faced hippies, brained by smoke and cheap whiskey, marijuana and politics. Frankly, I still loved to giggle and dance, still hated the fools in charge. Even the ones who said they were on our side. They drove me to drink, too. I didn't even hate the war anymore, or even all the wasted death, exactly. Loving the boy had washed the cynicism and anger right out of my blood. Hell, maybe I would become one of those ancient, almost wise old men who live for slow afternoon beers balanced against a single shot of good Scotch as the baseball game plays on a bad television in a cheap bar. That sounded better than a reptilian isolation in retirement.

Well, maybe not wise. And not so ancient, either. Occasionally, I still found a young woman touched by the company of the bad times and the old days. Maybe I wouldn't retire from that. Not just yet. Not that I had taken advantage of some kid's romantic attachment to sixties nostalgia. Nope. Actually, I hadn't slept with a woman since Wynona's death. Though taking comfort with that made me a little nervous.

But, Christ, that afternoon I had just gotten off a particularly ugly job, chasing a bail jumper for Harim through West Texas for nearly two months. When I brought the sly old man, one Jack Barstow, back to face sixteen counts of child molestation, Harim's secretary, a fortyish harridan named Lila, had been so pleased that she stuffed three tightly rolled joints into the envelope with my cash, saying, "Somebody has to smoke all that dope I keep taking away from my goddamned kids."

It seemed I hadn't had a day off from work or fatherhood in years, so maybe it was time to blow the pipes. But first, Baby Lester, always first.

I went by Wynona's mother's house, played with Baby Lester until he was crazy, then put him down for a nap. Mrs. Townsend promised me that the boy would sleep till dark, at least, then asked me to call her "Grammy" for the twentieth time, and told me to take a couple of days. When I argued, Mrs. Townsend whispered as she snuck a cigarette on the porch, "Sonny, you look like warmed-over shit. Get drunk. Hell, get laid—even if you have to go to Juarez. Wear a rubber, though. Grammy'll take care of everything."

All right, blame me. I fired up Lila's first number as I backed out of the driveway, promptly dropped it, then backed the van into the salt cedars that lined the driveway. When I looked back at the house Mrs. Townsend was laughing and waving, shouting something about the nature of fun, but sometimes the old lady didn't make any sense. And sometimes she did: She wouldn't smoke in front of her grandbaby; she stubbed out her cigarette before she went in-side where Lester, escaped from his nap already, clung to the screen door, shaking the frame, waving and laughing, as if encouraging me to let it all hang out. Just like the old woman.

Sometimes old people were a wonder.

Take Garciela Townsend. Wynona had told me enough about her mother so I knew that she was about a thousand ants short of a picnic, and often mean as a sow with a shoat stuck under the bottom rail, but as far as Lester and I were concerned she was sweet as strawberry honey.

I admit my amazement freely. Because Mrs. Townsend in-sisted on taking care of Lester, I was able to work the job as usual—skips and repos and jumpers, depositions and di-vorces, instead of night shifts at truck stops or the cracking plant or the smelter, the taste of dust, diesel, or arsenic thick on a cigarette-seared tongue. So I fired the *mota* again, pulled the van out of the brush, punched *Beautiful Loser* into the tape deck, and drove slowly away. This nostalgia was a frenzy that needed feeding. "God love Grammy."

And sometimes old people were a caution.

Take Jack Barstow. The old boy had spent his life as a fairly respectable and slightly boring high school history teacher, raised a small but normal family, taught thousands of students about Stephen F. Austin and old Sam Houston and others of that tribe. Then he retired.

The shit must have been stirring, but maybe Jack was too busy. Or maybe he had just never been caught. The acts Barstow had performed on his three grandsons and their playmates were so heinous that Harim made me leave my weapons in the bond office safe before I left on the chase.

When I finally caught up with Barstow in Ranger, Texas, and found the old bastard volunteering as a foster grandfa-ther at a church child care, I admit I was glad the Browning wasn't under my arm. As it was, when the old man didn't re-sist but did simper like a clown as he claimed his innocence, I slapped him so hard they never did find his false teeth.

Cruising the Upper Valley that afternoon, the weight of Jack Barstow almost lifting off my shoulders, I was drawn to the desert west of the Rio Grande. The great, rough emptiness filled something in me, something I couldn't name.

I nearly drove out there, thinking perhaps to drive the sandy tracks across to Columbus, New Mexico, then across the border to Palomas, where the whoremasters broke in the young girls bought in the high desert villages. No matter what they looked like, their beauty was in their hopelessness. Once, half-drunk in Palomas, I decided that when I wanted to commit suicide, I would cross the border, steal a vanful of young whores, and drive them home. Of course, they'd be back in the whorehouses before my body began to decay.

So this wasn't the time, not for Palomas, or the far desert roads. This was a time to watch the sunset flame out, watch the shadows creep across the valley, watch the Thunderbird glow blood-red across the face of the Franklin Mountains.

Wynona had been dead ten days over a year. As he grew from baby to toddler, Lester was almost too alive, too wild and crazy. But I never had any resistance to loving Wynona's child. The first time the kid heard Zevon chord into "Stand in the Fire," Lester, who could barely stand, ripped off his diaper and danced naked like a dervish. Lester was bound to be a rambler, a gambler, and a good-time car wreck. Just like his mom. Then I remembered that Wynona had died before we ever had a chance to dance. Shit.

Like all shiftless, rootless drinkers I sometimes thought of myself as a poet of the highway or a roadside philosopher, like my mad father. But he had also taught me a few things, a few ways to protect that core of being that makes you human. Sometimes people you love fucking die. You're supposed to feel bad. For-fucking-ever. And that is a gift. Most assholes, even if you gut shoot them, can't even manage to feel bad about their own deaths long enough to stop being assholes: that was sad. Feeling bad about the deaths of people you loved: that was hard, but not sad.

So I decided as the sun drifted down the western sky to head the van up the prehistoric banks of the Rio Grande, have a beer, smoke the last joint, cry a few tears, laugh, and think of Wynona Jones. Then when it was dark as ink, I'd go home, back to Lester and the old stone house where we lived. Yeah. Pick up some tapes. An old movie for me. *Out of the Past* would be perfect. Cartoons for Lester. His favorites, Tom & Jerry and Bullwinkle. And McDonald's. It sounded like a plan.

But the cooler was empty. I couldn't go to the sunset without a beer. Luckily I was just passing La Esperansa del Mundo—a tiny Mexican beer joint that seemed to capture all the horrible moments between Texas and Mexico, the wars, the lies, the naked aggression of a country led by the Protestant gods of capitalism against a country confused by the old gods and the Catholic Church, a country mad with beauty and despair . . . Yes. La Esperansa. "Poor Mexico," they say. "Too far from God and too goddamned close to Texas."

In my piss-poor border Spanish, hoping to be as polite as an aging hippie redneck can be, I ordered a can of beer to be drunk politely before I ordered a six-pack to go. La Esperansa could not be treated like a convenience store. Too much dignity. I nodded at the older Mexican farmers at the tables, men who had seen my passing act before and forgave it, who nodded like gentlemen acknowledging my effort. Since the valley still held the sun's heat and the shadowed bar was cool and peaceful, I ordered another beer. Then a third.

At some point a group of five young urban Chicanos slouched through the door, to everybody's displeasure, and surrounded the bumpy old pool table with its crooked sticks and chipped balls. The young men looked at me, the only gringo in the place, as if I were a sail-cat, a flat, sun-fried roadkill. A challenge issued. The tallest one, a wide-shouldered dandy with a thick moustache and snaky eyes, smiled too long. So I smiled back, hoping the smile indicated age and maturity, not lack of judgment, then turned away.

Nothing was at stake here, it seemed. But after a moment the bartender started shouting at the men, Spanish spit too quickly for my ear.

Well, fuck it, I remember thinking. God hates people who make trouble in bars. Particularly bars that mean something to me. So, half-stoned, half-drunk, and more than half ready to kick the living shit out of some asshole, I turned back to face the young men—planning, I suppose, to walk over to the tall one, talk to him or take him out quickly, whichever the kid wanted. If that didn't stop the others—well, hell, I'd worry about it later. They might kick my ass, but they wouldn't be getting a cherry.

So I moved, a fast but friendly, bold stroll between the tables, and the bartender screamed. The tall *cholo* had drawn a cheap pistol from his back pocket. Shit, and there I was with nothing but a beer can in my hand.

I had time to recognize the piece, a South American five-shot .38 revolver made by an arms company that supposedly started up with stolen CIA funds left over from the Reagan years, and even had time to think, *I guess you think odd shit just before you die.*

And afterward, too.

Sometimes my father claimed that I had been conceived in the back of a moving pickup truck outside Socorro, New Mexico. At other times he said a motel in Deming. And other odd places at odder times, too.

But if it had been a Deming motel, I hoped it had been a little sweeter room than Milo's. The walls had been slopped instead of painted, the carpet exhumed instead of laid, and the crooked curtains nailed to the wall for good reason. Two puke-plastic chain lights flanked the filthy bed with dim stagnant streams from forty-watt bulbs. A former tenant had tried to steal the cheap clock-radio off the murky wall, but it had resisted the theft and held on by a single bent bolt. Perhaps the same tenant who had snatched the television and plugged the toilet.

Among this chaos Milo couldn't have looked any more dead, flat on his back, unwashed, badly stitched, laid out in the stolen clothes. He had his right hand under the dirty pillow, and the stink from his exposed armpit smelled like death. Rubber tubes dark with age ran in a frenzy of snakes up his nose, into the back of his hand, and out of his dick. The old addict and his silent Mexican nurse had enough tubes in him to open a service station. The doc maintained that Milo was a dead man if he didn't pee soon; and nobody really wanted to deal with the paperwork and questions a hospital would require. Not even our lawyer.

"I've shoved that fucking tube up his dick until my arms are sore," he said, "and I ain't gonna do it no more."

The doc jerked the catheter out of Milo—who rose briefly then fell back on the dirty bed, his hand anchored under the pillow—and the ancient nurse started to gather their supplies, but Teddy put the doc in an arm lock and sat him heavily down. That was the end of that argument. I knelt over Milo and tried to talk to him. Without response. For a long time.

"What the fuck is wrong?" I asked.

"Maybe shock," the nurse suggested.

"Maybe that last jolt was a little too much," the doc whispered. "I've sorta lost my touch over the years."

I stripped the sleeve off the inside of Milo's elbow: tracks like the Union Pacific without a gold spike.

"You old fuck," I said, "if he's hooked . . ."

"It's all I had, son, and it ain't nothing he can't cold turkey," the old man said. "Hellfire, I've done it a hundred times myself. Maybe a thousand." Then he added, "But I can't make him pee."

"Put the goddamned catheter back in, you junkie bastard," I said quietly, and he tried. Without any success. Milo stirred again, briefly, his hand locked under the pillow. "What the hell's he got under there?" I said. "A piece?"

"Among other things," the doc said. "But I wouldn't try to take nothing away from the bastard. He'll hurt you." The old man lifted up his wrinkled shirt to expose three or four large bruises of various age and hue. "He's pretty tough for a dead man," he said quietly.

Jack held one leg, Teddy the other, as I tried as carefully as I could to pull the sodden pillow from under Milo's head. Weak and wasted as he was, he bridged his back to hold the pillow in place and wrestled so hard that Teddy had to get a leg over Milo's free arm so I could jerk on the other from under the pillow. Finally the struggle ceased. Milo flopped back and opened his eyes, his empty hand flexing like a dying snake, the right still buried under the pillow.

"Sughrue?" he croaked, and the nurse wiped his lips with a washrag wrapped around ice cubes. "Water," he said, "gimme some fucking water."

The old doc shook his head. "It'll kill him," he whined, "then you'll blame me. They always blame me. Then hurt me."

"Blame you," I said. "I'll peel your hide and pack you in rock salt."

"See," the old man said, and fell back in his chair, weeping junkie tears.

"Water," Milo whispered, grinning with a death rictus, dots of blood forming on his cracked lips. "Gimme some water, Sonny, and I'll give you something." I eased up on Milo's arm, and we watched in total silence as it slithered under the pillow. Even the doc muffled his sobs. But Milo didn't bring out a pistol. He handed me the half-rotten right hand of Xavier Kaufmann, then begged for water until he passed out, leaving the cold soft flesh for me to hold while he retreated into his near-coma.

Two hours later, Milo came out of it screaming, sitting up and howling like a man whose raw flesh was covered with black scorpions, whose blood crawled with fire ants. We thought he was coming down off the nod. But as a blackish stain dampened the bed, we realized he was just taking a leak. And, boy, did it sound like it hurt.

When he stopped screaming, we started laughing. Milo stared at us as if we were stone crazy. "Where the hell did you get this?" I asked him, holding up the hand, which Jack had placed in an evidence baggie. "And what the fuck was it doing under your pillow?"

"It's a long story," he croaked, then pulled the Glock from under the pillow, "and not very pretty." Then he grinned again and the blood ran down his chin. "Now get me a fucking drink of water."

The old bastard wasn't just alive, he was probably dangerous. Perhaps he'd given up his foolish dreams of living this life without occasionally shooting somebody.

Finally, the whales sound deep in the dark water, and Milo detaches the 25x scope from the tripod with steady fingers, then replaces everything in the foam-lined carrying case where the various weapons and surveillance gear are stored. He touches the case as if he can feel the automatic fire beneath the plastic. Milo had kicked cold turkey, but it wasn't nearly as easy as the old doctor promised. "I wish I could see them up close," Milo says, turning his back on the darkening swells, "maybe hear them sing."

I tell him I'm not sure these are the singing kind, but if he wants, we can take a guided boat tour.

"Can't," he growls. "I get seasick."

How the hell do you know? I ask.

"Korea," he whispers. "On the boat ride over, I threw up ninety-seven times. After I started counting. If I hadn't been a growing boy, I'd've been dead before I got there. As it was, Sonny, I told 'em I'd rather die in combat than climb back on that fucking troop ship."

I suggest that he was a sissy.

"No, I was a baby," he says, his voice deep and raw after three weeks of maintenance whiskey and constant cigarettes. I have been watching him closely but haven't seen a sign of the old style death-wish drinking. Just a guy trying to hang on to a bit of ease in a bad world. "Just a teenager," he muses. "Hell, I would have been a virgin, too, if it wasn't for Phyllis Fjosse. God love her. I've had this thing for cross-eyed girls since that afternoon." He puts the foam-lined case into the trunk of the Caddy. "I snuck out of the hospital in Japan and got laid a couple of times. But it was either too or-nate for my body cast—they wanted to stick stuff up my ass—or too commercial. So the next real piece of ass I found was when I mustered out in Frisco. A gap-toothed Catholic girl on her last free weekend before a one-way ticket to the convent . . ."

Milo pauses by the driver's door, gazing over the Caddy's roof, once more considering the cold Pacific, slate-gray now and rougher in the rising wind. The swells, so smooth in the distance, crash madly against the rocks below, spray flinging itself halfway up the cliff, fingers of icy foam clinging.

"Never felt the same afterwards," he whispers. "Not about gap-toothed Catholic girls. Or nuns, either." Then he smiles softly. "The way that girl loved to fuck, I suspect she didn't make Jesus a great wife."

I agree, and laugh politely. Once Milo was mobile, Jack moved us out of Deming to Silver City to hide out with an-other branch of the extensive Soames family, a retired cop who ran a bar, and we went to ground in his rambling adobe until the reports of Xavier Kaufmann's death were confirmed. I still wanted the guy who paid him to pull the trigger, wanted him like fire, but Jack and Teddy talked me into letting *la familia* cool down before we thought about crossing the border to look for the Baron, particularly around Enojada. After finding Milo in the motel, it only seemed fair to let my revenge slide for a time. We could look for his banker and the money, and check out the dead lady poet now; and I could wait.

Milo left me at home for a couple of days, resting up, while he drove to Southern California. Holding Whitney was like holding my heart in my mouth. Catching Baby Lester was like chasing a greased, rawhide pig. I suspect it hadn't been that way for Milo. He spent three nights with Maribeth at her condo in La Jolla. But he hadn't mentioned it yet.

"What time's that deputy supposed to be back at the substation?" he asks, as if he doesn't know.

"Now," I tell him, without glancing at my watch.

Americans seem obligated to erase the past. Wipe out the names, even. I suspect the seaside village of Highwave, California, had once been called Las Olas Altras, but now it sounds like a proctologist's chore. Just like the sheriff of Cocachino County. We spent all afternoon at the courthouse in Glory while Milo looked for the right way to kiss the sheriff's ass before the stumpy politico would let us even talk to the deputy, Don Henriksen, who'd been on duty at the Highwave substation when Rita Van Tasselvitch's body went off the bridge into the Copia River.

The substation must have been built before Proposition 13. Bulletproof glass and iron doors keep the visitors from the squad room, and the dispatcher issues official plastic visitors' badges to us before we are allowed to shove on the locked and barred door while she fucks with the buzzer. Finally, inside, we find almost new desks mounted with state-of-the-art computers and braced with soft-seated swivel chairs. The empty holding tank looks clean, almost comfortable, and the weapons racked along the rear wall look as if they've never been shot.

Deputy Henriksen is losing his blond hair, and with his

goofy grin he has the look of pure country, but it hasn't affected his cop face. I notice that right away. Just as soon as Milo asks him how he likes working in a small community, then plays his old Meriwether County deputy experience on the kid. Henriksen talks to Milo as if he's the sheriff's favorite uncle. When in fact, the sheriff is Henriksen's least favorite uncle. But this is an open murder case in one of the smallest rural counties on the North Coast, and Doug isn't anxious to talk about it. No matter how much and how easy the small talk. But finally Milo finds the key. Fishing. Milo invites him to come to Montana and go trout fishing on his ranch.

What ranch? I think.

Turns out that Henriksen's family had been commercial fishermen for several generations up at Fort Bragg, but between the government and the Japanese there were no fish anymore. So over the years the family had taken to law enforcement instead of marijuana farming, as most everybody else had.

"Yes, sir," Henriksen says, "the drug problem along this section of the North Coast is terrible."

"How's that?" Milo says.

Too many fucking cops, I think.

"Mexicans have moved in," Henriksen says. "Mafia is trying to corner the crops. The growers are carrying automatic weapons . . . It's a war out there."

Right, I think, *but the fucking government started it.*

"I take it, Deputy, that you think that Miss Van Tasselvitch's death was connected to this war?" Milo says softly, then adds, "I'm Russian myself, and I don't believe I've ever heard that name . . ."

"Oh," Henriksen says brightly, catches himself, then shrugs. It won't hurt to talk to us a little bit. "That was a professional name. She used to be a stripper down in the city. Had her name changed. Hard to believe, you know, after looking at the body . . ."

"Shotgun tore her up pretty bad?" I say.

"That's right. One big mess," he says, turning to me finally. Since I had taken off my gimme cap and let my ponytail fall out, Henriksen had treated me as if I were a redheaded stepchild. Or an idiot cousin. "Rita must have put her hands over her face when the guy popped a cap on her."

"I heard somebody tied her hands to her face," Milo says.

Henriksen stares at Milo for a long second. "Where'd you hear that?"

"The FBI."

"Oh. Well, it was a mess, whatever. No fingerprints, no teeth. A real mess," he says as if he's talking about the weather.

"How'd you identify the body?" Milo asks.

"Oh, easy," Henriksen says. "The tattoos, and her size, you know. She put on a few pounds since she twirled her tassels down in the city." Then he laughs like a boy. "About a hundred-weight, man. She was a big, big woman. Everybody knew her. Hell, everybody in the county had seen her hitch-hiking naked at one time or another. Last time I saw her naked was right over there in that holding tank. Couldn't believe it was the same woman my Uncle Leo . . . the sheriff . . . he had some pictures from the old days, of her, with her . . . tits showing. Uncle said her tits were so big his cowboy hat just barely fit on one . . . can't think what he was doing with . . ."

Milo and I look at each other.

"When was that?" Milo asks.

"Musta been twenty years ago."

No. When she was in the tank, I say. So Milo won't have to play the bad guy. Why was she arrested? And what made you think she was our Rita?

"Oh," he says, looking at me hard. "It musta been when she came back from Mexico. Four or five months ago," Henriksen says. "She got a hard-on at some damn Texan down at the Hog's Rest Inn. Thought he'd insulted her. Took six officers to get her off him," Henriksen says proudly. "Rita's about as tough as they come. Hit that damn Texan between the eyes so hard the shit ran out of his ears for an hour . . ."

Texans don't have a great reputation anywhere outside of Texas. And sometimes I wonder what we really think about ourselves at home.

". . . so when we got her back here, we stuffed her in the tank. And like always she took her clothes off. Stunk up the place, too. Don't know how those people slept . . . ah, lived in the same house with her."

"People?" Milo says. "Place?"

"Yeah," Henriksen says, sighing, "Rita's ex-husband gave her a place up the river . . . Oh, you know, the Copia ain't really a river. Just an estuary with a couple of freshwater springs at the head. That's where the place is. Only way you can get there is by boat. My cousin Oscar rents boats down at the Copia docks. But you better catch him before noon."

Milo stands up before Henriksen invites us home to meet his mother, then says, "Thanks, Deputy Henriksen. If you think of anything else, son, give us a call up at the Cliff Point Lodge."

"Oh, jeeze," Henriksen says. "Your client must have some heavy bread. When the sheriff sends me out of town, I'm lucky if I've got enough expense money to stay at Motel Six and eat at Burger King." Then he turns to me, saying, "Oh, and her social security number."

What?

"Our Rita had the same social security as the Rita in Montana."

"Well, thanks. And good luck with those job applications," Milo says as we hurry to the door, both thinking we might as well flee ahead of the game, and without reminding him that we had a lot of information the sheriff probably didn't mean for us to have.

"Oh, hell," Henriksen says, a wide, honest grin across his Nordic face. "San Francisco's too close to home, and LA's too damn far away."

Back at the hotel, faced with an extravagant half-eaten fresh seafood dinner, Milo sips a double single-malt, aching for a cigarette. The restaurant doesn't have a smoking section—hell, the state of California doesn't seem to have a smoking section anymore—but I don't want him brooding alone in his room, staring at his gray face in the bathroom mirror. He's gained a few of the lost pounds back and still looks dangerous, like a bad cop or an expensive hit man, but I worry about him. I had been out of town, working rustlers undercover for the Wyoming Cattleman's Association, when

Milo went over the deep end that last time, the time he gave up death drinks and live rounds, but I had heard enough about it from Chief Jamison not to want to see it happen again.

"Quit fucking worrying about me, Sonny," he says suddenly. "I think this expensive dinner is giving me the shits." He stands up, stretches, and grabs his down vest against the coastal chill. "Let's find a bar-burger and a place where I can smoke, and we can figure out who the fuck *this* Rita Van Tasselvitch really is . . ."

Fucking Milo. The old fart's pretty smart sometimes. Like that bit when he made me remember the afternoon I got shot. For a long time the last thing I remembered was singing along with Warren Zevon. "Heartache Spoken Here," I think it was. I remembered that. And the dusty film on Wynona's eyes. Dusty film with a piss-fir needle mired in it. At the hospital, they said, I sang that song over and over again. Until Whitney showed up. Someday, I suspect, I have to talk to her about Wynona's death. Milo told me that on the long drive from Fairbairn to Austin. Like I say, he's pretty smart sometimes.

But Milo had no more luck back in Meriwether breaking into the true identity of Rita Van Tasselvitch than the FBI did. Not that the Feds were any great shakes at finding people who wanted to stay hidden. Particularly if they weren't professional criminals. Supposedly, they had access to a lot of information that we, as private citizens, didn't. But luck wasn't their strong suit. It was mine.

We had to drive all the way across the Coast Range to Glory on U.S. 101 to find the bar that Milo wanted—right number of Harleys outside, right parts of the neon sign burned out—a place called "Tarzan's," run by a huge, handsome Hawaiian-Somoan whose mother had a twisted sense of humor, the bartender said, naming her son Tarzan. Milo laughs easily, and the bartender goes on. People just talked to Milo. Even when they didn't have much to say.

As Milo stuffs his gullet with a double cheeseburger and a double bait of Walla Walla sweet onions, I watch him load the information inside his head. After the burgers, he says about the only thing I hear about that time in the desert: "Best meal I ever had was a pound of stolen raw hamburger and an onion."

So, I say, you don't think this body is our Rita Van Tasselvitch.

"Don't know," he murmurs. "Could be, I guess. People said she was a tall pretty woman running to lard. During her time at Mountain States nobody took a picture of her. Nobody." Milo pauses for a cigarette. "And the only print they found was a partial thumb under the toilet seat in Jacobson's wife's bathroom. At least the feds think it's hers. Nobody really knows. Hell, the federal grand jury had to no-bill her for lack of evidence on the bank fraud. They had to go for some idiot RICO indictment or something." Milo thinks for a second, then waves for another pair of beers. "Actually, I'm just being nice. Not a fucking chance she was the right woman."

I nod at the speculation and decline the beer, since I suspect I'll be driving back across the winding mountain roads in the fog.

"All the people I talked to, Sughrue," Milo continues, "everybody had a different story. Students, faculty, friends—they all saw somebody different. Shit, one of those burned-out bush-hippie-vets you used to hang out with claimed . . . What the hell was his name?"

I explain that I know more than one burned-out veteran.

"The one you used to buy hash from."

Todd, I guess. He claimed to have a Chi-Com connection.

"That's him," he says, smiling. "Good hash, too," he adds, inhaling deeply, then letting all the air out of his lungs with a sigh. I suspect the memory of THC lingers in the body for years afterward.

"During one of his rehab periods," Milo says, "he worked out at the pulp mill. Anyway, he took a couple of classes at the college and said that he thought Rita was really a bartender named Lee Ann or Roy Ann or something like that, a tall, skinny woman who used to work out at the Pinetop Palace . . ."

Roriann, I correct him.

"You knew her?"

Light-fingered, bad-tempered skinny coke-whore bitch? I say, then add, I nearly fucking married her.

"I never knew that," Milo says with a smile.

You didn't know shit then, man.

"What happened?" he asks.

She wanted me to spank her, I say.

"What?"

I don't know, man, I admit. One night we're in bed and out of the blue she asks me, "Didn't you say something the other night about wanting to spank me?"

"What did you say?" Milo asks.

What the hell, I tried, I say, but she could tell that my heart wasn't in it. After that she didn't want anything to do with me. Even after I asked the bitch to marry me.

"Ain't love grand," Milo says, then nearly laughs as he orders a shot of schnapps. Which he guns happily, then smiles for the first time in a long time, until we leave several slow beers later.

Maybe it's in the blood, or the genes, but few men like to share their women. Roriann, on the other hand, simply refused to fuck one man at a time. Okay, she was good enough in bed . . . no, strike that. In the right mood, she was more fun in bed than any other woman I'd ever slept with. Period. Fun and dangerous as a wildcat. A sexual encounter with her usually left me covered with scratches, bites, and blood. And perhaps if she had been open about it, it might have been worth it. But her major mood was anger; her major thrust, deception. She could lie quicker and better than a criminal lawyer. And she loved to steal shit. Any shit. In the four months we were involved, I hated to take her out in public. I can't count the number of times I had to cover restaurant checks she tried to walk, twelve-packs of beer and giant bags of potato chips I had to pay for after she shoplifted them, or the ounces of cocaine she lifted from my stash. Once, over in Deer Lodge, she lifted a giant prison guard's gimme hat while he was in the can. Roriann nearly got me killed over that one.

And although she wasn't smart or educated, she was sly and quick. Somewhere, maybe television or drunk women, she had picked up some version of feminism and political correctness that was frightening in its simplicity: Whatever she did was right for women and politically correct.

"She nearly drove me mad," I tell Milo as I'm driving back to the inn. "Nearly got me killed."

"She ever show any poetic tendencies?"

"Only in bed," I admit.

"Probably not our girl," he says. "Woman like that, she'd have killed Jacobson," he says, then laughs at me again.

Some people recover from tragedy far too quickly for their own good.

The next morning about nine o'clock after a breakfast of French pastries and double espressos—not everything in California is a bad idea—Milo and I step out into the fog where we find Sheriff Henriksen leaning his bulky, rumpled body against the Beast, a deputy-driven patrol unit blocking our exit.

"Glad I caught you boys," he says, pointing the chewed-off nub of a short pipe at us like a zip gun. "I wanted to be sure to say 'thanks for visiting my county' and 'goodbye.'"

Milo excuses himself for a moment, grabs some cigarettes out of the glove box, then leans against a Mercedes parked in the space next to the Caddy, opens the pack of Dunhills, and offers one to the sheriff, who pauses, then takes it. Milo lights them both. I try to fade into the fog. Milo says that even in a suit and tie I look like a felony in progress.

"One of the really great things about California," the sheriff says, "is that everything happens here last." Milo raises a furry still-black eyebrow. "This morning, because of the time difference, sir, I had a chance to speak to both the sheriff's department in Meriwether County and the Federal Bureau of Investigation in Montana. You guys ain't exactly their favorite folks."

"What's the problem, Sheriff?" Milo asks calmly. "We haven't caused any trouble in your county, have we?"

The sheriff has a tiny hangover, I believe, just enough to make his cigarette smoke tremble in the cold, cloudy air and to make his beady eyes watery.

"You pumped my deputy down at Highwave as dry as an

old bone," he answers. "I'll have to prime that boy's pump with a couple of months of straight midnight shifts."

"I don't think that's a crime," Milo says quietly, "sir."

"Interfering with an active criminal investigation certainly is," the sheriff says, "sir."

"Obstruction of justice, I believe they call it, sir," Milo says. "But I don't believe we've even started to obstruct. And we have no intention of doing so. We're both licensed and bonded in other states, we both checked in with your office. Identified ourselves and explained what we were doing here. We've complied with the law. Sir."

"What happens, mister," the sheriff says as he steps around to the rear of the Caddy, "if I make you open this trunk?"

"Supposing you can get a warrant before I can call a lawyer?" Milo says. "Not a fucking thing. Sir."

"We're gonna follow you out of the county, buddy," the sheriff growls, then tosses his cigarette butt between his tiny polished boots and grinds it out, "and if you cross the white line, boy, we're gonna be on your ass like stink on squat."

Milo leans over and picks up the sheriff's cigarette butt and drops it in his shirt pocket, then takes out a micro tape recorder that he must have grabbed during the cigarette moment. "Actually, if I were you, Sheriff Henriksen, I wouldn't follow me anywhere," Milo says calmly, "because if I see you behind me, I'm driving directly to Glory, between the lines with my partner on the video camera, of course, and I'm going to find the last pissant lawyer who beat your socks off in court, then sue you to the death."

Then Milo switches off the recorder. "Or you can give us a couple of days," Milo adds, "have every piece of information we turn up, even go along with us, and walk away with a sizable contribution to your campaign chest."

"That sounds like a bribe to me," the sheriff grunts.

"Of course," Milo answers, "but a perfectly legal one."

The sheriff sputters, examines the gravel with his tiny pointed toes, then asks, "How much?"

"Legal limit," Milo answers, then switches on the recorder again. "And while you're thinking about it, Henriksen, let me add a couple of other things to think about: you've been to the FBI Academy at Quantico, and you don't like those tight-assed jerks any more than I do; they just want to close the case file to look good at budget time, and if the woman who helped steal my money isn't your Rita—and I'm convinced she isn't—it's their fucking ass hanging out, so you got the nuts on the resident agent the next time he tries to muscle you. As for me, you can't muscle a guy who's already dug his own grave. And believe me, Sheriff, I'm that fucking guy."

The sheriff takes a long look at Milo, then nods as if he believes the old fart.

Cousin Oscar Henriksen, captain of an electric flat-bottomed skiff with which he guides birdwatchers, doesn't have a drinking problem because Sheriff Henriksen pats him not-so-gently on his red cheek and takes the pint of Four Roses away from him on the dock. "Oscar," the sheriff tells him, "Mr. Milodragovitch here says he gets seasick real easy. So let's take it flat and slow . . ."

Flatt and Scruggs, I say, and realize it's my first words of the morning. Since I ordered breakfast. The sheriff, who's now our buddy, rode up front with Milo on the way down to the Copia River, and he looks at me as if I've lost my mind. As does Milo. So I shut up. And enjoy the boat ride.

Although I had spent several years snaring runaway kids in San Francisco during the late sixties and early seventies, about the only time I'd spent this far up the coast was the time I tracked a kid to a goat commune up in Mendocino County above Gualala.

The kid was from a family farm outside Slippery Rock, Pennsylvania, and he wasn't so much hiding from his folks as he was looking for fun. Up at the commune they milked their own goats, made their own cheese, and grew their own great marijuana, the first sinsemilla I'd ever smoked. I bought a pound for what an ounce goes for now, and got the kid to ride down to San Francisco with me ostensibly to peddle the smoke. But I really got him to come along because I told him that everybody else at goat farm was fucking their livestock. The kid looked so sick at heart that I realized I'd made a lucky, or unlucky, guess.

The kid climbed on the airplane home by himself, which wasn't usually the case, and last I heard he was happily working the farm and growing a little noncommercial crop for his own consumption. Farming high, he said, was about the only way to go.

I had done a little time on a tractor as a kid, pulling a stalk cutter and a disc over rows of picked cotton, turning the plants under to keep the pink bollworm at bay. That was in the old days, before chemical assistance became popular. Both among tractor drivers and cotton. I thought maybe the kid was right.

But nothing during that visit up the coast had prepared me for this foggy boat ride up the brusque reach of the Rio Copia. Once the flat-bottom boat drifts silently around the first curve of the estuary, we are someplace else. Because it's been a bird sanctuary for a long time, the redwoods still stand like old people on the steep slopes, their ancient thick-bark faces draped in the gray fluff of sailing fog in the stupendous silence, a quiet so perfect the tick of blood rumbles in my ears and my breath breaks like storm surf. I hear a blue heron lift its wings, feather by feather; the sputtering gasp of a sea lion resounds like thunder across the tree-clotted banks. And the water below does not stir before our passage.

Something happens to me: my heart aches, I think, with the tranquil beauty, and I long for the slim, tanned arms of my woman, the laughter of my child. They should see this. Hell, they will see this, someday, I promise. Christ, maybe I'm just homesick. And the lump in my throat is strapped to my body. Like the pistol under my arm. Shit. I grab a sob with a cough. It echoes like a gunshot.

"You okay?" Milo asks, and I nod. Truthfully. Milo smiles at me as if he understands.

"The Tiptons ain't exactly morning people," the sheriff says quietly as the boat drifts into thickening fog, and I realize that he's not the politically ambitious clown I thought. He grew up here. This is his place. "So let's try not to scare 'em into gunfire," he adds as a house beside the still water heaves into view like a floating shipwreck.

Oscar cuts the electric outboard and fires up a gasoline one. Christ, it sputters like an automatic weapon. Or a terrible alarm clock. A thousand unseen birds fling themselves into the air with an immense flapping din. But when it's over and Oscar cuts the outboard to drift to the waterlogged dock where he casually tosses a loop over a piling, no life betrays itself at the house. Opaque windows reflect the dull water and sky. The gray redwood shakes of the roof are green-grizzled with moss like the faded board-and-batten walls. This is a place nailed together for silence, a keep built for secrets. Even the front door, open to the cold morning, seems shut.

So when a giant naked woman with a mane of gray hair bursts from the black hole of the open door, clatters in a fierce run down the dock to cannonball a great sweep of cold water over the boat, I scream. Like everybody else. And whip the Airweight off my ankle.

"I'll pretend I didn't see that, son," the sheriff says to me quietly when the boat stops rocking enough for us to drag our sodden selves onto the dock.

I apologize to the sheriff, then explain that I didn't realize what I'd done.

He almost smiles, then shouts at the woman quickly disappearing into the remaining wisps of fog over the rolling water, "Goddammit, Nancy Tipton, I'm gonna fucking blow your ass off one of these days."

"Promises, promises, Leo!" the hard-stroking woman shouts back, then swims away.

"Shit," the sheriff says. "We might as well go in and make coffee. If Nancy's up this early, she's been up all night, and god knows when she'll be back."

"The goddess knows what evil lurks in the heart of men," comes a faint echo from the fog bank.

"You know," Milo says, "this is the only time I've been in Northern California, Sheriff. Unless you count the repo-depot in Oakland. And right now I'm just as glad I went on to Korea that time . . ."

Laughing, we tumble into the house like wet puppies. Although the outside doesn't look like much, the inside seems as neat and tight as I'd imagine a clipper ship's galley. The sheriff stokes the woodstove like a man familiar with it, and within minutes has cowboy coffee boiling over it. He douses it with cold water to drop the grounds, then quickly fills tin

cups and hands them to us. He pulls Oscar's pint from his
coat pocket, explaining, "There ain't never been no sugar in
the Tiptons' house, but I might be able to dig up some
honey."

Oscar says the whiskey will be fine, but he doesn't get
any. Milo doesn't want any, so the sheriff and I have a tot.

You're not the sort of man I ever thought I'd be having a
drink with, I tell him.

He nods as if the feeling is mutual, but smiles and takes
the sting off it. "This ain't a drink, son," he says. "Just coffee."

Milo tells a story about drinking rye and coffee with his
dead father while his mother broke every dish in the kitchen,
and I remember, but don't say, how old man Moody had the
old Indian retainer, Bald Coon, drive him from the Big
House across the Muddy Fork to show up almost every
morning of my childhood at my mother's shotgun-shack
kitchen table for bourbon and coffee. I realize the conversation has split around the cleft of my memory, and I say
What? as if I'm already drunk in the morning.

The sheriff looks embarrassed. Milo coughs politely. "Leo
was just saying, C.W., that he and Rita—his Rita—were old,
old friends." The sheriff blushes so deeply he finally looks
kin to Cousin Oscar. "It must have been a terrible chore to
identify the body," Milo says kindly.

"A fucking nightmare," the sheriff whispers.

We stand awkwardly around the neat kitchen in this time-
less place until our memories drive us out to the dock as the
sun clears the high ridges behind the house and fires a sheet
of quicksilver across the still waters of the false river, almost
sizzling the fog. Moments later, Nancy backstrokes through
that siren fire, her mantle of gray hair like a silver cape over
her broad shoulders, then bounds onto the dock like the
world's largest, oldest gymnast.

As she stands on the end of the dock, flinging water from
her hard body and wringing her hair like a mop, she and
Milo stare at each other like two old grizzlies preparing for
their last encounter. Love, maybe, or hate. Whatever, bloody
fun. Then Milo blushes and looks away. He lost the moment,
somehow, down in La Jolla with Maribeth, maybe. Shit, I

want to shout at him. It's okay. A guy gets a burning needle stuck up his dick, digs his own grave, and nearly dies because he can't piss, it's no wonder he doesn't get a hard-on the first time he tries. Try again. Fuck it, try again. With this one. I love it when I'm philosophical.

But before I finish the thought, she's lost interest and is looking at me as if I were breakfast. Or lunch. No, not a meal. A snack. I blush, too, and look away, feeling an odd desire to apologize. This is old hat for the smiling sheriff, and Oscar has curled into himself like a salt-sprinkled banana slug.

"This an official call, Leo?" Nancy says in a melodious voice full of laughter.

The sheriff shakes his head sadly, then explains that Milo and I want to talk to her about Rita. Nancy looks at us in a different light now. Distinctly, I hear the words "old fart" and "pipsqueak" but brush them from my mind. Just as she brushes the water from her legs with the side of her heavy, work-hardened hand. I steal another look at her naked body.

She's not fat. Not at all. Just huge. Everywhere. Her breasts only sag with age, and her rosy, erect nipples are as big as cherries. The blond thatch at her crotch is as white as straw, and her labia peeks pinkly through. I suspect her clit is the size of my little finger, but since I'm already as horny as a two-peckered goat, I'm afraid of looking too closely. For fear she'll show it to me.

The sheriff almost laughs as he introduces Milo and me to Nancy. As we shake hands with a large naked woman, we try to act as if it's all in a day's work. Nancy barks and leads us into the house, where she slips into sweat pants and a XXL Forty-Niners jersey that's a little too tight across the chest.

"Thanks," Milo says, smiling. "I appreciate that." The old fart hasn't given up yet, I think. They sit at the table alone, Nancy across from him. I lean against an inlaid redwood wall corner so snug it must be water-tight. The sheriff leans beside me. "Do you mind talking about Rita?" Milo asks politely.

"Why should I?" Nancy asks softly, then looks at me, and turns back to Milo. "How long have you and this cracker been buddies?"

Cracker? I say.

"I was born at night," she says without looking at me, "but not last night."

"We've been partners twenty-some-odd years," Milo answers.

"Well, Rita and I were friends," she says in that quietly musical voice. "Friends. Not buddies, not pals, not partners. But friends for almost forty years. We were born in Glory the same week. Our mothers were friends. We grew up together, we grew middle-aged together, pal. When she married my big brother, I told her not to; when she divorced him I told her to pluck him like a fryer. And if anything I can tell you will convince this bumbling fuck of a sheriff that she did not die in a drug deal, I'll talk to you till your dick falls off." Milo starts to say something, but she breaks in. "Get this straight first, man, Rita was batshit crazy all her life. But she did not lie, cheat, steal, or deal drugs . . ."

"Except to her friends," Leo interrupted.

"You never had a friend, Leo," Nancy says, "so what do you know about it?"

"Except Rita," he answers softly.

"Except Rita," Nancy agrees. "But she was crazy. See! Everybody loved her. Even the fucking law."

"So who killed her?" Milo asks.

"I don't fucking know," Nancy says, her voice breaking. "But when I find them, I'm going to twist their fucking little heads clean off."

The sheriff pours all of us some coffee. Milo takes a little sweetener this time. I don't. Oscar whines at the front door like a runt puppy, but it does him no good.

"What was she doing in Mexico?" Milo asks.

"Dealing drugs, according to the Federales," the sheriff says softly.

"Writing her autobiography," Nancy says. "Supposedly."

"Supposedly?" Milo says.

"It was supposed to be some big secret," Nancy says, "and for once in her life, she managed to keep it."

"Any idea why?"

"Had to be love. Rita didn't give a shit about money," Nancy says, "and she wasn't afraid of anything."

"Maybe she should have been," the sheriff says.

Nobody has a question for that answer, and in the silence we hear the creak of a bedspring, the thump of a heel, and a metallic clack that sounds very much like a pump shotgun jacking a round into the chamber. The sheriff grabs my right arm and shakes his bald head slowly. And then a voice drifts down the stairwell: "Who the fuck's down there, Nancy?"

"It's me, Aaron," the sheriff says, then turns to Nancy. "You didn't tell me he was back."

But Nancy just shakes her head. "I thought he was too stoned to wake up, Leo. The fucking shotgun is loaded with double-ought buckshot."

"Oh, shit," the sheriff whispers, then releases my arm.

"You got a warrant?" the voice floats down again.

"Just a friendly visit," the sheriff starts to say, but footsteps hurry across the ceiling and a tall, iron-pumped blond guy in swim trunks fills the stairwell, a pistol-butted sawed-off 12-gauge pump shotgun propped across his forearm and his finger curled white on the trigger.

"I don't take your visits friendly, Leo," Aaron says, the shotgun leveled at the sheriff.

"Son," the sheriff says quietly. "Get your finger off the trigger, open the breech, and set it on the stairs . . ."

Aaron laughs, his teeth white against his tan face, but his blue eyes not smiling. "Or what, you pus-bucket?"

"Do it, bro'," Nancy whispers, but it sounds more like a plea than a command.

"Who are these guys, sis? I don't even know these guys," he says, then swings the shotgun to cover Milo, "and I don't like them. What the fuck are they doing here? They feds?"

"They're helping the sheriff with Rita's murder," Nancy says calmly, then steps toward her brother, who's crying now, huge tears silently flowing out of his blue eyes, and reaches for the shotgun.

"Goddamn Rita!" Aaron screams, then slams the barrel of the shotgun against his sister's jaw and jerks the trigger.

Big as she is, Nancy drops like an empty sack, all slack muscles and loose skin, and the double-ought buckshot knocks huge hardwood splinters from the inlaid kitchen ceiling. One of them spears the sheriff between the neck and shoulder. I shove him aside, draw the Airweight, and fire two quick shots over Aaron's head, but he ignores them as if wadcutters are gnats.

Before he can reload, Milo is on him, struggling for the shotgun. It's not immediately clear who's going to win, and I don't want Aaron to have the sawed-off, so I look for a clear shot, but Milo holds hard to the shotgun, locks his feet into Aaron's midsection, and rolls backward, throwing him out the front door, where he rolls across the dock, smashing Oscar to the boards with his shoulder.

Aaron scrambles quickly to his feet, then dives into the water and swims away so swiftly that he leaves a wake as Milo watches from the door, the sawed-off hanging from his hand.

"Shit," he says, then unloads the remaining rounds and sidearms them out the door, where they splash into the Copia. Then we check out the mess.

Nancy is deeply unconscious, and, as far as I can tell, her jaw is badly broken. And she's in the best shape. Sheriff Henriksen has a six-inch varnished redwood splinter buried deeply in behind his collarbone, and massive amounts of shiny blood froth around the wood.

Outside, Oscar lies on the dock in the sunshine, holding his stomach and chest and rocking as if a piece of his viscera has been broken off. I remember the feeling, remember thinking that I could feel the bullet, feel every movement of it through my body. And hear in my bones the firing pin breaking.

Then Milo grabs my shoulders, shakes me once, and we go to work.

But not quickly enough to keep the cursing sheriff from jerking the polished redwood splinter out of his shoulder. A breathlessly red jet of arterial blood splatters the ceiling, and the sheriff hits the floor like a sack of seed corn. Subclavian artery, I guess, and Milo nods. "House like this must have an old hemostat roach clip," he says, and digs his fingers into the bloody wound. "Find it. And some tape."

I dump all the drawers in the house before I find one inside a cigar box on a night table upstairs. When I get back to the kitchen, Nancy has come around, but passes out again when she opens her mouth to say something to me and her jaw collapses like an old rotten bridge. Oscar still moans like death on the sunlit dock. And Milo looks as if he's been butchering hogs. I open the woodstove, jam the hemostat into the red-hot coals until it burns my fingers, then hand it to Milo, along with a clean dish towel and a roll of duct tape, the closest I could come to a field dressing.

While Milo tries to catch the bleeder, I slip the radio off the sheriff's belt, but can't raise anybody because of the deep valley. "See if you can get something between her teeth," Milo grunts, reaching deep into the wound. "Something wood. Then immobilize her jaw with the duct tape, man."

It ain't pretty, but it seems to work. As does Milo's jury-rigged bandage over the hemostat. I can only hope Nancy's jawbone doesn't splinter any worse as we load her beside the white-faced sheriff in the skiff. When we pick up Oscar, though, he wails like a fresh-cut shoat, hopelessly. Something inside is broken, and he screams louder than the fleeing flocks of birds as we ease the overloaded boat down the estuary.

Finally I raise the substation dispatcher when we are about five hundred yards from the dock, and she locates a passing Coast Guard chopper that meets us at the landing, where we transfer our load, then climb aboard behind them. I spent my Vietnam tour in the 1st Air Cav, so helicopters were nothing new, but Milo had never been up in one. As we fly to Glory, we discover that Milo doesn't just get seasick. He starts throwing up when the pilot throws the chopper into a banking turn, and doesn't stop until we land in the parking lot of the hospital. The paramedics carry the wounded to the ER, and the deputies escort Milo and me to jail.

Which makes me sick.

Thanks to Don Henriksen's clout with the chief deputy, we are only there a few hours. Which is a few hours too many.

The next afternoon, most of the blood and fear washed off and out of us, Milo and I drive to the hospital, where we discover that the sheriff is still unconscious in ICU because of the blood loss and shock. But Oscar has died in the night, Don Henriksen tells us, his ribs crushed into his lungs and his damaged liver and spleen destroyed by Aaron Tipton's shoulder, for whom there's a manslaughter APB being broadcast at that moment.

Milo invites the haggard deputy for cafeteria coffee, but not me. I know Milo's coming back to the waiting room. It only takes him five minutes. "Go see the woman," he says. "Don't tell her about Oscar's death. Or the APB. We have to find her brother before the law, Sughrue."

Why me, man?

"She liked you, boy," he says. "I could tell."

Fuck you, old man, I think. But take on the chore.

A nurse sits beside Nancy's sleeping bulk in the bed. At least I think it's a nurse. She looks like a nurse, even in a crew cut, nine earrings, and a pastel, flowered jumpsuit. She stares coldly up at me.

"Can I help you?" she whispers.

I need to talk to the lady, I suggest. She awake?

"You with the sheriff's department?"

Before I can nod, Nancy's hand slips out of the covers to grab the control and raises the bed. Her hair is matted in dirty clots, her teeth are wired together, and the bruise has seeped across her face and neck, but a sleepy smile flirts with her eyes as she nods at the nurse.

"He's come to wash my hair," Nancy says to her, teeth gritted, talking with just her lips.

"Well, isn't that sweet," the nurse says to me, as if I'm not just a child, but a dull child, "but I have to stay in the room. Nancy just had a shot of Demerol, and I have to watch her, you know." The nurse slaps a pair of wirecutters on the bedside table. "In case she regurgitates."

"He can handle it," Nancy grunts. "Now get the fuck out of here. Please."

The nurse looks only slightly ruffled, then asks, "You the guy with the duct tape?"

I shrug.

"I guess you'll do," she says, then smiles and steps softly to the sink and fills a washbasin with warm water, which she hands to me, along with a sample of shampoo and a small pitcher. "Don't be afraid," she adds, smirking, then slips quietly out the door on her rubber soles, while Nancy raises the back of the bed as far as it will go.

I'll bet you think I don't know how to do this, I say to her in the silence as I place the water between her legs.

But she answers with a wooden smile. "I fucking love Demerol." Then bows her head over the basin as if praying.

As I pour the warm water over her bowed head and work the shampoo into her matted gray mane, I tell her: My mother was an Avon Lady, a terrific gossip, and a secret cheap wine drinker. When I was a little boy, after my father left, she drank more, and some summer mornings when she had an earthquake of a head, the look of a woman with continental plates shifting in her skull, I would wash her long blond hair, then comb it dry . . .

"Until it started giving you a hard-on," Nancy says, in a tight-lipped yet soft voice. "I'll bet she loved Demerol, too."

When she was dying of lung cancer, I whisper, she loved it all. But she didn't have much hair to wash by then . . .

"I'm sorry."

It was a long time ago, I say.

"Nothing's a long time ago," Nancy whispers as a single tear splashes into the soapy water. "Nothing. My mother only knows it's Wednesday because I do her hair on Wednesday."

I'm sorry.

"Fuck it," she says, then tells me about her brother until I'm finished. Then she tells me how much she loves dreamy Demerol again and asks for another favor of a more personal nature. I can't refuse, not now. Wrapped in the painkiller, it takes a long time. Long enough for me to become involved. But when she's finished, I raise my head, wash my face, and kiss her slack, sleeping mouth, and promise to be back.

But the next day, after having heard about the sheriff's slim hold on life and Oscar's death, Nancy refuses to see me.

"It's pretty thin shit," Milo says a day later as we top the Grapevine and stare down at the rain-washed LA Basin. The air is cool, clean, the sun perfectly warm, all the way to

the heart of the Valley, the sort of day that once made LA
seem like paradise, but which you don't see much anymore.
"Pretty thin shit in a fucking huge town," Milo adds.

"But a beautiful day," I say.

At least we have three possible connections to Aaron Tipton: the name of a retired stunt man, Tim O'Bannion, that I
weaseled out of Nancy; a known criminal associate, one
Tom-John Donne, given us by Deputy Don from Aaron's rap
sheet; and a biker's nickname, Greasy Leg, that the bartender
Tarzan had let slip after a day of drink and drugs with Milo.
But no addresses, and not much of a lead on the cops.

By the time we get to the Sportsman's Lodge on the border between Studio City and Sherman Oaks, the day has
gone to hell—the sun unpleasantly hot through a hazy film
of smog—as has the Valley. Back in the old days when I occasionally chased runaways to LA, I stayed in the Valley because the place and the people had seemed a little bit country
and you could still find an occasional orange tree. But looking at it now, it is LA to the core. Strip malls stuffed with
bad yogurt shops, silly fingernail places, and other useless
businesses; cheap apartment complexes waiting for the big
one to turn them to plaster dust; and traffic hell, streets filled
with drivers who couldn't read signs or spell fuck.

At least the Sportsman's still seems a calm island in the
madness. Since Republic Pictures used to be down Ventura
Boulevard, John Wayne had had a drink or two and the odd
nap there in the old days, and occasionally you could still see
Gene Autry teetering in his tiny boots across the coffee shop.
We take a suite in the front building above the pool, then have
a drink or two and curl up for naps.

After I wake from a drowning sleep for a shower and
clean clothes, I find another new Milo in the Lobby Bar,
chatting up the black bartender and guzzling blended margaritas. "Just about to call you," Milo says expansively. Still
surly from my nap, I order a beer. Any fucking kind. "Make
him one of those margaritas, please, Joe," Milo says, already
on a first-name basis with the bartender. "We'll see if we
can't cheer him up."

"What if I don't want to be cheered up?" I say.

"Then you're an asshole," Milo says. "And you better be polite, Sughrue. Joe here's one bad rooster and he's already solved about half our problems."

As Joe puts together the first blender drink I've had in my life, Milo tells me all about it. Joe has an old friend who has just come back to town from Kentucky, somebody named Boots who has a current PI license, a chauffeur's license, and expired SAG and WGA cards, but a current AA membership.

"You'll like Boots," Joe says as he places the drink in front of me, "and, Texas, if you're just half as crazy as your buddy, you're gonna need Boots." Then he laughs in soft, southern tones as I sip the margarita. Pretty smooth, I think, and not too sweet, either.

"Not bad," I say, then turn to Milo, asking: "How the hell long have you been here?"

"Well, I couldn't sleep . . ."

"Don't blame him on me," Joe says, smiling fondly. "I found him like this when I came on shift."

"Strictly my fault," Milo adds, sniffling.

"You got into the fucking cocaine," I whisper.

"Boots can't show up until nine tomorrow, Sughrue, and it's Friday night, man, time for a night off," Milo says seriously. "It's fucking time."

What could I do but raise my glass, drain it, and order two more. "Whatever comes," I toast, but I've already ruined the mood. At eleven when Joe gives last call, Milo orders a double tequila and a beer, then goes to piss.

"Room service is over?" I ask Joe.

"But Jerry's Deli delivers," he answers.

So at least Milo has a half-pound of pastrami on rye in his gut when he rolls into bed. Which gives him something to throw up in the morning.

Over breakfast the next morning, Boots, a small, efficient black woman in working cowboy duds, lays it out for us. "This is Hollywood, boys; first we eat, then we talk."

"Is this a power breakfast?"

"Not hardly," she answers. "Too late."

Actually, she forks through a huge breakfast as she tells stories, all of which have the same point: because she's black and a woman, she's had to do it all, work all these jobs to stay around the business and raise her three fatherless boys in some decent fashion. And maintain her expensive hobby: horses.

"Are you telling us that you're going to be expensive?" Milo asks.

"That's right, cowboy," she says, then reaches for a piece of sourdough toast on Milo's plate, "if I work for you. And right now that's a big *if*." Then she gobbles Milo's toast with brightly capped teeth and, finished, snatches a piece of bacon off my plate.

"You must be southern," I say.

"I thought I'd lost the accent."

"Southern women always have to eat off somebody else's plate," I say.

She stares at me a long time, then laughs softly. "I don't think I've ever been called a southern woman before," she says, taking a shorthand notebook out of her purse. "Okay, boys, lay it out for me."

After Milo finishes, she reaches for his last piece of cold toast, asking, "You got two grand in cash?"

"I can get it in five minutes," Milo says.

"Go to the front desk, get an envelope to put it in, and rent me a room for tonight," Boots says quietly, "and I'll see what I can do for you boys."

"A room?"

"I want to go swimming when I get back," she answers, then stares at me as if I am going to deny her.

Milo shrugs as if to say *It's just money,* then takes off. While he's gone, Boots fills the void with aimless Hollywood chatter and gossip as the waitress quietly cleans the table. When Milo returns and hands her the envelope with the money and the key, Boots stands quickly, saying, "It's going to be a nice afternoon, boys, our last one for a while, so why don't you hang out around the pool and work on your tans—they could use some work, right?—and I'll be back before you burn."

Then Boots was gone, skipping away like a dreadful sprite, leaving us mostly speechless.

"Guess we should buy some new swimming trunks," I

suggest, and Milo looks at me as if I'm crazy. "It's SoCal, man," I explain.

So once the idea is in place, we both buy some new trunks that make us look like refugee tourists. And suntan lotion, too. As if Milo could burn through the dark curly pelt across his chest and shoulders. Or me through my West Texas tan. But I've never exposed the scar to people I didn't know, so I lather myself with it, too, as if the greasy sheen will hide the wound.

It's not like we think it's going to be, lazing around the pool in Hollywood—although Hollywood is more a notion than a place—taking the smog-filtered sun with Jewish families and car salesmen, unemployed aerospace executives and cocktail waitresses. California dreaming ain't what it used to be. No muscle boys with greased loins hang out, and not a single starlet lounges around us, although a fairly pretty Frenchwoman seems to be working on songs at the table next to ours.

After another pot of coffee and the *LA Times,* Milo finally turns to me and says, "This is fucking boring."

"It's Hollywood, Jake," I say. "You get the drinks, and I'll cut the lines."

Six hours later, we are chatting up the two cocktail waitresses from Phoenix when Boots steps out poolside, shining in a bikini, as slender and strong as an ebony bow, and slips into the pool without a splash, and does about thirty brisk laps before the gals from Arizona realize that we are watching her instead of talking to them. Milo and I feel like two little boys who have been caught farting in the bathtub and thinking about biting the bubbles. Boots climbs out of the pool and shakes her head at us, then grabs her towel and walks toward us, lovely and compact, not so much erotic as simply impressive.

Sometimes Whitney does that to me. She's lovely, that's for sure, so lovely that in the old days it never occurred to me that I could even talk to her. But that's not all she is. She's a lovely person. Sometimes Whitney does something so wonderful and generous of heart—jollies Lester, another woman's child, out of an angry funk, or hugs me just because she wants to—that I feel like a heartless worm, even if she loves me. Women, man, women.

Boots doesn't waste a moment on formalities, or even a smile, doesn't even dry the sparkling water out of her short, curly hair. Tim O'Bannion, the retired stunt man, owns a motel in the desert on the edge of the Joshua Tree National Monument. Greasy Leg's real name is Bill McGeorge and he has done time with Aaron Tipton at Chino; he probably could be found working the Boardwalk in Venice Beach or hustling drinks and running a jewelry scam in Santa Monica at either Chez Jay's or the Circle Bar. And Tom-John Donne has cleaned up his act, opened a dojo in Panorama City, and works now and again as a heavy in low-budget kick-boxing movies.

"So if you were us," Milo asks, "how would you start?"

"Frankly, boys," Boots answers quickly, "I'd start home. And just as fast as I could." Then she pauses and stands. "But I know you're not going to, so good luck."

"That's it," I say, "for two grand?"

"You want more," she says, turning on me. "Such as the fact that you assholes are both drunks and drug addicts? Driving around in a Caddy with New Mexican plates full of state and federal felonies? Working an open attempted murder case, no less?"

"Attempted?" Milo interrupts.

"It sounds like the sheriff's going to make it," she said. "Thanks to you. And if my friend Joe didn't like you two idiots, for inexplicable reasons as far as I can tell, I'd throw your money in your face and let you kill yourselves without my help. 'Cause I got too much to lose." Then she gathers a deep breath. "As it is, I just hope you're not too fucked up to remember what I told you, because I ain't about to write it down," Boots finishes, and almost spits at our feet.

"Fucking LA," I say, standing now, too. "Land of the expensively cheap thrill."

But Milo pulls me down sharply, saying softly to Boots before she can turn away, "Thanks for your help, ma'am. Maybe I understand how you feel about us. I sometimes feel the same way myself . . ."

"Speak for your own damn self," I whisper hoarsely.

". . . but we're just playing the cards we're dealt . . ."

"Fucking denial!" Boots shouts over the random echoes of the pool.

"Judgmental bitch," I mutter.

"Shut up, Sughrue," Milo says. "You weren't raised like that . . ."

"I can take you, cowboy," Boots says, her tone flat and mean and ready, "any fucking time."

"Maybe not, honey," I say, shaking off Milo's hand. "It might be fun trying."

"Sit down, children," Milo whispers, "you're scaring the tourists."

Boots and I glance suddenly around the shimmering pool, look at each other, and realize how silly we must seem. At last we laugh. Boots waves at us forgivingly, then walks away, shouting "Good luck, boys!" over her lovely shoulder.

I quickly find the chair with my butt and take a long pull on the margarita, still trembling with the adrenaline burst.

"What the fuck was that about?" I ask breathlessly.

"I don't exactly know," Milo says, "but I expect she's had some bad times with the cocaine and the drink. And maybe she's still having them. Maybe worried about her boys. I don't know."

"No, I mean, what's it really about?"

"Sexual tension, kid," he answers, "but don't worry. You could have taken her. Just like you took that asshole back in Kerrville. So come on. Let's get out of this piss-thin sunshine, go see Joe and have a last drink, a nap, then go to work."

"Be along in a minute," I say.

Jesus, I couldn't even remember that Howdy Doody motherfucker's name in Kerrville. But I remember that he gave me all I could handle. And more. His right foot at the end of a leg sweep that seemed to tear something in my thigh. A couple of body shots that hit like large-caliber rounds. If he hadn't missed with the big right hand, it would have been me stretched out to thump at will on the rich guy's lawn. But when he missed, I slipped behind the big bastard, locked my right arm around his throat, and choked him down. With my teeth locked into the back of his neck. Like some asshole bad-dog jail-cop. Shit, I was so scared of losing the fight that I nearly choked him all the way down to dead. And probably would have if the old rich guy hadn't grabbed an over-under shotgun out of the trunk of his Mercedes and aimed it at us, his hands trembling so badly I was sure we were bird-shot dead. It took a half-pint of vodka and two long lines for me to stop shaking enough to face Milo. Hell, I would have shot the coke into my arm if I'd had the works.

For the first time since I was released from the hospital, I feel the loss of the kidney, sort of a dull, lonesome ache.

Maybe Boots would have kicked my ass. Or me hers. Hell, I'd never gone at it with a woman, and lord knows I was scared. She was tough and smart and hit too close to the mark. Win, lose, or draw, my choices, it seems, were limited. _Smart,_ which I had always equated with sneaky, seems to be the only answer. Since _tough_ is out of the question.

Joe told us that Chez Jay's was an old-line chop house, so we made late dinner reservations for four so we could have some elbow room with our beef, then crashed until dark-thirty, which found us in our best cowboy duds rolling up Laurel Canyon in the El Dorado, making our own damn way through the traffic. Milo let me drive the Beast, and boy did I.

"Where the fuck are all these people going?" he asks as we wait at the light at Mulholland.

"I never figured that out," I say, "when I was spending time down here. Some years ago. And even if I had, it wouldn't matter. LA's a quick-change artist living on shaky ground."

"I ask a real question, boy, and you give me cheap poetry. What the fuck's the matter with you?"

"I've got to turn on my LA-mode, man, sharpen my attitude, just to survive the traffic."

Then the light changes to green, I floor the Beast and roar through the intersection, blow two cars off on the right, and drift swiftly down toward the LA Basin, the true belly of the beast.

"Jesus, Sughrue," Milo complains. "If you're going to drive like that, you better get that piece out of your boot."

"Shit," I say, "I can maybe plead to a misdemeanor for the .38, but that sap in *your* boot is a guaranteed felony bust."

"Maybe first thing Monday morning we should look for a seat cover man to build a hidey-hole for the Beast," he suggests.

"I'm surprised you haven't already," I say.

"Maybe I'm slowing down in my old age," he says.

But he doesn't want a response so we ride in rubberneck silence down to Santa Monica Boulevard and turn west toward the ocean, Ocean Avenue to be exact, where Milo directs me to the Loew's Hotel just across the street from Chez Jay's. We check in with a couple of new, empty overnight bags and valet park the Caddy.

His brooding silence takes over again and carries us through two drinks at the crowded bar under the television, then through dinner. Finally, after the waitress pours our coffee, Milo asks, "Who the fuck are these people?"

"I don't know," I admit. "Anybody can sound like a mover and a shaker out here. They can all talk the talk."

"Right," Milo grunts, "but walking the walk is another story. Especially for our wooden-legged friend at the bar. Greasy-fucking-Leg indeed."

The dude in question is tall and lanky, blond and beach-buffed, and not too many tattoos for a biker, dressed out for Saturday night in black and gold. Black jeans and boots, black silk shirt; an array of gold chains depend from his neck toward his large golden belt buckle, and gold nugget rings on his fingers. Clean-shaven except for a neatly trimmed moustache, his slightly puffy face still looks dirty around his hooded eyes, the kind of face you want to wash with your boots. And he keeps digging at his butt-crack, as if his jeans are too tight or he hasn't changed his shorts in weeks.

"You think he's our guy?" I ask.

"If he ain't," Milo says softly, "he knows him."

We pay the check, step to the bar, Milo limping slightly, and sip slow Absolut martinis on the rocks until we can work our way next to our guy.

"Anybody sitting here?" Milo asks him, smiling loose and friendly, half-drunk but polite.

The guy nods carefully. Sometimes Milo can't help sounding like a cop. Milo orders a round for us as I pull up on the stool beside him, then he offers the guy a drink, which he accepts with practiced ease. We tip our glasses at each other, when they come, and Milo introduces himself as Milton Chester. Me as his nameless driver. The guy says his name is George Hill, which is close enough for us.

"Never been here before," Milo says. "Nice little place."

"You guys from out of town?"

"Montana," Milo says, "where men are men, women are scarce, and sheep are lying little tramps." We drink to that as if we know what we're talking about. Then he says, "Did you know, my friend, that two-thirds of unsuccessful bank robberies are planned in bars?"

McGeorge looks suddenly nervous; the spray of blackheads across his forehead disappears into his furrowed brow. "I don't know anything about robbing banks, sir."

"I know too damn much, friend. I used to be a cop," Milo sighs sadly, then rubs his knee. "Till the goddamned telephone company bought me off. Then I took up ranching, fucking around, and chasing pussy." Milo has a sip of vodka, then drops the conversation and turns to me, chatting about bad horses, the cattle market, and last year's disastrous calf crop as he finishes his drink. "Pretty slim pickings, huh?" he says to me. "Let's get the fuck out of here, Sonny."

"Let me get you guys one before you go," McGeorge says, waving at the bartender. When it comes, he raises his glass, then says, "The telephone company bought you off?"

"Yeah," Milo says, smiling, "one of their fucking trucks ran over my leg during a bank robbery. Not once but twice. No more running after the bad guys for me."

"Jeeze," McGeorge says, slapping his wooden leg, "I know how you feel. A fucking semi took mine all the way off, but the fucking trucking company went bankrupt before I got a penny. Bastards."

"I nailed the fuckers for six million," Milo says.

"Well, good for you, buddy," McGeorge says, slapping Milo on the shoulder.

Now we've got the fucker. Of course, the fucker's got a hard-eyed Korean bodyguard, who follows us everywhere.

It takes three bars packed with expensive yuppies, a couple of cab rides, and enough vodka to make me feel as Russian as Milo before he asks McGeorge about his belt buckle. McGeorge says he made it, that he makes gold jewelry.

"I might like one of those," Milo says, "tomorrow maybe. But right now let's find a real bar, man."

McGeorge leads us to the Circle, which seems as real as a heart attack. I can't tell who anybody is here. When an ancient drunk tells me that the legless guy on a skateboard used to be a famous film director before he got hooked on crack cocaine and lost his legs driving his Ferrari into a school bus at ninety miles an hour, I almost believe it, until the old bastard tries to cadge a drink off me.

At closing time, somebody's having an after-hours party somewhere, but Milo declines, saying we've got an early flight tomorrow. Then McGeorge says he's leaving tomorrow, too, that perhaps Milo should take a look at his work, and slyly implies that the gold is hot, therefore cheap. So the three of us drift back to the hotel to break into the minibar in our suite, while the Korean goes to McGeorge's Mercedes for a short run to pick up the goods. It's only parked across the street, the creep says.

When we enter the suite, Milo saps him behind the knee so hard it sounds like an axe handle against a fence post, and I drop the butt of the Airweight at the base of his neck, and before McGeorge has a chance to complain, he's duct-taped to the furniture, a complimentary pear stuffed in his mouth, and his prosthesis stashed in the tub. We also dig a Walther PPK out of his right boot and rip a flat throwing knife off his wooden leg. When McGeorge comes to life after I pour a bucket of ice into his silk shirt, he doesn't know whether we're cops or rip-off artists, and we don't tell him.

"You guys ain't half as slick as you think you are," he says dreamily through the pear mush, then he spits, saying, "I'm connected and protected, and . . . and you fuckers can't rip me off!"

"Spare me the fucking melodrama, okay?" Milo says, then motions me behind the chair and tosses me the spring-loaded sap. "You're a two-bit jerk-off hustler, and if we wanted to rip you off, asshole, you'd be dead. So don't make me mad." Then Milo pauses for effect. "Break his left elbow . . ."

At least I manage to say *What?* with my eyes. I once specialized in that sort of interrogation. But it had been years. Too many.

". . . then his good kneecap." Milo laughs wickedly.

That seems to get McGeorge's attention.

"Wait a minute, man," he stammers. "We can work something out, right? Who the fuck are you guys, anyway? I need to know who I'm dealing with."

Milo holds up a hand to me, sighing, "An old fart who ain't got a fucking thing to lose. Not a fucking thing. And you're not exactly dealing from strength, either, asshole." Then Milo stops, drops his face into his hands. This time the sigh sounds real, deep and sad, bone-tired. "Mr. McGeorge, I'm going to say a name, and you're going to tell me everything you know about that name just as quickly as you can, or my boy there is going to fuck you up. Permanently."

With a born hustler's optimism—at least he wasn't dead, yet—McGeorge starts looking for angles. "Hey, man," he says, working on a sick smile, "I'm already permanently fucked up . . ."

Milo glances up at me. "Tell him."

"We'll wrap your hand around the Walther," I ad-lib, "and kill the Korean, beat the shit out of you, then call the cops on the way out."

"I don't think I'd want to be a one-legged white guy in the new California prison system," Milo says quietly. "Unless you can find a big bad white hubby who's into stumps . . ."

"Just gimme the fucking name, all right, and let's get this shit over with," McGeorge mutters.

"Aaron Tipton," Milo whispers.

"That crazy son of a bitch!" McGeorge barks, almost laughing. "Fuck, man, you didn't have to go to all this trouble. I'd roll over on that crazy, worthless bastard for a ten-dollar bill. Hell, maybe I'd've paid you ten dollars . . ."

Then it all comes out in a rush. Until we've got all we

need. Then Milo shoves the pear back into his mouth. We leave the knife and the empty pistol on the coffee table, plus five hundred-dollar bills, then leave the key in the door and go down the fire stairs, call for the car, and split like second bananas.

As we pull onto the Santa Monica Freeway, Milo points out that I had mentioned that surface streets were the answer to the LA traffic question. "Rush hours are over," I say. "They'll be empty this time of night."

Sure. When we pull onto the 405, it looks as if somebody opened the gate down in San Diego.

"The gate to the fucking asylum," Milo suggests, chuckling. It's a true nightmare: slow cars locked in the fast lane; drunks lane-hopping; stop-and-go traffic; enough jerks on carphones to break down the cellular network; and carloads of absolutely dangerous kids, their psychotic desires unhidden beneath their cocked hats and crack-muddied eyes. I slip the .38 out of my boot and nestle it under my balls. Milo laughs, then says, "Wake me if we get home, Sughrue." Then he tilts his seat all the way back, and the fucker goes to sleep. It only takes twice as long to get back to the Sportsman's from Santa Monica as it did to get there.

Tom-John Donne is easily found the next morning. His dojo is listed in the telephone book. It's Sunday, but we check it out anyway and find it surrounded by bikers in full regalia, hoods in shiny suits, and dozens of people in karate clothes, with a number of trucks and rough-looking guys in the alley for backup. We consider shooting our way into the dojo, but decide to at least ask a few questions before we start a firefight on a movie location.

A kid dressed out of L. L. Bean, carrying a walkie-talkie, stops us with a languid wave as we try to pull into the parking lot of the strip mall.

"I thought you guys had a convertible," the kid says, "and you don't fucking look bad enough to be cowboy hoods. And you're way early, dude. We don't have an extra penny of overtime in the budget . . ." Then he has an inspiration. "Hey, you've got your costumes in the trunk, right?"

Milo gets out of the passenger seat, walks around the Beast, then grabs the kid by his ear. "Listen, asshole, I've ridden more horses to death than you've fucked. So don't say I don't look like a cowboy. Okay?" The kid nods weakly. "I want to talk to Tom-John Donne."

"He might be . . ."

"Fucking now, kid," Milo says, giving his ear a final tweak that bounces him against the Caddy. "Watch the fucking ride," Milo growls.

"Right," he says, not bothering with his walkie-talkie. "They're probably setting a shot right now . . ."

I cut the engine, leave the car sitting where we stopped, and join Milo, saying, "I smell barbecue."

"Shit," Milo says, "Montana only needs two things to be perfect."

"What?"

"Less February and more barbecue."

"What about Mexican food?"

"Make that three things," Milo answers as the kid leads a medium-sized wiry guy out of the crowd. The guy's wearing makeup, a black *gi*, and a friendly smile. But there's something wrong with his smile. He's got a set of shiny teeth lodged in a crunched black Irish face that looks as artificial as his straight nose.

"You boys scared the shit out of my PA," he says, and holds his smile. "What can I do for you?" he asks in perfectly modulated tones. "You can't hold me up for more money. Either I finish this piece of shit today or the goombahs finish it for me, and I can promise you can't jerk them around at all."

"Take a hike, kid," Milo says softly, then turns to Donne. "We're not in the movie business, Mr. Donne," Milo says. "We're in the drug business."

"Oh, shit," Donne says, a cracker accent creeping into his voice, his feet sliding into a combat stance. "What the fuck do you guys want?"

"Just a minute of your time," Milo says, hooking his thumbs on his buckle. "And Aaron Tipton."

"Burned you on a deal, huh?" Donne says, then glances at the New Mexican license plate. "I heard he was doing business down your way. Shit. Where the hell did you get my name?"

"The sheriff of Cocachino County," Milo answers, "and a piece of shit in Venice Beach."

"Fucking McGeorge. Jesus, man, they oughta make a law against even talking to people like that," he says quickly, then adds, "Listen, man, Tipton is batshit crazy and the toughest motherfucker I ever met in my life. I wouldn't hit him with a fucking train. You better shoot him before you ask him where the dope is, and then kill him good."

"Where's the car?" Milo asks.

"Fuck, McGeorge gave you that? He used to be a stand-up dude. Even on one leg."

"We all get old," Milo whispers, barely audible against the sound of the traffic. "We'd like to take a look at the car."

"Sorry, man, we used it in a scene last night," Donne admits. "It's already being parted out in TJ. I went through it pretty good. Nothing there."

"You know a guy out in the desert named O'Bannion?"

"Yeah, you better shoot him first, too."

Milo reaches into his pockets, then shuffles through a sheaf of hundreds. "We need a favor, Mr. Donne, okay? The cops are right behind us. And they ain't happy. Tipton killed the sheriff's cousin. It was an accident, but the cousin's dead nonetheless. We'd appreciate it if you could stall them for a day or two."

"What do I get out of it?" he says, a shitty little grin opening his little mouth, exposing his brilliant teeth.

"You get to keep your fucking pretty teeth," I say.

Donne is not impressed, but he looks at me carefully.

"And two grand," Milo says quietly. "That seems to be the going price for favors in LA."

"Can be more, but it sounds good this morning. So you got a deal," he says, nodding, grinning all the way. "No big thing. We wrap this fucker tonight, I'll be on my way to the Big Island tomorrow. Take the fuckers a week to track me down."

Milo hands him the money, makes him shake his hand, then we climb back in the Caddy. But we do not depart friends.

"FYI, hard-ass," Donne says, leaning toward my window. "My pretty teeth came from the government while I was in jail, as did my lovely profile, so you ain't about to fuck up my livelihood, hard-ass."

"It's a date," I say, and he nods, then goes back to work.

"Try to stay out of trouble," Milo says.

"Goombahs," I say as we drive away, "in the movie business?"

"Everywhere," Milo answers. "Let's see if we can follow that barbecue smell to its source."

"I'm sure I can," I say.

"Follow your nose, Sughrue," he says. "Think he made the plate number?"

"Won't matter," I say. "I changed the three to an eight and the *E* to a *B* this morning. You're not the only sneaky son of a bitch on this job."

The night before, it turned out, Milo had blocked our trail at the Loew's Hotel by using a credit card with the Milton Chester name on it. In fact, I was quite impressed with his whole set of working legal papers—credit cards, a passport, a checking account—so I asked him why he hadn't gotten me one, too, and he said he assumed that I already had my own. Of course I did. But it was buried in an ammo box south of Fairbairn.

After lunch at a place that claimed to make Texas barbecue but put too much sugar in their sauce, we rent a couple of four-wheel drive Subarus with Milo's fake ID, cover a couple of other chores, then park the Beast at the Sportsman's, have a drink and a laugh with Joe, and head for the desert, loaded for bear.

Part Three
Milo

FOLLOWING THE MIRAGE-FLOODED INTERSTATE DOWN INTO the desert valley beyond Banning, I wondered again at the windmill fields stretching across the desert across I-10 from Palm Springs. I'd noticed them on the way back from San Diego when I was running from Maribeth—she wanted to mother me, and her boys wanted me to father them, which put a hell of a strain on our bedroom time, so I had to remove myself.

On the way back to West Texas to pick up Sughrue I cut over the mountains down into Palm Springs and found the windmill fields, the white windmills. Graceful, peaceful technology creating electricity out of air, something out of nothing. Perfect twentieth-century machine. And living proof that efficient beauty replicated is fucking ugly. But fascinating, nonetheless.

As the Beast rolled past them heading east that day, I had a sudden impulse to stop, to listen, I think, to the sweep of the great blades, a whole field of them—whoosh, whoosh, whoosh in the hot breeze—and perhaps sleep as if in a gentle black wind.

But I didn't stop then, and if I stopped now, fucking Sughrue would think I was crazy and start worrying about me again. Christ, it was like taking your grandmother on a bank robbery. But when he wasn't indulging himself in his mother-hen act, he was still great company. We hadn't become friends by accident. And in a bad situation, his friendship might be the difference between life and death. Not that I gave much of a shit. Not now. I just wanted to recover my father's money and take my revenge as quietly as possible, perhaps just cut their fucking heads off with a shovel as I would a run-over rattlesnake or a Mexican drug dealer's hand, and feel completely justified, then go somewhere where nobody knew my name and become a town drunk—the one who studies baseball encyclopedias and can give a passing stranger the roster of the 1924 Giants or the '54 Indians—then drink until I died in my sleep, peacefully strangled by my own vomit.

What I didn't want was Sughrue hurt. Not even a little bit. I didn't want to face Whitney and Baby Lester with his blood on my hands. And I didn't want him to face them with blood on his hands, not blood or bone chips or gray matter. After what happened to me, I was damn sure of that. I guess there's something to be said for hitting the hard-rock bottom of your life; a certain clarity of mind forms from the muck, forms and rises like life itself.

If I could have dumped him, I would have. But not only did he stick to my tail like a bad hound, he knew where we were going. And if I had told him what I had in mind, he'd ask, "Who's the fucking grandma now?" I wondered what sort of favor he had done for Nancy to make her come up with the O'Bannion name. Probably fun, I suspected.

I almost laughed. Still, I looked at the windmills with something akin to longing, thought of swimming with the whales, sleeping wrapped in Nancy's silver hair, sleeping without dreams.

O'Bannion's place looked as if it had been moved from the fifties and dropped against a rocky hillside among the cactus and Joshua trees, a pool shimmering blue in the center of a circle of rooms set over covered parking places, with a rambling faux adobe behind a steel fence and a locked gate about a hundred yards up the slope.

When I checked in, I found the rooms were clean and bright and shining with scrubbed formica and glowing chrome and white asphalt floor tiles. The walls seemed made of windows as clear as a mountain stream, and when I flopped on the large bed, I felt as if I had fallen into a god's perfect pocket.

Poor Sughrue. He had lodged in a motel down by the highway, one of those two, four, six, eight, we don't masturbate, much, establishments that didn't even have a bar. It did have a rough and wonderful empty space between it and O'Bannion's where we could set up an observation post.

O'Bannion's, on the other hand, had a great bar off the

restaurant, dark and cool and secret, with red plush booths and stools, the only hints of light the cool glow of real candles in smoked glass holders, the flickering reflections on the chromed stool legs, and the soft whiskey-flavored glow from the back bar.

After waiting moments for my eyes to adjust from the blazing sundown to the dim space of the empty bar, I spotted a bald older guy with the size and grace of an Alaskan brown bear leaning his great back against the bar as he watched a football game on the color television in the corner.

"What can I do you for?" he said as he dropped a coaster in front of me.

"I always like an empty Sunday night bar," I said as I climbed on the stool. "No amateurs." O'Bannion smiled politely. "Coors," I said, "no glass."

"Colorado Kool-Aid," he said, then turned to the cooler.

"A thin bitter beer for the end of a hot afternoon," I said, then nodded toward the television. "I'd've guessed black and white," I added.

O'Bannion smiled, ran his hand over his barren pate, then said, "Don't make 'em much anymore. Not big enough to see, anyway. You staying at the motel?" I nodded. "First one's on me, sir. How about a knock to hold that thin beer down?"

"Jameson's," I said, and the large grin widened across his face. "Thanks."

"How'd you find this place?" O'Bannion said as he poured both of us a shot of the Irish whiskey. "I don't advertise."

"On my way to Twenty-Nine Palms," I said, "and turned off the road looking for a beer. Saw this place, sir, like a dream out of my youth. Ought to be a museum. It's fucking beautiful."

"Thanks," he said. "Built the place with my own hands."

"Damn good job," I said.

"What's in Twenty-Nine Palms?" he asked.

"Looking for a warm place to retire."

"Jesus, friend. You an ex-Marine?"

"Army," I said, "but I'm a retired deputy sheriff from North Dakota."

O'Bannion laughed, raised his glass, and said, "Well, here's a go, partner." After we drank, he said, "No offense, but I think you can find a better place to retire. And cheaper. And warmer. And more fun than hanging out with a bunch of jar-heads."

"Where's that?" I asked.

"Mexico."

Lord knows what I expected after hearing that magic word again—hell, I hadn't even crossed the border yet—but what I didn't expect was a long discourse on the American retirement communities of Mexico, the value of the American dollar against the Mexican peso, the youth and beauty of Mexican whores, and the joys of warm afternoons on the square in Chihuahua conversing with ancient, sun-wrinkled cowboys retired from all over the American West, all of this punctuated by endless shots of Jameson's, a whiskey I'd never liked that much, laughs, jokes, and stories of our misspent youths, his spent as a stunt double in Hollywood, and mine as a lawman in an almost mythical Grand Forks, North Dakota, a city I had visited only once many years ago to set up a false identity.

I finally walked into the chilly desert night before I became hopelessly drunk and lost track of my lies. And, taking as a commandment that you shouldn't shoot your friends, before O'Bannion and I became new best friends.

After he saw the light in my window, Sughrue came in from the night, dressed in the desert camo fatigues we had picked up before leaving LA.

"Working hard, old man?" he said as he grabbed a beer from the cooler.

"Irish whiskey is a fucking chore," I said.

"What'd you get?"

"Drunk."

"And?"

"A long lecture on the benefits and joys of a Mexican retirement," I said. "And the distinct impression that the big son of a bitch is the toughest and the most criminal of all the bent bunch we've seen in the past few weeks . . ."

"But you liked him?" Sughrue said as he cracked another beer.

"He wanted to kiss me when I left."

"Nothing solid, though?" he said.

"Just a drunken impression," I admitted, "that Tipton is here, O'Bannion is nervous, and we're in a slippery load of goose shit."

"He's not in the house or the motel," Sughrue said. "How you want to work it?"

"If he doesn't lead us to Tipton by tomorrow afternoon," I said, "I think I'll just be straight with him. We don't have much time to play cute before the cops show up." Sughrue considered that, shook his head once, then nodded. "Leave me a map so I can find where you're set up," I said, "and I'll order some room service, pass out for three hours, then relieve you till daylight."

"Sounds good."

"Leave me a little bump," I said, "so I'll at least be awake for part of my watch."

Sughrue stared at me for a long moment. "You all right?"

My grin didn't quite fit my face, but I answered, "Just try me, kiddo."

"Don't forget your long johns, old man," Sughrue said. "It's cold out there."

Thanks to slow room service and the snooze-alarm, I didn't relieve Sughrue until almost two A.M., but he didn't complain, just smiled and nodded.

"Mr. O'Bannion lumbered up to the house about midnight," he said, "and nothing's moved since then. I'll see you in three."

"Take six," I suggested. "I'm hungover and wired. So I'll be awake anyway."

Sughrue grinned, then slipped into the desert shadows as I slid between the two crinkly camo space blankets. Of course, I'd forgotten my long johns and nearly froze to death crouched over the spotting scope in the light of the three-quarter moon. But it's no more than I deserved.

At nine the next morning when Sughrue showed up with a thermos of coffee, I'd already stuffed the space blankets back into their sacks and I was glad I'd forgotten my long johns. The sun had come up like a flamethrower, chasing the night chill into the shadows behind the rocks, and the desert smog began to form, spreading across the depression of Palm Springs like a guilty conscience. But not mine.

"You're bright-eyed and bushy-tailed," Sughrue said, "and not visible from the highway." He jerked his chin downhill to the highway where an endless line of traffic snaked through the rough hills. "Nothing happened?"

"Quiet as a graveyard," I admitted.

"And from the looks of the smog," he said, "it'll be one before long. How do you want to work this?"

"Shit, Sonny," I said, "I don't exactly know. Can you see the turnoff from your room? Without the scope?" Sughrue nodded. "Why don't you set up there? He's got a green Toyota Land Cruiser and a red and white 1952 Buick—he showed me pictures yesterday—so tag him if he leaves. If he doesn't, I'll meet you in the bar at, say, three-thirty, and I'll lay it out for him.

"Sounds like a plan," he said, then laughed.

But not a great plan, I thought, maybe not even a good plan.

After I'd finished my story, O'Bannion sighed, cleared the bar with an exterminator story, then brought me another Coors. Sughrue had ducked into the john instead of out the front door. O'Bannion shook his head, said, "Goddammit, I hate liars," then reached into a stack of towels and pulled out a gigantic horse pistol. "Colt's Dragoon," he said, talking to the pistol, "1848 model. Forty-four caliber. Percussion conversion to black powder cartridges. Fucker weighs more than an M-1 carbine, kicks like a ten-gauge single shot, and it will put you down. For good."

"Fuck you," I said quietly.

O'Bannion took a step backward, then leveled the horse pistol at my chest with both hands. "Finish your shitty beer, buddy," he said, "and don't even bother checking out of the motel—I'll take the loss—then I don't want to ever see you again, because if I do, you're . . ."

"Hey, excuse me," I interrupted. "Do I look like the kind of jerk who'll do whatever some asshole says just because he's got the gun? That ain't my style." He considered that a moment. "Besides, it ain't even cocked." So he cocked it.

"To hell with it," I said again, then kicked the bar with the pointed toe of my boot. "You've got a gun, I've got a gun, and he's got a gun . . ."

O'Bannion glanced into the corner where I knew Sughrue had the Browning dead center on him.

". . . so let's all get a gun and we can all be cowboys. Fuck it. That hand-loaded cannon could misfire, my forty-caliber Glock might not make it through the bar, but my man over there ain't going to miss. So if you're going to do it, man, do it. Or put it up."

O'Bannion smiled, slid the horse pistol back under the towels, and picked up the Jameson's and three shot glasses, then started to walk around the bar.

"I'll have a schnapps," I said.

"Make mine tequila," Sughrue said. "The Herradura."

"Next thing you know," O'Bannion said, laughing, "I'll be dragging out the blender for you pussy tourists . . ."

We gathered at the corner of the bar, drinking silently for long moments. "Did you know Rita?" I asked to break the silence. "I know there was some sort of bond between Tipton and Rita but I never had the pleasure of meeting the woman."

"Meeting Aaron Tipton wasn't exactly pleasure?" Sughrue asked.

O'Bannion gave Sughrue a long, hard look, then started talking. He had been taking care of Aaron Tipton for twenty years, ever since the afternoon the awkward teenager showed up on the Coast Range location of a horse opera where O'Bannion was doubling for a faggot movie star who couldn't stay in the saddle. Except with a key grip.

"The kid wanted to be a stunt man. For some fucking reason," O'Bannion mused over an empty shot glass. "I told him to come back when he grew up, put some meat on his bones. That's when he started lifting weights and gobbling 'roids. For some fucking idiot reason, I gave the kid my address and telephone number."

We had sipped several shots at the corner of the bar, which O'Bannion had locked after all the firearms had been put away.

"Six months later he shows up on my front porch pumped

to the gills, crazy as a loon, and looking for work in 'the industry,' " O'Bannion said, his bartender instincts filling our glasses again, freshening our chasers. "Fucking 'industry,' my ass. I got him some work standing around coke whores in beach-bunny flicks. But the poor fucking kid couldn't stand still and chew gum at the same time. Strong as an ox, but not nearly as graceful." He paused, then said sadly, "So Aaron went from steroids to cocaine to crank in about three years. The next step was working muscle for a Texas bookie . . ."

"Remember his name?" I asked.

"Not offhand, but I've got it somewhere," he said. "It was only another quick step to cooking crank, then knocking crank labs over, burning guys on coke deals, stretches in the can . . ." O'Bannion gunned his shot. "I've spent a fortune on detox doctors and criminal lawyers."

"Where's he now?"

"Up to his ass in deep shit," O'Bannion said, pouring again. "Even if he cops a miracle plea on the sheriff's cousin, he's going in for a long time. So I got him stashed in an old shack I own up toward Barstow. Maybe I can get him out of the country, get him in a hospital in France or someplace . . ." Nobody believed that.

"You think he'll talk to us?"

"On the telephone, maybe," O'Bannion said, "but I wouldn't try it in person. He can be pretty touchy."

"No shit," I said, "we were there—with the sheriff's permission—and we heard that the sheriff is going to make it and Tipton's sister isn't going to press charges. We could make it sound like an accidental discharge. If he's willing to help us . . ."

"I'll give him a call," O'Bannion said, lifting a tiny cellular telephone out of his shirt pocket, "give it a try."

"I could even help with the defense fund," I said.

O'Bannion waved his meaty hand at me. "Money's no problem, buddy. I made my first million smuggling grass thirty years ago, when it was still almost a million dollars. I just stayed with the stunt work because I liked being around movies, man." He laughed. "Just like the dumb-ass kid." He punched in the number. "Damn, it's busy." Then he thought about it. "Let's drive up that way. Maybe he's been taking his Prozac."

"Let's hope so," Sughrue said.

O'Bannion told us to fill up a cooler behind the bar with beer and ice while he walked up the hill for his Land Cruiser. As we were doing it, Sughrue asked me if I thought the old man was straight.

"He could be carrying us into a trap, Milo."

"We could always shoot him," I said.

"Several times, man," he said, then slipped the Browning and a spare clip out of the back of his jeans where it had been hidden by his Hawaiian shirt. "You're not supposed to tell the bad guys that you've got a piece when you don't," he said as he handed it to me.

"I can't tell the bad guys from the good anymore, Sonny," I said.

"Well, I still can," he said, then slammed the lid of the cooler shut.

Other times, it might have been a pleasant late-afternoon ride with slow beers and fast conversation. But every time O'Bannion tried the shack's number, he got a busy signal, which clearly made him more nervous each time. Then as sunset drifted into its daily desert theatrics, he found that his combination didn't work on the locked chain around the steel gate at the turn off Highway 247. "Shit, this ain't my lock," he muttered, and began to climb the gate. "You guys still carrying?"

"Yeah," I said as we joined him. "How far is it?"

"Two miles of deep sand and rock," O'Bannion said, then struck off up the track toward the stone-crested ridge to the west.

"Let's don't walk in this sand," I said, pointing toward the fresh tire tracks. Going in and coming out. O'Bannion looked at me. "I didn't lie about being a lawman once," I said. "Whatever has happened has already happened." I convinced him to dig a flashlight out of his rig first, then we moved into the rougher traveling off the track, circling toward O'Bannion's cabin.

The weathered board-and-batten shack might have once provided a shaded refuge for a desert rat or a religious hermit, but when we topped the last shallow rise, it looked as if it had been hit by a tornado. Or a bulldozer. Large portions of the wall had been punched out, the flimsy roof tilted crazily, and a large naked body lay in the front doorway. Even in the swiftly fading light, the black bloody smears were visible. O'Bannion sobbed, then started to trot down the ridge. I stepped in front of him, but not hard enough. He brushed me away like a gnat. I held on to the thick, sodden arm, waving in the cool air like a child. Sughrue grabbed the other arm, and for a few steps the old man carried us downhill, until his already tired legs gave out and we tumbled into the rocks, sand, and cactus.

"You gotta think, man," Sughrue said quickly.

"We gotta work this out, O'Bannion," I added, then helped him to his feet and made him look me in the eye. As best he could. His eyes were pouring tears into the sweat of his face.

"You okay?" I asked. He nodded slowly as if his head weighed a thousand pounds. "Sughrue," I said without looking at him, "go over there about a hundred yards, cut me a switch with more leaves than thorns, cut it below the surface of the sand, and cover up your tracks on the way back."

I heard Sughrue turn and walk away. O'Bannion knocked my arms off his shoulders, saying, "You're so fucking smart."

"Smart keeps you out of jail," I said, "and the fucking cops aren't going to leave this alone. Not for a second. So we have to be smart. Okay?"

O'Bannion nodded again, but the look he gave me would have frosted the balls off a lizard.

"I'm sorry," I said.

"Fuck you," he answered.

Eventually he calmed down enough to let me cover the scene, carefully trying to conceal my tracks. It seemed to take forever. Then I trudged back up the sandy rise, brushing out my boot prints behind me. O'Bannion knelt in the sand, staring up at the winking stars in the black sky. Sughrue stood behind him, his shirt open for easy access to the Browning.

"I'm going to give it to you straight," I said, "and you've got to take it, then walk away."

"Fuck you," he said without looking up.

"You ever been inside, old man?" He shook his great stone head. "Then shut up and listen. Sit down and listen." Sughrue and I helped him get comfortable on a nearby flat rock, then I gave it to him.

"This is only a guess," I began, "but it's my best guess . . ."

"And he'll be damn close," Sughrue said softly.

"Tipton came to the door in his shorts, carrying the cellular telephone," I said, "and somebody wearing running shoes shot him at least three times in the face with a twenty-two. Then stopped to put a round into the phone as maybe Tipton went for the shotgun, which was on the kitchen counter next to a dozen lines of pretty good cocaine. He didn't make it. He took another three or four rounds in the lower back. That's when he crashed through the side wall.

"The killer walked through the house, which was stupid, because he left tracks in the dust . . ."

"Fucking kid never was much of a housekeeper," O'Bannion muttered. "Christ, I had to muck out the place every time I came up here . . ."

". . . then the shooter put several more rounds in Tipton's gut, and one up close in his nut sack. Which just made him mad, as far as I can tell. Whatever, he ripped his shorts off, got up, staggered back into the shack and across it, where he took out the corner post on the back side, and fell down again. Then the killer kneecapped him. Twice. Tipton crawled back in the shack, destroyed the table, some chairs, a shelf of tapes and the player, crawled all the way to the front door. Where he gave out on the stoop.

"There, the killer put two or three in the back of his head, one in his ear, maybe even one in the mouth, then the rest of the clip into his back. I don't know in which order," I said, then added, "They used one of those little Grendel carbines with a thirty-round magazine. They used every one of them. Wiped it clean and tossed it on Tipton's back."

"Professional hit?" O'Bannion asked quietly.

"I don't know," I said, "but whoever did it certainly wanted to make a point."

"I'll give you guys a hundred grand to find out who did it," O'Bannion said. "Or make it two hundred. Put it in escrow tomorrow morning. Plus expenses. Whatever you need . . ." Sughrue barked a quick laugh, hard and clipped, the sort of sound a coyote might answer. "What's so fucking funny, kid?"

"Actually, there's a little more than that involved," I said, "but thanks, anyway."

O'Bannion looked at me with his great head cocked on his thick neck almost to the breaking point. "Who the fuck are you guys, anyway?"

Sughrue and I looked at each other and shrugged as the crooked, waning moon topped the desert mountains to the east.

"I guess we're your new best friends," I said, then helped the weary old giant to his feet.

As O'Bannion eased along before us, occasionally sobbing softly, backtracking our way to the gate, Sughrue and I brushed out our tracks as best we could by the shrouded moonlight. At the second rest stop, O'Bannion flopped to the ground about ten yards in front of us, his legs splayed like an abandoned doll's.

"Wish the fuck I'd thought to bring a beer," Sughrue said. "How's it going?"

"I'm hanging in there," I said, "but I'd sure as hell rather not seen that one."

"Mind if I ask how you knew the cocaine was primo?"

"I rolled up a bill and did two of the lines," I said. "It kept me from puking. Then I left the rest of the lines and stole his stash."

"Was that smart?"

"Necessary," I said, "which is sometimes the same thing," and handed Sughrue the plump baggie.

The moon was almost down, the sun almost up when we reached the gate, half-crazy, double-tired from half-carrying O'Bannion's bulk. The three of us emptied a six-pack and started on another in minutes. It picked up O'Bannion enough for me to get his private number and to tell him what to do before he collapsed into the backseat. I let Sughrue drive us back to the motel, then we crashed until we decided it was either wake up or die.

Then it was back to LA as soon as we could safely check out of our respective rooms. Finally, we rid ourselves of the rented Subarus and tumbled into our beds at the Sportsman's and stayed there, living on room service food and despair, with occasional side dishes of pool time and margaritas until O'Bannion had time to finish his chore.

At one point, Sughrue turned to me while we were baking beside the pool to say, "Have you noticed that every time we look for somebody, we find them dead?"

"I've noticed a few bodies along the way," I said, "but at least none of them are us."

"Yet."

"Or O'Bannion's," I said. "Though he didn't sound all that lively when I talked to him this morning, at least his lawyer's faxing a copy of his cellular bill to the front desk. Said he had to get a lawyer to get the fucking telephone company to give him a printout of his calls on that number. And check the reverse directory."

"What about the body?"

"Tomorrow. He's going up tomorrow afternoon with an ex-cop buddy of his to find it."

"Then what?"

"Why don't you fly home for a week or so," I said carefully. "Spend some time with the family while I hang around out here and check out Tipton's telephone calls."

"Surely you're not thinking about wandering around without backup," he said.

"I hate it when you call me 'Shirley,' " I said.

"Arlene," he said, laughing, then lifted himself off the lounger, no longer quite so self-conscious about his scar. "I think I'd best stick to you, old man."

"We're not joined at the hip, kid."

But we might as well have been. We picked up the fax, retired to the Lobby Bar, and tried to decide what to do next. After shaking our heads over the fax until our necks hurt, we still didn't have a clue. Or maybe too damn many clues leading in too many directions to too many places we had already covered. According to the fax from O'Bannion's lawyer, Aaron Tipton had made six calls from his cellular telephone. Two to Seattle, one to a hotel and another to a restaurant; two to a pay telephone in El Paso; and two to a Donell Wilbarger residence outside Austin, the bookie for whom Tipton had once worked as muscle. Tipton had received only one call at the shack. From another pay telephone in El Paso. Two days before he died.

So we packed our gear, sat our butts in the soft leather seats, and drove east. On the drive I tried once again to talk Sughrue into taking some time at home, but he refused. Unless I'd stop there, too. So I said yes. Then dropped him at the store late the next afternoon, telling him that I'd see him after I checked back into the Cuero Motel. But I left him standing there, hugging Whitney in the parking lot, while I headed for the interstate. Later, I knew he'd curse me and the fact that he'd never catch me in the old pickup.

Austin looked like a different place in the gray November rain. The norther had stripped the trees, seared the grasses, and washed the colors off the damp stone outcroppings. Even the pastel capitol building seemed pale and sickly in the ashen air. Just another midsize middle-western city locked into the embrace of early winter. Nothing I hadn't seen before.

"I hate even the suggestion of cold weather," Carver D said through the dingy cloud of Gitanes smoke when I finished bringing him up to date over a dark table in Flo's. He looked a bit washed out, too. "Anybody with a lick of sense would be down in ol' Mexico loungin' on the *playa* watchin' the beach boys' butts and drinkin' brandy 'stead of this shit." He waggled his pudgy fingers at the dim afternoon air.

"Be all too happy to drive you, boss," Hangas said, his smile the brightest point in the joint.

"Irony is wasted on fat people," Carver D said quietly, staring at me, "and advice on fools." Then he paused. "Ain't you livin' a bit large, Mr. Milodragovitch, after the events of your last visit?"

"Just stirring up the shit," I said, "see which floats and which sinks."

"Love it when shit happens," Hangas said, his grin broader. At least he was happy to see me.

"What the hell does that mean?" Carver D asked, ignoring Hangas.

"I don't know," I admitted, "but that's how I work."

"Well, you're damn well overpaid for it."

"You want to tell me why you've got the red ass, Carver D?"

The fat man's sigh sucked all the air out of the room. He lit a new cigarette off the smoldering butt of the old one, then picked up the bourbon bottle at his feet and made it bubble. "Success," he said finally.

But I just waited.

"Goddammit, I've kept that pissant little newspaper afloat for twenty years on my family's ill-gotten gains—Galveston whorehouses, East Texas land frauds, and the sweat of illegal aliens—but for the last five years, the son of a bitch has made money . . ."

Again I waited.

"And last week a syndicate of alternative rags just offered me more money than I've got in it. Even countin' all the years of losses."

"So what's the problem?" I asked.

Carver D heaved himself out of the chair and waddled toward the restroom. "Who the fuck knows?" he muttered over his shoulder.

Hangas answered for him. "All the years of hard living have caught up with him finally," Hangas said softly. "He fainted last week while they were putting the paper to bed. Doc told him to quit drinking, smoking, and staying up late at night with teenage boys."

"So he's thinking about taking the offer?"

"Damn straight."

"What do you think, Hangas?"

"Me?" he said, then laughed. "You know, Milo, my people been working for his people since before the War of Northern Aggression," he said with a slow grin, then sipped at his beer, "and Mr. Carver D, he took me in when

I give up the Corps and put all six of my children through college. They're all professionals now—two doctors, two lawyers, a CPA, and a set designer at the San Francisco opera—and they all ask me, 'Daddy, what for you driving that fat ugly white boy around every day?'" Hangas set his beer down carefully, then stared at me. "A man retires from what he loves, it's just like a death sentence," he said, "and I love that fat ugly white boy and he loves that paper."

"You tell him that?"

"Why, hell no, man," Hangas chortled, "he'd fire my ass in a New York minute."

"Waxahachie," I corrected him, and we laughed.

We were still chuckling when Carver D came back from the john.

"I tell you what, gentlemen, a swollen prostate ain't nothin' to laugh about," he said, then slumped heavily into the chair. "Fuck it, a man's gotta do what a man's gotta do," he added, groaning, then added, "then live till he dies. What the hell you and that crazy Sughrue want now?"

"Sughrue's all the way out of this part," I said.

Carver D stared at me for a moment, then smiled. "At least there's some good news," he said, then laughed until he almost cried.

According to Carver D's sources, the former bookie, Wilbarger, had gone legitimate recently and was a major silent partner in several cable franchises around central Texas and an upscale development in the hills west of Austin, Castle Creek Country Club Estates, executive homes built around a thirty-six-hole championship golf course. But he still lived like a gangster, surrounded by stone walls, electronic security systems, and well-dressed hoods.

Carver D suggested that breaking into a bank might be easier than talking to Donell Wilbarger. And even that would be easier than breaking into the encoded information on the floppy disk I had taken from Ray Lara's laptop. As far as his skateboard punk could tell, the disk couldn't be copied, or even read again without the proper password, or it would destroy itself. The Lara killings were still buried at the cop shop as a murder-suicide for some reason that none of his police contacts could explain.

Keeping my profile high, posing as a prospective buyer with more money than sense, and dropping the Wilbarger name as often as possible, I made an appointment with one of the sales agents, Irene McDormand, a lovely, highly buffed middle-aged divorcee wearing more gold than a television actress, who sat me in a pink golf cart and gave me the grand tour of the estates and golf course.

All the houses fronted on the golf course, all came with pools, and the smallest ones had at least three thousand square feet of living space. I couldn't imagine who could afford to live like this. From what I'd read in the local paper, Austin was surviving the slump in the oil business with a surge of Silicon Valley clones, rising neatly from the ashes again. But I didn't know how anybody lived the way they did. Hell, all the people I knew were criminals, drunks, and bad-dog lawyers. I didn't really know anything about normal life and supposed I was a bit long in the tooth to find out about it now. But as Irene showed me how they lived the good life in central Texas, I found myself thinking about it. Thinking even about golf. God, I'd not only lost my purpose but perhaps my mind.

Then I nearly blew the whole afternoon's work as we puttered past Wilbarger's elegant fortress. "Mr. Wilbarger must live there," I said. After which Irene suddenly remembered a pressing engagement that would woefully interfere with the rest of the tour and our tentative dinner plans.

But as I drove past the manned gatehouse, the guard told me that Mrs. McDormand had called and asked me to wait. Irene showed up in a pink and gold blur, breathless and extremely nervous, to inform me that perhaps we could meet for a late dinner at a place on the other side of the lake, Hudson's on the Bend, where we could dine on exotic game over a couple of bottles of really good wine. Who was I to deny her? What the hell, I'd gotten Wilbarger's attention without gunfire. Better than a poke in the eye with a sharp stick. Or a needle up the dick.

Hangas covered my back outside while Irene and I dined on lies and quail, antelope pâté and wild boar medallions. Not only was the dinner great, she plied me with three bottles of a fair Texas vintage and so much steamy implied sex that I nearly forgot what I was doing. Once again. Even with two of Carver D's giggling buddies, whom he claimed ran a tae kwan do academy, watching our every move from a nearby table.

As we lingered over coffee and cognac, Irene excused herself to go to the bathroom, leaving her sweater and purse. An act that seemed oddly familiar. At least she hadn't offered me a blow job.

A tall, athletic type wearing a cashmere blazer and a neatly clipped moustache over a hard grin stood up from a nearby table he shared with two of his bodyguards, two large gentlemen who affected Birkenstocks and Glocks, limped over, and sat down in Irene's chair without asking. He stared at me without speaking. I tossed him the leather folder with the dinner check in it.

"What the hell is this?" he said as he caught it.

"From the looks of your operation, Wilbarger," I said, "you can afford it."

Wilbarger chuckled, then said, "Jesus, Milodragovitch, do you have any idea how little your life is worth right now?"

"I'd say with your juice you could sell me out for about ten grand," I said. "But given the trouble I could cause, it would hardly be worth it."

"Snap my fingers, dude, you're a puddle of piss and puke."

"It's been tried," I said, and found myself smiling as if I meant it. Perhaps I'd been infected with the Sughrue disease. Life was the ultimate insult. "And found wanting."

"I'll just bet it has," he said, then slapped the folder against his long thigh. "So what the hell do you want with me, old man?"

"Aaron Tipton," I said. "And don't call me 'old man.' "

"I knew somebody would be coming around," he said,

"asking about the asshole, but I expected the law dogs, not some crazy old . . . boy." This time he laughed deeply, then tossed the check folder to one of his thugs, telling him to take care of it. "Can I buy you a drink?" he asked. "Then you tell those dangerous little faggots over there to relax, and I'll tell you a little story."

I nodded, but Carver D's friends had stopped giggling and were so tightly strung I could almost hear their trained muscles humming.

After the waitress brought new cognacs, Wilbarger launched into his tale. "First off, man, the word on the streets had it that you were looking for the dudes who tried to ice your buddy, then you somehow came up with Ray Lara and the money laundry scam out at the Pilot's Knob Bank. Ruined their whole deal and dealt them a ton of grief, right?"

A question I didn't bother to answer.

"Then you show up alone, man," he continued, shaking his head, "nosing around my shit. Well, lemme tell you something. After I blew out my Achilles' tendon in college, I started a little sports book, that got me into a sports wire, then titty bars, massage parlors, and some motels. That was the sum total of my scam, man. Drugs were fine with me, but drug deals were way too exciting, too dangerous, too many guns . . ."

"But you know those people?"

"Sure," he said, "what's not to know? But I never did business with them. And I never took a fall, so when I made enough bread, I went legit. When I heard you were asking about me, friend, I checked you out, and when I found out who you were, I didn't know what to do. Really."

"So you arranged this little dinner?"

"Well, at first Rennie was just supposed to pump you, but I decided to play it straight."

"Thanks," I said, almost meaning it, "but Tipton called you a couple of times from California. What did he want?"

"I don't know," he said, "I didn't talk to him."

"Don't give me that shit," I said.

"No, really," he answered, leaning across the table. "Listen, five or six years back I had some extra change and a buddy of mine talked me into financing a low-budget movie.

They shot here. A football movie. Maybe you heard of it. *Pigiron?*" I nodded. "Didn't cost shit," he continued, "and did a little business. Made some actual money. For the fucking distributors. Those bastards are real criminals. I just barely got out with my ass intact.

"Learned my lesson, though," he said, then laughed and waved for more cognac. "That's how I met the Tipton kid. He came out from Hollywood for a bit part. As a 'roid monkey. Talk about type-casting. So we hit it off and started hanging out. His career, as he called it, wasn't going anyplace, so I gave him work."

"Collecting?"

"He was the best I ever had, man, because he was truly fucking crazy," Wilbarger said. "Which is why I didn't take his calls."

"What'd he want?"

"That's the funny part," he said. "I'm not quite sure."

"What's that mean?"

"Well, my boys told me that he was asking about a broad who played a hooker in the movie," he said. "I mean I did a little number with her on location, but shit, man, she was just too fucking crazy and dangerous for me. Pure mean. Even had a mean name. Darcy Stone. Plus, she tried to run a scam on me. So I shit-canned the bitch and haven't heard from her since. Can't even exactly remember what she looked like."

"What sort of scam?"

"She wanted me to finance her *movie project,*" Wilbarger said, "but what the hell. Everybody on the fucking job pulled a project out of their asses when they found out that I had a bunch of cash stashed. That's the way those people are, man, real fucking greedy when it comes to *projects.*"

"That's what they say," I said, without really knowing who *they* might be. "Can I ask you one last thing?"

"If I can ask you a favor."

"What's the favor?"

"Analise Lara used to cut my hair. She was a sweet kid. When you find out who did her, friend," Wilbarger said softly, "call me. I want to talk to the bastards. Personally."

"That shouldn't be hard," I said.

Wilbarger stood up, shook the kinks out of his bad leg,

picked up Irene's purse and sweater, then paused. "You had another question?"

"You've already answered it," I said.

He smiled sadly, then limped back to the protection of his new life. "I'll call."

None of my backup help wanted to take off, but after the Wilbarger crowd disappeared, I managed to convince them to leave me alone. I left shortly, then spent the night drinking 7-Eleven coffee and letting the Beast drive me around Austin. Maribeth was supposed to come to town in a couple of days, without her boys, but I needed to decide where to go and what to do. And how to apologize to Sughrue. But my wanderings seemed to have some purpose. Twice I drifted past the Laras' house. And just as a gray line gathered at the cloudy eastern horizon, the Beast carried me to the Emergency Vet Clinic in north Austin for the third time that night, by which I supposed I had something in mind. So I parked, hesitated for a long moment, then buzzed the night bell.

"Dr. Porterfield?" I asked when a soft voice answered the bell.

"Betty," she said.

"Remember an old Lab bitch named Sheba?" I asked.

"Yes."

"Well, I'm the guy who dropped her off," I said, and she buzzed me inside. Bravely, I thought. Later she told me she had a stun gun in her sweater pocket and a Ruger .40 double-action automatic in her belt pack.

Once I was inside the clinic that morning, the door locked behind me, the vet leaned on the counter, the portable telephone in hand. "I've already dialed the nine and the first one, bud," she said, "now convince me not to dial the last one."

"Do I impress you as the sort of asshole who would . . ."

"Bud, I don't have any idea what kind of asshole you are," she interrupted calmly.

". . . shoot a dog with a twenty-two?" I asked.

"You don't know how little that kind of shit impresses me."

"I'm going to empty my pockets," I said, then did.

She poked idly through the change, money clip, Buck

pocketknife, and keys, then thumbed through my wallet. "How would I know if this stuff is real?" she said. "All I can tell is that you drive a new Cadillac with New Mexico plates, have a Montana driver's license that's about to expire, and carry too much cash to be trusted."

"I can explain that," I said.

"I'll just bet you can," she said. "Explain the dog."

So I tried to make up something she might believe, a story about bikers and dopers and cops, a good story. Maybe because of the way she looked. Betty Porterfield looked to be in her late thirties, had a large heart-shaped face, a spray of freckles across her cleanly weathered skin, and a wild thatch of light red hair gathered at the back of her neck with a ribbon. Her nails were short, her hands blunt and serviceable, the sleeves of her sweater pushed above her elbows. She listened to my lies without interruption, bright blue eyes shining, her right thumb occasionally touching her right cheekbone, rubbing a narrow unfreckled line of a scar that angled across the cheekbone almost to her ear; the sort of flaw, I suspected, that would make her face even more lovely in smiling repose. Should she ever decide to smile at me.

"Which side were you on?" she asked when I finished the lie. "Criminal? Or cop?"

"A deputy sheriff once," I said, "and a private investigator later."

"And now?"

"Just a friend, I guess," I admitted. "Actually, I guess I was just trying to help a friend come up with . . . some version of revenge that we could live with."

"I can understand that," she said thoughtfully. Then she paused. "But you took the time to bring in the Lab. Why?"

"I couldn't leave her there," I said. "Did she survive the gunshot wounds?"

"If you'll hang around until I get off," she said, "I'll let you see for yourself just how well."

When she left the emergency clinic at eight, Betty Porterfield nodded at me without speaking, jerked her head for me to follow, then climbed into a battered Toyota four-wheel drive pickup and led me west for an hour or so while the rest of the norther blew itself out, led me through a little town called Blanco, across a low water crossing, then onto a dirt road. Six locked gates and two creek fords later, she stopped at the end of the road beside a tin-roofed stone house with a gallery running along the south side. The house sat on a bench on the side of a limestone ridge that overlooked a small, narrow valley with a clear-running creek down the middle. Except for a Quonset-hut-shaped barn built from rough cedar poles, all the other outbuildings were constructed from the same flat rock. Even the chicken house and the hog pens. Everything looked carefully used, I thought as I stepped out of the Beast, perfectly preserved and in its element.

Like Betty Porterfield. Who greeted me outside the Beast with a combat stance and the Ruger .40 automatic unwaveringly pointed at my thorax region.

"Assume the stance," she said quietly.

"Say 'please,' " I said.

"What?"

"Say 'please,' " I repeated. "I'm not in the habit of taking orders from people. With or without guns."

"Are you crazy?"

"Maybe."

"Assume the position!" she screamed. "Please! Before I blow your balls off!"

So I assumed the position. She patted me down carefully, not avoiding the afore-threatened gonads, then stepped back, still holding the pistol on me.

"I guess you're clean," she said. "But I couldn't watch you in the car, so I had to make sure."

"Change your mind on the way out, lady?" I asked, standing and facing her now.

"Not exactly," she said, "but I decided I wanted to hear the whole truth."

"It's not pretty," I said.

"Believe me, bud, I know some ugly stories."

So I told her most of the whole truth. She listened without flinching. Not even when I told her about the intrusion into the Laras' murder scene or Tipton's death. But she did slip the pistol back into the belt pack holster.

"So you're sort of a cop, sort of a criminal, sort of a fortune hunter . . ."

"My fortune," I pointed out, but she didn't smile.

". . . and seeking some sort of wild justice," she said. "So what did you want with me?"

"Just wanted to find out about the dog," I said, "and maybe hear your voice again . . ."

"Give it a rest," she said.

". . . and maybe convince you that I hadn't shot the dog."

"You at least did that," she said, "'cause if I thought you had, bud . . ."

"If I had, what?" I said.

"Maybe I would have taken you down to the spring hole, popped you there," she said, then looked at her scuffed cowboy boots, "gutted you, then filled your body with rocks. Drop your fucking land barge on East Sixth . . ."

"You can talk the talk, lady," I said, "but can you walk the walk?" I didn't know exactly what it meant, but Sughrue said it a lot.

"Bet on it," she said calmly, then pointed at a heart-sized rock twenty yards away already stained with lead fragments. "Watch this, Buster Brown," she said, then drew the pistol so quickly I didn't see her hand move and emptied the clip against the rock. The echoes filled the small valley. When they stopped, a thin whine came from the door of the house.

"Pretty impressive," I admitted, "but rocks aren't coming at you and don't shoot back."

"That won't bother me a bit," she said, replacing the empty clip, then turned toward the house, adding, "Let's see if Sheba remembers you, bud. While I rustle up some breakfast."

Betty scuffled random chickens and lazy cats out of the way, stepped up on the gallery, opened a screen door, and a black quivering mass circled her feet, whimpering and yipping with happiness as Betty scrubbed Sheba's head with her knuckles. Betty pointed at me, then escaped into the house. The Lab paused, then came for me, prancing and dancing with joy. I knelt to greet her, but her rush knocked me on my ass. Maybe she just recognized my supine posture, and maybe she just loved humanity in general, but she nuzzled and licked my face until she convinced me it didn't matter.

The screen door opened long enough for a tennis ball to bounce out. Sheba turned her attentions to the ball and let me get off the ground. But not off the hook. She dropped the ball at my boots and whined until I threw it. My arm wore out before she did, so I took refuge in the house.

The long, single room contained the kitchen, the living room, a futon against the far west end, and hundreds of books shelved along the walls. And a dozen sleeping cats. All the heat came from the wood cookstove, which Betty worked like a native, a compact sheepherder's stove at one end, and a stone fireplace at the other. No electric lights, no telephone, nothing from the modern world.

Breakfast smelled like nine hundred dollars. Betty poured coffee into a heavy mug, didn't offer cream or sugar, and waved me out of the way. I leaned against one of the rock pillars that held up the roof beam and watched Betty work. Her movements had an economy and grace that transcended beauty. I reached for a cigarette.

"Outside," she said without turning. "Please," she added, then gave me a smile that dimmed the winter sunshine.

During a breakfast of fried eggs from her free-range chickens and smoked venison sausage from her own smokehouse, neither of us spoke. We just sat across a handmade cedar table and ate in a comfortable silence until it was all gone. Then we took our coffee out on the gallery and sat quietly in carved cedar rocking chairs until long past noon.

"Thanks," I said. "That was great. And thanks for letting me see Sheba."

"Anytime," she said, leaning over to scratch Sheba's head. "Thanks for bringing her in."

"I've got to be going, and quite frankly I don't come this way much," I said, "but would you mind if I called the next time I'm in town?"

"Anytime," she repeated. "Call me at work. I'm there from ten to six, three nights a week, midnight to eight the other two." Then she stared across the valley and suddenly began to talk. "My great-great-grandmother and my great-grandmother were born in the barn over there. It used to be half-barn half-house. It was the Spivey place then. My grandmother and mother were born in this house. I was born in Breckenridge Hospital in Austin. My mother took up with a doctor's son who used to have a deer lease up here. That's all this land is good for—deer leases—but I don't need that money anymore." Then she paused. "Want some more coffee?" She went inside for the pot without waiting for my answer, filled our mugs, then put the pot back on the stove and stopped just inside the screen door. "I was going to be a doctor," she said, "but I lost my faith in humanity. When I was in . . . medical school."

"How's that?"

"You come back," she said, "maybe I can tell you. You've got a face a woman can talk to."

"Count on it," I said.

"Please," she said, then stepped out of the door and gave me another sunrise of a smile. "Be careful," she added, "and get the hell out of here. I've still got morning chores."

"Don't you ever sleep, lady?"

"Not in a long time, buster," she said, "not in a long time." She touched my cheek with her work-hardened hand, kissed me lightly with dry lips, then moved her hand to the back of my neck, held me for a moment, held me so hard I felt my bones creak, then shoved me roughly away.

Betty stomped to the end of the gallery, her hands stuffed tightly in the back pockets of her faded jeans, then turned angrily. "You better call me, you son of a bitch," she said, stalking back, "or I will shoot your sorry ass the next time." Then she chuckled and said, "I'll bet I'm not the first woman who threatened to shoot you." She laughed again. "Just the latest."

"I've been shot at," I admitted, "but never hit."

"We'll fix that," she said as she walked me quickly to the Beast, said goodbye without touching me again, then hurried off to her animal chores.

Back in Austin at the Hyatt, I called Sughrue at the store, but got Whitney instead. Laughing, she told me that they had a telephone now and gave the number, but when I tried it, nobody answered, so I called her back.

"Tell him I'm sorry," I said, "and . . ."

"Don't be, Milo, please. It was wonderful to have him back," she interrupted.

". . . I'll be in Fairbairn tomorrow night."

"Stay with us this time," she said. "It'll be all right."

So I agreed. Then slept until daylight, slept long enough to miss Betty at the clinic, slept long enough so that I didn't remember my dreams, then headed the Beast west one more time, faced with the endless expanse of West Texas again, armed only with a cooler full of Negra Modelo and a couple of ounces of a dead man's cocaine. It was enough to take me to Sughrue's front steps.

Part Four
Sughrue

Fucking Milo. First he dumps me at the store without a word, then shows up four days later a little bit haggard, road drunk, and half-coked, but he didn't act like a man who had been having fun. He didn't even argue with me when I offered him the guest room. Just said sure, now that we've got a telephone, then he took a forty-eight-hour nap, broken only by these mysterious midnight telephone calls that he won't talk about, a nap that wiped the circles from under his eyes but not the solemn look off his face. Then he pulls this other crazy shit.

The third morning Whitney takes Lester to the store with her so Milo and I can hammer out the next moves while we're sitting on the steps drinking coffee and watching the wet, cold wind work the brush.

"It smells like weather," I tell him.

"What would you think, Sughrue," he says, "if we gave up all this shit?"

"I don't know. Why?"

"I'm thinking," he says, "maybe I don't need all that money. Maybe you don't need revenge. Not like we did when we started."

"What's changed?"

"I don't know," he says. "I was just thinking—maybe we don't need this shit."

"I hate to point this out," I say, "but this was sort of your idea."

"Yeah, I know," he says. "Fuck it, let's just do it."

I don't have the heart to ask the old man exactly what it is we're doing.

It's snowing like mad at dusk when we reach El Paso. The local radio tells us that schools and businesses are closing and the city is buckling down for six or eight inches of snow in the next twelve hours.

I suggest we should change cars at the airport, perhaps pick up a four-wheel drive unit. Milo glances at me as if I'm crazy. Like most Montanans Milo has never seen a snowbank he couldn't bust through with a slick-tired worn-out beater and never seen an icy road he couldn't drive.

"You know," I say, "lots of people here are going to remember this car. And you. I'd like to be sure that Whitney and Lester stay out of this shit."

"Christ, Sughrue, you live three hundred miles from El Paso."

"West Texas only looks big," I say, "like Montana."

"You're right," he says, "I'm sorry," then takes the airport exit.

At two o'clock the next morning, one of the bartenders from Mateo's is facedown in a shallow snowbank and Milo is banging the other one's head against the running board of a rented Jeep Cherokee in a parking lot in the Upper Valley, and we don't even have a motel room yet. Shit, we haven't even had dinner yet.

I finally pull Milo off the bartender, shove him in the Cherokee, and flee through the blowing drifts down Doniphan to Mesa while the old man seethes with tequila and cocaine in the passenger seat.

"Jesus," I say, "there's an all-night taco place at Sunland Park. And maybe we can come up with a couple of rooms down at that Holiday Inn across from the racetrack. Or maybe we should drive up to Las Cruces."

"Whatever," he says. "I'm sorry, Sonny."

But it seems like a waste of time to forgive him. And god knows the bartenders probably won't call the police.

The fax from O'Bannion's lawyer only gives us the number of the pay phone and an address on the north end of Doniphan, and it takes us a little time to find the telephone hanging off the outside front wall of a neighborhood bar called Mateo's. We play it cool, we think, hanging out and sipping slow beers at the bar for a couple of hours, checking out the scene, a mixture of Chicano and Anglo working-class guys who don't have to go to work tomorrow, and chatting up the two bartenders, Rudy and Paul, who are splitting the shift behind the stick.

We're doing fine, I think, until the lanky blond cocktail waitress, a middle-aged charmer named Laurie, takes a shine to Milo, who leans on the bar next to her station.

"You know," she says to him while waiting for a drink order, "this white guy and this Mexican guy are takin' a leak out back in the irrigation canal one winter night, and you know how guys are standing around next to each other with their dicks in their hands—they kinda gotta say somethin' so the other guy don't think they're a fuckin' faggot.

"And you know, I'm sure, sir, how sometimes when you guys finish takin' a leak, you guys kinda shiver, you know, and it's colder than a witch's tit in a brass brassiere out back so the white guy really shivers. So he's zipping up while the Mexican guy is still draining his lizard and he turns and says, 'Pretty chilly.'

"'Thanks,' the Mexican guy says."

Then Laurie grabs her tray and sails off into the melee while Milo laughs like a madman.

"That's the funniest joke I ever heard," he says, sniffling.

"I've heard it," I say, then realize that the old fart has clipped a bit of Tipton's cocaine and has been in the john shoving it up his nose. Neither telling me nor offering me any. Both bad signs. Sometimes, when a guy stops thinking of the blow as the people's cocaine, he opens his mind to all sorts of greed and foolishness.

Then he elbows me in the ribs and points across the bar. "That's that tequila you've got, right? The one with the blue horseshoe?"

"Herradura," I say.

"By god, let's have a shot," he says, then offers Laurie one when she steps back to the waitress station.

"Let's not," I say, but it's too late by then.

About ten I manage to slip out the back door and drive down the street to a convenience store, where I call the pay phone outside. After about twenty rings, somebody picks up.

"Shoot," a male voice says.

"Tell them to call Tipton," I say, and give him an LA number.

"Gotcha," the voice says, "but they still owe me for the last one."

"You're covered," I say, then hang up.

Back in the bar, Laurie and Milo want to know if I've been outside freezing my chile in the snowstorm.

"I hear they're easier to skin after they're frozen," Laurie says, then honks wildly like a wounded goose. My faithful Russian companion joins her.

After about an hour of such hilarity I finally get Milo's attention and hand him the Jeep keys.

"Maybe you better do it," I say, "while you can still drive."

"Try to relax and have a little fun, Sughrue," he says, then stumbles toward the back.

I guess I don't care if he makes it this time, so I have a shot of Herradura of my own, but just as I finish it, the outside telephone rings. Rudy and Paul look at each other. After ten rings, Rudy grabs a pencil and paper, checks his shirt pocket for the earlier message, and heads outside. When he comes back a few moments later, he gives Paul a shrug, then they confer at the cooler, without, it seems, coming to any conclusion.

Milo returns a few moments later. Laurie wants to know if he's been playing in the snow.

"I haven't stuck my pecker in a snowbank since I left my third wife," he says, then laughs and orders more tequila.

"Remember what happened the last time you got drunk in El Paso," I remind him, foolishly.

"Don't you fucking worry about me, little buddy," he says, suddenly as sober and as mean as I've ever seen him. Then he nods to Laurie, and they disappear into the back rooms of the bar, only to return a few minutes later with shining eyes and snotty grins.

She takes off at one o'clock with a sad smile and an empty promise to meet her at Carrow's for breakfast. We manage to string out last call until we are the final customers in the bar.

Milo guns his last shot, chases it with a swallow of beer,

then stands and slaps a one-hundred-dollar bill on the bar. "I understand I owe you boys some money," he says soberly.

Rudy and Paul turn as one, Rudy from the cash register, Paul from the door. They aren't big guys, or even particularly tough-looking guys, but they've pounded their share of drunks in their time, so they aren't even vaguely worried or afraid.

"What's that for, sir?" Rudy asks. "You've already had last call."

"Twice," Paul says.

"For the telephone number," Milo says.

"I'm sorry, buddy," Rudy says, "but if Laurie didn't give you her number, I ain't about to. Now let's go." He comes quickly around the bar.

"For the telephone message," Milo says. "You guys didn't get paid last time. Isn't this enough?"

Rudy grabs the bill, stuffs it in Milo's shirt pocket, and says, "I don't know what the fuck you're talking about, buddy, but let's take it outside. Okay?"

"Take it easy," I say, "he's just drunk." Then realize that maybe I am, too. "We can talk about it tomorrow," I say.

"Right," Rudy says.

Milo is as docile as a kitten, letting Rudy lead him to the door, waiting silently for Paul to unlock it and usher us through. Then as we are all standing outside in the blowing snow, Milo tries once more for rationality.

"Look, guys," he says, "we know all about the telephone message drop. You can talk to us about it, even make a little bread on the side, but you can't . . ."

Rudy has had enough. He puts his hands on Milo, saying, "Get the fuck out of here, old man."

Rudy never even sees what hits him. Actually, neither do I. Milo bounces him off the front wall of the bar, breaking plaster with Rudy's head, and tosses him like a piece of garbage into the nearest snowbank. Before I can stop Milo, he has Paul down in the parking lot and has banged the kid's head against the Cherokee's running board so hard that I hope he's not dead.

But maybe it's all an act. When I pull at his shoulders, Milo comes away easily and doesn't resist when I open the passenger door and shove him inside. Neither does Paul, who's still dazed when I pick him up and brush the dirty snow off his shirt.

"You assholes be here at three tomorrow afternoon," I say, "and we'll figure this shit out."

"You fucking-A right we'll be here," Paul shouts, but he's talking into the north wind, looking in the wrong direction.

As I pull away, Rudy is gathering himself from the snow. And Milo is steaming in the seat beside me. Maybe it's not an act.

By the time we're checked into the Holiday Inn with our bundle of tacos, Milo is calm enough to convince me to call Laurie at Carrow's and apologize for our drunken absence. But even through the thick walls of our connecting rooms, I can hear the old man laughing drunkenly on the telephone. I'm glad Milo's happy. Hell, I'm happy to be alive. Not to be in jail.

But that doesn't last long. And the news isn't all bad.

The first piece of good news is that the DEA agents actually knock politely on our motel doors instead of breaking them down, which gives Milo time to dump the remains of the coke on the carpet and grind it with his foot, swallowing the wadded-up paper of the bindle, and gives me a long moment to lock the Airweight and the Browning Hi-Power inside the plastic carrying case. Unless they had real bad-guy warrants, we were fairly clean.

The second bit of good news is that they sent the suits. Or at least the sport jackets. Badly fitting ones designed for house apes instead of gorillas. But they ask for ID, say please before they casually toss the rooms, and don't cuff us for the ride down to interrogation.

They don't take us to the federal building. They take us to their compound, where they try to impress us with the technology they use to protect the border against the dreaded influx of drugs, stuff that didn't work worth a shit in Vietnam, either, then they lock us in separate clean, anonymous rooms and ply us with fairly decent coffee and greasy doughnuts. After a couple of hours, they drive us back to the motel before checkout time without asking me any questions. They act as if they already know all there is to know about me. And they probably do.

When I first came to El Paso, the DEA already had my name in their computers, thanks to a fucking lie from a drug lawyer in Meriwether who was supposed to be my oldest buddy from the war. Setting me up like a ninepin. Then when Joe Don Pines, that scum-sucking pig with more shadowy government connections than a Mexican power plant, went out his office window, the government bastards put a permanent star beside my name. But lucky bastard that I am, I came out of the mess with no warrants and Baby Lester on my hip.

At the motel, Milo doesn't say a word as we load our gear and check out, doesn't have anything to say until we finish our *huevos rancheros* at Victor's Cafe, then he says, "So much for keeping our heads down, Sughrue. Those assholes at Mateo's can wait. Let's go to Seattle."

"Can I at least call home?"

"Just don't tell her where you're going," he says calmly, then grabs the check and heads for the door.

It may be winter in El Paso, but Seattle is having something like Indian Summer on the edge of winter. When the flight circles into the landing pattern, the snowcapped Cascades and Olympics gleam in the moonlight, Rainier shines like another moon being sucked from the heart of the mountain range, and the Sound stretches among the dark islands like a sheet of hammered silver. Milo had made some calls while we laid over at Salt Lake and arranged for a rented Cadillac and two rooms at the Inn at the Market with the Milton Chester ID, the hotel to which Tipton placed one of his calls. The other, placed a few minutes later, had been to a restaurant, Campagne, which turns out to be just across a small courtyard from the hotel. As we check in we can see that the bar is still open, so Milo suggests a nightcap.

We ride up in the elevator to stash our gear, and I point out that Milo hasn't said a word about the DEA interrogation.

"Later," he says, and leaves it at that.

The small bar is fairly lively for midnight in the middle of the week, but we manage a couple of stools at the end of the bar, and Milo orders a couple of double baits of the Macallan, which makes the curly-headed blond bartender smile.

"The twelve-year-old or the eighteen, sir?" he asks.

"The twelve," Milo says. "Six ice cubes."

"That's my drink," the bartender says.

"So let's all have a taste," Milo suggests. And we do.

The customers seem mostly upscale and attractive kids, art and advertising yuppies perhaps, except for two large middle-aged men at a table who are sharing several bottles of champagne with a young girl with a notebook who seems to be interviewing them. The two guys—one in a chambray work shirt, the other in a ratty sweater—don't fit the scene, but they seem perfectly comfortable in it. They're either rich or famous or both. One of them has a wild eye that doesn't seem to point the same way as his face; the other, a large crooked nose with the same problem.

In the lull as the bartender changes the CD from Etta James to Johnny Cash, I hear the young girl ask, "Is it true that you guys once ate a whole deer by yourselves?"

The men chuckle in unison, then the one with the nose answers, "It was just a little deer." Then laughs wildly and orders another bottle of expensive French champagne.

We have a couple of more drinks waiting for the bar to clear out, as it does just before last call, except for the two guys at the table, abandoned by the young girl.

"I hope last call is a little calmer than last night," I say.

"So do I," answers Milo, then motions the bartender to fill our glasses one last time. When he's finished, Milo asks, "Were you working last Thursday night?" The bartender nods. "Do you remember somebody staying at the hotel getting a call just before midnight?"

Before the bartender can say anything, the answer comes from behind us. "That'd be that Howdy Doody motherfucker, Jim," the bent-nose gentleman says. "Ed Forsyth," he adds, unnecessarily, "but he left yesterday."

"The fucking DEA acts like they know everything," Milo says later as we have a final drink in his room, "but they don't. They're running some kind of scam on us. I just can't figure out what it is. Plus, they offered me a deal."

"A deal?"

"Right," he says, then pauses for a long time. "I roll over on you and I walk. On everything. Whatever everything is."

"What did you say?"

"I told them my lawyers could whip their lawyers," he says, chuckling. "But they bought it too quick, too easily. They've got something else in mind."

"What?"

"Well, I'm not sure, and that worries me. But they did suggest something pretty strange," he says, then takes a long pull on the Scotch.

"What?"

"They think your shooting is connected with my money."

"That doesn't make any fucking sense."

"They're not stupid," he says, "just narrow-minded." Then finishes his drink. "So we have to think about it."

"That's never been our long suit," I tell him, and he laughs as he hasn't in days. "And there's this, too," I add. "What's the connection between Eddie Forsyth and Aaron Tipton? I can't figure that out."

"Well," Milo says, "let's see. Connie's married to a banker with shady connections. Connie's dead, crooked brother-in-law is both a banker and connected to one of the border *familias*. Maybe Western art and banks are good places to hide drug money . . . Shit, I don't know."

"So why kill the fat woman? Keep her from singing?"

"And blow off her fingerprints and teeth," Milo adds. "And Tipton. Nothing fits, dammit. And I don't see any way to come up with the answers. Much as I'd love to bounce Eddie around again, he ain't the kind who's gonna give us shit.

"Maybe I'll just ask him straight," he says, "I've had a little luck lately not being either cute or mean."

"You mean like last night?"

"Oh, hell, those assholes didn't know anything," he says. "They're just a dead drop. And I lost my shit. I told you I was sorry. If you want, I'll go back and apologize."

"When?"

"Tomorrow night."

Then the telephone rings.

"Who the hell could that be?" I ask, but Milo just answers the telephone and tells the caller to hang on.

"So what am I supposed to do?"

"See if you can't get us on the early Delta flight, and I'll drop you at home tomorrow," he says. "And try to get a nap."

"You're the boss," I mutter as I go out the door, but Milo is already lost in his phone call.

And I discover that I don't mind the idea of home at all. Not one bit. Then it comes to me that perhaps Milo didn't tell me the whole story about his encounter with the DEA. But after his interrogation at the hands of the Kaufmann brothers, I'm careful about asking him any questions.

Part Five
Milo

SUGHRUE AND I HAD DOZED ON THE FLIGHT TO SALT LAKE, then again on the shorter hops to Albuquerque and on to El Paso. He hadn't even put up a token resistance when I dropped him at the store. So when he invited me to stay for an early dinner at the Lionheart, I accepted.

It was sort of a silent aimless meal. Since we didn't know anything, we didn't seem to have much to discuss. Whitney picked at her food and Baby Lester colored his placemat. Sughrue had gathered up a handful of newspapers at the store—Alpine, Fairbairn's slim weekly, Midland, Odessa, and El Paso—and rattled through them as we ate.

"So what do we do," he asked, "if Howdy Doody won't talk to you?"

"I don't know," I said, suddenly tired to the bone. "Maybe we should take a vacation. Stuff you and Whitney and Baby Lester in the Beast and let you guys show me this country," I said. Baby Lester liked the idea better than Whitney did. "I could get to like this desert shit, you know. Maybe we should call up Kate, too. Take the kid to dinner, then fly her to Montana. Hell, I don't know. Maybe we should all go to Mexico for a real vacation."

"You want to quit again? What the hell are you thinking about?" he asked me quietly. "You can't afford to let this go."

"Maybe I can," I said, wondering how to leave Sughrue permanently behind, then glanced at Whitney and Baby Lester, but they were lost in a Little Golden Book. "The guy who did you is dead . . ."

"That's what they say."

". . . and my father's money is gone with the goddamned wind, so maybe we should just relax."

"Right," he said bitterly. "Listen, man, if you're afraid to brace Forsyth, I'll do it."

"I don't think you have the right to say that to me, kid."

"Hell," he continued, his voice a bitter snarl now, "maybe even take *real* jobs. You and me, man, we could chase bail jumpers for Harim. Or maybe even go to work as security guards." Then he rattled through the newspapers again and held up the classified ads. "Those Hollywood jerks," he said, "that Rattlesnake Productions, they're taking bids for a qualified security outfit. We qualify, right?" Then he crumpled up the paper. "Fuck you, man. Maybe you started this shit, but by god I'm not afraid to finish it."

"If you boys have to have another fistfight to make friends," Whitney said, "get yourselves a new audience and leave me the hell out of it." Then she and Baby Lester hit the door like people running from a fire.

"I get the point," I said, tossing my napkin on the table. "I'll be back in a couple of days and we'll finish this shit."

"But your heart's not in it anymore, man."

"I left my heart in San Francisco, dipshit."

"Or outside Columbus, New Mexico," he said suddenly, not smiling, "along with your nuts."

I took a deep breath, and we stared at each other over the dead silence. "Your call," I said, "in the parking lot, in the desert where you hide, or on the fucking moon."

Sughrue sighed, rubbed his face as if he could wipe the stubble off his face. "Hey man, I'm sorry," he said. "I don't know what the fuck I'm thinking about."

"That's fairly clear."

"Look, I'm going to loan you the Airweight, man," he said, "and I want you to promise me that if that Howdy Doody motherfucker comes at you, you put him down. Put five rounds in him without a single fucking word."

I didn't say yes. But I didn't say no, either. I guess we'd been spending too much time together. But whatever had almost happened was over.

"By the way," he added softly, "Whitney says Kate's been calling. Every day. Why don't you stop by?"

"Maybe," I said, then paid the check and climbed into the Beast. In my rearview mirror, it looked as if Sughrue and Whitney were shouting at each other in the fading light. It was probably my fault, but I didn't have either the time or the energy to try to fix it.

Since I had all night on the interstate no matter what, I decided to drop in on Kate. Once again the ranch house looked deserted. The General seemed to be asleep at the wheel of his large pickup parked at the far corner of the house. The Rattlesnake Productions 4Runner was parked at the front door, and the old *vaquero* squatted on his heels, leaning against the wall. The cowboy gave me a brief smile as I climbed out of the Beast, took the thin, hand-rolled cigarette out of his drooping moustache, spit off the porch, then spit a mouthful of Spanish at me, *"Que quiere tu, gringo?"*

"Kate," I said. I had been listening to Sughrue's border tongue and reviving my teenage dreams of Robert Jordan's Spanish Civil War. *"Es aqui?"*

"Peladita," he said, laughing, "the little bald one." Then he banged on the door once with his fist.

As if she had been waiting behind the door, Suzanne opened it quickly. She'd dressed in black again, cowboy boots this time, crinkly new black Levi's, jeans and jacket, an expensively aged work shirt, and a silvery silk scarf knotted at her long smooth column of neck. She touched the scarf with professionally red nails and asked in a hard flat voice, "Can I help you?"

"Is Katie around?"

The woman narrowed her eyes, then turned without answering me. "Katherine!" she shouted. She walked back into the dark empty hollow of the house without inviting me through the wide-open doorway. She settled herself in a director's chair before a laptop computer at the large table in the dining room. Sam Dunston and the preppie kid sat on the other side. The click of her nails on the laptop keys filled the silence of the house for several minutes. Then the woman glanced up, her eyes as hard as malachite chips, staring at me as if she had never seen me before.

"Katherine!" she shouted again. Her partners flinched. "Gentleman caller!" She made the phrase sound like "white trash."

Kate danced out of the kitchen doorway, music clamped on her ears, a can of Tecate beer in one hand, a bomber joint in the other, wearing a long, yellow T-shirt that said FUCK KARMA . . . on the front, and on the back . . . BEFORE IT FUCKS YOU.

"Uncle Grandpa," she squealed when she saw me, then boogied over and threw her arms around my neck. "Where the fuck you been, man?" she whispered, then added loud enough for her sister to hear, "You got any blow, Daddy-O?"

I didn't even bother to answer.

Kate introduced me to the *vaquero,* Juan-Jose, who drifted silently away, oddly shy and polite now, then Kate waved at her sister. "Say hello," Kate said. Suzanne gave us a sixteenth of an inch of a cold smile.

"She's been working in Hollywood too long," Kate said by way of explanation. "She doesn't have time to be polite. So fuck her. Listen, we're having a big fajita cookout for my birthday Sunday week, so you gather up that worthless Sughrue and his wife and kid and make them come . . ."

"Katherine," Suzanne said quietly. "It's a private party."

Kate ignored her. "She's bringing her *stars* and her famous ass wipes," she burbled, "and she's afraid the great unwashed will ask them for autographs and all that gooey, goony shit . . ." Kate paused for breath, then addressed her sister out of the corner of her mouth. "Mr. Milodragovitch is too rich to be an asshole . . ."

"I'm sure, sister dear . . ." Suzanne said without looking up from the screen.

"I promise I won't ask for any autographs," I said, catching Kate's high, "unless I can have nekkid pitchurs, too."

". . . and it is *my* birthday."

Without looking up from her laptop computer, Suzanne smirked, "Only by accident."

I led Katherine out to the car and we climbed into the front seat so I could make a small bindle of Tipton's blow for her.

"How's it going, kid?" I asked.

"Same as always," she said. "Shooting and screaming; barking and backbiting . . ."

"Your dad and Suzanne?"

"And me in the middle," she said softly. "It's always been bad but it's the worst it's ever been." Then she paused. "I think my father's got money in this movie deal . . ."

"How's that change things?" I asked.

"You don't know the General and money," she said. "The ranches sometimes cost more to run than they make, and his retirement doesn't go as far as it's supposed to . . . Hell, I don't know. He's always been funny about money."

"Katie, honey," I said, folding the bindle into her hand, "you hang on, and if I'm back from Austin in time, we'll be here for fajitas. And maybe even a couple of laughs."

Then the kid almost smiled as she hugged me goodbye, scattering tears on my neck, whispered "Come back," and fled back into the house. It made me wonder why some families didn't just get out of each other's hair. Even those who didn't have any.

I had my hand on the ignition key of the Beast when the General wandered toward me from the far side of his pickup with a bottle in his hand. I climbed out to at least say hello.

"Mr. Milodragovitch," he said politely, "I've never probably thanked you for bringing Kate home. Thank you. You have any children?"

"No," I lied. I saw no reason to discuss my life with the General.

"They'll break your heart," he said, then raised a dusty bottle to his lips. He must have gone deep into his cellar for it. Then he offered it to me. "I'm sure Kate told you that I have a wonderful cellar. This is a Napoleon, an 1846, I think, out of Somasa's basement. As an officer and a gentleman, can I offer you a knock . . ."

"No, thanks," I said, "I wasn't an officer."

"I must apologize for the lack of a snifter," the General drifted on, "but somehow it seemed superfluous on a day like this . . ."

"A day like this?" I said.

"One of my daughters is as mean as a rabid fox," he muttered, "and the other a stone dyke . . . I wonder what I did to deserve this . . ." He didn't want an answer. He sat down on the raised sill of the porch. "I know you weren't an officer," the General said out of nowhere, turning his lean, weathered face to look up at me. "You were a child, a goddamned child . . ."

"True enough," I said. I had turned sixteen in basic and

seventeen huddled in a cold, muddy trench. "But how did you know that, sir?"

The General grinned slyly. "I've still got friends at the Pentagon, you know."

"I'm sure you do," I said. Like most investigators I didn't like people digging into my past. "But what's the point?"

"You mind if I ask you a personal question?" the General asked, suddenly almost sober as he raised the bottle. Before I could answer, he asked, "You've been in combat, right? It changes a man, doesn't it? I missed Korea and Vietnam, but I saw a bit of trouble during my years in Central America. Enough to know that it changes a man, makes him a better man . . ." The old man stood up and wandered over to lean on the fender of the Beast.

"That wasn't my experience, sir," I said, which was true. "I knew a bunch of World War II combat vets in my outfit. Some of them were great guys. Some of them were pieces of shit wearing stars and bars and stripes. But what's the point? It was a long time ago."

"No point," he said calmly, then drinking, "but what the hell, let's have a drink. We'll never have another chance . . . well, you'll never have another chance because I'm going to drink the whole son of a bitch." Then he raised the bottle to his lips and had a decent taste. "Goddamn," he said, trying without much success to be one of the guys, "if pussy were honey and it was on fire, it'd taste like this."

The General offered me the dusty bottle again, and this time like a fool I took it. His estimation of the brandy wasn't too far off. Nor my estimation of the foolishness of having a drink with him.

"Have another," he said. "You've brought Katie home, and I owe you . . . more than you know."

So I had another knock. Perhaps the brandy should have been served in a candle-warmed snifter—I don't know—but even out of the bottle it made me feel as if I should be wearing a morning coat, a top hat, and an ascot, a woman on my arm as lean and troublesome as an Afghan hound.

"Nice," I said.

"Have another," the General said, and I did. But when I handed the bottle back to him, he asked, "I'm sure Katie told you that the bastards tried to indict me over that Iran-Contra mess?"

"She mentioned something about it," I said carefully.

"A lot of great soldiers—combat soldiers, great Americans—were tarred with that ugly brush, you know," the General said, handing me the brandy again. "Tarred by bastards who never heard the sound of gunfire," he added. "I'll never feel the same about this country again . . . Those soldiers did their duty."

"I'm not sure I believe duty included lying to Congress . . ."

Before I could finish, the General grabbed the bottle out of my hand. "What the hell do you know about it?" he asked.

I hesitated with my answer. He was Katie's dad.

"What?" he asked. "What the hell you know about duty?"

"Not much," I said, taking the bottle back without his offering it, "But I did what I thought was my duty . . ."

"But you never led men, never faced the insidious political problems . . ."

"That's true, sir," I answered, then had another hit of the brandy. "General," I said, "forgive me for being blunt. But I spent ten months in Korea serving in a line infantry outfit and goddammit I did my duty . . ." I had to stop to get a breath and hold back the unbidden anger. "But it didn't make me a fucking liar."

"But it was a different time," the General said, almost begging, "the rules were different."

As always the West Texas sky was moving. Clouds and light and hope for rain. I wrapped the cognac in his hand. He didn't resist.

"The rule is," I said, "you eat their salt and do their bidding but you don't fucking lie for them when they fuck up." There seemed to be a dark moment when the General had a light in his eye as he told me, "You've never been in charge. You don't know what the hell you're talking about."

People in charge have been telling me this shit all my life.

Think of it this way: you're in the third wave at Tarawa, and some dolt misread the tide, so your landing craft lodges on the reef; every second Marine in your LST dies during the thousand-yard struggle through the surf; or you're trapped on

that black slithering sand at Iwo Jima and some fucking nut
in a tank runs over your buddy; or it's Korea when the pow-
ers that be decide that jets can do close infantry work; you
put out the purple panels and the smoke of the day, and still
the F-86s come slithering through your positions, hammering
you with rockets and .50-caliber rounds as big and ugly as
your thumb; or your squad had laagered on a ridge in In-
dochina, eating some shit out of a can left over from a war
nobody remembers, and some kid who flunked out of East
Jesus State misreads the elevation on the 81mm and everybody you knew on this tour has turned to bloody puddles
without ironic final lines.

"I don't mean to be impolite, sir," I said politely, "but I
saw more atheists in foxholes than I did Republicans."

"I'm not sure what that means," he said, then smiled like a
man for whom foxholes were an abstract notion.

"I'm not sure, either," I said. "You take care, sir."

So I nodded goodbye and climbed into the Beast leaving
him with his bloody bottle, thinking perhaps I needed a long
rest and a detour to Blanco.

I had to wonder, though, if perhaps Sughrue wasn't right: I
was afraid to face Howdy Doody. I was supposed to have
come home from the war years ago. But sometimes it follows you home like a bad dog.

During the long drive to Betty's house I took the time to
reconsider the DEA encounter in El Paso one more time. I
hadn't exactly told Sughrue the whole story. If I had, there
would be no way to leave him behind when I had to cross the
border. And I had resolved, during the interview with the
DEA agent, to do just that.

The agent—a tall, lanky bald man in his fifties, a knobby
piece of work, more gristle than muscle—who finally let
himself into the small interrogation room, introduced himself
as "Chuck Johnson."

"This is going to be your copy," he said in a soft southern
voice as he pulled a microcassette recorder from his pocket
and placed it on the table between us and switched it on.
Then he held out his broad hand, which I ignored. He actually looked hurt. "It's going to be that way, huh?"

"You're fucking right," I said, "Mr. . . . What was your name? Hiram Walker? Or was that Fred Flintstone? And please. Tell me that's the only recording device in this room. Jesus, give me a break."

"Mr. Milodragovitch," he said quietly, propping a hip on the table, "of course this isn't the only recording device in the room. But everything else is turned off. That's why I want you to have your own copy."

I was interested by this ploy. So I played along, checked the tape and the sound level, then replaced it between us.

"Now what?" I said.

"First, don't fuck with me. A couple of dances with me, and you'll be begging for the Kaufmann brothers."

"Who's that?"

The agent stood up, turned in a quick, frustrated circle, then slammed his palms on the table and leaned into my face. "Listen, you dumb son of a bitch," he hissed, "I'm not some fucking bureaucrat with a gun. I got more time on the street than you got in the crapper, and I know everything there is to know about you and your jerk-off buddy, Sughrue. Everything. You fuck with me and you two will never see daylight again . . ."

"Why don't you just cut the pissant melodrama and tell me what you want?"

After a long pause and the deep, hard-bitten sigh of a man too long in a shitty, losing war, "I want Emilio Kaufmann alone on this side of the border," he said calmly.

I let that one lay there. But something sick and greasy slipped among my viscera as I waited for his explanation.

"Listen," he said, "this isn't your usual border trash snake-shit. I can't touch him in Mexico. He's one slick son of a bitch. Our own Special Forces trained him when he got out of high school and he served a couple of training tours in Central America before he came back to the States to do a Ph.D. in pharmacology from the University of Washington, a Harvard MBA—his family owed the Cruz Azul chain of drug stores—so he's damned smart, dirt mean, and without conscience."

"Sounds like Superman's evil twin, Skippy," I suggested.

"Smarter and tougher than that," he said. "Most of the cocaine that arrives in America is transhipped through northern Mexico. Emilio Kaufmann controls most of the cocaine that crosses the border in this sector. He's done it for years, survived all the changes in the Colombian drug lords because he's the best at what he does. And he's especially hardnosed. He loses a shipment, everybody connected with it dies. Everybody. And all their families. And he's heavily connected politically, virtually unindictable on either side of the border."

"Send in the troops," I suggested. "That worked with Noriega. Like a charm."

"Hey, asshole, don't make jokes when you don't know the whole story."

"Right," I said, "since I'm a civilian, I'll never know the whole story. So what the hell does the DEA want with Kaufmann?"

"It's this way, Mr. Milodragovitch," he said pleasantly. "We have it from a very reliable source that Kaufmann is about to change businesses. From smuggling to designer drugs."

"So?"

"Word is that he's perfected a new drug that can be smoked, ingested, or injected. The high of cocaine, the peace of heroin, and the price of crack," he said. "Think what the inner cities will look like once that hits the street."

"Right," I said, "chaos, war, and the DEA budget triples. Quit blowing smoke up my ass, Mr. Jack Daniels. What does the DEA really want?"

After a long pause, he decided to tell me another version of the truth. "Not the DEA, Mr. Milodragovitch," he said, sighing, then sat down. "Me. I want him. Kaufmann has only made two mistakes in his life. Some years ago he killed a man on the docks in Puentarenas, Costa Rica. In broad daylight. An American tourist, a young girl on a trip with her Sunday school, took a videotape film of the murder. Her father was a police officer in Reston, Virginia, and she was a tough kid. She stayed calm, took steady pictures of the killing." Then the agent paused, sighed again, and I didn't have to ask who the young girl was. "Kaufmann killed her, too," he continued quietly. "Through a long series of misadventures, the tape recently came into my hands. If I can get him to Costa Rica, I've got his ass forever. For-fucking-ever."

"What was his other mistake?" I asked.

"What? After Harvard, he applied for American citizenship. His father kicked him out of the legitimate *familia*. That's when he showed up in Enojada to take up with his mother's family, the Hurtados, who own the Castellano Ranch."

"What makes you think I can do something by myself that you can't do with the whole fucking government behind you?" I asked. Then when he didn't answer, I said, "Let me answer that for you. Because he's a CIA asset, right?"

"I wouldn't know anything about that," he said slowly.

"Jesus," I said. "What the hell was he doing with the Special Forces in Central America?" He didn't answer. "Okay, what do I get out of this?"

"Well, let me see. First, I can keep Sughrue out of prison."

"What?"

"Some of my colleagues took the mysterious death of Joe Don Pines pretty seriously," he said. "So there's been a lot of overtime hours put into that investigation. Unofficially, you understand."

"And?"

"I lucked into the key," he said. "The fat boy who brokered Sughrue the bamboo vipers got popped in Vegas when I happened to be there. Ten ounces of primo blow. Enough for twenty-five years without parole. So Mr. Dahlgren sang me a sad song. It wasn't hard after that. I've even got the guy who made the copies of the clay ducks he used to get the snake into Joe Don Pines office . . ."

"The Mexican Tree Ducks," I said to nobody in particular.

". . . and I've even got the guy who stole the UPS truck he used to deliver the packages . . ."

"Okay," I said. "You've made your point. What do I get?"

"What do you get? Well, just let me just say that Sughrue's shooting in New Mexico and your missing money are directly connected . . ."

"What the hell does that mean?"

"That means that maybe I can show you how to get your money back."

"I wish I believed you."

"You better believe me," he said quietly. "You don't have any choices anymore." Then he reached into his jacket pocket, brought out a small leather packet and an 800 number on a slip of paper, which he handed to me. "This is the works. The same drug the Kaufmanns used on you. He'll be immobile for at least four hours. And you can reach me at this number anytime. Day or night. And I'll meet you at the Castillo airstrip within the hour."

"Why don't you just let us shoot him? Hell, given the right weapon, Sughrue can probably stick a round in his ear at eight hundred yards."

"Dead's too easy. I want the bastard in a cell in Costa Rica."

"Let me guess," I said. "You're getting close to retirement, right? And maybe the Costa Rican federal police need an experienced American cop . . ."

"I wouldn't know anything about that," he said again.

"Perfect," I said, glanced at the number on the slip of paper, then popped it into my mouth, chewed, and swallowed it.

"What the hell are you doing?"

"Eating the evidence," I said.

He laughed, honestly. "I guess that's better than stuffing it up your nose . . ."

We stood up. Once again he reached out his hand. And once again I ignored it.

"Listen, buddy, I don't know what you're after, but you fucking people make me crazy," I said. "You want to win the war on drugs? It's fucking simple. Take the goddamned money out of it. Legalize the shit. No money, no crime. No harm, no foul. Declare the war won, and let's go home. If you really want to help, take your budgets and give them to jobs programs and rehab hospitals . . ."

"Simpleminded liberal bullshit!" he snarled. "You don't know what the hell you're talking about."

"Well, that makes two of us, sir," I said. "You keep your people out of my way, and I'll see what I can do. But you fuck with Sughrue, and I'll spend the rest of my life and all my money making your life a living hell. Remember, I've got nothing to lose. Absolutely nothing."

"You can say that again," he said, then led me out of the room.

As they drove me back to the motel I wondered what had happened to that teenager who couldn't wait to get to war, who had raised his hand to swear allegiance to country and Constitution and commander-in-chief. I also wondered what had happened to said country, Constitution, and president that had left the sullied and aged remains of that teenager feeling as if he possessed some of the last bits of moral integrity in this troubled world. Or perhaps I was just wondering, *Why me?*

"Looks like you're going to have an open winter," I said to Betty Porterfield as we sat on her gallery sipping slow morning beers and rocking. I had nearly killed myself getting there but had made it in time to meet her at the first gate for the beginning of her weekend. It had been a long time since I wanted to see a woman that badly. A very long time.

"What's an open winter?" she said.

"No snow."

She laughed quietly, a sound that made the six-hundred-mile drive worthwhile. "Sleet or freezing rain is about as close as we usually come to snow, bud," she said, then tucked a stray strand of fine red hair behind her ear and looked away, adding so softly I almost didn't hear it, "But you should hear it on the tin roof."

"I think I'd like that."

She turned back to stare at me and considered that. Sheba stirred briefly on the top step, then stretched out in the weak sunshine, one eye on me, one eye on the Rock Island Red hens pecking and scratching in the pale dust of the front yard, their soft peeping voices murmuring through the cool morning air. A thin cloud of cedar smoke from the banked fire in the cookstove filtered across the small valley.

"Maybe," she said, then looked away again.

"I thought you said 'anytime,'" I answered lightly.

"That was breakfast," she said, perhaps more sharply than

she meant. We were like a pair of sore-footed old geldings testing our friendship in a new corral.

"It was good," I said, "thanks again. But I've got a bunch of shit I'm supposed to be doing, and if you don't want me here . . ."

But she watched the woodsmoke drift toward clarity and didn't respond for a long time, then she pondered the hens and said, "You know how I keep Sheba off the chickens?"

"Force of will," I said, and got the beginnings of a smile.

"I let her kill one," she said, "then I tied the feet around her neck and let the dead chicken hang there until it rotted off. She'd starve to death before she'd eat an egg."

"Are you as tough as you sound?" I asked.

"Is anybody?" she asked, then thought about it and smiled. "Maybe I am, though," she said. "I've seen some shit."

"Is that why you dropped out of medical school?"

"Maybe," she answered. "Maybe. I told you I lost my faith in humanity. A long time ago. People bother me. Shit, I can't even deal with people enough to have a normal small animal practice. But other than that, bud, I'm plenty tough."

"Hell, I've dug my own grave," I said, trying to sound light again.

"Haven't we all," she said calmly, then stood up and walked to the end of the gallery, slowly this time, then turned around. "Let's lie down," she said softly, "to sleep."

"I thought you didn't sleep," I said.

"I think I need to," she answered, then walked over to touch my nose with her finger. "Can you?"

"I can try."

"Cocaine makes me nervous," she said. "I don't like it very much."

"Me either," I said, "but it was the only way I could get here as quickly as I did."

"You could have flown."

I hesitated for a long time, then told her the truth. "I don't want to be on record as having checked a handgun." Sughrue had loaned me his Airweight, and I still had the Glock hidden in the trunk of the Beast. "It could come back on me."

"Are you here to kill somebody?" she asked, suddenly serious again.

"Not unless I have to," I said. "It's not much fun."

"It's not much fun even when it's supposed to be," she said without explanation. "Humanity, decency—it's not all it's cracked up to be." Then Betty took me by the hand and led me into the house and across the kitchen to the corner where the futon rested. Sheba followed with soft clicking footsteps on the plank floor, then curled up on the bottom of the futon. The dog tried to stay as still as I did as we waited for Betty to lie down.

She didn't even take off her boots as she stretched out beside me on the futon and rested her head on my shoulder. She talked into my neck, telling me the sorry story about how she lost her faith in humanity.

She was in her second year of medical school in Houston, a fairly normal young woman, raised by decent people, her dad a pediatric cardiologist, her mother a good country woman without pretensions, and Betty was in love with and engaged to a young black med student from Conroe, who was himself raised by decent people, his dad a high school principal and his mother a third-grade teacher.

Then early one evening Betty answered the doorbell. The young black man she saw through the peephole wore a three-piece black suit and a rep tie and carried an expensive leather briefcase. An insurance salesman, perhaps, or a graduate student taking a survey. And to inquire might seem a betrayal of the man she loved and planned to marry. So she took the door off the chain and opened it.

"Then once it was opened," she said softly, "he hit it with his shoulder, hit it hard enough to knock me down in the middle of the living room.

"He grabbed my hair and dragged me to the bedroom and threw me across the bed before I knew what was happening," she said, "then he took out a pissant little twenty-two derringer—Christ, I had a thirty-eight Colt Detective Special in the night table drawer that my mother had given me and taught me to shoot—but he took this cheap little fucking toy pistol and stuck it in my ear and told me that if I did everything he wanted, he wouldn't kill me, told me in a very calm, almost amused and highly cultured voice, then he asked me please not to make him kill me.

"Hey, what the hell," she continued, turning away from me, "I was a grown-up lady, bud, I wasn't some prudish country girl, so I said 'Okay, but please don't hurt me,' and he agreed so nice and polite.

"Jesus fucking Christ, what a fool I was. Shit, I even apologized for pissing my pants when he started hurting me, my breasts, and he let me go to the bathroom and clean up, let me change the sheets, but then he hurt me, hurt me bad, and hurt me for what seemed hours.

"Oh, Christ did he hurt me," she said as calmly as she could, but even Sheba heard the tone in her voice. The dog crept up from the bottom of the futon and licked her face. Betty pushed Sheba away, then apologized to the dog, turned away from me, and gathered Sheba's muzzle to her face, then Betty tried to go on in a normal tone as she rubbed Sheba's face and pulled at her loose underlip.

"You know she has a number tattooed on her lip," she said, "but it wasn't an American Kennel Club number. I checked." Then she paused for a long breath and went on with the story, hugging Sheba's body to hers.

"Oh, shit, he was huge and iron hard," she whispered, "and he stuck that goddamned thing in me over and over again. Any place he could find a hole. Oh, hell, bud, I was bleeding everywhere, even my throat was full of blood, and I tried and tried to get him off, anything to make him come and stop, please stop."

"Then he stopped and told me what I had to do to make him come," she said, then paused. "I had to believe he was going to kill me or he couldn't come. Christ, he was crying and apologizing when he told me that, but he told me that if he didn't believe me, he was going to kill me, and I guess I believed him. He stuck that shitty little gun in my mouth and jacked off over my face. He demanded that I watch him, told me that if I closed my eyes when he came, he'd pull the trigger.

"I guess I didn't care by then," she said. "I just wanted him gone, and I was willing to do anything to have him gone. So I did what he said, did it without complaint. And then, then the worst part, the fucking worst part.

"He got a warm washrag and cleaned my face, cleaned it

as if I were a baby, kissing his come and my tears off my face," she said as she rolled toward me again, then grabbed my beer and guzzled the rest of it, and turned away from me. I eased her back into the circle of my arm.

"I guess I was still crying," she continued, "as he got dressed, because the bastard stood there at the end of my bed and asked me in this perfectly normal voice why I was crying. I don't know what I answered, but it must have been wrong, because the bastard smiled sadly, then took the fucking little twenty-two out of his coat pocket and shot me in the face. Shot me right in the face, then laughed and tucked that piece-of-shit pistol in his coat pocket."

Betty shrugged off both Sheba and me again, sat up against the wall, and hugged a pillow to her chest. Then she touched the faint scar across her cheekbone.

"I don't know what would have happened to me if he hadn't shot me," she said, her voice muffled by the pillow. "Just don't know. And don't know what would have happened if that twenty-two short hadn't glanced off my cheekbone and skated around to my ear, if it had punched through the sinus as it should've and scrambled my brains. Don't know."

Betty was silent, her face buried in the pillow, so long that I finally asked, "What happened?"

She raised her head, glared at me as if I were mad, and said, "I jerked the thirty-eight out of the nightstand drawer and put two rounds into his butt before he got to the bedroom door," she said calmly, "then I put another one between his shoulder blades as he scuttled toward the living room. Then I leaped out of bed, kicked him until he rolled over, then I called him a 'fucking nigger' and shot him in the face. Twice. Then put the derringer in his hand and called the police."

Betty threw the pillow aside, jerked the ribbon out of her hair, and tossed it as if she were trying to scalp herself.

"I don't know," she said, cocking her face at me. "It was just like shooting myself . . . I might as well have shot myself."

"Well, you're sure as hell a good enough shot," I said, trying for an echo of her line the first morning I'd been out at her place. But it was the wrong note.

And oh, hell, was I sorry. Before I knew what was happening I was politely but coldly escorted out the door and into the Beast.

The last thing she said was: "Don't call me, you son of a bitch, and I won't have to hang up on you."

Blame it on the coke, I told myself as I drove away, or blame it on an innate lack of sensitivity in my character, or blame it on the fucking bossa nova. Whatever, I was looking forward to visiting with Mr. Ed Forsyth.

As I drove toward Kerrville, sleet began to rattle my windshield, and I almost felt sorry for Ed Forsyth. The Chicano kid had warned us that Forsyth was a sucker puncher, and I planned to be the puncher rather than the sucker. I slipped the sap into the liner pocket of my jacket. But I never got it out.

The desk clerk at the motel remembered me, so she told me that Mr. Gish had died and then she called Connie up at the house, who said come on up, so I did.

Ed Forsyth greeted me at the front door with his goofy smile, then escorted me into the living room to see the "grieving widow." As we waited for Connie, he even made me a drink. But when I reached for the sap as if reaching for a cigarette, Eddie tried to kill me without another word.

I managed to roll over the couch, land on my feet, and chunk the heavy crystal glass at him before Forsyth leaped the couch and planted the heel of his boot in the middle of my sternum, then landed lightly, bouncing on his toes. When I recoiled off the stone wall, it felt as if my heart had stopped. What the hell, surely I was dead. Forsyth was fifteen years younger, thirty pounds heavier, and had a worse attitude than Sughrue.

"I'm gonna let you up, old man," he said, his goofy grin sparkling, " 'cause you're easy."

"Thanks," I whispered. I didn't realize I'd been lying down so I levered myself off my side and wobbled to my feet in front of him. "Come on," I said hoarsely, "you Howdy Doody motherfucker."

"Stop it, Eddie," came Connie's tired voice from the back of the room.

I got in a single right hook somewhere near his kidney before I blocked his sweeping kick with my left arm. Even blocked, the kick seemed to crush most of my remaining unbroken ribs. Crashing into the bar took care of the rest of them.

"Eddie!" came a shout. Out of the corner of my eye I saw that Connie had snatched a small stainless steel automatic pistol out of her purse.

But Forsyth ignored it, grinned more broadly, and came after me. I lifted a bar stool between us, feet aimed at him, but Forsyth chopped the rungs out of it without effort, leaving me holding a bundle of kindling, which I tossed into the air, then tried to kick him in the crotch. He twisted slightly and caught my foot on the rock-hard slab of his thigh, then came on, knocking me to the floor with another leg sweep.

"Eddie!" Connie screamed.

"Fuck you, bitch," he answered half-turning, still grinning at me.

Perhaps if he hadn't called her "bitch" Connie might have fired a warning shot over his head. As it was, she fired the whole clip at him. Mostly she missed. But one of the rounds caught him right in the side of his cheek and blew his toothy grin all over me as I scrambled once again to my feet.

Losing most of his teeth distracted Forsyth long enough for me to brain him with a heavy silver ice bucket.

"Are you all right, Montana?" Connie asked, her voice shaking as she sat down on the floor, legs akimbo.

"Fine," I said, not really believing it. "What about you? You ever shot anybody before?"

"No, but I knew I wouldn't have any trouble pulling the trigger."

"Good thinking," I said, trying to draw a breath without bone splinters stabbing my lungs.

"Is he dead?" she asked.

"Probably not," I said, "but he's sure fucked up."

One of the Chicanos showed up before the echoes of the gunshots rattled out the broken plate-glass window.

"Get that *chingadero* out of here, please," Connie said, slipping the .25 back into her purse and standing up. "He's bleeding on a thirty-five-thousand-dollar rug. And call an ambulance."

"Do all the women in Texas carry guns?" I asked.

"Just the ones who count," she answered. "What the hell did you want with Eddie?"

"I just wanted to talk to him," I said, "but I don't . . ."

"I think I've got enough clout in this town to make a good case for an accidental shooting," Connie said, more to herself than me, or to the two kids dragging Forsyth off the rug. She grinned broadly when she saw his ruined mouth. "And he'll probably be ready to talk when he gets out of the hospital."

"Don't worry about it," I said. "I think I know almost everything I need to know." Which was true. Somehow kneeling there in that cloud of blood and dental dust, the key fell into place and the lock turned as if oiled with money. "Except for one thing. Did Ray Lara ever work for your husband?"

"First job out of the Army," she said. "Rincon Norte State Bank in El Paso."

"Hey, Connie, many thanks," I said by way of goodbye. "And even more thanks for taking Eddie off my back."

"Anytime," she said with a casual wave, as if this had been all in a day's work. And perhaps for Consuela Navarro of Del Rio, Texas, it was.

A couple of hours later with my new knowledge and sore old body, I eased into Austin, rented a cellular telephone, then checked into the Hyatt again. The telephone was important. It allowed me to sit in the Jacuzzi and make dozens of telephone calls while the hot, swirling waters worked the aches and pains. At least the ones on the outside. It had taken too many telephone calls before Betty Porterfield returned one, and our conversation had been heartbreakingly brief. But once that was done, the rest was easy, except for two quick trips—one back to Meriwether, where the weather was anything but, and another down to sultry, sandy Port Arkansas—and I worked out a way to jerk Emilio Kaufmann across the border, keep Sughrue out of prison, and maybe put some of my own money back in my pocket.

Part Six
Milo & Sughrue

SUGHRUE

"MILO," I SAY, "THIS IS FUCKING CRAZY. WILL YOU TELL ME what's going on?"

"The perimeter's secure," he says, ignoring my question, "so you just circulate among the guests. Keep the peace quietly. And keep your ears open."

"What the hell am I listening for?" I ask.

"I'll know it when you hear it," Milo says, then turns to leave.

"Okay," I said, "what if some asshole wants me to get them a drink?"

"Get it," he says quietly. Even behind his dark glasses his eyes are basalt hard. Just as they've been since he returned from Austin. And told me that we were going into the security business. It's as if I made an angry joke over dinner, and fucking Milo made it come true. Without telling me why. His eyes just saying, *Do it, Sonny, or get the fuck out.*

"What the fuck, I'll get the drink . . ." I start to say.

But Milo limps away from me, leaning heavily on a cane, a result of the Eddie Forsyth interrogation, he says, but he looks solid and official in khaki gabardine and a banker's Stetson, the brand-new tooled-leather pistol belt and cowboy boots creaking as he parts the crowd of partygoers watching the *vaqueros* sweating over the barbecue pit.

Before it died, the sharp edge of the northwest wind scrubbed the West Texas sky to a pellucid pastel blue wash and left the air so clear that the rocky peaks to the south on the Mexican horizon seem as close as the lower mountains just on the edge of the Kehoe ranch. Although it hadn't been visible from the front of the ranch house, a greensward half the size of a football field—the smooth sweep of grass broken here and there by rock and cactus gardens worked into the folds of the lawn like fairway traps—stretches behind the house all the way to the barns, stables, and corrals. Around the edges of the huge lawn the General has erected a party tent, dozens of rented tables, staffed bars, and a barbecue pit as large as a small house trailer.

It looks as if the Kehoes have gathered more people in expensive cowboy leather than I ever knew existed. It's as if they drew a line from Dallas to Santa Fe and invited every rich phony south of there to the ranch for *fajitas,* a dish invented by *vaqueros* because the skirt steak was the only scrap of beef left for them when the *patrons* butchered. Now it has become southwestern yuppie food. America the beautiful gobbling up low-rent Mexican beef.

The General isn't just a general and a large landholder, he's also a big West Texas Republican, so his highfalutin buddies are here, along with a fine showing of northern Mexican ranchers, senior officers from the Mexican military, and retired smugglers; fascists to a man, I suspect. Also the General seems to have invited a dozen or more local peace officers decked out in dress uniforms and fancy sidearms.

As I drift through the throng Kate slips up to take my arm, shakes her head, smiling in a happy stone, and informs me about the Hollywood part of the crowd. Since Suzanne is directing her first movie and her film experience is limited to a couple of bit parts and three short workshops, she is leaning heavily on the shaky old legs of a supposedly dry Sam Dunston to produce. Suzanne has also gathered the experience of a bevy of aging ingenues with tight-skinned faces and desperate eyes to fill the leading roles and a pantheon of character actors to give it the illusion of character. All the faces are familiar in a frightfully vague way, but the names completely escape me.

Of course, the film crew, who buffed and decked out might have passed for actors themselves, gather at some distance from the actors, and closer to Kate, who seems to have good connections among the West Texas drug and music trade, and she leaves my side to stand surrounded by long hair, runny noses, and the demon stink of primo *mota.* That's the crowd I might have joined. Along with Whitney and Lester. If Milo hadn't forced us into these idiot uniforms and this silly job. I feel like a fraud with my ponytail stuffed under the Stetson and dressed like an expensive rent-a-ranger.

Even Lester looks at me oddly as we drive, earlier, to the highway from the trailer. "Daddy," he asks as we rattle past the miniature horses, "have you ever eaten a horse?"

"Not that I know of," I admit. "But the Apache ate them all the time. You know what they used to say out here: a white man would ride a horse until it foundered, then leave it there; a Mexican would come along and ride it another twenty miles, then steal the saddle; an Apache would come along, ride the horse to where he was going, then eat it."

I glance at Lester while I'm chuckling at the story. From the look on his face it's clear that I've answered the wrong question. It happens, I've learned, with children. Whitney is choking on stifled laughter. "What?" I say.

"Could you eat one of those little horses?" he asks solemnly as we drive past the tinytown ranch.

"With enough hot sauce, sure," I say. "But it might piss off our neighbors. Why?"

"Just wondering," he says. Just like Whitney when she doesn't want to tell me why she wants to know something.

"What the hell is going on?" I ask, but Lester's admiring the new cowboy boots we've bought him for the barbecue.

"He's worried about the uniform," Whitney says quietly.

"Why?"

"He thinks you took this job because we need the money," she says between giggles, "and wonders if we can eat the little horses when we run out of food . . ."

Whitney fluffs Lester's long blond hair hanging free, smiling. The faint blush of the port wine stain is nearly invisible after the laser surgery and under the deep tan. His face is as clear as my memory of his mother's eyes, as clear as the love in Whitney's face.

"That's crazy," I say.

Whitney says, "Don't blame me. He was crazy when I got here."

"Who?" Lester wants to know. "Who's crazy?"

"Your daddy," Whitney says.

"No. He's not crazy," Lester says quietly. "He's funny."

"Sometimes," Whitney says calmly as we turn onto the highway.

Suzanne seems to be the only person drifting freely between the various groups. She's resplendent in a black fringed suede jacket dripping with silver conchos, the rodeo queen from hell, the only sparks of color a glint of hard green eyes below the brim of her black cowboy hat, a snicker of a silver hatband above, the blood-red slash of her smile, and a faint but dark blush rising from her cleavage to her slender neck. In the hard desert light I can see that what looked like Irish cream skin in the shade has a distinct duskiness glowing through. But I still can't place her in my memory.

Milo sneaks up on me while I'm watching her.

"Keep away from her, Sughrue," he whispers. "She's mine."

"You're welcome to her, cowboy," I whisper. "When I look at her she reminds me of grief and misery, heartache, pain, and cocaine, lies and dying young. I just don't know why."

"It's your guilty conscience," Milo chuckles, then slips back into the crowd. This is supposed to be my part of the world. But something about the party makes me as jumpy as a domestic cat stalked by coyotes, while Milo seems perfectly at ease. Maybe it's the uniform. It makes him look like the law. Before we left the trailer, standing in front of the bedroom mirror, I told Whitney that the uniform made me look like a burned-out hippie dressed up for Halloween. She told me I looked good, good enough to eat. Which she suggested and did before we left for the party. The depth of her love amazes me, comforts me. So I shouldn't be quite so much on the edge. But I am. Right from the beginning.

When Kate greets us, almost demure in this crowd in a burgundy wool suit and a short blond wig, greets us with wild, happy laughter and enthusiastic hugs, she charms Lester and Whitney with a smile and takes them away, saying, "Stick around, boys, the real party begins after dark."

After the Mexican waiters have passed through the crowd with pitchers of frozen margaritas, shots of Herradura tequila, bottles of Mexican beers, and trays of nachos, the separate groups mingle a bit more, the conversations become a bit more interesting, and the peace a bit harder to keep quietly.

One of the young Mexicans—dressed by Rodeo Drive but probably the son of a rancher—accuses the East LA Chicano hairdresser on the film of being a *maricón* because he doesn't want a shot of tequila. Without hesitation, the hairdresser kicks the Mexican in the balls, shouting, "*Maricón* that, you fucking greaser!"

So much for *La Raza* that afternoon.

Milo escorts the Chicano to the crew van, leaving me to convince the young Mexican that he can't beg, borrow, or buy the Browning Hi-Power I'm carrying as I assist him into the house. By the time he's convinced, two shots of tequila and snootful of coke later, he wants me to party with him. It takes a little longer to convince him that duty calls. So I'll just indulge him. A short shot and a smaller line. He's placated, we're *compañeros,* and the hairdresser is history.

By the time I'm back outside, Milo is moving toward a wild-eyed musician who looks as if he's been shooting crank into the corners of his eyes and who is shouting something about politics at a Republican state senator, a rawboned old fart who is just about to knock the kid back to the sixties. But Milo catches the old man's punch and takes the musician away with a wristlock that's so painful the kid almost comes back to reason.

Then there's the rattlesnake. Maybe eighteen inches long. Nobody knows where it came from. Maybe out of one of the small rock gardens. Or why it chose that moment to awake and flee. Maybe strolling musicians woke it. Whatever, one of the women spots the serpent snaking through the grass. She screams, right, just as you might expect; screams, then jerks an S&W Ladysmith-Auto out of her purse and pops the rattlesnake's head off. Close range, right, but moving, too. At the sound of the gunfire, pistols appear in everybody's hand. The whole crowd is packing. Then the pieces disappear and everybody laughs. I seem to remember why I left Texas in the first place.

But for the most part Milo catches the trouble before it begins. When the voices elevate, he's there to soothe the hackles before they begin to rise. I notice several of the law officers look him over with a professional eye. But Milo's on the job and will not be engaged in nostalgia. Thankfully, after the crowd settles down to their plates and the sun cools toward the horizon and the wind falls, peace reigns supreme. Milo tells me to grab a plate and sit down with Whitney and Baby Lester.

"You're the boss, boss," I say.

"Not for long now," he answers.

"Captain-fucking-Cryptic," I say to his retreating back.

While we're eating, a black Suburban with Mexican *Frontera* plates pulls beside the house. Three bodyguards step out of it, flanking a tall Mexican, slim and elegant in a dark tailored suit, who steps lightly out of the rig. The bodyguards, who look as if they have been trained by the American Secret Service, gather about him as if protecting royalty. The General insinuates himself into the group and exchanges a formal *abrazo* with the Mexican gentleman, who's obviously looking over the General's shoulder for somebody else. Then he sees Suzanne, brushes off the General, and heads toward her. She acts surprised in that phony, Hollywood way, then quickly bored, as the Mexican gentleman tries to pull her aside by the elbow. Suzanne jerks her arm out of his hand, then stalks into the crowd, leaving the Mexican gentleman pissed.

"Who's that?" I ask Kate as she kneels to offer Lester a honey-filled *sopapilla*.

"Don Emilio Kaufmann," she answers. "He's the big cheese across the border, the Baron of Enojada." Somehow I'm not surprised. Then I am. "He's my uncle," Kate adds.

Fucking Milo. He's conveniently disappeared.

By sundown most of the crowd has retreated. El Ricos back to their side of the border. Don Emilio's visit was as brief as his retreat was showy. The Republicans, of course, head back under their rocks. The actors, except for a large, villainous-looking heavy who remains at Sam Dunston's side, have fled back to their lonely trailers to drink or drug or twelve-step among their scurvy sycophants. And the rich trash in their gaudy cowboy duds have run back to whatever holes they profane. Except for one blowsy blonde in red and white leather who claims to be the junk queen of West Texas and who drunkenly wants to know when the fucking party is going to start.

The General draws Milo and me aside to tell us that our jobs are over and since we're Kate's friends that we should join her party, laughing and drinking in the tiki lamps flickering in the hazy dusk.

"Actually, sir," Milo says, "we're working for the movie company."

"Fuck the movie company," the General says softly. I realize that the old boy, although erect and eloquent, is as drunk as a dancing pig.

"Thanks for the invite, General," Milo says. "But Sughrue has to take his family home. The real job starts tomorrow, you know. But I'll be happy to have a drink with you. Just as soon as I walk Sughrue to his truck."

At this, Milo takes me by the arm, leads me to Whitney and Lester, then to the truck. After they are in the cab, I pull Milo behind the pickup bed.

"Okay, man," I say. "What the fuck is going on?"

"Just trust me," he says. "And work the job."

Before I can ask him what the hell the job is, Milo limps into the shadows toward the table where Suzanne stands over Sam Dunston. Even at this distance I can hear the icy wind of her words.

"Haven't you had quite enough to drink?"

Dunston's deep, rumbling voice answers: "It's in my contract, Ms. Kehoe. Saturday nights I can drink all I want. The rest of the week I'm pure, clean, dry, and yours. But Saturday night, honey, I belong to myself."

"No. No. You belong to the whiskey."

I've heard that tone of voice myself. Then Suzanne turns and marches into the house as I climb into the truck, where Lester is already sleeping with his head in Whitney's lap.

"What was that all about?" Whitney asks as we drive away.

"I don't know," I answer. "Nobody ever tells me anything."

"I'll tell you this," she says. "It's certainly nice to have you at home again. All of you."

"It's nice to be home," I say, then wonder what the hell Milo's got up his sleeve.

MILO

FROM THE SAG OF HIS SHOULDERS BENEATH THE LASH OF Suzanne's voice, I could tell that Sam Dunston did belong to the whiskey. I should know; I once belonged to it myself. Suzanne's eyes flared in the smoky light, and the reflected flames flickered up the shiny black leather of her tight pants. Her gaze swept the table so hard that her drunk father slipped away like an egg-sucking dog.

But Dunston seemed made of stronger stuff. At least at this whiskey moment. He ignored her stare, turned and held out his glass toward the actor, whose name I couldn't remember, who filled it with four fingers of Wild Turkey. Suzanne nearly stomped her silver-toed boot like an angry drugstore cowboy. But she restrained herself to a single angry sigh. An angry blush rushed like fire up her slender neck, then she tossed her sin-dark hair and stormed toward the house. The back door slammed, then the front, then a car door, and we listened to the gravel-spitting roar of her 4Runner as Suzanne fled south toward the location.

When she was safely away, I rested my cane on the table and sat down across from Dunston, who glanced at me with bright, angry eyes, asking, "So, Mr. Rent-a-Cop, have you come to monitor the old buzzard's intake?"

"Actually, Mr. Dunston," I said, "I sat down to see if I might share a glass of that unblended whiskey with a man whose movies I've always admired."

"Flattery might get you a small measure, Mr. . . ." he said, and I introduced myself. "Jesus, partner," Dunston said to the actor beside him, "fella with a name like that surely deserves a full measure." And he complied. Then we raised our glasses. "Absent friends," Dunston said, "magic time, and that fucking Kehoe bitch." I guess I hesitated because the old man explained. "Hey, son, I ain't got nothin' against her. Except she should've let me direct this damn movie. And she should've starred in it instead of that jiggle-butt bimbo."

"I didn't know she was an actress," I said.

"A fuckin' natural," Dunston said. "Best untrained talent I've ever seen. We could've made a fortune. She's a real fuckin' beauty . . ."

"But she wanted to direct?" I said.

"Even the fuckin' road signs in LA want to direct, son," he said, then sipped his whiskey and went back to bemoaning his fate in the hands of Suzanne Kehoe. "And I'd bet horse turds against hand grenades that the camera just loves her. But no pictures. Of any kind. That's one of her many rules. Never knew a director, not even me, who had so many fuckin' rules on the set."

"She's got a lot of rules for a beginner?" I said.

Dunston suddenly stared at me. The old man had survived for a long time in a business not known for suffering the foolish. He might be half-drunk but he was more than half-smart. And he knew he was being pumped. Suddenly, for no good reason, other than meanness, perhaps, he decided to let me prime the pump. But his bodyguard gave me a look meant to freeze the silver off my belt buckle.

"She's no beginner," Dunston said slowly. "I don't know dogshit about her but I know she's not a beginner. Hell, all I know is that she showed up at my trailer on the beach up in Cocachino County with a damned good script and almost enough money to make this fuckin' movie . . ."

"Almost enough?" I said.

"Damn near," he said. "So you don't have to worry about your paycheck, son. In a couple of weeks we'll have enough film in the can for a European presell. If I can keep that idiot DP from shooting old jiggle-butt from the rear . . ."

"Especially in the saddle," the other guy suggested quietly. "From that angle you can't tell which is the horse's ass."

He and Dunston laughed as quietly as they could, then Dunston slapped his companion on the back, saying to me, "Hey, you remember this old boy?"

"The face is familiar," I admitted, "but the name escapes me."

"Roy Jordan," Dunston said. "Starred in my first movie."

"Demon Ride?" I said. "Sure. I see it now. Nineteen fifty-four. Great movie."

"Downhill since then," Roy said, but he didn't sound too sad about it.

"Speaking of downhill," Dunston said, "you boys drink on without me for a bit. I'm going over there and lean on that wall until my fuckin' prostate surrenders and lets me piss and hope it runs downhill into the fuckin' Rio Bravo del Norte." Then Dunston pushed up from the table, Roy watching him like a night nurse, and staggered to the side of the General's house, where he leaned like a permanent addition to the adobe.

"What the hell happened?" I asked Roy. "I thought he was dead."

"Damn near is," he answered quietly. "Three bypasses, a minor stroke, and a long, continuing bout with pancreatic cancer."

"Damn," I said, "that's rawhide tough. Is that why he quit working?"

Roy thought for a long time before he decided to answer that one. "I guess it doesn't matter anymore. After he shot his wife and the hyphenate, everybody—studios, independents, even foreigners—was afraid to hire a director who was willing to shoot the fuck-ups instead of just firing them." Roy smiled like a man who wished he had discharged a few rounds himself.

"I guess I missed that," I said. "Dunston shot his wife in the hyphen?"

Roy laughed as if I were an idiot child. "We were making a movie down in Durango when Sam caught the star-producer-pissant, the hyphenate, porking his wife. Hell, it had been going on for weeks, and Sam didn't much care. The shoot was going well, and Sam always cared more about the movie than he did about pussy. And what the hell, we were running whores in tandem all over Durango every night our own damn selves.

"But one afternoon Sam was setting a shot. One of those

complicated moments when twenty-five people, ten horses, the clouds, and the sun have to hit the mark the first time. Mr. Asshole Star chose that particularly ill-chosen moment to run his link sausage up Mindy's ass.

"Well, you can imagine. She screamed like a stuck shoat. The trailer rattled like a six on the Richter. It fucked everybody's concentration. Even the fuckin' horses were glancing over their withers. So Sam gets in his limo, rams the trailer, turns it over, then grabs his sweet-sixteen double-barrel, loads it with nine-and-a-half bird shot, and when the star and Mindy hightail it into the desert, Sam peppers their butts until they were out of sight.

"Then Sam came back to the set, did the shot, the sweet-sixteen-gauge loaded and propped on his shoulder, then we wrapped," Roy concluded. "The son of a bitch could always get the shot."

"I don't think I know this movie," I said.

"Sure you do," he said. "The studio fired him, and the fucking hyphen finally directed it, recut the shit out of Sam's stuff. I can't remember the title—*The Hard Rock,* or something like that—one of those psychologically sensitive bullshit westerns." Then Roy paused, smiling, poured a small measure of whiskey in our glasses, and said, "But at least he had sense enough to keep Sam's shot. Best fucking shot in the film."

Before he lost the mood and Dunston staggered all the way back to the table, I asked, "Why did you guys finally decide you needed security?"

"Wetbacks and rattlesnakes," Roy said simply. "The wetbacks were stealing us blind. Hell, they even stole the front tires off Sam's Winnebago while he was sleeping in it. Sober. Then Ms. Kehoe found a rattler in her 4Runner. Sam convinced her to give up on the people she had hired—moonlighting law dogs—and hire some real help."

From the wall, we heard Dunston yelp like a coyote, then laugh happily.

"Success," Roy said.

Dunston rejoined us, and we drank and talked about the joys of old age, old movies, and old whiskey, until Kate came to get me.

"Milo," she said, calling me by name for the first time I could remember. "The General is down. Will you help me get him to bed?"

The General was down in one of his fake bunkers, quietly curled in the sand, his skinny shanks jerking in the firelight. If the old fart had been grinning, I might have thought he was dog-dreaming of *conejos,* chasing bunny rabbits through the brush. I gathered the old gentleman's shoulders and a guy stepped over from Kate's fire to get his ankles. As we stood up, I got a clear look at the guy's face in the firelight. "I thought you were in Hawaii," I said.

"It's a long story," he answered, a sick grin on his face.

"Maybe you can tell me about it over a beer," I suggested. He nodded grimly, and Kate urged us toward the house with her father.

A few minutes later, the old man safely abed, still sleeping drunkenly, Tom-John Donne and I faced each other across a tiled breakfast bar in the large Mexican kitchen while Kate grabbed a couple of beers out of the built-in refrigerator.

"You guys know each other?" she asked. When both of us nodded, she added, "Is it cool?"

Donne took a long pull at his beer, then grunted, "I'm chill, kid, as long as it's cool with Mr. Milo-whatever-his-name-is . . ."

"Milodragovitch," I said, hoping it sounded like a threat rather than a spelling mistake. Then I turned to Kate, thanked her, and excused her. "You said it was a long story," I said to Donne as soon as Kate left, and he raised his beer to his mouth.

"Yeah, right . . ." he started to say.

"By the way, Donne," I interrupted, "somebody chopped off Aaron Tipton's head."

"That's not what I heard, man," he said as soon as he had another swallow of his beer.

"What did you hear?"

"Actually, I read it in the *LA Times* . . ."

"When you got back from Hawaii?"

"You got it, man . . ."

"Are you doing stunts on this fucking movie?"

"Hey, I'm the stunt coordinator, man," he said quickly,

"the second AD, and the third male lead." Then he paused to suck on his beer. "This film is my big break, my SAG card and the whole bit. Makes all that fucking cheap prison dental work worthwhile." Donne sounded too happy and proud to be lying.

If he wasn't, I didn't know enough about the business to brace him with it. I wanted to go into his history with Tipton, but suddenly I was tired of questions and answers and lies. Perhaps even tired of people telling the truth. Betty Porterfield came to mind.

"Fuck it," I said, "just forget it." The son of a bitch looked hurt. So I grabbed my beer and headed back to Dunston's table.

But when I got back, Roy and Dunston were gone, so I took my leave, too, walked over to the Blazer with the Sawyer Security Systems logo on the door, and headed south toward the location.

Most of the crew had been lodged at distant motels from Castillo to Marfa, but all the head hogs were in fancy motor homes parked near the adobe ruins of an old ranch headquarters three miles off the highway. Most of the movie was being shot there, at nearby exteriors, and at a mock Mexican village that had been jury-rigged just over the next rise. So I had three guards roaming the perimeter, and a relief manning a small frame guard shack on the road into the location.

When I got to the shack Suzanne Kehoe's 4Runner sat beside it, engine off, headlights glowing faintly as if the battery had worn down. In the flash of my headlights I could see her head rise from where it had been slumped over the steering wheel, and in the harsh light of the shack's single bulb I could see the relief man tilted back in his chair, his head hanging at an impossible angle.

Oddly enough, setting up the security company, with Maribeth Williamson's friendly assistance, had been the easiest and perhaps the cheapest part of putting this scam together. A friend of her dead husband's already owned a security company that specialized in the oil field, so for a nominal price, a stiff bond, and an insurance rider, he loaned me the logo and some of the equipment necessary to bid for the job. As far as I could tell, nobody else wanted it. Not after the initial interview with Suzanne Kehoe, when they found out that a major duty was rattlesnake patrol. Ms. Kehoe didn't want to see any snakes. Ever. Of any kind. But I had good reason to kiss deep ass, though I never understood why she let me. Pure arrogance, maybe.

But Suzanne Kehoe's face was twisted by pure fright as I leapt out of my rig and rushed to her window.

"The flies," she gasped, quickly rolling it down, then nodded toward the shack, ". . . the flies . . ."

I glanced over at the shack. A dozen large and black flies crawled slowly across the guard's face. I darted to the shack, but as soon as I opened the door the smell of cheap bourbon, instead of fresh death, rolled out on a wave of heat. The worthless bastard, a local redneck deputy sheriff, had passed out with the small space heater turned on high enough to hatch the flies out of the wood. They hung tightly to his face even when I propped his limp body in the rear corner of the shack. Then I checked on my other three guards. At least they were sober enough to answer their radios, and sensible enough not to complain when I cursed them and told them that they had to finish the night shift without a relief.

Then I heard Suzanne Kehoe grind her weak battery. When I got back to her her face was composed, her voice trembling but calm as she explained that she was fine. Except she kept a constant pressure on the ignition key, held it there until the dim headlights died and the battery clicked against the starter like a dying cricket. I reached in through the window and took the keys as gently as I could.

"I'm sorry," she said softly, her cold fingers on my wrist, her breath hot against my cheek. "I'm sorry, I didn't know I was doing that. . . . Is he dead?"

"Drunk," I said.

"Would you be so kind as to accompany me to my quarters?" she asked with hysterical calm.

"Bette Davis?" I guessed, as I opened the door of the 4Runner. But the blank look she gave me told me that she didn't have the vaguest idea what I might be saying. So I helped her out of her 4Runner and into my Blazer, then drove around the other dark and silent motor homes, which were huddled around a single mercury vapor lamp, to her quarters, which sat apart on the edge of the stark shadows.

After I'd unlocked and opened the door, I handed Suzanne her keys. She took them, smiling as if she had just recognized me, saying softly, "You said something about a drink . . ." Then she took my hand and led me into the darkness.

In my late middle age it comes to me that women often take advantage of my good nature. But it's nobody's fault but mine. So blame it on me. Or the sudden release of tension when I discovered that the guard wasn't dead. I'm weak. Always have been about women. And my life hadn't exactly been a Doris Day movie lately. But that's no excuse for what happened. Given what I knew about this woman, I might as well have agreed to crawl into a sleeping bag full of diamondbacks. But what the hell, I told myself, even a rattlesnake deserves the benefit of the doubt.

By the time Suzanne and I finally got around to the drinking part, my moustache still smelled of her crotch and my knee was bleeding. When she'd come—sitting backward on top of me, holding on to my half-raised knee with one hand as she fingered her clit with the other hand and I pounded inside her until I thought I might die—she'd screamed and buried her expensively capped teeth into my knee. The release, to say the least, was terrifically intense. At least for me.

Suzanne flopped on the bed beside me, pressed her lean body against me just long enough for her spasms to cease, then rolled away to scoop up a tiny hit from the pile of pink Peruvian flake sitting on a small mirror on the nightstand in a long, red fingernail. She hit it twice, then did my nose, but only once, before she picked up the Stoli and shaved ice with a lemon twist I'd made her when we'd first come in the motor home.

I rolled off the bed, grabbed my beer, stepped to the back door of the motor home, the one on the dark side. The black desert sky glittered with stars as distant and cold as my head. The cool night air moved lightly against my wet, naked skin as it seemed to dry individual hairs on my chest. I felt fucking great for the first time in a long time. So I roared into the night, roared from someplace deeper than my diaphragm. A horse whinnied and a pack mule brayed from the corrals. Then I stalled on the hard ground, the warm piss foaming and splashing in the dust. I roared again, deep and longer this time. The hardpan of the corral clattered with nervous hooves as the remuda snorted and whoofed.

"That's certainly lovely," she said as I turned back into the small space. "If you're one of those assholes who smoke after sex . . ."

"Some parts of me are smoking, lady," I interrupted, smiling so hard my cheeks hurt. "That's for damn certain sure."

". . . then please do it outside," she continued flatly, not even a hint of a smile cracking the smooth planes of her face.

What the hell. She'd given as good as she'd gotten. I'd done my job, and now I was no more part of her life than the tissue she used to wipe my jism out of her crotch. "Excuse me," I said and reached for my pants.

"Forgive me," she said quietly, "I can be a bitch . . . afterwards."

I didn't need to ask what she meant by that.

"Loss of control and all that," she added.

So I put my britches back on the chair and sat on the bed beside her. Even in the dim light, I could see that Suzanne was closer to forty than thirty, could see the almost invisible scars in front of her ears and along her hairline.

"A woman has to work with what she has," she said softly, watching me look at her, "and my body is a weapon." Then she cupped her small perfect breasts. "State of the art, though," she said.

"And a fine and lovely work of art it is," I said, then took the soft pebble of her nipple between my lips.

"Thank you," she whispered against my hair, and once again I was fucking lost. And soon bleeding from another slice of Suzanne's ecstasy.

SUGHRUE

As THE MOVIE WINDS ITS TROUBLED AND WEARY WAY TO-
ward a pre-Christmas wrap, the weather grows unseasonably
warm, almost early-summer hot, and the rattlesnake patrols
take more and more time. The poor spade-headed, forked-
tongued devils slither in thick, dark streamers from their
deep rocky sanctuaries to laze on flat rocks in the unexpected
sunshine. Two or three times a day shotgun blasts split the
windy silence, and the heap of bloody serpent scraps fills the
narrow refuse pit the effects guys had blown in the stony
ridge between the adobe ruins and the fake village, bodies
that clog the stone slit and writhe to decay under each day's
ration of lime that holds down the smell of rotting snakes.

Fucking Milo not only refuses to answer any questions
about what the hell we're doing on this job, he doesn't even
talk to me anymore. He hasn't for days. It's the goddamned
woman. And probably her cocaine, too. Rumors among the
crew say it's primo. Which is dangerous for the old man.
Each morning I wake horrified to face the day.

Even Kate is horrified when I tell her.

Kate's driven over to our place to bring Whitney and Baby
Lester back from an afternoon's horseback ride on the ranch.
She refuses to stay for dinner, but will share a beer with me
after I change out of my uniform and work on the tiles for
the rear patio as she watches quietly. I'm not exactly sure
why I bother. The place doesn't even belong to us. Harim
picked up the title, along with the convenience store in Fairbairn he lets us run, when an old coke dealer jumped bail on
an ancient conspiracy beef.

Thanks to the lovely DEA. Once you come to their attention, they never forget. And with the blunt force of manda-

tory sentencing, they can make your mother roll over on you.
Hell, I'd done a lot of drugs in my misguided life, but never
sold a bit, and knew, thanks to Joe Don Pines, I was still
somewhere on their list, still wearing a gold star. A list bearing Milo's name, too, now.

"You've got a great life here, Sughrue," Kate says softly
to my back. "What's the matter?"

"Milo and Suzanne," I say. "I'm worried."

"Oh, no! He's not sleeping with my sister?" Kate says.
"Oh, my god, he is! What the hell's he thinking?"

"Thinking's not exactly the first word that comes to
mind," I say. "Besotted, that's the first word that comes to
mind."

"Is he in love with her?" she asks. "My god, that would be
awful."

"Well, maybe not," I lie.

And lie again because I don't tell Kate that I strongly suspect her sister is also sleeping with Dunston, the DP, the
preppie AD kid, and maybe even the Chicano hairdresser
who's providing her with cocaine. Hell, even the aging starlet lead spends a lot of time in Suzanne's motor home. I
don't know where she finds the time. Like everybody else,
Suzanne's working long, hard days. Maybe even longer and
harder than everybody else. The only people I've ever seen
work this hard was a grunt patrol on a useless jungle hump in
Vietnam.

"Suzanne can be trouble," Kate says, her voice trembling
as if she's talking about a terminal disease. "If he's not in
love with her, I don't think he should be fucking her . . ."

Everybody's fucking her, I think as I tap a red tile into the
sand, but only Milo's blindly in love. But I don't tell Kate. I
don't tell her lots of things. So she hugs me goodbye, and I
retreat into the house, send Baby Lester from his homework
to the shower, and, once alone, suggest to Whitney that perhaps we should find another way, another place to live.

Whitney leans on the edge of the sink for a long moment,
long enough to make me worry. I step forward, cradle her
slim waist in my hands, bury my face in the sweet tumble of
her golden hair.

"C.W.," she says without turning. "C.W., if I hadn't come

when you called, you would have let yourself die in that damned hospital. So you owe me, right? Big time, right?"

The question doesn't need an answer.

"Finish this thing," she whispers, "then we'll talk about the future. And the past." Then Whitney pauses, turns, smiling, into my arms, asking, "You mind?"

I do, but know I can't say so. I know what it will take to get Milo away from Suzanne and back on the job. Maybe even save his life. I just hope Whitney will forgive me later. I know the old man won't.

MILO

THE FIRST THING THAT CAME TO MY MIND WHEN I SAW HIM swagger out of her motor home was: so this is how it happens.

Suzanne had sent me off that morning with the wranglers, the horses, and the stunt doubles to bodyguard and snake watch the second unit while they covered a complicated horse chase. She didn't trust anybody else, she told me, and it was important that all these shots were covered in one day. Even after two weeks on location, because they shot out of sequence, I still didn't have much idea of what the movie was about.

I just did my job, did it perfectly because if things fucked up—if an actor found a stash of pills and blew a line or the hungover cameraman missed a shot on the last take before the light failed—she wouldn't sleep with me, ignored me with a passion. Except for those wild moments when she accused me of sleeping with the assistant hairdresser. Or the makeup girl. Or the only aging starlet who didn't treat me like passing offal. Even when she didn't want me, Suzanne acted as if I belonged to her. She would have driven a younger man, less patiently desperate, completely insane. As it was, she made me crazier day by day. And she would have bled the heart out of a man with thinner skin.

I did everything I could to sleep with Suzanne every chance I got. And thanks to her endless supply of cocaine—which she seemed to use as a working drug instead of a happy one—I wasn't sleeping in my bed much, either. I spent my nights roaming the desert beyond her trailer, waiting for the sound of her voice crackling through the night, spent my days keeping my part of the job working clean and tight. But lately I felt as if I was worn down to the gut strings, as if a coil of barbed wire occupied my chest.

It was all complicated by my refusal to talk to Sughrue. I knew he wouldn't approve of the way I was fucking it up— my money, his revenge and salvation—but I believed I could work it out, could have it all, believed if we could just get through this goddamned movie, everything would be all right. I suppose, in that way, I wasn't much different from the cast and crew. Surely they wouldn't have worked this hard if they hadn't believed that some magical thing would happen to them at the celluloid finale.

So that last day went perfectly and quick. Even though I stayed with the wranglers to help unsaddle, cool, and load the horses, it was still midafternoon when we got back to the location. The first unit was setting a reverie of a gunfight in the adobe ruins, but Suzanne's chair was empty. I limped quickly toward her motor home, but Dunston, sitting on the steps of his adobe, called me over and insisted he couldn't have a beer unless I joined him. Fuck his contract, he shouted.

What the hell, I thought, I could borrow his bathroom to fix my nose, and beer with the old boy was always a pleasure. As long as we could stay out of the tequila.

As he lifted the third Herradura, Dunston said, "Let's hear it for that great movie."

"What great movie?"

"Tequila Mockingbird," he said, laughing and choking down his shot.

I slammed my half-empty shot glass on the table, stared at my trembling fingers, and interrupted the old man. I had already been in the bathroom. Twice. "What the fuck is *this* movie about, Mr. Dunston?"

"You don't know?"

"Women on horseback without shirts, and a little gunfire?" I suggested, then laughed and stood to leave.

"Sit down, son," he said, pouring another shot and slicing another piece of Mexican lime, "and I'll tell you."

"Okay," I said.

"Okay," he said, then lifted his glass. "It's like this. These out-of-work women gunfighters . . ."

"Have hit the glass ceiling?" I joked as I finished my tequila, which Dunston refilled immediately. "You're going to get me drunk," I said, laughing, touching my cane, thinking I might need the support this afternoon.

"You're going to need it," he said, then continued, "Okay, listen, they're not really gunfighters, these women. They're gamblers and camp cooks and whores and whatnot. But they have all killed their men. Well, not their actual men. Just killed a man. Or two."

As Sam sipped at his drink I thought of Betty Porterfield, which sobered me somewhat. Even though I told Suzanne that our brief moments together were the best part of my long, ruined life, which I even made myself believe in spite of everything, I never stopped thinking of Betty Porterfield.

"So they get hired by this rich rancher, whose wife has been kidnapped by this Mexican revolutionary, to take the ransom money to Mexico and bring his wife back . . ."

"This is beginning to sound familiar," I said.

"Right," he agreed. "And when they bring her back . . ."

"They learn the truth," I interrupted, pouring my own shot this time, "and turn her loose to go off with Jack Palance?"

"Something like that."

"Jesus," I said, stunned. "She never saw *The Professionals*?"

Dunston took a long time to answer, considering his darkly aged tequila in the sunlight slanting through the top of the curtained window. "Son," he said, "to tell the truth, I don't think Suzanne's ever seen a western movie. Not even one of mine."

"You didn't say anything?"

"Don't get me wrong, kid," he said, "crazy whore that she is, the bitch wrote a great script and she's making a fucking wonderful movie." Then the old man paused, then continued in an aged whine. "You have any idea how long it's been since I've been on a film? Ever'body in that fucking town thought I was dead. Except for those bastards who hoped I was."

"I guess I thought you were dead, too," I said.

"Well, I'm fucking not!" he shouted, standing.

I stood up, too, but Dunston wasn't looking at me. He was

staring out the window. Then he reached over to push me back into my seat.

"Fuck it," he said, "let's have a drink to commemorate my resurrection . . ."

But it was too late for both of us.

Through the narrow uncurtained space at the top of the window I watched Suzanne clatter down the steps of her motor home and stride toward the location, talking into her handheld radio, her shadow as black as her shining hair and leather pants, black against the pale desert dust. And behind her, Sughrue, standing in the doorway, wiping his nose, tucking in his shirttail, and scratching his nuts.

"I'm sorry, son," Dunston said softly, but I wasn't there anymore.

If I hadn't paused in the doorway after I kicked the door open, paused to reach back for my cane, which had been the most expensive part of this goddamned scam, I suspect I would have hit Dunston's steps with my pistol in my hand and emptied the clip into Sughrue's chest without thinking about it. As it was I used several thousand dollars worth of cane to immobilize his right arm with a shot to the elbow before I dropped him in the dirt with a right hook that should have put both of us in the hospital. He stayed down, touching a trickle of blood from the corner of his mouth. But he wasn't out.

"Now she's made us both bleed, Milo," he said.

"You chickenshit son of a bitch," I hissed, "you're fired. Don't let me see your ass around here again."

"More than fine by me, man," Sughrue said as he stood up slowly. "By the way, she wants you to drive her to Enojada after this shot."

"Fuck you."

"And also by the way, man," Sughrue said as he turned to walk away, "before you cross the border with her, do me a favor. Just say 'Roriann,' man, say 'Rita Van Tasselvitch,' and be sure to say 'dumb fucking old man.' Say that loudest, Milo."

"You stupid son of a bitch," I said, "you think I didn't know?"

For once in his life, Sughrue didn't have anything to say. He just left. I wish I could say I had planned it that way.

SUGHRUE

OKAY, SO NOW I'M THE FUCKING STUPID ONE, CARRYING A mouthful of sore teeth as I follow Milo and Suzanne across the border into Enojada in the vain hope I could keep him out of trouble. Trouble I'd started, somehow. Once he'd started sleeping with her, I knew his eyes would be blinded by her whipcorded body and his ears filled with the angry buzz of her screaming, bloody orgasms, and that he wouldn't listen to me when I told him who Suzanne really was. Or who she really wasn't. But by the time I remembered where I had heard that whiplash of a voice she used on poor old Mr. Dunston at the fajita party, it was already too late.

When I saw him the next morning coming out of her motor home, I didn't know what to say. Then I didn't have a chance because he wouldn't talk to me. Right then I decided Milo wouldn't listen to me unless he thought I'd fucked her. Which I guess I nearly did. I suppose, technically, a blow job counts, even if you don't come. As I said, I guess I'm the fucking stupid one now.

When Milo shouted at me while I was lying in the dust that he already knew, I was nearly as shocked as I was by Suzanne's reaction when I told her that I knew what she'd done. She didn't turn a hair. Just lifted the corner of her mouth and said, "I should have had you killed."

"They took a pretty good shot at it," I said.

"That was just an accident," she said. "Or maybe a problem with the language."

"Jesus, you're not just a liar, you're fucking crazy."

She just smiled sweetly, watching me in the mirror as she

fixed her makeup, saying, "You know what they say. When you're a schizophrenic you never have to be alone . . ."

"You're not a schizophrenic," I said, "you're just a bitch."

". . . and when you're a manic-depressive, you don't have to be unhappy too long."

"Jesus wept fucking blood," I muttered. "You are crazy."

"What did you say, C.W.?"

"I said you're a fucking bitch."

"Comes with the territory," she said calmly. "But you're a man. You wouldn't understand."

"Right," I said. "I never killed anybody for money."

"If you think this is about money," she said, "you're dumber than I thought. Besides, I never killed anybody . . ."

"You didn't have to, did you?"

"Nope," she said, "they all lined up. And everybody fell down on cue."

"Maybe I lined up," I offered, "and maybe I fell down, but I got back up."

"Not exactly," she said quietly. "You got out of the investigation business. Which was all I wanted."

"But Milo got me back in," I said, but I'm remembering the sound of the firing pin shattering in my ear. "And he's still standing up."

"Not exactly, honey," she said, her pure West Texas twang returning to hum like a strand of barbed wire in the wind. "Your precious Milo fell the farthest. And landed right on top of my lovely body. You remember that, don't you?" Then she paused, turned, and continued as if none of this had happened, "And you know, Milo's the one I might keep around. I think he loves me." She smiled at me in the mirror and chilled my soul.

"Poor bastard," I said.

"When Milo comes back with the wranglers, please tell him that I need him to drive me across the border to my uncle's place when I finish the gunfight reverses."

"How the hell does somebody end up like you?"

"I don't know," she admitted. "That's not my worry. Perhaps I just accepted my station in life. I'm a second-class citizen, dumb-ass, so I learned everything I could learn about how to live in a man's world." Her smile sparkled like a frozen river. "I could have made you come, you know. No matter how hard you tried to resist. I could still do it." Her hand reached for my fly. I jumped back as if touched by a snake. Her laughter sounded like a wall of mirrors breaking. "See," she said, laughing. "I *do* know how to live in a man's world."

"A man's world?"

"But then you wouldn't know anything about that, would you?" she said. "Face it, C.W., you're not a man. You're just a kid. A mind full of nonsense, a head full of silly macho romantic notions. You're a child. Wandering around with your dick in your hand. Speaking of which, if I were you, I'd button up my pants before I talked to Milo. I suspect he won't understand."

"No more than I did," I said, remembering how she seemed to enjoy my humiliations when I tried to love her.

"Nor any less," she said, "I pray," then she went out the door like a woman in a movie. Leaving me to follow like the fourth stooge . . .

. . . all the way to the gate of Don Emilio Kaufmann's estate up a small river canyon outside of Enojada. A half-mile or so below the gate, I nearly overrun them while Milo stops his rig for something. Maybe a long piss. I don't know, can't see anything but the right rear of the Blazer. But finally they drive on to the gate, with me following, and I drive past as they pull through the gate, then park the Blazer.

Unfortunately, the stakes are immediately raised. The gate stays open long enough for a black Suburban with smoked glass to roar out and tail me. But not very far. Maybe two miles, then in my rearview mirror I spot a guy with a mini-Uzi rising through the sunroof. As I see the flashes of automatic fire and feel the rear tires go, I grab the emergency brake, lock up the rear wheels, whip the pickup into a bootlegger's turn, then slam head-on into the left front fender of the Suburban.

If our bumpers hadn't caught and locked, the Suburban would have tumbled off the narrow track and into the canyon without me, but as it is, clinched together like love bugs, turning slowly in the afternoon air, I have plenty of time to think about stupidity.

MILO

AFTER WE CROSSED THE RIO GRANDE AND THE BRIEF INSPEC-
tion at Mexican customs, Suzanne glanced up from the open
briefcase on her lap long enough to direct me down the rough,
crooked main street of Enojada, a small ruined town where it
looked as if even the halt and the lame carried automatic
weapons concealed beneath their rags. The only signs of pros-
perity were a liquor store just across the border, a new motel
built over a dance hall, and the Chevy dealership. Pale dust
drifted like gunsmoke in the air. I drove very carefully and kept
my eyes to myself. Suzanne had made me empty the Blazer of
firearms before we left the location, and I missed the weight of
my pistol belt. I also particularly missed having Sughrue to
cover my back. But that was the deal I had made with myself.
I'd cross the border naked, or not at all.

But I couldn't imagine what made Sughrue go into her
trailer. Of course, he'd nearly married the woman. Or would
have married her, I remembered, if she would have had him.
Hell, I might have married her myself, if I'd had any hope of
gracing her bed more often. At least Sughrue's out of it, I
told myself. Whatever happens.

As we bounced through the rocky potholes around the
zócalo, Suzanne told me to turn onto a thread of rough pavement that led out of town and upriver and to the small
canyon where the Rio Estigma flowed into the Rio Grande.

"You don't know the way," she said as she shut her briefcase, "do you?"

"Quite frankly, my dear," I said, reaching into the cooler
in the backseat for a beer—the drinks I'd had with Dunston
had been washed out by the single blow of Sughrue's betrayal—"I've never crossed the border before . . ."

"I should have guessed."

". . . and I don't plan on coming back."

"I would think you would fit perfectly in this culture," she said, not meaning it as a compliment, I was sure. And the insult began the uncoiling of the razor wire in my chest.

"Can I ask you a couple of things?" I said.

"You know me: I can't promise to answer," she said.

"Can't? Or won't?"

"Does it matter?"

"I don't guess so," I said, almost laughing. "Why did you bring me along?"

"You look good in a uniform," she said. "And although my uncle loves me, he is a businessman and a Mexican. If I didn't bring anyone, he would not treat me with proper respect. What was the other thing?"

"If you don't like me, Suzanne, why the fuck do you sleep with me?"

She smiled coldly, saying, "I suppose it's your facility with the language."

"And I suppose they pulled your polite gene out with your ovaries . . ."

"How did you . . ."

"Just a lucky guess," I said, really laughing this time. "How much money does your father have in the movie?"

"My father?" she said, surprised.

"Yeah. Kate suggested he might have put up some of the money."

"Listen, you bastard," she said sharply, "I raised every fucking penny myself."

"Sorry," I said, thinking, *I should know.* "You're cute with your dander up, honey," I added, "waving gently in the air."

"Now you're just trying to be offensive," she said, ignoring me.

Now that I had the enemy where they wanted me, I truly had nothing to lose, so I drank beer and chuckled to myself as we wound up the canyon, out of the chaparral, and into the thin mountain pines, Emilio Kaufmann's mansion rising like a bad moon over the ridges above us, its white walls lung-blood-pink in the fading afternoon light. Suzanne sulked in silence beside me. Often it seemed that she hated to see anybody have any fun. Even herself. Maybe that's why she was such a bitch after an orgasm. I finished the beer and tossed the empty can into the backseat.

"Would you get me another beer, please?" I said.

"What?" She acted as if this were the most insulting thing ever asked her. "What?"

"Get me a fucking beer. Please."

"Kiss my ass!"

"Do we have time?" I asked. "Please don't act as if I haven't kissed it before, from the hairy hole to the shit hole and everything in between," I said politely. "And please don't forget the beer, either."

"As soon as we get back to the location, buster," she fumed, "your ass is fired."

"Why wait?" I said, then slammed on the brakes. Her briefcase flew off her lap, and she barely had time to get her hands up to keep her face off the dashboard. "Why fucking wait?" I bluffed, knowing that what she needed at her uncle's, she needed badly enough to put up with this.

"What *are* you doing?"

"Get out," I said, reaching over to open her door. "This is my rig, lady, and I don't fucking work for you anymore."

Suzanne started to protest, saying she'd get the goddamned beer, but I jerked the emergency brake, shouting "Walk or fuck!" and bulled her out the open door, grabbed her flailing fists at the wrist, dodged a flying nutcracker knee, turned her around, gathered a fistful of thick hair, bent her over the seat, and wrestled the tight leather pants down her slim hips.

"You wouldn't, you son of a bitch . . ." she muttered against the seat covers as I popped the string of her thong bikini.

"Oh, but I will, lady," I said. Then planted a long, wet kiss at the crack of her lovely ass, laughed, and let her go. I jumped back behind the wheel before she jerked her pants up. As she started to climb back into the rig, I held up my hand. "I thought you were going to get me a beer, honey."

Suzanne got the beer before she settled into her seat, but from the look on her face, anger firing a flushed glaze across the high cheekbones, I suspected she thought she might have preferred rape to the humiliation of getting me a beer. At least I didn't make her open it.

But as I drove away, I reminded myself that this wasn't any fucking John Wayne movie where Maureen O'Hara's just been waiting for this moment of physical domination to fall back in love with me. Nope, pilgrim. If I turned my back, this woman would fancy nothing more than burying an axe between my shoulder blades. Or nestling a sawed-off 12-gauge at the nape of my neck. But, hell, I'd always known that about her. And the sorry truth—sorry for both of us—was in that angry moment we'd never been closer, never been more of a single mind.

Suzanne was perfectly composed by the time we reached the gate. Dunston was right—she could have been a great actress. She even smiled when Kaufmann's guards, dressed like guys who had seen too many Peckinpah movies, waved us through, then aside to a turnout to let a black Suburban pass us on its way out. Then they went over the Blazer with mirrors, bomb-sniffing dogs, and a finely toothed cock's comb. Just in case they'd missed something, they drove us up to the *casa* in an electric cart, one guard carrying Suzanne's briefcase, another my cane, and a third a Benelli M-3 12-gauge shotgun.

At the front door we had to pass through a metal detector, Suzanne's briefcase and my cane through an X-ray machine, and a more serious set of guards who looked like Secret Service agents. Emilio Kaufmann stood smiling, thirty yards away across the tiled foyer, safe behind a portable plexiglass shield. Suzanne's briefcase was restored to her, but the tall guy who seemed to be in charge held on to my cane as he conferred with his shorter partner. Then they X-rayed the cane again, conferred, and that tall guy stepped over to whisper to Kaufmann. After a moment, Kaufmann spread his arms and his smile.

"Forgive me, my dear *sobrina*," he said pleasantly, his English without accent, "for these foolish precautions. But your call came so suddenly . . ."

"Please forgive me, *tío*, but a matter of considerable importance has arisen."

"Of course, of course," he said, even more pleasant, "whatever it is we will take care of it directly . . . but it seems that your employee . . . something is not right about his cane. . . ."

"Milodragovitch," I said. "That's my name, Señor Kaufmann, and my cane's just a stick with a flask in the handle. Unscrew it. There's a couple of large shots of tequila in there. Herradura *anejo*."

The shorter guy started to unscrew the handle, but before he could there was a shout—*"Cuidado!"*—from the tall one. Once again Kaufmann begged forgiveness. From me this time. And suggested that I step outside the double doors and do the honors myself.

"No problem," I said, then limped through the still open doorway, followed by the shorter guy with my cane. He handed it to me, told the guy with the shotgun to cover me, then stepped back inside. The double doors closed heavily, thumping with a weight more like steel than oak. Two closed-circuit television cameras over the doors buzzed like angry insects as they focused on me as I unscrewed the handle of the cane and took a sip.

"Nothing but the best," I said, raising the cane to the camera. "Perhaps you'll join me, Señor Kaufmann . . ."

"Drink it all, gringo," came a metallic voice. So I did. Then held the flask upside down so they could see the last few drops splatter darkly on the stone steps. Then replaced the handle.

"Please, sir," came Kaufmann's voice over the intercom, "you will join me in a *copita* . . . I have some tequila that will make your Herradura taste like horse piss."

"My pleasure, Señor Kaufmann," I said. "I have been told that business affairs in Mexico proceed at a more deliberate and polite pace. But no one mentioned that I would have to drink horse piss."

Kaufmann's laughter seemed honestly amused, if slightly tinny. But when the doors opened, the metal detector, X-ray machine, and plexiglass shield had been moved aside. Suzanne and I were conducted into a large office off the main hall where Kaufmann sat behind a desk worthy of a pope, a narrow, pristine expanse of ancient Spanish oak broken only by a cellular telephone, a Toshiba laptop, and a silver tray containing a black bottle, a silver dish of cut limes, and three silver shot glasses. Suzanne and I were seated in bishop's chairs, and Kaufmann poured the tequila and dismissed his guards with a wave of his soft hand, then picked up a shot glass. *"Salute,"* he said, then we drank. Finished, Kaufmann leaned forward, elbows resting lightly on the dark oak, his manicured fingers steepled.

I set the cane in my lap and twisted the handle counterclockwise until I felt the tiny trigger nestle against my finger.

"Now, my dear Suzanne," he said, "what service may I perform for you?"

Suzanne opened the briefcase, slipped a folder across the dark oak, and said, "This is the fax I received this afternoon when I attempted to transfer funds into my production account."

Kaufmann opened the folder, glanced at the single sheet, then frowned. "But how can this be?" he said, then turned to his laptop.

"That's my question," Suzanne said.

Kaufmann's fingers flew over the computer keys, then waited as the machine buzzed, then beeped as it connected him to his bank in Panama. After a moment, his fingers flew again. Whatever he saw on the screen, Kaufmann obviously didn't like. He reached for the telephone, saying, "I'll call the bank personally, and we'll . . ."

"It was my fucking money anyway," I said quietly, then slapped my cane on the expensive desktop and pointed it directly at his face.

Kaufmann rose from his chair suddenly, his light hand held in front of his face as if he could ward off the cane.

"No, you stupid sons of bitches," Suzanne grunted. But we were too busy to be insulted.

And I pulled the tiny trigger.

Quick as a striking snake the coiled wisp of carbon fiber spit from the ferrule of the cane, and a loop made of wire almost as tiny as a spider's strand and even stronger than steel cable settled gracefully over Kauf-mann's head. I released the trigger and let the spring ratchet just long enough to tighten the loop. The fingers of Kaufmann's right hand clawed at the scant fiber as it tightened nicely into the soft flesh of his neck.

"Gotcha, motherfucker," I said.

Behind me I heard the scurry of feet, the racking of semiautomatic pistol slides, and the snicker of safeties moving to the off position.

"Shoot the woman," Kaufmann said without hesitation.

"Loan me a piece," I said, laughing, "and I'll shoot the bitch myself. But if you want to live another ten seconds, Kaufmann, you best keep those fuckers off my back."

Kaufmann held up his free hand. The noises behind me stopped.

"This is how it is," I said. "If my finger slips off this little trigger, nothing you can do will stop the spring. And nothing you have will cut the carbon wire. First, the ends of your fingers will pop off and scatter like grapes across this lovely desk. Then the blood to your brain will cease. But the spring is so quick and so strong that chances are you'll still be conscious when it cuts off your head."

"What the fuck do you think you're doing?" Suzanne asked, confused.

"Did you think it would be funny to have me watch my fucking money move around on a computer screen?"

"I don't know," she said in a small voice that sounded almost sincere.

"And if you want to walk out of here alive and well and with any chance to finish your movie, you better keep your ass in the chair, honey, and your mouth shut," I said. "For a change."

"But I would have put the money back . . ." she blathered.

"I told you to shut up," I said, easing around the desk to shove Kaufmann back into his chair and stand behind him. If I was going to be shot, I wanted to see it coming. "Tell your men to unload their weapons and take off their clothes. Pile them on that couch over there. Except for one loaded Glock. Which I want right here by my left hand. Then tell them to stretch out on the floor, facedown, with their fingers laced behind their heads."

I had to give him this—Kaufmann didn't shit his pants or start weeping. He took a deep breath, then said calmly,

"Should I speak to them in English or Spanish, Mr. Milodragovitch?"

"Hey, you're the one with your nuts in the wringer, Señor Kaufmann," I said. "Tell them in Urdu if you want to." Then I let the spring slip a notch. When the ratchet clicked into place, everybody jumped. And Kaufmann rattled Spanish at his men.

The men complained. But not for long. Another burst of Spanish stopped that. Suzanne looked up once as the tall guy placed his pistol on the desk between us, then, as he joined the pile of naked guards, she sighed as if it were her last breath.

"Movie business too tough for you, kid?" I said. "Or is it embezzlement that makes you sigh?"

She had no answer, except for her trembling fingers clattering against the hard leather of the open briefcase.

"All right, Mr. Milodragovitch," Kaufmann said, a slight quaver in his voice now. "What can I do for you? It seems you already have your money back, plus a considerable amount of mine. Surely we can negotiate some sort of deal . . ."

"This ain't about money, asshole," I said, "and dead men don't make deals." Then I picked up his cellular telephone, dialed the number the DEA agent had given me. He answered almost immediately.

"I got him," I said, "but you need to clear me through the U.S. Customs and Immigration at the border. Okay? White Blazer. Sawyer Security Service logo on the doors. Black-headed bitch driving. Kaufmann in the front seat beside her. And me behind him."

"You got it," came his quick answer.

As I clicked off the phone and set it down, Suzanne suddenly stood up as if she'd gone mad.

"Listen, Milo," she said hotly, "I'm really sorry about your money, and even sorry about Sughrue, but I don't think I'm really involved here. And even though this piece of shit was going to have me shot to save his rotten life, I'm sure as hell not going to help you get him across the border. In fact, I'm out of here right . . ."

I picked up the Glock with my left hand. "There was a

time, honey," I said, "when I was nearly as good with my left hand as my right. But that was a long time ago. I might not be able to put a round in a nonvital part of your lovely ass."

Suzanne stared at me. Maybe she wondered if I would actually shoot her.

"You owe me a pound of flesh," I said.

"I hope you take a long fucking time to die," Suzanne said as she sat down.

Kaufmann cleared his throat. "May I ask who you called?"

"Some fucking DEA jerk in El Paso," I said, unable to think of a reason to lie.

"I'm afraid you've made a terrible mistake," Kaufmann said, visibly relaxed. "The DEA is not interested in me. We have a deal . . ."

"I don't think this guy is interested in a deal, either," I said. "I think he wants to fly you to Costa Rica . . ."

"Puntarenas . . ." Suzanne said.

"That fucking Dickerson," Kaufmann said.

"Hey, I've seen the tape," Suzanne said quickly, "and my uncle had nothing to do with his daughter's death . . ."

"You have the tape?" Kaufmann said, amazed.

"Her ace in the hole," I said.

"It's in a safety deposit box in LA," Suzanne admitted.

"What do you bet it's sitting next to a copy of your lab files and the formula for the wonder drug?" I asked Kaufmann.

"My god, is there no loyalty anymore . . ." he said, then turned to me. "Dickerson killed his own daughter," Kaufmann said. "It was an accident, I am quite sure. But still, he pulled the trigger. Not me."

"What does Dickerson have to do with you?" Suzanne asked me.

Once again, thinking I had the upper hand, I told the truth. "He promised to bury the evidence of a murder and keep Sughrue out of prison," I said.

"Oh, no," Suzanne said. "You fucking fool . . ."

"Xavier!" Kaufmann shouted.

Xavier Kaufmann, who didn't seem to recognize me in my sunglasses, Stetson, and different name, stepped smartly through a side door into the office, smiling and very much alive, wearing a state-of-the-art prosthesis very much like a real hand and holding a small automatic pistol in his other. Eddie Forsyth, with his metallic smile and bandaged cheek, followed him, pushing a bound and gagged Kate in front of him, a large automatic pistol dangling insolently from his hand.

"Now let's see whose nuts are in the wringer, asshole," he hissed through wired teeth.

"Howdy Doody, motherfucker," I said. And I took Forsyth out of the equation with a single round to the face. The 10mm round must have been a jacketed hollow-point because most of the back of Eddie's head blew into the next room and he hit the tiled floor like a sack of freckled shit.

But Xavier, quick as a snake, dodged behind Kate and had his pistol lodged at the base of her skull before I could pop him.

Sughrue

Fucking Milo. He was always crazy about seat belts. Wouldn't ride with me if I didn't buckle up. So the seat belt saves my ass. That and the failure of the Suburban's bumper, which rips like pot metal while the two vehicles are turning in the air. When the vehicles land on their wheels, I stay in the seat, while the four Mexican *banditos* fly like broken dolls through the open doors of the Suburban. My GMC pickup is a total loss, which I hate, the rear axle propped on a small boulder in the shallow river, but I'm mostly okay. Nothing important broken, no arterial bleeding. The Suburban rests nose-down in the middle of the river, but its four occupants are scattered like so much trash on the steep slope above.

As I scrabble up to check the bodies, I hope they're all dead, skin bags of shattered bone, burst viscera, and blood. But one isn't. He's dying but not dead, his flight broken by a clump of prickly pear. And he opens his eyes long enough to see me. I can't have that, so I take his mini-Uzi, thinking I will do what I have to do. This is no time for ceremony. Although there's no fire, the explosive dust from the wreck rises like a firestorm in the afternoon sky.

Even as I have the sights of the automatic weapon aimed into the middle of his forehead, the Mexican's eyes cloud over. Goddamn, I'm tired. Fucker meant to kill me. But I close his sightless eyes before I leave, and find myself jerking a cluster of barbed pear spines from his forehead. Finally, I make myself leave when a red ant crawls between the slack lips. Jesus. For a moment I understand how Milo must have felt when he gave up gunfire. But Milo only has himself to think about. I hammer the license plates off the pickup, hoping it will slow the pursuit, grab a pair of running shoes out of the tool box, wash my bloody head in the river, stretch my legs, then go.

I leave the Uzi behind because I know where to safely cross the Rio Grande after dark, know where my paranoid stashes of weapons and supplies are cached, know I can run to Whitney and Baby Lester before daylight, pray I can beat the bastards to my home.

MILO

IT APPEARS YOUR LEFT HAND STILL SHOOTS QUITE WELL," Kaufmann said to me quietly. "As does Xavier's."

"Yeah," I said, "but is he willing to die?"

"Please," he said, then nodded carefully toward Suzanne. "I know you wouldn't care if this one died," he added. "Even though I love her deeply . . ."

At this Suzanne snorted.

". . . she is a viper the world could do well without. But I suspect you have slightly different feelings about her sister." When I didn't respond, Kaufmann continued, "So I am confident that now you have good reason to negotiate."

"It looks like a Mexican standoff," I said, laughing. "But before we get into deals, I'd like to know what's at stake here."

Suzanne and Kaufmann looked at each other for a long time.

"If you don't release this infernal device," Kaufmann said quietly, "Xavier will kill Katherine."

"How about I give you a couple of notches," I said, "and you tell me what the fuck is really going on."

In order to have a weapon that wouldn't set off a metal detector or show up on an X ray, it had taken a gunsmith, a watchmaker, an aeronautical engineer, and a robotics technician. And the cost had been almost prohibitively expensive—I flinched when the guy who made Carver D's shotgun cane told me the price—but once I had the key to the financial machinations on Ray Lara's floppy disk, money was no longer a problem. Instead of trusting his memory, since a second wrong attempt would wipe the information, Ray Lara had it tattooed inside the dog's mouth. Good old Sheba. She'd held the key all that time. And once I convinced Betty Porterfield to return one of my several calls, it was no problem to have Carver D's computer friends trace the remainder of my father's money to several numbered accounts in Panama, then transfer it, plus a healthy chunk from some of Ray Lara's other skimming operations, back into my trust account in Meriwether. Only this time, I had to be at the bank in person to remove or move the money. In case I didn't make it back across the border, my new will left almost everything to Baby Lester.

And now it looked as if I wasn't going to make it back.

"First, I'm sorry to disabuse you of the notion that I control the cocaine smuggling in this section of northern Mexico," Kaufmann said, "although at one time many years ago, when my father saw fit to cast me out of the *familia,* in revenge I invented the marijuana distribution system sometimes known as the Dallas Parkway and made quite a bit of money, enough so that, once my father died, I was able to buy back into the family business . . ." Kaufmann paused. I'd given him enough slack to ease his fingers from beneath the filament cutting into his neck. He took a deep breath. "And frankly, even before cocaine smuggling seized the border, I found myself troubled by the violence and removed myself from that area of business."

"So what was that shit earlier about how the DEA couldn't touch you?" I asked.

Obviously, this was a question nobody wanted to answer. Kaufmann coughed, Suzanne squirmed, and Xavier spoke for the first time.

"I grow weary of this nonsense," Xavier said quietly. "Release him, or I'll kneecap this skinny little dyke. Now."

"You'll be dead before she hits the floor, kiddo," I said. "I'll blow your nose right out the back of your head."

"Xavier, please," Kaufmann said. "I know it is not your nature, but please stay calm. We can work this out." Then he tried to shift his head to look at me. "Perhaps Mr. Milodragovitch will release my throat just a tiny bit again. As a gesture of good faith?"

"I think it's only fair to warn you," I said, "that if I release the spring too much, you face a much more horrible death."

"What could be . . ."

"AIDS," I said. "Too quick a release triggers a small plastic dart filled with the HIV virus."

"Jesus, you're sick," Suzanne sputtered. "Sick."

"I didn't start this shit, lady," I said, then gave Kaufmann two clicks worth of slack, a quarter inch. He flinched and might have fallen out of the chair if he could have. The AIDS thing was an ugly idea that Carver D had added. The part about the dart was true, but not the AIDS part. But it insured that even if Kaufmann escaped the noose, the rest of his life was ruined by the worry. "I didn't steal any money, didn't have anybody shot," I continued, "didn't start any of this shit. But believe me, I'm going to have the last word."

"What do you want?" Kaufmann sighed as he touched his throat. "Just tell me."

"First, Xavier puts his pistol down," I said, "then . . ."

"Not a fucking chance, gringo," Xavier said.

"So much for negotiations," I said.

"Xavier!" Kaufmann shouted.

"You old fool," Xavier said, shaking angrily. "I should have killed you a long time ago."

"You tell me what it's like to jack off with a plastic hand, *culo*," I said to Xavier, since it seemed the asshole wasn't going to recognize me, "and I'll tell you what it's like to dig your own grave."

"You!" he shouted.

"Katie, hit the floor!" I shouted, and had two rounds into Xavier's face before he pulled his trigger, gouging a short furrow of flesh out of the back of Kate's shoulder.

"I hope he wasn't one of your favorite sons," I said to Kaufmann, who shook his head slightly as Suzanne vomited into her briefcase. "Now let's get this shit over. I want some answers."

Kaufmann nodded and murmured, "He's not my son."

Suzanne wiped her mouth, went to Kate's slack, unconscious body, tugged her out of the gore, then untied and ungagged her and pressed a silk scarf against her bleeding shoulder.

"Who killed Rita?" I asked Kaufmann.

"Eddie," Suzanne answered breathlessly from her knees.

"Why?"

"He loved me. We met on that dumb fucking football movie in Austin. And he just decided he loved me," Suzanne said mournfully. "And when I told him . . . asked him to lean on Rita—she got homesick in Mexico—and she wanted more money to stay down there and let me use her identity. Plus the fat bitch told Aaron what was going on . . ."

"And he wanted money, too?" I suggested.

"Not money," Suzanne said. "The stupid bastard wanted a part in my movie. Can you believe it? He couldn't stand still in front of an empty camera."

"Did you ask Eddie to *lean* on Aaron, too?" I asked.

Suzanne nodded slowly, as if she were actually filled with remorse.

"So where the hell does Jacobson fit into this shit?" I asked.

"Andrew belonged to me," Kaufmann said like a man suddenly awakening from a long, blurry nap. "Dead-end job in a small-town state-chartered bank, married to an ugly woman . . . You know how it is . . . He and Raymundo were in the Army together . . ."

"So who the fuck's idea was it to steal my money?"

"Jacobson's," they answered in unison. A bit too quickly to suit me. "It was his way out."

"And the other money?"

"She convinced him to steal from me, too," Kaufmann said. "She fucked him stupid."

"Jesus," I said to Suzanne. "Who haven't you fucked to make this movie?"

Suzanne turned to face me, her face proud and angry and beautiful. "Myself," she said. "I haven't fucked myself." Then she stood up as Kate began to stir.

If it had ended there, perhaps she would have been right. But I'd made a crucial mistake. I'd sold the old boy short.

The barrel of the street-sweeper shotgun tapped against the carved wood of the doorway, tapped softly like a small branch against a rain-dark window, a light tap, but as insistent as death's final pointed knock, then the real Baron of

Enojada stepped over the bodies in the doorway and into the office, tall and erect as if in dress blues, a military Colt .45 automatic carried loosely in one wrinkled hand, a large smile almost softening his weathered face.

SUGHRUE

THREE OF THEM MAKE THE MISTAKE OF WAITING OUTSIDE.
Three city guys in baggy suits and street shoes waiting in the
brush around the double-wide, their black Suburban only
half-hidden behind the tin shed where Milo's Caddy is
parked, the smoke of their cigarettes hanging in the still air
of the desert dawn. A dark blue roil of clouds threatens just
beyond the mountains to the north. I could wait for the wind
and rain. It would be easier in the rain with the wind to cover
the sound of my movements. But I can't wait.

I strip off my bloody and torn uniform, dress in my
breechcloth and knee-high moccasins, and take them one at a
time with the Bowie. It's all I can do to keep from taking
their scalps. A knife makes you think that way.

Luck is with me. Through a crack in the living room cur-
tains I can see Whitney and Lester bound and gagged on the
carpet, a sleepy thug on the couch, another goddamned mini-
Uzi resting on his knees. I watch for a moment. Whitney and
Lester look exhausted and terrified but awake and alive.
Thankfully alive.

There's a silenced .22 in my gear, but I can't kill him in
front of my family. Can't. So I crawl beneath the steps,
crouch, waiting, occasionally tapping on the aluminum door
with my blade, tap until the bastard steps outside to see
what's happening.

When I cut his throat, I nearly take his head off.

I can't go inside covered with blood, can't scrub the blood
off me with sand, can't leave the bastard's body sprawled at
my front door. So I stash it in their Suburban. And the others,
too.

Then I head for the horse trough to wash away the dark

smears that cover my body. I don't know how long I stand naked in the water. Long enough for the blue norther to triumph over the dawn, arriving on blistering gusts of wind and needles of sleet. Long enough to remember the long float down the irrigation ditch, muddy water thick in my mouth, my blood leaking like sand. Long enough to know I'll never be afraid again.

Only then do I retrieve my gear from the brush, dress, and climb the steps as if climbing a gallows into my house.

Now, goddammit, now nothing will ever be the same.

Lester is the easiest to calm. The long silent Apache hours we've spent in chaparral have paid off. He's tough, no longer a baby. He drinks the hot milk and coffee, then goes to pack without asking a question. Just a few things, I tell the boy. You have to choose what you can't leave behind.

Whitney, on the other hand, tough as she is, has a lot of questions. Too many. But after a few minutes of long, hard holding, she, too, throws a few things together she can't bear to leave behind—a picture of her parents in a canoe in the Boundary Waters; a perfect obsidian arrowhead she once found outside Terlingua; our marriage license—then waits for me at the door.

"You're not taking anything?" she says.

"You and our son," I answer. "That's all I need."

Whitney hugs me until my ribs crack.

"Fucking Milo," she whispers fondly. The boy hears and grins.

Before we can leave, we hear the sound of a car, its springs creaking over the rough road. Not coming fast. But coming.

"Shit," I say, picking up the Uzi. "If anything happens, go out the back door and run. Lester knows the way."

The car, an anonymous gray sedan, stops in front as I step outside. It's the rawboned guy from the DEA compound. He climbs out of the car, not even glancing at the Uzi, ignoring it as he does the freezing rain in his face.

"Where's your buddy Milodragovitch?" he says.

"I don't know," I admit. "Exactly. Maybe dead in Mexico. Why?"

"He called me late yesterday afternoon," the agent says. "Told me he was bringing Emilio Kaufmann across the border."

"What for?"

"For me."

"What for?"

"To keep your sorry ass off death row," he says. "But he didn't show."

"Shit," I say, too tired to think. "Look, I'll make you a deal. If you'll take my family to a safe place," I say, "I'll go get the son of a bitch for you."

"Which one? Milodragovitch or Kaufmann?"

"Whatever," I say.

"Deal," he says.

"Deal," I say, then sigh. "Isn't that what law enforcement is all about?"

"Sometimes," he answers tiredly.

MILO

EMILIO," THE GENERAL SAID SOFTLY, STRIDING AROUND THE desk. "For a smart man you lack the capacity to pour piss out of a boot with the instructions engraved on the heel. I didn't survive all that time in the Army to lose everything now over a stupid cowboy and a dumb fucking western movie." Then he pressed the pistol against Kaufmann's cheek.

Nobody will ever know how Emilio Kaufmann intended to defend himself because without another word, the General pulled the trigger as Suzanne screamed, "Daddy, no!"

I have to admit that I flinched, deafened by the muzzle blast, blinded by the bloody splash as Kaufmann's head exploded in my face. Kaufmann bounced off me, then flopped onto the desk, jerking the cane out of my hand. The General, nearly as covered as I was with blood and brain matter, but completely undaunted, stepped forward, clubbed my wrist with the .45, then stepped back and aimed it directly at my nose as the Glock clattered across the desk.

"Milodragovitch," he said, "too many people know you're here, and I would prefer not to put a round into you. But as you can see, I'm more than willing. So please don't force me to fire."

"It seems I'm out of options," I said, trying to wipe the gore off my face. "What now?"

His daughters whimpered behind him, and he snapped at them, "You girls shut up!" I understood where Suzanne got her whipcrack voice. "I understand," he said to me, a sparkle in his watery blue eyes, "that you have a great deal of my money."

"I just took back what was mine," I said. "And maybe a little for my trouble . . ."

"I had nothing to do with that," he said calmly.

"What about the movie?" Suzanne asked as she rose to her feet, leaving Kate to weep dark tears upon the tiled floor.

"Fuck the movie," he said.

"I've heard that somewhere before," I said.

"Either restore my money, Mr. Milodragovitch, or I will kill you and everybody you ever cared about."

"I can't let you do that," I said.

In that long silence afterward, the guy with the street sweeper stepped into the room to cover me. The four body-guards in their baggy shorts struggled off the floor and hurried toward their clothes, which seemed more important to them than their weapons.

"Then you're a dead man," the General said calmly.

And except for Kate, I would have been.

"Daddy!" she screamed from her knees, Xavier's small automatic braced familiarly in her hands. The joys of military life. "Daddy, no!"

The old gentleman didn't flinch at her scream. But he did drop the .45 without pulling the trigger after she shot him in the elbow. I grunted as if punched in the gut. The guy with the street sweeper was half-turned when she put three rounds into the side of his chest. He did pull the trigger before he stumbled into the desk, but only the computer and the cell phone died. I had the shotgun before he hit the floor. But before I could cover the half-naked bodyguards, they were out the door.

Within moments unaimed automatic weapon fire tore through the open front door.

"Can't you stop them?" Suzanne screamed at her father, who had fallen into Kaufmann's chair, his arm hanging at an ugly angle, arterial blood pumping in gouts from his arm.

"Not a chance," he said with the calm of shock. "We've fallen into the den of snakes . . ." Then he fainted.

I grabbed Suzanne's hand, placed her thumb against the pressure point in her father's armpit. "Hold that!" I shouted into her blank face. But her hand fell limply away. I slapped her, cursed her until she kept her thumb there. By then I could see men circling. "Help me!" I shouted at Kate, and we slammed the oak shutters over the wide window behind Kaufmann's desk.

Then I scrabbled under the desk until I found the Glock and the General's .45. As I handed them to Kate, I told her, "I've got to shut the front door. You just reach around the doorframe and fire out the front door until I get it closed. You hear me?"

She nodded, so I didn't look back, just rolled out of the office into the great hall until I got behind the plexiglass shield and rolled it to the door. Fucking rounds were hitting everywhere. And Kate was covering me like a pro, crouching and aiming her fire until I got the steel doors shut, and we retreated into the office.

Automatic fire had begun to splinter the heavy shutters, and Suzanne had pulled her father to the floor for cover.

"We have to get out of here," Kate said.

"Where?" I said. "And fucking how?"

"The basement," Suzanne said. "We'll be safe there."

With nothing to lose, I gathered the shoulder holsters, pistols, and clips off the couch, wrapped them over my arm, then folded the General over my shoulder and followed the women across the great hall, down a winding set of stone stairs to a large solid door. Suzanne grabbed a key ring off the wall beside the door, unlocked it, and led us to her version of safety. A large, expensively furnished stone-lined chamber, more like a tomb or a bomb shelter than a living space.

They couldn't get in. We couldn't get out. But Andy Jacobson poked his head out of the bathroom, wondering what the hell was going on. I set the weapons on a library table, doubled up my fist, and knocked the little bastard into the bathtub. I wrapped a tourniquet around the General's arm, then stood under the shower over Jacobson's unconscious body long enough to wash most of the blood and shit off me. I sat down in a soft leather chair with the shotgun across my knees, leaned back prepared to bleed to death. The round that Kate put into her father's arm hadn't stopped there. It was floating around somewhere in my guts.

"Get that piece of shit out of the tub, Katie," I said, "and fill it up before they figure out to turn off the water."

"It's not bleeding much," Kate said later, washing my sweaty face with a cold washrag.

"Thanks," I said, not saying what I thought. *Not much on the outside.*

Suzanne huddled over her father on the large bed, tending the tourniquet, trying to save his arm. A lost cause, I suspected. As lost as we were. Jacobson drooled, strapped into a chair in front of me. Kate had found me a bottle of brandy, which I sipped and tried not to swallow. Occasionally, we would hear muffled sounds through the oak-shrouded steel door. But when I wondered why the bodyguards didn't blow the door, Suzanne pointed out that they needed the General to get to the money.

"They want to kill you," she said, the bloody planes of her face staring over her father's slowly heaving chest. "Not him. Or me. Or Kate."

Kate leaned her forehead on my knee, whispering, "I'll die before I let them kill you."

"Thanks, kid," I said, my hand on her close-cropped head, "but that's not necessary."

"Oh yes it fucking is," she said, raising her face to me. "What was it you said? I always wanted to fall in love with somebody I couldn't fuck."

"You people are sick," Suzanne said, as she hurried into the bathroom for another towel.

Kate and I laughed. Laughed loud enough to make Jacobson stir in his chair. His eyes followed Suzanne like a sick puppy's.

"Beautiful woman, hey?" I said to him.

"Frankly, I liked her with a little more meat on her bones," Jacobson said. "Suzanne," he whined as she passed him again. But she ignored him. Kate and I were still giggling.

Kate staggered into the bathroom to wash her face. Somehow the General's corrupt blood had missed her.

Or maybe it wasn't in the blood. Maybe the General had learned corruption. At great government expense. Or maybe all the years in Central America had found the real bastard beneath all the breeding and education and gentility. Too often it seems that way. We send our legions among the savages in the name of democracy, and they learn violence and torture in the name of United Fruit. I wasn't sure, now, if we had created General Kehoe, or he us, but I knew that we had created Emilio Kaufmann . . .

And now all the bad guys were dead. Except for me. And I supposed I was dead, too. Shot by the only decent person in the whole fucking deal. And it was never about drugs or money. It was always about a goddamned western movie. In some way I didn't exactly mind dying. As I drifted away, I heard the sounds of rushing air, felt the force of moving water, heard the great beasts singing . . .

"Look!" somebody screamed at me, slapped me. "We've been here all night. So what the fuck happens now?" Suzanne asked, standing over me, pointing a pistol in my face. A muffled pounding came from the door.

I suppose I had drifted a long way, that the pounding had been going on for a long time. I meant to put a load of buckshot into Jacobson before I died. But suddenly it seemed too much trouble. You step on pissants. You don't shoot them.

"What?" was all I could say.

"What happens now?"

"We survive this shit, love, which seems a long chance," I said dreamily, "your father dies in prison, and you wander the earth like a pariah dog. Again."

"But you loved me, dammit," she demanded. "I fucking know you did. I can tell."

"Maybe I did," I said. "I even put enough of Ray Lara's money aside for you to finish the movie . . ."

"I knew it," she said. "I knew you loved me. I'll give you the Puntarenas tape. Give you the formula. Just tell me how to get the money. Come on, goddammit, you love me . . ."

"I'm not completely responsible for my character flaws," I said, then looked into those hard green eyes. "Or yours. Maybe I'd've felt differently if you hadn't put all thirty rounds into Aaron Tipton and your father hadn't been such a scumbag."

"My father's dead."

"Tourniquet mismanagement," I suggested, then laughed.

Suzanne clubbed me across the face with the pistol. "I'm going to give you to them," she said. "They'll make you talk about the money . . ."

"No, you're not," Kate said, leaning over her father's body, her shining face dripping tears. Then she walked over to stand in front of her sister.

"Fuck it," I said. "Let her, Katie. It's fine. It's a fair price . . ."

"The General's dead," Suzanne said flatly. "It's our only chance."

"Please," I begged, "let her give me up. Please . . ."

Perhaps it was the begging. Who knows? For the first time in a long day and night of blood and guts, Kate collapsed, her forehead again on my knee. I could hear the rain on Betty Porterfield's tin roof as I drifted away again, could hear in the background the pounding against the door as Suzanne struggled with the locks.

Then somebody else was slapping my face and cursing me.

"Goddammit, Milo, you fucking son of a bitch."

And I knew it wasn't the angels.

SUGHRUE

FUCKING MILO.

Dickerson and I find the gate to Kaufmann's compound wide open and not a soul in sight. Which explains the pickup loads of furniture we had met on the road up. The small plane intended for Emilio Kaufmann has carried Whitney and Lester to El Paso, where they are safely locked in the DEA compound. Dickerson can't call in backup and I don't know anybody who might help Milo. Maybe not even himself. Like the open, unguarded gates, nothing makes any sense anymore.

And the front doors of the mansion are wide open, too, the dark burns of an explosive charge scarring their width. Once inside, for the first time in my life, the phrase "charnel house" comes to mind. The place is stripped to the walls. Except for the dead bodies. The buzzing of carrion flies is as heavy as the smell.

We work the house like a rifle squad, and the fear makes the air heavy. We breathe like gut-shot lions, our breaths louder than our footsteps. Until at last we find the basement stairs, the trail of blood black and fly-specked on the pale stone steps. Then the locked door, scarred with gunfire and sledgehammer blows. Covered by Dickerson, I pound on it with my foot until we hear the sound of the key in the lock.

When it opens, Suzanne stands as if struck dumb as we brush past her, ready for anything. Except what we find. The dead General, Andy Jacobson bound to a chair, Katherine weeping, and fucking Milo holding a bottle of brandy against a blood-soaked towel, grinning like a happy drunk.

MILO

The first thing I did when I got out of the hospital was to buy Sughrue a new pickup. A loaded Dodge Ram 4x4 with a club cab. I hadn't been gut shot as badly as Sughrue, but I had been gut shot and couldn't help them load the truck; I supervised as he gathered his goods and family to head back to Montana, their Texas experiment over. Katie rode along to take care of Lester and, as she said, "Check out the broads in Montana." Whatever Sughrue planned, I could tell that he was finished with this part of life.

Suzanne has disappeared again. Even before her father's funeral. They buried the old bastard with full military honors at the Fort Bliss cemetery. Hell, Ollie North walked on Iran-Contra, so why shouldn't a dead man? Maybe we shouldn't teach our soldiers how to smuggle.

Of course, Suzanne has the formula for the Kaufmanns' super drug and her witchy ability to become anyone she pleases, so I fear the world hasn't heard the end of her. She also has the real copy of the Puntarenas tape, which I suspect implicates her father as much as Emilio Kaufmann.

As far as Dickerson can tell, neither Kaufmann nor the General will be much missed in the drug trade, and nobody seems even vaguely interested in revenge. Maybe they're just happy for the opportunity. Such is life along the border. Another kingpin smuggler slips into place as easily as a snake sheds its skin.

Dickerson has postponed retirement to fight what he thinks is the good fight at the border. I tried to talk him out of it over several dinners, but he's a good cop and refused all my arguments. The lost war goes on. Greed beats good sense every time.

As soon as I was out of the recovery room after they dug the little .32 slug out of my viscera, Sam Dunston was standing at my bedside. Because I'd made Sughrue call him. For a piece of the movie, I provided enough money to finish the shooting and postproduction. Sam was as happy as I'd ever seen a man. Unfortunately, the old bastard died three weeks later of heart failure in the middle of a shouting match with the assistant director. Roy Jordan brought me one of the old man's favorite bolo ties, the braids of dark sweaty leather held together with an obsidian spear point. He thanked me for making the old man's last days happy.

Of course, the preppie kid took over the movie, cut a politically correct piece of shit out of it, and somehow I lost the money I put up. But it wasn't exactly my money anyway. I understand that's how Hollywood works.

And once they removed the clips from my belly, I settled my affairs in El Paso. I shared a bottle of tequila with the Soames brothers over Rocky's grave.

Then in Austin I had many drinks with Carver D as I told him the promised story. He thanked me, then told me he had no place to publish it anymore, even if he could. "I'm sorry," he said. "Someday the bastards will own it all." I didn't have to ask who the bastards were. The fat man seemed hugely sad as I left, and I promised to come back.

Outside the beer garden Hangas climbed out of the Continental to let me know that all was not lost just yet. His boss had put most of the money from the sale of the *Dark Coast* into a foundation for alternative newspapers and investigative reporting.

Then it was time to heave my sorry ass into the Beast and drive to Blanco. Take the long chance.

Maybe Sheba heard the Beast rumbling over the last cattle guard. Or maybe Betty heard it. They never told me. But they met me at the last locked gate, Sheba prancing in the bright morning sunshine of the open winter, the tennis ball in her teeth, and Betty Porterfield with a small but true smile on her face.

"Hey, bud," she said, "you look rode hard and put up wet."

"Right," I said. "Remember I told you I'd been shot at but never hit?"

"Yep."

"Can't say that now," I said.

"If I'd known you were coming, bud," she said, "I'd have fixed breakfast."

"It's not too late," I said.

"I guess it's never too late," she said, then opened the gate.

Welcome to the Island of Morada—getting there is easy, leaving . . . is murder.

Embark on the ultimate, on-line, fantasy vacation with
MODUS OPERANDI.

Join fellow mystery lovers in the murderously fun MODUS OPERANDI, a unique on-line, multi-player, multi-service, interactive, mystery game launched by The Mysterious Press, Time Warner Electronic Publishing and Simutronics Corporation.

Featuring never-ending foul play by your favorite Mysterious Press authors and editors, MODUS OPERANDI is set on the fictional Caribbean island of Morada. Forget packing, passports and planes, entry to Morada is easy—all you need is a vivid imagination.

Simutronics GameMasters are available in MODUS OPERANDI around the clock, adding new mysteries and puzzles, offering helpful hints, and taking you virtually by the hand through the killer gaming environment as you come in contact with players from on-line services the world over. Mysterious Press writers and editors will also be there to participate in real-time on-line special events or just to throw a few back with you at the pub.

MODUS OPERANDI is available on-line now.

Join the mystery and mayhem on:
- America Online® at keyword MODUS
- Genie® at keyword MODUS
- PRODIGY® at jumpword MODUS

Or call toll-free for sign-up information:
- America Online® 1 (800) 768-5577
- Genie® 1 (800) 638-9636, use offer code DAF524
- PRODIGY® 1 (800) PRODIGY, use offer code MODO

Or take a tour on the Internet at
http://www. pathfinder.com/twep/games/modop.

MODUS OPERANDI—It's to die for.